In this work of fiction, the characters, places, and
events are either the product of the author's
imagination or used entirely fictitiously.
Any resemblance to actual persons,
living or dead, is purely coincidental.

To the Paiges in my life,
to my own Monster-in-law,
to my parents, to my hubby,
and to my Skattie
And to the victims,
To the survivors and,
To all of those trying to keep their head above water

# The Long Road Home

J. H. Morgan

ISBN: 0-578-50749-1
ISBN-13: 978-0-578-50749-1
LCCN Imprint Name: JH Morgan

# Chapter One

"**S**hit!" Emily Winter swore quietly under her breath, but apparently it wasn't quiet enough, for the moment the word had left her lips, a disapproving sniff came from behind her.

Nigel Bellaroux was really starting to get on her nerves. The weedy museum manager had been breathing over her shoulder every moment she had been in the security office.

"Problem, Mademoiselle?" He asked in his haughty voice, his French accent thick.

Swallowing the urge to ask him how often he practiced his accent, since she had researched him before accepting this job and knew damn well he was from Queens, she took her fingers off the keyboard and turned around in the swivel chair she was sitting in to face him.

"As I have repeatedly explained," she told him, her annoyance starting to show through, "your server has been breached by someone who knows exactly what they're doing. I warned you that this would take me a while and that I need to check every possible way in which the hacker may have gained access." Emily took a deep breath to keep her irritation at bay, "I have thousands of lines of code to go through and most of them will not be the route he used, in which case, I will occasionally get a little frustrated. I didn't realise that you would be hovering over my shoulder every second."

Nigel sniffed again and flicked his bleach-blond fringe out of his eyes. "We were told you were the best and that it wouldn't take you long to secure our system."

"I am the best," Emily snapped at him, "But your system is so outdated that it's taking me a long time to repair. I'm working non-stop for you but if you would prefer to get someone else in, be my guest."

Without waiting for a response, Emily turned back to the computer and carried on with what she was doing.

On the screen, she saw to her relief, the reflection of the annoying man walking away from her and slipping out the server room door.

An hour later she was leaning back in the uncomfortable swivel chair and watching the ones and zeroes move across the screen. She always found it oddly mesmerising. She was unconsciously running a finger along the thin scar that ran from behind her left ear down to the front of her collar bone then down and disappearing into the neck of her shirt. Normally she kept her long, dark hair loose so that it would fall over the scar, and she didn't have to think about it or notice people looking at it, but the server room was hot and she had given up several hours ago and used a pencil to pull her hair into an untidy bun behind her head. Her thoughts drifted to her hotel room, with its high balcony overlooking the city of Paris, where in the distance, the Eiffel tower could be seen when she sat outside. More than the balcony, she was thinking it was one of the few places she had been since she arrived that she was allowed to smoke. She had left her cigarettes in her room that morning thinking that the day would be over by now and knowing that the pretentious manager would complain if he smelt smoke on her clothing.

The door behind her snapped open and Nigel came back into the room.

"I thought everyone in Paris smoked." Emily said in way of greeting.

"It is a filthy habit." He replied stiffly and dropped a torn page of a notebook on the table in front of her, "I am not your secretary Mademoiselle."

Confused, Emily picked up the paper and saw the words, 'Phone Glynis NOW' scrawled in posh writing.

"Glynis is my assistant. Perhaps if you had allowed me to bring my phone in here—"

"Security of this museum is my top priority as well it should be yours." Nigel interrupted.

"Oh relax Nigel, this isn't the Louvre." Emily said irritably, "I need to use a phone please."

Nigel was already looking insulted and scowled further, "The phones are for museum related communication only."

"Glynis knows not to call unless it's an emergency. And if you didn't want me to ask for the phone, you wouldn't have given me the message. Now give me the phone."

Nigel sniffed his annoying sniff once more and took the cordless phone from its holder on his fancy couture belt.

Taking it from him, Emily dialed her office number and waited while it rang across the world.

"Winter Consultants," Came the clear voice of her assistant.

"Glynis, it's me, what's up?" Emily turned away from the manager once more and played with the note in her hand.

"I'm sorry to have called you on site, but I didn't know what else to do." Glynis started.

"Just tell me what's going on." Emily interrupted the apology, she didn't like the sound of concern in the older woman's voice.

"It's your friend Paige. She's been trying to get hold of you desperately. When I told her that you were in Paris she became frantic, saying she needed to speak to you immediately."

"I'll call her now, thanks Glyn." Emily disconnected the call before the other woman had a chance to respond.

Ignoring the irate huff from behind her, Emily dialed another number and once more held the phone to her ear.

"Hello? Emily?" Paige sounded distraught.

"Paige, it's me, what's wrong?"

"It's Casey." Paige said, even though the connection wasn't as clear as it had been with Glynis, Emily could hear that Paige was crying.

"What happened?" Emily asked urgently.

"She's been backpacking with friends around Europe and her friends said she disappeared a few days ago." Before Emily could respond, Paige continued, "We've been calling every government and embassy around trying to get there, but my passport has expired and they won't let me come until tomorrow."

Emily sat back again, "I'm not sure what I can do Paige? Do you want me to trace her mobile?"

"No, no," Paige held back a sob, "She was found this morning. They've got her. They are trying to get her out of some tunnel she was in. The police said once she's out they'll take her to some Holy Spirit hospital in Frankfurt. But I can't get to her."

Emily stood up, "I'm on my way. Text me whatever details you have."

"Oh, thank you Emily."

"Text me." Emily repeated, disconnecting the call. She was uncomfortable with emotional people at the best of times and Emily had only ever heard Paige upset once in her life, the rest of the time, Paige McKenzie was the calmest person she knew.

Emily grabbed her jacket from the back of her chair and passed the phone back to a shocked looking Nigel.

"You have a job to finish!" He spluttered, his French accent slipping.

"Actually, I don't." Emily told him, "It's finished. You'll get my bill and instructions on how not to screw it up in due course."

Without a second glance, Emily left the bewildered manager gaping after her.

Emily hadn't had time to do anything more than collect her bag from the hotel and rush to the airport, so it was only when she was in her seat on the plane that she realised her hair was still in its makeshift bun. The flight attendant had tried not to stare, but Emily noticed her gaze lingering on the scar on her throat as she walked down the aisles greeting people and checking their seatbelts.

As soon as the plane was in the air and the seatbelt sign had been turned off, Emily went to the small toilet and splashed cold water on her face. Pulling out the pencil holding her hair up, she tried to brush her hair with her fingers to make it look less like it hadn't been brushed since that morning.

The pencil had left kinks in her straight hair, and no amount of fiddling with it would smooth it. Emily sighed and decided it would have to do.

Emily didn't look at her reflection for a moment longer than necessary. Usually she avoided looking at herself in the mirror at all, and when she did, she usually concentrated on a specific feature instead of herself as a whole. She made sure her hair covered the scar then, without another glance in the mirror, she left the cramped cubicle and returned to her seat.

The flight was quick, but trying to find her bag was a different story. After nearly an hour, Emily finally threw her bag into the back seat of a taxi and climbed in after it. Giving the driver the address she had been texted, Emily sat back and stared out the window.

She had been ignoring the nagging feeling growing in her chest but found that the closer she got to her destination, the harder it became to ignore.

If Emily was honest with herself, she really didn't want to be in a car heading towards Casey. Not that she didn't like Casey, she had always had a soft spot for the kid, but because she didn't want to know what she was about to find.

Anything that made Emily confront her own past was ordinarily off limits. If it had been anyone besides Paige that had asked for help, Emily would have refused without a second thought.

Emily looked down to check the time and realised she had been scratching a scar on the palm of her left hand subconsciously. The scar had left her with no feeling where her index finger met the hand, all the way to the thumb pad. Normally it didn't bother Emily, but her scratching of the area had drawn blood.

"Shit." She said out loud, earning her a quizzical glance from the wizened looking taxi driver.

Emily dug around in her laptop case for a tissue, finding one and holding it tightly in her left fist to stem the bleeding.

She was still holding the soiled tissue when she arrived at the hospital. She paid the driver in Euros and thanked him distractedly.

Grabbing both her laptop bag and her suitcase, Emily wheeled the suitcase towards the entrance thinking it must look strange to see a perfectly healthy-looking woman walking into a hospital as though it were a hotel.

The nurse at the reception spoke English fluently. She informed Emily that Casey had been brought in less than an hour before and she directed Emily down the hall, up the elevator and down another hall to room four-oh-five.

Emily made her way slowly up there, as if she went slowly enough, she could avoid her destination all together.

Halfway down the final passage, Emily heard screaming. She looked at the door to her left and saw that it was four-oh-two. She immediately knew the screaming was coming from four-oh-five. Running the last few yards, Emily burst into the room without knocking. It took a moment for her mind to take in what she was seeing.

A doctor was leaning over a bloody mess in a bed while three nurses tried to hold the writhing, screaming patient down.

The screaming and pleading from the bed set off something primal in Emily. She threw her suitcase and laptop bag to the side, and she ran towards the bed, shoving both nurses on her side of the bed out of the way roughly. One nurse flew backwards and lost her balance, landing hard against the portable blood pressure machine, knocking the entire machine to the floor.

The other nurse stared at Emily in shock while the doctor was screaming at her in German.

Emily ignored them. She stood close to the side of Casey's head and grabbed the hand that was thrashing around defensively.

"Casey, it's me Emily. I'm here. No one is going to hurt you."

Casey continued to writhe and scream. The doctor and nurse had been joined on their side of the bed by one of the others Emily had pushed aside and were still trying to hold Casey down. The doctor had a syringe in his hand, a furiously determined expression on his face.

"Please!" Emily yelled at them, louder than even Casey's screaming. "Look at her, she's terrified!"

The nurses looked at Emily, then down at Casey and finally at the doctor.

"Ve are trying to calm her with a sedative!" The doctor yelled back. "Ve do not vish to hurt."

"Just leave her for a moment," Emily pleaded, "she doesn't want to be held down. She's been through enough."

The doctor stared at Emily and opened his mouth as if to argue, but seemed to think better of it and closed it. Motioning to the nurses, he took a step back.

"You have five minutes to calm her." He told Emily, his accent lessening now that he was calmer, "If not, I give her the shot."

Emily nodded gratefully.

Casey had an unbreakable grip on Emily's hand, but the screaming hadn't slowed. Emily leaned over the bed and looked the girl in the eyes. One of Casey's eyes were swollen almost completely shut, blood was still oozing from a cut above that eye, and the white around the girl's blue eye that Emily could see was a brilliant red.

Casey's eyes were darting frantically around, not seeing anything. Emily could clearly see the terror in the girl's face.

Leaning over her still, Emily squeezed Casey's hand and stared unblinking into the blue eyes. "I'm here Casey. No one is going to hurt you. I won't let them. It's over."

Finally, the screaming settled into anguished whimpers and Casey's blue eyes met Emily's green. Emily watched as Casey's breathing slowed and she quieted still more. The girl was still gripping her hand tightly, but now that she had locked onto Emily's unwavering gaze, she didn't blink.

Emily saw not only terror in Casey's eyes. She saw the eyes of a pathetic child who was desperate to be comforted and told that everything was going to be okay.

Emily was shocked by her own reaction to the situation. Sedating Casey would have been the far easier thing to do, but Emily also knew that when you had been in a situation where you didn't have control of your body, when you finally got it back, you didn't want anyone going near it or taking away your control again. Not for any reason.

She stared into those pitiful eyes for a long time, eventually lifting her other hand to slowly stroke the hair out of Casey's face. Casey flinched but didn't stop her.

Emily saw the doctor coming closer to the bed again out the corner of her eye.

"Casey, the doctor needs to help you. He needs to clean your wounds."

Casey shook her head violently, her blue eyes never leaving Emily's.

"I won't leave you." Emily promised.

Slowly she saw the panic leave Casey's eyes and she stilled once more. With her gaze unwavering, Emily nodded towards the doctor.

The doctor approached the bed once more. "I need to insert an IV so that ve can start a drip and antibiotics. Ve also need to give her something for the pain before I can start to clean the vounds."

Emily nodded and held Casey's hand tighter, "I won't let them hurt you unnecessarily. They have to do this to help. I won't leave you."

Casey nodded weakly, though she never once loosened her grip on Emily's hand.

Emily ignored the commotion around her as the doctor and nurses started attending to Casey. Her focus was on Casey alone until she heard one of the nurses gasp.

Emily looked up to see that they had cut Casey's filthy floral summer dress open and pulled the ragged pieces aside, exposing Casey's chest and stomach. The girl's chest was covered in bloody bite marks, and there were dark purple bruises covering her entire abdomen, getting darker as they moved towards her pelvis.

Emily swallowed a sudden urge to throw up. She squeezed her eyes shut and tried to fight the nausea threatening to overwhelm her.

Taking a deep breath, she told herself that it was Casey lying in the bed and that Casey was the only concern she had right then. Emily told herself this wasn't the time to deal with her own demons. Forcing her eyes open, Emily once more locked gazes with the broken girl in the bed and tried as best she could to reassure her, occasionally whispering encouragement, but for the most part, being a silent guardian.

A while later the doctor coughed quietly to get their attention. Emily nodded to let him know she was listening.

"I have to do the test kit now." He said quietly, motioning towards the trolley next to him.

Emily didn't need to look to know what he was talking about.

The doctor unlocked the wheels for the bed Casey was lying on and pulled it away from the wall a bit.

"Perhaps you should stand by her head." He suggested to Emily in a deep, kind voice.

Emily moved to the head of the bed, still looking at Casey, who seemed to realise something was about to happen.

The younger girl reached up with her other hand and Emily grabbed it tightly.

Casey's lips were moving, but Emily couldn't hear what she was saying.

Emily leaned closer her until her head was almost on the pillow besides Casey's.

"I'm so scared." Casey whispered, her voice quivering.

"I know." Emily whispered back. "I'm so sorry Cas, this is going to really hurt."

Casey tucked her head into Emily's neck and pulled their hands up to her chest tightly.

Emily pulled herself closer to the girl below her, allowing Casey to hide her face in her own neck and hair. She heard rather than saw the doctor preparing the speculum and squeezed Casey's hands a little tighter.

Emily felt the girl stiffen suddenly and the agonised scream that came out of Casey chilled Emily to the core. She could feel the degradation and violation from the girl she was holding.

Hot tears touched her cheek, and she heard Casey's ragged sobs.

"Shh, it's almost over." Emily whispered, hoping she wasn't lying.

Casey's stare was blank when the doctors left the room. Still, she held tightly to Emily's hands, but it was as though the life had left her.

Emily knew the feeling and was, for the first time in many years, close to tears. She could feel the burning behind her eyes, her throat closing, but she also knew the tears wouldn't come. She felt completely empty and drained. While she didn't move or look away from Casey, Emily felt herself disconnect from herself and the room around her. She forced her mind to go blank, trying to forget the last few hours, trying to ignore the smell of sweat and disinfectant that had been clogging her senses since she had arrived.

∞

The last week had been the longest of Paige Mackenzie's life. The embassy had come through so quickly that it was nothing short of a miracle, but what Paige hadn't considered was the feeling of helplessness she would have on the trip. Once she had been given the go ahead and had made it to the airport, she had been forced to slow down and wait. The trip had taken an emotional toll on her that she hadn't begun to expect.

The fourteen-hour flight to London seemed to take a lifetime. Paige felt as though she were crawling out of her own skin, willing the plane to go faster. It was only the calming presence of her husband, Daniel, that stopped her from having a total meltdown on the flight.

Then their flight from London to Frankfurt had been postponed and no matter how much Daniel tried to convince her, Paige had been unable to eat or rest.

Now they were finally in a taxi, on their way to the hospital and Paige couldn't get her leg to stop shaking.

She had been trying to get hold of Emily for hours, but her calls had gone unanswered. Daniel had reminded her that Emily probably wasn't allowed her mobile in the hospital and that if she wasn't calling back, it was because she wasn't leaving Casey's side, which wasn't a bad thing.

They hadn't been given many details about what had happened to Casey, but what they knew had left them both totally distraught. Daniel put a comforting hand on her knee. Her darling husband was always able to face the storms calmly. She knew that inside he was as upset and desperate to see their daughter as she was but looking at the profile of his face in the passing streetlights, the only tension she saw was in the taut muscles in his jaw.

When they finally entered the high-care hospital room their daughter was in, Paige had to stop a moment to adjust her eyes from the bright hospital corridor they had just been escorted down.

The lights were low in the room. A machine beeped near the bed, the green lines on the monitor casting a surreal glow on the room's occupants.

Casey's eyes were closed, and she appeared to be sleeping as Paige slowly approached the bed.

There was a large plaster on her daughter's forehead, covering her right eyebrow. Paige could see the eye below the plaster was swollen and black. Casey was covered in a hospital blanket, with only one hand showing. There was a tube running into the back of Casey's hand, and her only child was grasping tightly to Emily's hand, even in her sleep.

Until that moment, Paige had barely registered the other woman in the room. She saw Emily sitting in a hard plastic chair, her hand in Casey's, her expression unreadable in the dim light.

Although Emily didn't acknowledge the new arrivals or even seem to notice their entrance, she gently removed her hand from Casey's grasp and Paige took her daughter's hand in her own.

She looked down at the torn and bloody nails and felt hot tears pouring silently down her face.

She felt Daniel's reassuring arm around her shoulder. He placed his hand over his wife and daughter's joined ones and stared at Casey as though he didn't recognise her.

Casey whimpered quietly and Paige bent close to her, brushing her hair back and whispering to her.

Casey woke slowly and started sobbing the moment she realised her parents were really there.

Paige held her gently in her arms and sobbed with her, Daniel cradling them both.

None of the occupants in the room noticed Emily collect her bags and slip silently from the room.

# Chapter Two

# Two Months Later

The room was cold and dank, light filtering through the few slits in the wooden floor boards above her head. She was mesmerised by the floating dust mites illuminated by the weak sun beams that had managed to break through.

Her arms ached, her useless left arm hung awkwardly from the shoulder socket and any movement set off a spasm of pain through her body.

The stench of urine, body sweat, and cheap whiskey had become so constant that the girl barely noticed it anymore. She was lying on the concrete floor, both wrists strapped above her head and shackled to a large old-fashioned bolt in the wall.

She heard footsteps above her and watched as more dust was dislodged through the cracks above. The usual terror that filled her didn't appear. She wondered weakly to herself if it meant she was dying, or just didn't have the strength to care anymore. A trap door in the distance rattled as the large padlock was unlocked. She considered trying to sit up, but she knew it would only hurt and she wouldn't be allowed to stay in a sitting position for long. The trapdoor creaked open, and she saw the shiny black dress shoe on the top step. Followed by black trousers, then a white dress shirt over a thin, wiry body. The man closed the trap door behind him, shutting out the light once more as made his way casually over to where Emily lay.

She could only see the silhouette of him approaching, but she could sense his smile and it filled her with the until-then absent trepidation and disgust.

A hand came out of the dark, fingers grasping for her face, the smell of whiskey and lavender coming off his body.

∞

Emily sat up suddenly, breathing hard and still smelling the faint scent of cheap whiskey from her nightmare. She pulled her knees up towards her chest, completely disorientated for a moment.

Dull yellow streetlight lit up the small room through the cheap curtains. She could see the fluorescent motel sign flashing across the parking lot as the night's memories came flooding back in a drunken haze.

Looking next to her she saw the back and profile of the man she had met earlier in the bar. His light hair was tousled, and he looked much younger in his sleep than he had earlier in the lights of the crappy bar.

Emily pulled the scratchy sheet off her legs with irritation and headed to the bathroom. In the overly bright light of the bathroom, Emily looked at her reflection in the mirror. Her dark eyes were bloodshot, and her hair was a mess. She ran her hands through her long hair, trying to comb out the just-fucked look.

Splashing cold water on her face, Emily into the eyes staring back at her.

"You can't keep doing this," she whispered angrily to herself.

She crept back into the room, picking up her discarded clothing as she went. She couldn't find her panties, so she pulled on her jeans before picking up her shirt and slipping it over the undershirt that hadn't been removed.

The man in the bed stirred, reaching across to the empty side of the bed. He groaned once then rolled over and sat up, gazing at her with sleepy eyes.

"Hey." Said the man.

"Hey." She replied without looking at him. She pulled on a boot and reached for the other.

"Come back to bed." The man said with a smile, "I'm ready again if you are."

Emily pulled on the other boot without answering. She was looking around for her bag and keys when he got out of bed and, naked, tried to pull her towards him.

Emily slapped his hands away.

"What's your problem?" The man asked, grinning as though he thought she were playing.

"Sorry guy, I have to go. My kid is at home." Emily said, digging in her bag for her keys and not looking at him.

"Hey, I like kids, boy or girl?" He asked with his boyish enthusiasm. "Come on, it's the middle of the night and the room is paid for." He reached for her again, "Come back and we'll make the most of it."

Emily slapped his hand away again and opened the door. "Sorry guy, not tonight."

"Jed," he said, "My name is Jed, I told you at the bar." His boyish face looked crestfallen.

"Doesn't matter," Emily said with a wave, zipping up her jacket as she got to her bike. Her helmet was strapped to the handlebar, so she undid it and started pulling it on.

"Hey!" Jed shouted, "Don't I even get your name?"

Emily turned around and looked at him. She couldn't help but admire his physique. The chest and stomach she was so recently running her tongue along was beautifully lit up in the neon lights.

Emily mounted her Ducati Supersport and started the powerful engine.

Shouting over the noise of her bike, Emily yelled, "It doesn't matter." once more then pulled away, not caring whether he heard her or not.

Although Emily definitely didn't have a kid waiting for her at home, she always found it the quickest way to get out of these situations, usually her bed partners recoiled in horror at the prospect of a single mother. Poor Jed, she thought to herself as she changed gears, what a sweet boy, he should be on a farm chewing hay or something.

Emily loved the high of riding her bike through the city in the early hours of the morning. The streets were mostly deserted, and she could really open up the engine. She loved the feeling of power and freedom being on a motorcycle gave her.

She was almost disappointed when she arrived back at her apartment less than a half hour later.

She always made sure not to go drinking near her own place; Emily had a rule never to let her one-night stands know where she lived.

Emily let herself into the building and waved distractedly at the security guard sitting at the front desk. Once she was in the elevator, she pulled her phone out of her jacket pocket to check the time. She had left her work mobile in her apartment, but always kept her personal one on her, just in case. Almost no one had the number so Emily was surprised to see a notification lighting up the screen.

She had missed a call from an unknown number. She wondered for a few moments who the caller could have been, but by the time she had let herself into her apartment, the call was forgotten.

Emily headed to her room, stopping in the kitchen long enough to grab a bottle of half-finished tequila out the freezer on her way past.

Kicking off her boots and throwing her jacket and jeans onto the floor in the corner, Emily pulled on a fresh pair of panties then made her way to her bed, sitting down cross legged on top of the blanket. Pulling her laptop onto her lap and powering it up, Emily took a deep drink of her bottle, wincing as the hard liquor burnt her throat. Taking another sip, she waited for the burn to subside.

Since she didn't feel like sleeping, Emily figured she should at least get some work done.

She had been working as a freelancer with First National Bank for the last few months. As a freelance IT security consultant, Emily spent her time trying to hack into high tech security systems to make sure their security was the best it could be. So far she had been finding easy back doors into the banks new online profile system and had been creating codes for them to prevent someone like her from getting into accounts for more nefarious reasons.

Emily loved her job, the pay was excellent, she was able to work weird hours and the best part was that she seldom had to actually interact with people. More than anything, she loved the challenge of finding ways through the toughest programs out there.

Glynis Rodrigues opened the front door to the apartment at nine the following morning. The office was set up in what should have been the living room and Glynis was not surprised to find it empty and the blinds still closed.

Sighing quietly to herself, Glynis went to the fridge to collect a can of Redbull before making her way to the bedroom. She found Emily exactly where she expected to, lying on her back on her bed, her left arm and leg hanging over the side, still dressed in yesterday's undershirt.

Glynis walked into the room, picking up the discarded jacket and boots on her way to the bed. She leant over her passed out boss and called her name without touching her. She had learnt early on in their relationship never to try wake Emily by shaking her. She had no idea what Emily had gone through when she was younger, but she knew it must have been something awful. Normal people didn't react to being woken the way Emily did.

She looked at the ugly scar on her boss' inner thigh and wondered for the hundredth time if it was the cause for the reaction Emily had.

Glynis opened the can of Redbull and left it on the bedside table, calling Emily's name a little louder. Emily groaned and pulled a pillow over her head in protest.

Glynis went into the bathroom and turned on the hot tap in the shower.

"Up and at 'em!" She called cheerfully from the bathroom. Emily grunted again and turned over.

"Come along Boss, you have work to do and clients to impress. Not to mention it smells like a stale brewery in here and I want to open the windows."

"Don't you dare!" Came Emily's muffled reply.

Ignoring her boss, Glynis crossed the room once more, this time collecting the empty tequila bottle off the floor and tut-tutting and she pulled open the dark, heavy drapes, allowing the bright morning sun to light up the bedroom.

Emily groaned audibly and pulled the pillow tighter over her head. She muttered something about firing mean people, but Glynis just laughed her bawdy laugh and headed back out the room, the empty tequila bottle tucked under her arm. "As if you'd survive without me darlin'. Your juju is next to the bed, and you better get your butt in that shower before the hot water runs out."

Emily heard the bedroom door closed and rolled onto her back irritably. She couldn't have had more than three hours sleep and that crazy old goat was always coming in so damn happy. It wasn't right.

Emily sat up and waited a second for her head to stop swimming before taking a big sip of the energy drink left on her bedside table. She had two more sips before dragging herself to the bathroom.

She pulled off the undershirt and underwear she had fallen asleep in and threw them into the overflowing laundry basket next to the sink.

Turning on the cold tap, she climbed into the shower while it was still scolding, muttering about Glynis the whole time. Letting the water flow over her head and down her naked body, Emily leant her forehead against the cool tiles and closed her eyes.

She knew the old woman meant well. Glynis always did.

Emily had technically never actually hired her. Glynis was fired from her job at an insurance company for embezzlement. All the money that disappeared was traced, electronically at least, right back to Glynis. Emily had done some work for their online security before but barely remembered the older Spanish woman that ran the secretary pool in the claims department. So, when Glynis showed up unexpectedly at Emily's home, Emily hadn't taken it so well.

But Glynis had refused to leave until she was heard. Emily had closed the door on her face, but the older woman had just kept right on banging and yelling her side of the story through the door. Out of total frustration, Emily had eventually let her in. After hearing her story, Emily had done some digging of her own and discovered that someone had in fact been using Glynis's online identity but was doing it from a separate branch of the company, half a continent away. Emily hated hackers who took advantage of people this way.

Emily remembered the old woman faffing around in her office, straightening things up and throwing away rubbish while she worked, but it hadn't meant anything to her at the time. She assumed Glynis was just upset because her job had been helping put her granddaughter through college.

Emily had done a full report and hand delivered it to Glynis's boss.

Glynis was offered a full apology and her job back, with an impressive bump in salary, but the stubborn old mule had told them where to stick their offer. She instead demanded a tidy severance package and left smiling.

Emily had assumed that was the end of it and went back to her own life. Until the following morning when her doorbell rang incessantly once more. She had opened it, still feeling drunk from the night before, and found Glynis on her doorstep again.

Glynis had decided that Emily was in need of an assistant, and had taken it upon herself to take the job. Emily had been too bewildered at the time to refuse her and after the first week or so had realised that while she didn't like having people in her space, Glynis had been a big help. She answered the phone so that Emily had to deal with people even less than before, which suited Emily's anti-social personality perfectly. She also got Emily's paperwork and diary up to date and running smoothly, which Emily had to admit had made a difference. Emily had been known to forget to pay her electricity bill or telephone account on occasion, which is something Glynis would never allow.

The older woman had taken a liking to Emily and over the last two years had become more than an assistant. Like this morning, she was always there to clean up the mess without complaint. While she would occasionally chastise her boss' drinking habits or housecleaning abilities, she never judged and tried to make things as easy as possible for Emily where ever she could.

They hadn't even discussed salaries until the end of the first month and Emily had asked Glynis what she wanted.

Emily washed her hair and scrubbed her body until her skin started to redden. She never truly felt clean, no matter how often she washed. She got out of the shower and started drying herself vigorously. She wiped the mirror with her towel and looked at her naked reflection. Running her fingers down the jagged scar that ran from underneath her right breast to her pubis, Emily sighed. The tree tattoo that started below her belly button and finished underneath her breast hid it to some degree, but she could still feel it under her fingertips. She supposed she was lucky to have such a good figure with her lifestyle, she was slim, but defined. Her breasts weren't large, but they were big for her build and while one nipple was completely gone, an angry scar in its place, they were still firm, even now in her mid-thirties. Another scar, the long, thin one that ran from behind Emily's left ear, past her collarbone and down to her armpit. She hated that one the most. More because it was one she couldn't hide as easily as the others, but also because it was the one she had to see every time she looked in the mirror. People asked about it too, no one seemed shy when it came to scars, something that got Emily really irritated.

Her eyes travelled down her naked self, until she saw the scar on the inside of the left thigh. Shutting her eyes tight to stop the flashback that inevitably hit her when she thought about her scars, Emily took a deep breath and held it.

When she opened her eyes again, she looked directly into the dark green eyes of her reflection. She felt angry with herself, she wrenched her eyes away from her reflection and brushed her teeth a little more aggressively than normal and went back into her room to dress.

Emily's scars were one of the reasons she never took her vest off if she could help it. The people she spent the night with never got to see what was underneath. Emily had spent more than half her life trying to pretend they weren't there, and avoided looking at them as much as she could.

After putting on her underwear and a grey vest, Emily pulled a clean pair of black jeans from her cupboard and a checked black and grey button up shirt.

She was still buttoning her shirt with one hand when she entered the living room, her Redbull tucked under her elbow.

"Morning." She said to Glynis, "Thanks for the bull."

Her assistant smiled from her desk, "As always Boss. The coffee is on, it should be ready by now."

Emily took the last swig of her can, walked to the kitchen to toss it in the bin, then took two cups out of the dishwasher and filled them with coffee from the coffee machine.

Adding cream to both, but only sugar to her own, Emily carried both cups back through to the office. Glynis thanked her and handed her a file.

Sitting down at her own desk, Emily opened the file. It was a company profile. She paged through it while drinking her coffee, jotting down some notes on the edge.

"Do you ever get bored with this sort of job?" Glynis asked, gesturing towards the open file.

"Sometimes," Emily replied without looking up, "but boring pays the bill. This kind of digging is easy and there's not as much pressure as the banks." Emily powered up her laptop, assuming Glynis must have taken it from the bedroom when she had woken Emily up. "Which reminds me by the way, the First National site had more back doors than I could count. They need to look at changing their IT person before they make the security changes they need to make to the code."

"I'm sure they'll request that you recommend someone to do it." Glynis said then added, "Their IT director quit the day after you were hired."

Emily snorted, "Well, we know why."

Emily worked in silence for a few hours, not even looking up to acknowledge when Glynis refilled her coffee. It was after two when the older woman shut Emily's laptop.

"Hey!" Emily protested.

"It's already after two and you haven't eaten a thing." Glynis said, placing the wrapped tuna mayo baguette she had brought back from her lunch break.

"Thanks," Emily replied grudgingly. She unwrapped the food and realised how hungry she was the moment she smelt the tuna. Taking a large bite, she chewed and swallowed then looked at her assistant across the room. "Thanks", she said again, meaning it this time.

Glynis smiled and waved her thanks away, turning back to her own computer and her own work.

Emily had just finished her sandwich and was scrunching up the wrapper when her private mobile rang again. Looking at the screen, Emily wondered again, who with a private number would be calling on her private mobile.

She pushed the green button, an unpleasant feeling in the pit her stomach and held the phone to her ear. "Hello?"

"Hi Emily."

Emily recognised the voice immediately. "Hi Paige."

"I'm sorry to call you out of the blue like this, but I didn't know who else to turn to." Paige said, her voice cracking slightly.

"Is it Casey?" Emily asked, hoping it wasn't.

"She won't talk to anyone." Paige said miserably. "Ever since she's been home, she just hides in her room."

"Well that's to be expected don't you think?" Emily replied, doodling on the back of an envelope. "Why don't you get her to see a therapist?"

"We've done that." Paige said, "We've had three people out to see her and she won't connect with any of them. She won't talk to us either."

Emily sighed, "I don't know what you think I can do Paige, I'm not exactly good with people."

"But you're good with her." Paige pointed out, "You were there for her when I couldn't be." The older woman was openly crying now. "I'm so sorry I haven't called before now to thank you for what you did Emily."

"Don't worry about it." Emily said quickly, not wanting to discuss it.

"It's not that I didn't think about it," Paige continued, ignoring Emily's protests, "But I realised how hard it must have been for you and I thought you might be better off with me not reminding you about it."

"You weren't wrong." Emily responded quietly.

"Which makes me feel even worse asking this of you Emily. If there were any other way at all, I would do it. But I need your help. Please." She pleaded.

The phone call ended soon after, Emily looked up from her phone towards Glynis.

"You've gone pale, what's wrong?" Glynis asked.

"I have to go to Hawthorne." Emily replied. The reality of her returning to that place bringing a queasy feeling to her stomach.

"Hawthorne as in your childhood home?" Glynis asked, a look of shock on her face, "You said you wouldn't set foot there again if your life depended on it."

Emily sighed. She had mentioned her hometown to Glynis before, but never her reason for leaving, and to her relief, the older woman had never pried about it.

"Is it that Paige woman again?" Glynis asked carefully.

Emily nodded, powering down her laptop.

"Now you know I never get involved in your personal life," Glynis began, holding up a hand to prevent Emily from stopping her from saying anything more, "But ever since she called you in France, you haven't been the same."

Emily shut her laptop and started packing it away, trying to ignore her astute assistant.

"I don't know what happened there, but it made you angry. Well," she corrected, "angrier than normal.

You're sleeping less, drinking and going out more. I'm worried about you Emily."

Emily slammed her laptop case on her desk in irritation, "You're not my mother." She snapped at the older woman.

"I know, but that doesn't mean I can't care about you. Whatever it is with that woman, it's brought something up that should have stayed well and buried."

Emily sat back in her chair, frustrated. Softening, "You're not wrong." She said for the second time in fifteen minutes, "If it were anyone but Paige, I wouldn't go. But I owe her my life Glyn."

Glynis watched her for a moment before leaving her seat and heading through the kitchen towards the passage.

"Where are you going?" Emily called after her.

"To start packing for you. I hope there's enough clean clothes to get you through."

Between Emily and Glynis, the bags were packed and loaded into Emily's black, '69 Mustang within half an hour. She seldom drove her car, but Emily loved it almost as much as she loved her bike.

"Don't worry about things here," Glynis was telling her, "I'll call you and keep you up to date with everything. And you can finish the First National report from there."

Emily nodded distractedly, patting her jean pockets to check she had both phones. "Thanks Glyn. I'll be back as soon as I can."

Emily lit a cigarette as soon as she pulled out of the underground parking. Opening her window slightly, she turned on her sound system, turning the old-school rock music as loud as her ears could take it and headed towards the highway.

Once she was out of the city and onto the open road, Emily felt her anxiety rising once more. She knew the increase in nightmares and insomnia over the last few months was because of her trip to Germany. Just that morning Emily had thought about her scars for the first time in longer than she could remember.

She had spent more than half her life trying to forget Hawthorne and the memories it held.

When she was fifteen, Emily had run from that town and everybody in it; vowing never to return, no matter what. Now here she was, more than fifteen hours away, but getting closer with every mile she travelled.

It would have made more sense to fly, Hawthorne, small though it might be, had its own little airport because of its large forestry industry, but Emily needed to know that she had a way of leaving whenever she wanted to. And there were no such things as taxis in Hawthorne, at least not when Emily lived there.

Emily had been born in Hawthorne, her mother had been a schoolteacher and the most caring, wonderful woman. Claire Winter had devoted her life to her daughter, baking with her, playing with her, reading to her or just being with her. Emily had felt like the happiest little girl in the world. Emily's mother had died of cancer when Emily was only seven, leaving her alone with her alcoholic father. Mitchell Winter was not a bad man, he went to work in the forest every day, then he came home and sat on the sofa and drank until he couldn't get up. Either his drinking got worse after Emily's mother died, or Emily had been so absorbed in her mother that she didn't realise it was a problem until he was the only parent she had.

It was soon after her mother's death that young Emily realised that the clothes her mother had made for her by hand and the jerseys she had painstakingly knitted had a more practical reason than random gifts of love. Her family was broke. Her father never had any interest in working more than he had to and had always been a tree-feller, never once getting a promotion. So long as he had beer in the fridge and cigarettes in his pocket, he was a happy man.

The year following her mother's death had been hard on Emily. She was teased at school for her too-small clothing and her unruly hair.

That was when she had first met Paige. Emily had been in grade three when she was called to the office. She would never forget how scared she was when the headmistress had ushered her into her office. Sitting inside was a woman around her mother's age, maybe a little younger. Dark blond hair framed her face, a mass of messy curls. She had kind eyes, a greenish grey that young Emily had been fascinated by.

The headmistress had introduced the woman as Mrs Mackenzie from social services and had promptly left her office, leaving Emily alone with the smiling woman.

Paige had told Emily to call her by her first name, and while it took a long time for the woman to gain the grieving girl's trust, she had done so. She arranged clothes every year for Emily and to this day, Emily still wasn't sure where they had come from. Paige used to get to school every morning before everyone else to braid Emily's hair so that she wouldn't be teased by the other children. She had helped with homework and took her out for special occasions. She had even gotten permission from Mitchell to take Emily to Sunday school every weekend.

With that memory, Emily shook her head and forced her mind back into the present. Some things just weren't worth thinking about. That church was one of them. For a moment, she could see his smiling face in front of hers and she shut her eyes tight and slammed on her brakes. A loud honking from behind brought Emily back to her senses. She put on her hazards to apologise and pulled over.

She rested her head on her steering wheel for a moment before anger got the best of her and she started pounding the steering wheel with the side of her fists. Wanting to yell and scream and cry, Emily hit the steering wheel a few more times before calming down.

Taking a deep breath she sat back, gazing out the windscreen into the waning daylight. She lit a cigarette with a shaky hand and gave herself a mental shake. If she was going to fall apart before she even got to town, she wouldn't be any help to anyone. Taking a long drag on her cigarette, Emily put off her hazards and got back onto the road.

It was after midnight before Emily started looking for a place to spend the night. The snacks and energy drinks she had bought earlier at a rest stop had been finished hours ago and Emily was hungry and tired. She hadn't been sleeping well and while she loved her car, it wasn't the most comfortable drive after seven hours straight behind the wheel.

Emily drove past a few seedy looking motels before deciding she better pick something before she drove past the entire town. Nothing in this town looked clean. There was trash, crumpled papers and broken bottles lining the sidewalk. Most of the streetlights didn't work and a lot of the shop windows seemed to be boarded up completely. Stopping at the one motel that had the least gaudy neon sign, Emily parked her car outside the reception and went inside asking for a room.

An old man in his eighties glared at her for interrupting his show but handed her a key and pointed in the vague direction of the rooms. Emily thanked the man, but he was already shuffling back to an ancient armchair in front of an even older television.

Emily checked the number on her key and drove her car to the respective parking slot. Getting out and looking around, Emily was glad to see a gas station on the street behind the motel. She quickly took her bag out of the car and went to unlock her room.

The room was clean enough, but obviously hadn't been updated in decades. Faded, floral wallpaper covered every corner of the tiny room, and a matching bedspread was paper thin from years of use. Emily dumped her bag on the bed before going back outside and walking to the gas station.

The station wasn't well stocked, but it had chips, a slightly stale looking pie and best of all, booze. Emily took the only bottle of gin and added it to the chips and pie, giving the cashier her credit card to pay. The woman smiled at her with missing teeth and handed over the packet.

Once back in her room, Emily kicked off her jeans and boots, sat cross-legged on the bed and opened her pie. While it was definitely stale, Emily still ate half of it before opening the bottle of gin. Taking a small sip, she gagged on the burning taste of the cheap liquor. It took a few more sips to get used to the taste and then she wasn't bothered by the burn. She powered up her laptop and went through her emails, taking swigs of the bottle every few moments.

By the time she shut down her computer and put the bottle on the bedside table, it was almost empty. Looking at the cheap clock next to the bed, Emily saw it was already after three. She put her head back on the lumpy pillow and was almost instantly asleep.

∞

"Please," Emily whimpered, "please don't."

There was a cruel laugh in the darkness. "Don't tell me you haven't been begging for this. Praying for it every night." The man whispered near her ear. She could feel him running cold steel between her breasts, past her belly button towards the mound of hair between her legs.

Emily tried desperately to roll away from the knife, but he held her side down with a strong hand. "Don't be naughty," he said sternly, his face moving down past her stomach towards her legs. Emily tried frantically to kick, managing to knee him ineffectively in the side of the head. The man roared with anger and without warning bit down hard on Emily's inner thigh. She felt his teeth tear through her flesh and screamed.

∞

Emily woke with a yell. She looked around panicking, but her motel room was empty. Emily pulled down the sheet and looked at her thigh.

The scar was in the exact place he had bitten her in her dream, and it ached as though the wound were still fresh. Still panting, Emily looked around the room, identifying its features: chair, laptop, door, bathroom, and mirror. She repeated the names of the objects until her breathing slowed and her heartbeat calmed. It was the only grounding technique she had ever learnt, and it had become second nature to her.

Kicking off the blankets completely, Emily looked at the clock and was shocked to see it was after ten in the morning. The gaudy curtains had kept out the daylight and she had slept right through her alarm. Rushing to the bathroom, she turned on the shower and undressed. She rinsed out the taste of cheap booze from her mouth before washing her hair.

After her shower, Emily dressed hurriedly and threw everything she owned into her bag.

Loading her bag back into her car, Emily drove to the reception where she handed the keys to a slightly younger replica of the man from the night before. The sun was nowhere to be seen, thick grey clouds hung low, making the late morning feel like dusk.

Stopping once more at the gas station to buy a cup of bitter coffee and a chocolate bar, Emily headed back to the highway towards the town she hated.

# Chapter Three

She had been slipping in and out of consciousness for a while, and when she opened her eyes she was completely disorientated. Trying to lift her left hand up to her face, the girl gasped in pain, the memory of her arm pulling out of her shoulder socket coming back to her with sickening clarity. She had been so sure that if she had kept fighting, they would leave her alone, but they had just held on tighter. She had tried to wrench her left arm out of his iron-like grasp and had heard the sickening pop as her arm ripped free of its socket.

She rolled her head to the side and threw up. She hadn't eaten in days and the acidic taste of the bile burnt her tongue and throat terribly. Tears ran down her face as she asked God where He was and why she was still there in that disgusting room. She had begged Him to help her, over and over, but He never did. At first, she had been so sure that if she prayed hard enough, He would save her. He would smite those who tried to hurt her and that He would comfort her. She wasn't sure how long she had been shackled to the wall, but she knew now that no miracle was coming. No God was going to save her.

As a spasm of pain ran through her stomach from hunger and vomiting, the girl rolled onto her back again and waited for the relief of darkness to take over once more.

∞

The second day of driving had taken longer than expected, a jack-knifed truck held Emily up for over an hour.

As she approached the outskirts of Hawthorne, the hair on her arms stood up uncomfortably and Emily felt her breathing quicken.

Taking her personal phone off the passenger seat, Emily quickly sent a text to Paige.

*Almost in town, where must I meet you?*

The reply tinged almost immediately.

*Do you remember where the old steakhouse is? I'm here.*

Emily read it quickly and replied, *See you in five.*

Throwing the phone back onto the seat, Emily drove down the main road, looking around.

Not much had changed in Hawthorne since Emily had left. The drug store was still there, the sign a little updated, but the window display of antique medical equipment was just as she remembered.

The dentist's office was still there too, but the name of the dentist had changed. The blue blinds were pulled down, revealing a picture of a smiling white tooth that used to scare Emily when she was a child and her mother had brought her in for check-ups.

The supermarket was still the same and Emily was surprised to see Molly's Burgers and Shakes was still there. Looking through the window as she drove past, Emily could see the leather booths were all still blue and bright pink, but instead of seeing Molly, there was a young man behind the counter. Emily wasn't surprised. Molly must have been in her late sixties when Emily left town so she would have to be retired or dead by now.

Emily pulled into the gravel parking outside The Steakhouse and turned off the engine. She sat for a moment, trying to summon the courage to open her door.

The door of The Steakhouse opened, revealing a young couple, holding hands. There was a yell from inside and the man wrapped his arm around the young woman's waist and yelled something back into the restaurant. There was a burst of laughter from inside before the door swung shut again.

Emily sighed and got out of her car. She pulled on her leather jacket, there was a bite in the breeze and it was starting to drizzle softly.

It was late already but The Steakhouse was still busy. Emily looked around when a waitress approached her.

"Table for one?" She asked smiling.

"No, thanks," Emily replied, "I'm looking for someone. Do you know if Paige Mackenzie is here?"

The girl nodded and pointed towards a glassed off section. "She's in the smoking section over there."

"Thanks." Emily smiled briefly and headed towards the smoking section.

The room was deserted except for the furthest booth. Emily could see the top of Paige's head; the older woman had her head down and was wringing her hands, a cigarette in her fingers. She didn't notice Emily approach.

Emily pulled the cigarette out of the older woman's hand, startling her.

"Why on earth would you be smoking? You had cancer remember?" Emily asked, stubbing the half-smoked cigarette out in the ashtray.

Paige looked up and Emily was shocked to see how old she looked. She had dark rings under her eyes and her hair was in desperate need of a cut and colour.

Paige looked as though she wanted to smile but couldn't.

Paige had beaten breast cancer five years earlier and while Emily had only visited her in the hospital twice while Paige had been receiving treatment, she had never once looked this bad.

"I feel like I've lost my only child." Paige said, her voice breaking.

Emily sat heavily in the bench opposite. Without saying a word, she opened to box of cigarettes on the table and removed two. She lit the first one and handed it wordlessly to Paige, who took it in silence, pulling on it and inhaling deeply.

After Emily had lit her own, she started to say something but was interrupted by the waitress arriving at her elbow.

"What can I get for you?"

Emily saw that Paige had a glass of white wine in front of her and pointed to it.

"A bottle of that please."

The waitress nodded and smiled, turning and leaving the women alone.

Emily and Paige looked at each other, both unsure of what to say. Emily's cigarette was almost finished when Paige finally spoke, "You look good Emily."

"Thanks," Emily replied uneasily, "I wish I could say the same for you."

Paige gave a weak laugh, "Your honestly has always been refreshingly blunt." She sighed as the waitress returned. "I don't know what to say or do." Paige said, lighting another cigarette and pouring them each a glass of wine from the bottle the waitress had delivered.

Emily lit a cigarette of her own. She waited quietly for Paige to continue, not sure what to say.

"She's not eating, she's barely sleeping, and when she does, she wakes up screaming. Just like you used to." Paige continued.

Emily winced.

"Sorry," Paige said quickly, "I didn't mean to bring that up."

Emily shrugged a small shrug, swallowing a large sip of wine, "I wouldn't be the one you called otherwise so I figured it would come up."

Paige took a sip of her own glass, then with her free hand, grasped Emily's hand. "You're the only person who knows what she's going through Emily. You're the only one that will be able to help her."

"Because I'm the poster child for survival?" Emily said sarcastically.

"You are a survivor." Paige pointed out quietly.

"I'm the most fucked up person I know," Emily said irritably, she hated that term, "and you think I'm the one to help her?"

"I'd like you to try." Paige said.

"Look, I will try, but since I haven't got the best track record when it comes to therapy or recovery, I don't think I'm going to be much help. If anything, I'm going to do more harm than good. She'd be better off dealing with qualified people."

"I've tried. You know I have." Paige pushed, "Casey won't talk to anyone! She just kept saying that no one knows what she's been through. And she's right. You're the only person I know that's been through something this bad."

Emily waved the waitress away irritably as the young woman approached.

"I don't think you realise what you're asking." Emily said stubbornly.

"I know how hard this will be for you, and I feel terrible asking you. I feel terrible asking you to come here at all, but I don't know who else to turn to. If there were any other way at all, I wouldn't have bothered you at all."

"You don't get it Paige," Emily said, her irritation rising, "I don't think I'll help because you and I have opposing views on this." She held up a hand to stop Paige from interrupting. "You think I'm a survivor, you think Casey is a survivor. I don't. The daughter you knew and loved is gone."

Emily heard a sharp intake of breath from across the table, knowing she had upset Paige, she continued regardless, "Whatever comes back from this won't be the Casey you knew. Survivors aren't the same as before, there's no returning from something like this. Survivors aren't the people that they were before. They are just the people who weren't allowed to die. There's a difference."

Emily watched Paige struggle with something, then the other woman said, "That's not true Emily. I know in the hospital you may have wanted to give up. But you're still here. You're successful, you work hard, you have a life you're living."

"Paige, do you remember coming to get me from the hospital after I overdosed?"

Paige was surprised, "Of course I do. I stayed with you for a while." Paige lit another cigarette, "But that was an accident. Even the doctor said it was an accidental overdose."

"It was supposed to look like an accident," Emily told her calmly. "If that idiot from the underpass had just stolen my shit and left me alone, it would have been fine. But it had to be the only homeless person in the city with a conscious who found me and called for help."

"I don't believe that." Paige said quietly, shaking her head. "I was with you for weeks after that and never once thought you seemed suicidal. Depressed, certainly, but suicidal? You always had more fight in you than anyone I'd ever met." Dragging on her cigarette, she continued, "Besides, if you had truly been serious about it, you would have done it again."

"I didn't because of you." Emily said quietly, looking down at her glass and not meeting Paige's eye.

"What do you mean?" Paige asked, bewildered.

"Oh come on Paige, did you seriously never realise this?" Emily asked, "You took me out of that shitty state hospital, rented me an apartment which you paid for upfront for a year! You bought me clothes and groceries and took care of me. I owed you too much." Emily lit another cigarette, just to keep her hands busy then carried on. "I owed you a lot of money after that, but it was more. You took time away from your own family to try and help me. I couldn't let you down like that. You would have found some way to blame yourself."

Paige looked at Emily in astonishment. "I never expected anything in return Emily, you know that. You were the one who insisted in paying me back."

"That's not what I meant Paige. It wasn't about you wanting it back, it was about me not wanting to be indebted to anyone."

Paige emptied the wine bottle into their glasses, ignoring the comment about being indebted as she knew that much about Emily to try and argue with her about it. "Do you really think I would have blamed myself?"

"You already felt way too responsible for what happened." Emily stated simply.

"That's not true. Trying to help you didn't mean I blamed myself."

Emily shook her head with a weary look on her face. "One of the days you were at the hospital, the first time, not the overdose time. I was pretending to sleep because I didn't want to talk to you and I heard you talking to the nurse outside my door. Telling her that it was your fault for pushing me to be part of the church, pushing me closer to him."

Paige put her hand over her mouth in horror. "Why didn't you ever say anything? My personal feelings about what happened were not your responsibility."

Emily shrugged again. "You had enough unnecessary guilt on your plate."

"So what?" Paige exclaimed, louder than she meant to, "I was the adult, you were a child."

"I wasn't a child!" Emily snapped back, equally loudly.

"You were fifteen years old." Paige said in a much quieter voice.

Emily didn't want to get into this debate again. They had argued about it so many times years ago and never saw eye to eye. She sat back in her chair and swallowed the last of her wine.

"So what do you want me to say to her? Do you want me to tell her what I believe, or do you want me to tell her what you believe?"

"Can I ask you one more question before I answer that?" Paige asked, her calm self once more.

Emily toyed with the stem of her empty wine glass. "Shoot."

"Why are you still here then? You paid your debt to me a long time ago."

Emily's hand fell still. "I don't know." She answered honestly, not looking up.

They were silent for a little while, both lost in their own thoughts.

"I think," Paige finally said carefully, "That I would only ask you to tell her what you believe will help her through this, regardless of whether or not I agree."

# Chapter Four

Emily left the restaurant before Paige. They had talked about less serious matters, but neither of them had it in them to keep the conversation going.

By the time she got into the car, Emily's frustration and anger at herself was starting to bubble over and she slammed the driver's door closed with such force that the windows on both sides of the car rattled.

Emily started the engine then paused before putting the car into reverse.

She felt bad for what she had said to Paige, not because she hadn't meant it, for she truly had, but because of the pain and grief she had seen on the woman's face. She had been too harsh. The only thing Paige was holding onto was hope that her daughter could recover and be the same girl she had been before the attack, and Emily saw the exact moment that hope was destroyed.

She sighed heavily and put her car into reverse. She wanted to be out of the parking lot before Paige left the restaurant.

Paige had rented Emily a room at Martha's B&B, knowing that Emily would not want to stay with anyone, so Emily headed in that direction.

Martha's B&B was on the outskirts of town, the opposite direction from which she had come. It had been an impressive country estate at one point, but when Martha had inherited it decades before, she had turned it into a luxury bed and breakfast, claiming that as a single woman with no kids, she didn't see a point in being in such a huge house all by herself.

Emily was greeted at her car by Martha herself, who insisted on taking her bag and showing her through the communal areas of the house before showing Emily to her room.

Emily was relieved to see that Martha didn't appear to recognise her. Not that she had spent much time at the estate when she was younger, but in a town this small, everyone knew everyone else.

Emily put her bag on the bed and declined the offer of food from Martha. Once Martha had left the key with Emily and wished her a goodnight, Emily walked to the window and opened the velvet drapes.

The room was definitely an improvement from the night before, the bed was a large king size with thick down blankets and plump pillows. She had her own flat screen television in the corner next to a kettle, a few sachets of expensive coffee and two matching mugs, the same shade of burgundy as the carpet and drapes.

Emily's window gave her a spectacular view of the entire landscaped lawns. The lawn was scattered with statues and sculptured hedges. There were spotlights under each of the hedges, lighting them up from the bottom. With the evening mist swirling low to the ground, it created an almost fairy-tale like ambiance.

Emily sat in the overstuffed armchair near the window and stared out at the night sky, her mind in turmoil. Her first instinct was to get into her car and get the hell out of this town and forget this trip ever happened.

She thought about Paige's parting request, to at least try. While Emily thought it was a waste of everyone's time, it was also more because it was a part of Emily's own life she didn't want dredged up.

She thought about those dark days after being released from the hospital after she overdosed when Paige had been with her. Emily had been strung out and dealing with awful withdrawal. She had taken her rage out on Paige, never telling the older woman that she had never intended to survive the overdose.

Paige had left her family and life for a month, dropped everything to help Emily, something she didn't have to do. Paige had been looking out for Emily since Emily's mother had died and while Emily might wonder some days why she carried on, she knew that her life now was because of Paige.

Emily had vowed to pay back every cent that Paige had spent on her and had spent the first two years after the overdose working towards that. One of the bosses Emily had worked for had taken a liking to her and while Emily had been working as a temp, she had been sent on computer courses. That's when Emily found her calling. She was a natural with computers and programming and within three years had left the company and started her own business doing online security. She was now so busy that she was turning away clients.

Emily never spent money on herself. Her apartment was in a nice area, but she kept it sparsely furnished. Emily bought few clothes, and her only big expenses had been her car and bike. Her savings had grown so much that Emily knew she didn't have to work very hard anymore, but she also couldn't imagine not being busy. Being alone with her own thoughts was usually a dangerous prospect for Emily.

Emily never dated either, not in real life anyway. She would usually find people online that she could spend the night with and was able to investigate them properly before hooking up with them. She never gave her real name and wasn't interested in conversation. Emily's one night stands were all the socialising she was willing to do. Glynis was the only person Emily ever spent any extended time with and Glynis knew when to keep quiet. They could go a whole day without more than a greeting.

The only other person Emily had felt comfortable with as an adult had been Paige. Emily sighed, thinking about the conversation she had walked away from earlier. She thought about the pleading look on Paige's face and could imagine all too well what Casey was feeling.

The sky was lightening from black to pink by the time Emily finally stirred from her position. She put her elbows on her knees and her face in her hands. She knew she couldn't leave. She knew that no matter what Paige asked her to do, Emily would do it, no matter how painful it was.

Running her hands through her hair, making it look messy and unkempt, Emily made herself a cup of coffee and watched the sun come up fully while drinking it.

It was just after seven when she picked up her phone and texted Paige.

*Can we meet? Somewhere away from Casey for now.*

Within moments a reply came through.

*Molly's? I'll buy you breakfast.*

Emily sent a thumbs up and went to shower.

It was raining steadily by the time Emily left the bed and breakfast, the early morning sunshine completely hidden by a thick layer of grey. Emily jogged from her car to the door of Molly's, relieved to feel the warmth of the restaurant's heaters as she entered.

Nothing about Molly's had changed, the counter was still chrome topped with pink and blue stripes running from the counter to the floor, the stools and booths all had matching pink and blue striped pleather upholstery. The table tops were either pink or blue, but fortunately a lighter shade than the seats. Emily couldn't see Paige anywhere so she walked down to the furthest table, near where the ancient Pac-Man arcade still stood.

Emily had just slid into her booth when a young, high school aged girl with blonde hair and a pretty face deposited a menu on the table and offered Emily coffee.

The waitress had just finished pouring a cup when Paige sat down opposite Emily. Paige also asked for a coffee then gave her attention to Emily.

"Thanks for meeting me again." She told Emily with a small smile.

"I want to apologise," Emily said. Paige tried to protest, but Emily raised her hand to prevent the interruption, "Whatever my belief may be about what Casey's been through, I didn't need to be so harsh with you. I'm sorry."

Paige shook her head, "You told me what you believe, and I appreciate the honesty. I know I've been holding onto some hopes that are nothing short of miraculous, but at the same time, I've always believed in miracles."

Emily stirred sugar into her coffee, "Even now?" she asked. She wasn't being sarcastic, she was just genuinely surprised.

"Without my faith," Paige smiled at Emily again, "I wouldn't be able to get out of bed in the morning."

"Fair enough." Emily said, taking a sip of coffee.

Paige looked like she wanted to say something but they were interrupted by the arrival of Molly at their table.

"Paige, nice to see you." The old woman smiled warmly at both of them before winking at Emily, "And if it isn't Miss Winter, home at last."

Emily was surprised. "You remember me?" she asked.

"Of course I do pet. Your hair may have changed and you're certainly no teenager, but those eyes of yours are just the same."

"I can't believe you're still here." Emily said without thinking.

Molly laughed her loud bawdy laugh that Emily remembered so well, "Oh honey, heaven don't want me and hell's too hot!" Molly patted Emily on the shoulder, "It's nice to see you turned out so good. I've thought about you often over the years."

Emily muttered an embarrassed thanks.

"What are you all eating this morning?"

Both Paige and Emily ordered the easy breakfast and Molly left them to it.

Emily took a sip of coffee, "I'm shocked someone remembered me."

"I think you'll be surprised how many people will Emily. You lived here a long time."

"Yeah, a really long time ago." Emily pointed out.

"Nothing interesting ever happens here. You were quite the enigma for a long time after you left." Paige said, turning her coffee cup in her hands.

"Glad to know it was considered interesting." Emily replied darkly.

Paige shrugged, "You need to remember that no one knows the truth of what happened. The rumours that went around went from plausible to ridiculous, but few came close to the truth."

Emily looked down at her own coffee, "I remember Liam's version of events." She said sourly.

Paige sighed. "Yes, that was the most popular rumour. I had wanted so many times to set the record straight but you specifically asked me not to."

It was Emily's turn to shrug, "I don't care what people think."

Paige knew that Emily statement wasn't completely truthful, but she didn't comment.

Emily looked up from her cup and back at Paige, "How's Casey?" she asked.

"The same," Paige told her, "Daniel's with her now. I've mentioned to him that you might speak to Casey for us."

"How much does Daniel know about what happened to me?" Emily asked. She knew Paige had a very close relationship with her husband.

"Pretty much everything I know," Paige admitted, "I'm sorry Emily. He's the only person I've ever spoken to about you. I don't hide things from him."

Emily shrugged once more, "I figured."

Their food arrived and for a few minutes they ate in silence. Emily noticed that Paige spent more time playing with her food than actually eating.

"You're going to have to eat if you're going to help Casey. You can't let her see you going to pieces, it won't help her." Emily pointed out bluntly.

Paige sighed and took a bite of bacon.

"How much does Casey know about my past?" Emily asked after they had eaten in silence for a while.

"Just the rumours mostly." Paige said. "She asked me about it years ago and I told her not to believe anything horrible anyone said about you."

Emily chewed on her bottom lip, a habit she'd had since she was a child. Then she nodded. "We have to agree though, if she doesn't want to talk to me, I won't go. I'm not forcing her into anything."

Paige nodded too, "Absolutely, that's fair."

They were quiet again, the waitress came to clear their table and pour them more coffee. Emily took a sip of the fresh cup and looked out the window down Main Street.

"He's still here you know." Paige said, a slight smile in her voice.

"Who?" Emily asked, still looking out the window.

"Liam," Paige answered, "Well, he left, but now he's back."

Emily turned and glared at Paige, "Why would I care?"

Paige shrugged. "I just thought I'd mention it. He lives –."

Emily cut her off, "Let's be clear, I don't care where he lives, what he does or who he does it with."

Paige put her hands up in surrender, "Ok, ok, message received. Sorry, I thought you might be curious."

"I'm not." Emily snapped, "I have nothing to say to him."
Emily took a deep breath to calm herself. "How long do you
suppose this will take? Talking to Casey, I mean."

Paige shook her head, "I can't know that. It will depend on
the two of you. Maybe she chases you out and you wasted
a trip, maybe it takes you an afternoon. Who knows, it
might even take weeks. I don't think she's the only one that
needs healing."

Emily rolled her eyes but said nothing.

"Can I ask you something?" Paige asked timidly.

"So long as you realise I probably won't answer."

"Do you still have a relationship with God?"

"That's a stupid question Paige. I told you a long time ago,
God hasn't been there for me, I have no interest in knowing
Him."

"But you believe He's real?" Paige asked.

"I don't know," Emily shrugged, "Probably, I just don't want
anything to do with such a cruel God."

Paige looked like she wanted to argue, but pursed her lips
instead.

"Why are you suddenly concerned for my soul?" Emily
asked.

"I've always been concerned for your soul," Paige said with
another small smile, "But what made me think about it is
when we arrived in Frankfurt, Casey was silent most of the
time, except once to ask Daniel how God could let this
happen."

"That's a question she'll always have, and not one I will ever
be able to answer," Emily replied, "Do you still live in the
same place?" she asked, changing the subject.

"Yes, we're still there," Paige answered, "What time do you want to come past?"

Emily shrugged again, "Might as well get it over and done with," Emily paused, "but maybe you should warn her that I'm coming?"

"Give me an hour?" Paige suggested.

Emily nodded and took some cash out to pay the bill.

"Please, let me." Paige started, but Emily waved her away.

"It's on me." Emily told her.

# Chapter Five

She woke up to the sound of the Lord's Prayer being whispered in her ear. She wrenched away from the voice as hard as she could, slamming her head into the wall she was lying against. She heard laughter from the man kneeling beside her and felt nausea rising.

"Aren't we a little jumpy today." He mocked quietly.

"Why are you doing this?" the girl asked desperately.

"Because you asked me to." The answer came as though obvious. "You were given to me, as I was chosen for you."

"You're crazy." She blurted out.

"I'm not crazy!" He screamed in her face, spittle spraying her in the face. Even in the darkness, she could see the veins in his neck sticking out as though straining to break through. His dark eyes were open wide, his teeth bared. He looked completely demented.

"He gave you to me!" he kept screaming, over and over.

The girl wanted to clap her hands over her ears, but she couldn't. All she could do was lie there and listen.

∞

Pulling up the gravel drive of Paige's home two hours later, Emily tried to convince herself she was doing the right thing, but she honestly couldn't think of a single positive thing she could contribute. They knew nothing about each other, how could sharing a traumatic experience connect them?

Daniel was waiting outside the front door when she pulled up and he walked down the steps to greet her as Emily got out the car.

It looked for a moment as though Daniel wanted to give Emily a hug, but she put her hands in the back of her jeans pockets so he stopped a few feet away instead.

"Emily, it's nice to see you. Thank you so much for coming."

Emily nodded awkwardly. "Hi Daniel."

"Come on in," he gestured for her to walk past him, "Paige is upstairs, she made some lunch for Casey. I'll let her know you're here."

Once inside, Emily watched Daniel disappear up the stairs to the right. She stood awkwardly in the entrance hall until Paige came down, carrying a plate of flapjacks.

"Sorry, I was really hoping she would eat something. I made her favorite meal from when she was a kid, but she wouldn't even look at it." Paige looked as though she was about to start crying again.

Emily wasn't sure what to say, so she followed Paige to the kitchen. Paige put the plate down on the counter then put both hands down flat on either side of the plate and bowed her head.

"Does she know I'm here?" Emily asked in the silence.

Paige nodded, but kept her head down, "I told her that you were coming, but I didn't really get a chance to explain to her all the, you know."

Emily nodded and swallowed, she had a horrible lump in her throat and wanted desperately to run away. She was used to Paige being able to deal with anything. She had never seen the older woman fall apart and it was making her feel very uncomfortable.

Paige sighed loudly and ran both hands through her wild blonde curls. Her thick hair was streaked heavily with grey now, something Emily hadn't noticed before.

"I wish I could take this away from her." Paige said, the agony obvious in her voice.

"I'm sure." Emily murmured.

It took a moment for Paige to compose herself, but then she sniffed and gestured towards the roof, "Want me to take you up and do the introductions?"

Emily shook her head, "I'll find it."

Emily walked slowly up the dark wood stairs, her heart starting to pound. She ran her fingers up the smooth banister as she climbed and imagined Casey going up and down these stairs thousands of times before now, toddling up them when she wasn't supposed to as a small child, running down them on the first day of school, getting ready for prom, descending the stairs slowly in her dress and high heels, a beatific smile on her face as she saw her parents and date waiting at the foot of the stairs for her, pure love and pride in their eyes. Running down the stairs when the mailman arrived, desperate to see if she got into the university of her dreams. So many memories these stairs must hold, Emily thought, looking at the photos that lined the wall on the way up. Casey and her parents and different stages of their lives. Emily wondered how it must have felt to walk up those stairs to her room when Casey came home this last time. If Daniel or Paige had to hold her steady as she climbed them.

Reaching the landing on the second floor, Emily took a deep breath and started towards the room Casey had as a baby.

Taking another breath, Emily knocked once then opened the door slowly.

The room was dark, the only light coming from the door she had just opened. The curtains were shut, and Emily could just make out a huddled figure under the blankets on the double bed.

"Casey?" Emily asked gently. There was no response from the lump in the bed.

Emily stepped into the room and turned on the light. The bedroom was completely different to when Emily had last been there, there were posters from her college on the wall, the dressing table was full of photos and an old teddy, and by the window there was an old rocking chair with more teddies. The double bed had a thick navy comforter on it. Flowery throw pillows were lying on the floor near the rocking chair as though thrown there.

"Turn the light off." The muffled demand came from under the blankets.

"Sorry, I can't see where I'm going and don't want to fall over anything." Emily replied in a careless voice, trying to hide her own nerves.

"Then get out." The voice replied.

"Sorry, I can't do that either." Emily said, "It would be nice if you could take the blanket off your head though. I'm not big on talking to disembodied voices."

Casey sat up in bed irritably and immediately wrapped her arms protectively around her knees. She looked sullenly at Emily, but didn't meet her eye. "Happy now?"

"It's an improvement to the lump under the blankets."
Emily saw the newly healed cut above Casey's right eye, her
eyebrow had been shaved for the wound to be stitched and
was still growing back in. It gave her a rather comical look,
but Emily didn't find it the slightest amusing. Instead, the
memory of holding Casey's hands so tightly when that
wound was still new came back into her mind with such
sharp focus that she could almost smell the blood and
disinfectant.

Emily gestured towards the scar, "How have you been
healing? Are you still in any pain?"

"They're just scars." Casey answered stubbornly.

"I wasn't just talking about the scars," Emily said, "but I
think you knew that."

"I'm fine!" Casey snapped, "I wish people would stop
asking me."

"I know how irritating it is having people bring it up all the
time, believe me." Casey said quietly.

"Then why ask about it?" Casey snapped, pulling her knees
closer to her body.

"Because you can't run from it! Trust me, I've tried. You
have to get to a point where people asking you doesn't
bother you anymore."

"Or people could just respect my privacy and stay the hell
away from me." Casey responded sullenly.

Emily didn't say anything for a while, she leant back against
the wall next to the door and slid down until she was sitting
on the floor, her knees also drawn up.

Casey didn't seem at all interested in making conversation,
she turned her head away from Emily and was staring at the
closed curtains.

Emily shifted slightly, "My scars still hurt sometimes, more like a tingly ache than pain, but it's there."

"How awful for you," Casey mumbled, although it was loud enough for Emily to hear the sarcasm in the girl's tone.

Emily sat quietly, playing with the scar on her hand absent mindedly.

"Why are you here?" Casey asked after a while.

"Because your mom asked me to come." Emily answered simply.

"I don't want to talk to any more therapists or shrinks." Casey sounded like a petulant child, not wanting to do something, but there was a desperate tinge to her comments.

"Ha!" Emily responded, causing Casey to flinch in fright. "I'm no shrink."

"So why are you here?" Casey asked again, "Why did my mom ask for you? I don't need someone else asking me stupid questions."

"Your mother asked me to come here because she's worried sick about you," Emily answered with slight irritation, "She asked me to drop everything and come to a place she knows I loathe because nothing is more important to her than you are."

"So I should be thanking both of you?" Casey snorted, "Just because you were always her favorite kid in service. Because she always saw you as her surrogate pity case?"

"That's not why she called me." Emily asked, surprised and a little hurt by Casey's comment.

"Then why?"

Emily shrugged, "Maybe because we have something in common?"

"So we're sisters now?" Casey asked sarcastically.

"That's not what I—" Emily started but Casey cut her off.

Suddenly screaming as though hysterical, "Just because you were there doesn't make you anything of mine! Just because you held my hand, doesn't mean you're suddenly special to me! I don't need you!"

Emily was taken aback by the outburst, but Casey clearly wasn't finished.

Casey scowled. "I heard the stories in high school. When I told friends that my mother had disappeared for a month when I was younger and who she had gone to rescue, they told me all about you. How you were screwing the pastor and destroyed his family. How you got caught when you were in an accident and he was killed outright. How my own mother tried to defend you to the pastor's wife."

There was so much venom in her voice, Emily was dumbstruck. It took a barely moment for her anger to rise, but she swallowed it with difficulty, "Yes, your mother came to help me when I needed it. I didn't want her, I certainly didn't appreciate her, but still she came. Because she's a good person." Emily stood up and put her hand on the doorknob, "And for the record, you got the wrong story in high school. That piece of shit destroyed my life!"

Without another word, Emily left the room, slamming the door behind her. She rushed down the stairs and stormed out the front door, ignoring the shocked look on Paige's face as she passed her.

She drove out of the driveway with the intention of heading straight to the highway, but then remembered her bag and laptop were still at the bed and breakfast. Emily slammed on the brakes came to a dusty halt on the side of the road. She slammed her fists into the steering wheel again, wanting to scream. Making a decision, she turned her car around and headed back to the main road.

She arrived at Dusty's Pub a few moments later and went inside.

Taking a seat at the deserted bar, Emily waved the bartender over. "Tequila," she said abruptly and the burly man behind the counter didn't bother greeting her, instead he grabbed a bottle from behind him and poured her a double.

There was a couple of old men in the corner nursing drafts and playing cards, but otherwise the bar was empty. Emily swallowed her drink in one go and motioned for another.

The bartender poured it, but when he tried to move away, Emily grabbed his wrist. "Leave the bottle," she told him, "and bring me an ashtray."

The bartender shrugged and put the half empty bottle down next to Emily's tumbler and pulled an ashtray from under the counter.

"I remember you." He said in a gruff voice.

"Good for you." Emily replied, downing her second drink and pouring a third.

"What brings you here to Hawthorne?" He asked, pulling a lighter out of his pocket when he saw Emily's wasn't working.

"Stupidity mostly." Emily replied, taking the lighter.

"Ok then." The bartender replied completely unperturbed by her shortness, "If you want crisps or something, let me know. I don't do peanuts in this bar." He came out from behind the bar and joined the old men in the corner.

Emily sat staring at the bottles lined up behind the bar, drinking in silence. After a while she pulled out her work phone and checked her emails. She replied to one from Glynis about invoicing a client then shut off the phone once more, placed it on the bar counter and lit another cigarette.

Emily had ordered a second bottle after the first hour and by late evening, it too was almost empty. Emily was playing pool with a crowd of rowdy forest workers, laughing and feeling more than a little drunk.  She was flirting with one of the forest workers when the bartender pulled her aside.
 "I think you've had enough, don't you?" He asked her, not unkindly.
Emily wrenched her arm away, "Don't touch me!" she complained, louder than she had meant to.
"Leave her alone Nick." The guy she had been flirting with agreed with a drunken guffaw.
"Maybe you should go home to your wife Matt." The bartender retorted angrily then turned back to Emily, "I can organise you a ride home? These aren't guys you want to get mixed up with."
Emily laughed, "As if I should be scared of them. I'm just looking for a good time Nick." She slurred his name slightly, "Unless you want to show me a better one." Emily ran a hand down the bartender's chest but he slapped it away.
"Behave yourself or I'll throw you out." He told her sternly.
Emily laughed and turned back to her new friends, throwing up her arms in triumph. Matt, or maybe it was another one, pulled her into a hug and kissed her, his tongue exploring her mouth. She kissed him back with

enthusiasm, before another man pulled them apart and went in for a kiss of his own.

Emily took a sip straight from the tequila bottle and kissed the second man.

Suddenly, the man was pulled off and Nick the bartender was yanking him towards the door.

"Hey!" Emily yelled, wanting to stop him but finding it hard to balance and walk at the same time.

By the time Nick got back inside a few minutes later he had a bleeding lip and looked furious. "Out!" he yelled at the rest of the forest workers.

None of them seemed to want to argue with him. Grumbling, they all shuffled out past him.

"You." He said, advancing angrily on Emily pointing a finger at her, "You just lost me a whole lot of money. None of them paid their tabs!"

Emily took a wary step back, "You kicked them out," she said defiantly, "not me. I was just looking for a good time."

"Matt's married!" Nick snarled at her.

"That's his problem, not mine!" She yelled back.

"Matt's married to my sister!"

Emily snorted with laughter, grabbing the pool table to steady herself, "That's your sister's problem then." She said through her laughter.

Nick stalked angrily to his bar to serve some shocked onlookers.

Emily stopped laughing when she realised suddenly that she didn't feel so good. She looked around for the bathroom but didn't see it. She stumbled towards the door and out into the street. The cold night air hit her and for a moment she felt better. Then she doubled over and puked on the sidewalk.

A strong arm grabbed her upper arm and pulled her to her feet when she was done. Emily hadn't noticed that she had landed on her hands and knees. She was pushed face first into the wall and the man started checking her pockets.

"Hey!" she protested angrily, "Get your hands off me you freak."

She was pulled around just as roughly and found herself face to face with Liam, her high school boyfriend. Liam, wearing a county sheriff's uniform and a very unfriendly look on his face.

"Oh," Emily said, slumping a little against the wall. She had just realised her hands were cuffed behind her, "It's you."

"Yeah," he said, the unfriendly look on his face turning to anger, "it's me. And I'm arresting you."

"What for?" Emily asked glumly.

"Public indecency. We had a report of someone causing trouble in the bar, and here you are, puking on the pavement."

Emily looked towards the police jeep next to her car, the back door already open tor her, "Fuck." Was all she said as Liam led her to the back of the car and had to help her in.

# Chapter Six

**E**mily woke up and blinked groggily in the bright fluorescent light. It took a moment for her to remember where she was and how she got there. Sitting up made her head swim and she was already nauseous again. She put her elbows on her knees and her face in her hands, waiting for the wave of nausea to pass. "Shit." She said aloud to herself. She was sitting in a small holding cell, with only a toilet to one side and the bed she was sitting on. The plastic covered mattress had holes everywhere, the cheap sponge sticking out, and the thin blanket on the floor looked like it hadn't been washed in decades.

Emily heard voices from somewhere outside her cell. This must have been the sound that woke her up. She was desperate for a glass of water but stopped from calling out when she recognised Paige's voice. She sounded irritated.

"You know damn well this is being done out of spite." Paige said to someone.

"I did what the law told me to do." Came the indigent reply. Even after all these years, Emily recognised Liam's voice immediately. Her stomach gave an unpleasant flip.

"What rubbish," Paige told him in a stern voice, "You never arrest any of the locals for stumbling around drunk! You take them home and laugh it off."

"That is not a local!" He argued, and Emily could just imagine him pointing disdainfully towards her cell.

"Just let her out please Liam," Paige voice was quieter, Emily had to strain to hear it now. "She's here at my request. It hasn't been easy on her."

Emily didn't hear his muffled reply, but soon she heard a door open and footsteps heading towards her.

Liam stood in front of the cell, dislike showing on his handsome face. He looked older, his short dark hair was streaked with gray and he had stubble on his strong jaw, but his intense blue eyes were exactly the same. The expression in those eyes was the same as the last time she saw him too, on that fateful day he came to the hospital and called her a whore.

Without a word, he unlocked her cell and opened the door. Not wanting to push her luck, Emily stepped passed him out the cell and hurried down the corridor, her ruined jacket clutched in her hand. Paige was waiting for her in the reception area, still dressed in the clothes from the day before, even though it must be almost morning.

"You okay?" Paige asked her, looking concerned.

"I'm fine," Emily replied defiantly, "You didn't have to come down here."

"Of course I did." Paige said distractedly, scratching around in her handbag for her car keys, "Come on, let's get out of here before he changes his mind and throws us both in jail."

Once they were in the car, Emily realised they were heading in the opposite direction of the bed and breakfast. "I'm not going back to your house." She told Paige in a slightly panicked voice.

"No, you're not," Paige told her, "Martha called me and asked me to collect your things. She heard about what happened last night and said she'd prefer if I found you alternative accommodation."

"Oh," Emily said, feeling abashed for the first time. "So are you taking me to my car?"

Paige shook her head. "I was hoping you would stay a little longer."

"Why?" Emily asked, her head throbbing painfully, "Casey isn't going to open up to me and I'm not the right person to help her."

"She asked me to apologise to you." Paige told her, "She said she was taking things out on you and it wasn't fair." Paige looked quickly at her passenger then back at the road, "I told her the truth about what you went through. She feels awful for the things she said. She knew that something must have happened, which is why she already felt bad about saying you ran off with Stan, but she never had any idea about the severity of it."

"Hmm." Emily muttered.

Paige pulled into the driveway of a small house. Everything was in darkness.

"We bought this place a few years ago to help out a struggling family, but they've moved on now. We rented it out for a while, but Daniel felt it was too much of a hassle in the long term, so it's just sitting here." Paige handed Emily a key, "It's furnished, but I'm afraid there's no food in the fridge."

Emily nodded and opened the passenger door. "Thanks Paige."

"I'll leave you to sleep for a while then will come and fetch you later. Your bag and computer is just inside the door. I'll take you to your car and get some groceries for you once you've rested and cleaned up." Paige's voice was kind but it only made Emily feel worse.

She nodded at Paige and got out the car, using the key to let herself into the house.

The front door opened directly into a small living room. There was a small flat screen television against the wall and two blue sofas facing each other. Between them sat a glass topped coffee table with a pile of magazines on it. The kitchen was directly to the left, all open plan, separated only by a small dining table and four chairs. There was a small fridge, a built in gas stove and a few cupboards. Emily looked for a glass and drank two full glasses of water before checking the other cupboards. Besides a kettle, microwave and toaster, the kitchen was empty. There were some plates and cutlery, but nothing to eat or drink. Emily put her empty glass in the sink and went to fetch her bags. Opposite the kitchen was a small passage that lead to two bedrooms with a bathroom between them. Emily chose the slightly bigger one on the left and dumped her bags on the bed.

Taking out her toiletries, she went straight to the bathroom and had a shower. She felt disgusting and wasn't sure which smell was worse, the musty smell from the blanket she used in the cell or the smell of stale booze, smoke and puke that seemed to engulf her.

Emily dressed quickly and considered walking to the drugstore to get something for her headache. Looking out the window, she saw the sun had only just come up and thought better of it. Instead she lay down on the bed and was asleep within moments.

Loud knocking woke Emily from a dreamless sleep. She sat up suddenly, looking around. Her headache was better, but she still had a dull ache behind her eyes and a queasy feeling in her stomach.

Opening the front door, she saw Paige had obviously showered and changed as well.

"Did I wake you?" Paige asked, concern in her voice.

"No problem, I hadn't meant to fall asleep anyway." Emily told her, "Let me brush my teeth again quick and we can fetch my car."

Paige nodded, "I'll wait for you in my car."

Emily hurriedly brushed her teeth for the second time that morning and left the house, locking the door behind her.

Paige reversed in silence, but as she turned onto the road she spoke, "So, about last night, is that a regular thing for you?" There was no admonition in her voice.

"Not usually that bad." Emily replied vaguely.

"Do you have a drinking problem?"

"I drink a lot," Emily shrugged, "sometimes it's easier than being in my own head. Whether or not I have a problem is up to interpretation I guess."

Paige pursed her lips but didn't reply. She pulled into the parking lot of Dusty's pub and turned the car off. "Do you want me to go with you to get groceries or are you leaving town?" She asked Emily.

"Don't worry about coming with me," Emily told her, "but no, I'm not leaving yet. If Casey wants to talk to me again, I'll try. But if she says no, then I'll head home tomorrow."

Paige laid a gentle hand on Emily's arm, "I'm sorry Emily. I'm sorry I'm putting you through this."

Emily pulled her arm away equally gently, "Not your fault Paige, I chose to come."

Emily got out of Paige's car and got into her own.

Since the grocery store was just down the road, Emily considered walking, but decided she didn't want to leave her car at the bar, in case she ran into anyone from the night before. Parking outside the grocer, Emily went in and took a trolley. Usually she ordered her groceries online and had them delivered or Glynis would pick up what she needed, so it felt weird for Emily to be in a store again. She walked up and down the aisles, buying far more than she needed, but she was hungry and figured whatever she didn't have could be taken home. She was happy to find her favorite brand of coffee was in stock and bought a few ready cooked meals. Deciding she wanted pasta, Emily bought the ingredients to make herself a proper lunch later. Adding toilet paper, sugar and cream to her growing pile of groceries, Emily went to the check out. She added a few boxes of cigarettes to her things and paid with her credit card.

After packing her groceries into her boot, Emily went into the bottle store next door without really thinking and bought a few bottles of wine, some gin and tequila.

Emily had already made one trip inside the house with the groceries, she was heading back to her car to get a second lot when she found a young girl standing next to her car. She had curly blond hair and the brightest blue eyes Emily had ever seen.

"Hi." The girl said with a huge smile on her face.

Emily found herself smiling back. "Hi to you too." She said.

"I live next door." The little girl pointed to the slightly larger house to the right.

"Didn't anyone ever teach you not to speak to strangers?" Emily asked her, still smiling.

The girl rolled her eyes, "All the time," she said in an exasperated voice, "but I asked Nanny Bee if I could come say hello." She pointed back towards her own house and Emily saw an older Spanish woman looking out the window towards them.

Emily gave the older woman a small wave and turned back to the girl. "My name is Emily, what's yours?"

"I'm Sophie." The little girl said with another smile, "I'm going to be seven soon."

"Wow, good for you." Emily told her.

"Sophie, time to come inside." The Spanish woman was standing by the front door, calling out.

"Well, bye." Sophie waved at Emily and skipped away.

Emily took the rest of her shopping inside the house and made herself a cup of coffee before unpacking anything else.

She went outside the back door and sat on the step with her coffee in one hand and her cigarettes in the other. Lighting one, Emily inhaled deeply and looked towards the forest behind the house. There was no fence in the back yard, just an open field with the massive pine forest behind it. Emily used to love the forest when she was younger. It was her favourite place in the world until... Until she didn't love it anymore. Looking into the distance, the trees seemed menacing and cold now. Emily pulled her jacket tighter around her and finished her coffee and cigarette before going back inside.

Emily made herself some pasta with fresh tomatoes and herbs. While she didn't cook often, she quite enjoyed herself when she did. It was a nice distraction when she needed to keep her mind occupied on something other than her own thoughts.

She poured herself a glass of white wine then went to fetch her mobile from the bedroom before sitting down to eat. She found her personal mobile in her jacket pocket, but she couldn't find her work phone anywhere. She dug through the pockets of her jeans and jacket, even checked her shoes, but it wasn't there. She must have left it at the bar she realised with another lurch in her stomach. She knew she would have to go back and fetch it.

She was walking back towards the kitchen, wondering if she could call Paige and ask her to fetch it when there was a knock on the front door.

Assuming it was Paige, Emily opened the door without checking out the window.

Nick the bartender stood at the door. He was dressed in black, stonewashed jeans and a tight short-sleeve t-shirt, despite the cold.

"Oh." Emily said when she saw him.

Nick held out her mobile, "You forgot this last night."

Emily took the phone, "Thanks. How did you know I was here?"

"Martha told me that Paige Mackenzie collected your stuff, so I took a chance." Nick grinned at her, "Thought you might need that, it's been ringing all day."

"Thanks." Emily said again, checking the screen and seeing a lot of missed calls from Glynis.

"Whatever's cooking smells great." Nick said suddenly.

"Look, I want to apologise for last night. I'll happily pay the outstanding bills from the guys that left." Emily said, ignoring his comment.

"Nah, don't worry about it. It could have been worse, I know where all of them live. I'm sorry you got arrested. He's never arrested anyone from the bar before. Usually just takes them home."

"We have history," Emily explained wryly.

"So you've been to town before?" Nick asked.

Emily looked up at him, "Of course. You even said last night that you recognised me." She was confused.

"Yeah," he said, also looking a little confused, "I remember you from Lunar Security Tech. You came in to help with some clients."

Lunar Security Tech was a private, personal security company for the very wealthy. Emily was often called in to make sure their clients' home security was impenetrable.

"Oh wow, okay." Emily said, "I'm sorry, but I didn't recognise you."

Nick shrugged, "That's the point of a good security guard I guess, blending into the background." He smiled again, "Look, I'm not trying to be forward or anything, but it's getting kinda cold out here and I am starving. If you want to catch up about old times, you could at least offer a man lunch."

Emily looked sceptical, but he smiled again, "Don't worry," he told her, "I'm not taking you up on last night's offer if that's what you're worried about."

Emily again felt embarrassed about her behaviour the previous night, but opened the door wider and let him in.

She went to the kitchen and dished up two plates, before pouring Nick a glass of wine and taking the plates to the small table. Nick collected his wine glass and joined her at the table.

Nick took a bite and swallowed, "Tastes better than it smells." He told her.

"Thanks," Emily said, taking a sip of wine. "So why did you leave the security business to open a bar in the middle of nowhere?"

"When I got out of the military, the private security sector seemed like the obvious choice. Most of my buddies had married and settled down, but I was still looking for some excitement, you know?" He looked at her and smiled a little, "There isn't much excitement being the bodyguard of puffed-up idiots with money as it turns out, but the pay was good and the hours weren't terrible, so I was able to live a little.

Then, when I was guarding this real douche bag, someone tried to take a shot at him. Some ex-employee whose life the guy had ruined. Anyway, the boss was fine and the guy was arrested, but that night, I realised I didn't want to put my life on the line for people like him. So I quit.

Came here to see my sister, Sarah and her kids. While I was here, she mentioned Dusty's was up for sale, so I bought it. Never went back."

While they ate, Emily took in his story and found herself watching him while he ate. His gruff voice was soothing to listen to, and she had to admit to herself, he was very attractive. He was massive, probably close to seven foot, four and all muscle, but there was no cruelty in his brown eyes or expression.

"So you're from here then?" He asked her, pushing his empty plate aside and finishing his glass of wine.

"I grew up here," Emily told him, "But I left a long time ago and never thought I'd be back."

"Why are you back then?" He was filling both their glasses from the bottle he took from the counter behind him.

"A friend needed me." Emily shrugged.

"Must be a good friend." He remarked with a smile, "Paige Mackenzie?"

Emily nodded. "You know her?"

"Not really," Nick shook his head, "just from around. Small town you know."

Emily pushed her own plate away and nodded, "Yeah, I know." She got up from the table, "I'm going to call my office quickly, I'll be back now."

Emily went to the room and called Glynis.

Coming back a few minutes later, she was surprised to see that Nick had cleared the table and was washing the plates.

"You didn't need to do that." She told him, picking up a cloth and drying the plate he had just washed.

"I don't mind. You cooked, I clean. That's fair." He passed her the other plate then leant against the sink and crossed his arms, "Besides, the wine is finished and I wasn't sure if I was welcome to open another one."

Emily watched his stomach muscles move under his tight shirt while he spoke. When she looked back up at him, she saw that he was watching her with a small smile.

"Why not?" She said, taking another bottle out the fridge.

Emily sent Paige a text saying she needed a time out and that she would call her in the morning to set up a meeting with Casey, then turned her phone off and went to sit on the couch. Nick joined her and brought their glasses through. Emily filled them both and sat back, kicking her shoes off and putting her feet on the coffee table.

"So." Nick said, that same boyish smile playing on his face.

"So what?" Emily asked, surprised to find herself comfortable in his presence.

"You going to be here a while?"

"Probably not," she told him, shaking her head slightly, "Once I'm done helping Paige, I'll head back to the city."

"Have a guy pining for you back there?" He asked with a grin.

"Nope." Emily replied, looking into his eyes and feeling the attraction for him growing.

"Girl?"

Emily laughed, "No. No girls either."

"You ever been with a woman?" His tone was playful.

"A couple," Emily shrugged, "I'm not fussy."

Nick laughed. "I noticed." His expression turned serious, "Look, I'm not looking for any kind of relationship, but if you're bored while you're here or need someone to warm your bed, I'm happy to oblige."

Emily laughed, "Well, at least you're up front." She told him.

"And a better choice than Matt." He said, his smile back in place. He downed his glass in one gulp and leaned across towards her.

Emily met his kiss. His mouth was cool from the wine, gentle but persistent. He put his arm around her waist and pulled her close to him.

Emily wrapped her arms around his neck and deepened the kiss. Placing a hand on her hips, he lifted her onto his lap with ease, not breaking the kiss.

Emily straddled his lap and pulled his shirt off. Running along the right side of his body from his neck to his jeans was a burn scar, the skin mottled and shiny. Emily wanted to pause but Nick didn't let her. There was a tattoo of a dragon on his left chest starting where the skin met the scar and she pushed him back so that she could run her tongue along the body of the tattoo. Nick reached up to pull her shirt off, but she pushed him away gently. She pulled her own shirt off, leaving her undershirt on and kissed him again. He slid his hands under her shirt, but she grabbed his hands. "The shirt stays on." She whispered seductively into his ear.

He nodded and abruptly stood up, wrapping Emily's legs around his waist, he turned around and placed her down on the couch, her legs spread eagled. He knelt on the floor and kissed her again.

Pushing her back gently, Nick undid her jeans and pulled them and her panties off, dropping them of the floor next to him. Running his tongue up her right thigh, then teasing her and making his way back down her left. When he got close to the ugly scar on her inner thigh, Emily put her hands on either side of his head and guided him towards her for another kiss. Emily could feel his excitement through his jeans.

She pushed him into a standing position, unbuckling his belt and pulling his pants down. She reached for her bag on the coffee table and pulled a condom out the side pocket.

She opened the packet and slid the condom onto him, making him groan softly. He took her hands and pushed them above her head, pushing her back down against the couch and nudging her legs open with his knee.

"Are you sure you wanna do this?" He asked her in a husky voice, biting her earlobe.

"I never do anything unless I'm sure I want to." Emily responded.

He slid into her then, pushing his whole length into her in the first thrust. Emily gasped out loud and grabbed her shoulders, pulling him closer to her.

After an impressive three orgasms, Emily left Nick in the lounge and went to the bathroom to clean up. She wrapped a towel around herself and came back to find him putting his belt back on. He grinned at her as she entered the room.

"Gotta go. Have to open the bar." Nick kissed her gently on the forehead and bent down to fetch his shirt. "You know where to find me." He called out before he opened the front door and headed out into the chilly afternoon.

Usually Emily had to be the one to leave, making the moment feel unusual, but she told herself it was better this way, neither of them needed to pretend they wanted anything more. Somehow though, there was a slight feeling of rejection she couldn't shrug off.

Emily went to shower again, the hot water pounding her skin. She thoroughly enjoyed her time with Nick and decided that she would take him up on his offer. Having someone to call while she was here wasn't a bad thing. Her rule was to never have sex with anyone more than once, but since she had no intention of staying in Hawthorne for any more than a few days, she felt it was okay to bend her rule just this once.

Dressing, Emily heard the doorbell again. This time she checked out the window to see who was there.

Standing on her doorstep was a woman with long straight dark hair. Emily was sure she didn't recognise her. She opened the door warily, hoping it wasn't Nick's wife or something. Despite her behaviour the previous night, Emily had a rule never to hook up with married men.

The woman smiled at her, her makeup was perfect, and her hair fell well below her waist.

"Hi. I'm Amy from next door." She held up a bottle of wine, "Thought I'd welcome you to the neighbourhood."

"Oh, you must be Sophie's mom." Emily said, opening the door wider to let her in, amazed to find that small-town hospitality was still alive and well in Hawthorne.

"Other next door," Amy smiled, pointing to the house on the opposite side to Sophie. Amy went inside and saw the wine glasses on the coffee table. "I'm not interrupting anything am I?"

"No," Emily said, picking up the glasses and taking them through to the kitchen. "Come on through, I've got an opener here."

Emily put the glasses in the sink and took clean ones down from the cupboard. It was so strange for her to invite any stranger into her space, let alone two in one day. Being in Hawthorne was doing weird things to her.

Amy handed over the bottle for Emily to open and once they both had a full glass, they clinked them together.

"Would you mind if we sit on the step outside?" Emily asked, picking up her packet of cigarettes.

"Lead the way." Amy said with a smile.

Once they were both sitting on the step and Emily had lit her cigarette, she turned and looked at her new guest. "I take it you're not from around here." She said.

Amy laughed, "Do I stand out that easily?"

"Not at all," Emily told her, "Just that most of the people I've run into, I recognise."

"So I guess you are from around here." Amy said. "Why on earth would you come back?"

Emily was the one to laugh this time, a slightly hollow laugh. "I'm not here to stay, just came to help a friend."

"Oh okay, I don't blame you. I want to run away from this place at least twice a week."

"So why don't you?" Emily asked her, taking a sip of wine. "Or why did you come here in the first place? You look more like a city girl."

"I'm going to take that as a compliment," Amy grinned. "My husband, well ex-husband, got offered a really good job at the felling plant and dragged us out here. I took a job at the school teaching so I wouldn't die of boredom, but once we got divorced, I realised I couldn't leave yet. My son is settled and happy in school here and it's a better place for him to be than the city."

"How old is your son?" Emily asked.

"Sixteen."

"You have a sixteen-year-old kid?" Emily asked incredulously.

Amy laughed again, "I'm definitely taking that one as a compliment. Yes, Zavier will be a senior in the fall. Got pregnant in high school and married too young."

"Was it an ugly divorce?" Emily found it refreshing to speak to someone so open.

"God no! Erik is a sweetheart and I'll always love him. I just wanted something more out of life, you know?"

Emily nodded, "But if you're staying for now, wouldn't it make sense to make the marriage work for a while? It's not like this town is flooded with talent."

"Well," Amy flicked her hair back over her shoulder and emptied her glass, "I realised the moment I had to stay that I should probably make another go of it. But I wanted him to work for it, you know? Well, apparently I played a little too hard-to-get, because the next moment, he's dating his boss' niece and they've been together ever since."

"Ouch." Emily commented.

Amy stood up and held her hand out for Emily's glass, then went inside to refill them both. "It was ouch at first," she called from the kitchen, then made her way back out, "but she's far more his speed. She's happy with this small-town hick life and happy to have dinner waiting for him when he gets home. I was always more of a professional wife. I liked making money. I liked high pressure jobs and deadlines." She shrugged and sat back down. "And that's the life I'll go back to once Zavier graduates."

"What about you?" Amy asked her, "Married, divorced or hate men?"

Emily laughed, "None of the above. Spend too much time working I suppose."

Amy nodded sagely, "You have the right idea."

They chatted a bit about the town and superficial things when Amy suddenly stopped, "Hey," she said, "Do you know Stacey Green?"

Emily shrugged, "I don't think so."

"Wait, what was her maiden name? Puffer I think? Does that sound like a name?"

"Stacey Puffer? Actually yes, I think I do know her. She was in my year at school. She was a total bully if I remember right."

Amy clapped her hands, "That's definitely her then."

"Why do you ask?" Emily lit another cigarette, the image of an overweight girl coming to her. Orange, frizzy hair and bad skin she remembered. And mean to everyone she deemed poorer than herself.

"She's the deputy head at school and I swear, one of these days I'm going to shove a blackboard duster up her left nostril."

Emily laughed. "Geez, I can't believe she's still here. Or married for that matter."

"Why not?" Amy asked, "She's freaking hot, and she knows it."

"Stacey Puffer hot? Are you sure we have the same person?" Emily asked wondering if she was remembering the wrong person.

Amy pulled her mobile out her back pocket and logged into her social media account. Scrolling down a bit and then clicking, she showed Emily the screen.

The blonde woman smiling in the profile photo definitely didn't seem like the girl Emily remembered, but as she scrolled down further, she saw a picture of Stacey with a little girl. An overweight little girl with orange hair and a pouty expression on her face. "Oh that's her alright," Emily told Amy, "That kid is the spitting image of Stacey."

"Ha!" Amy said triumphantly, "I knew she wasn't as popular in school as she likes to pretend."

They finished the bottle of wine, sharing stories about Stacey and a few other people they both knew, but soon the sun had gone down, and Amy got ready to leave.

"I have to get home and feed the teenager, before he starts gnawing on the furniture." Amy put her glass in the sink and smiled at Emily, "It was really good to meet you Emily, it's so nice having someone with a decent sense of sarcasm around."

Emily walked her to the door, "Same here. I was beginning to feel ostracised by all the holier-than-thou women here." Emily joked.

When they had said their goodbyes and Emily was alone again, she realised how quiet the little house was. Getting irritated with herself, she went through to the room and collected her laptop. Setting it on the small dining table, she reminded herself that she liked being alone and powered up the computer so she could get some work done.

# Chapter Seven

Across town in one of the largest homes in all of Hawthorne, Cathy Richards sat with her son and granddaughter eating dinner at the dining table, as they had done every week since her son had moved back home.

"So I heard that Emily Winter has returned to town and already caused a scene," Cathy said to her son.

Liam looked up from cutting his daughter's food. "Yes, she was in lockup last night actually."

Cathy smiled, "I hope you were the one to throw her in there."

Liam nodded, "But I let her go. Paige Mackenzie came and got her out just before dawn."

"Why would anyone want to get that piece of trash out of jail?" Cathy asked abruptly.

"Mother!" Liam admonished, gesturing towards his daughter, "Could you not?"

"Sorry dear," Cathy said, "I was just hoping that girl was out of your life for good."

"She is out of my life." Liam said harshly, thoroughly irritated.

"Okay, okay," Cathy said, handing him a napkin for his daughter. "Settle down William."

"It's Liam." Her granddaughter corrected her cheerfully.

After Liam had left for the evening, still in a bad mood, Cathy had called Christian to come over. Christian Stone was the local doctor in town, about ten years Liam's senior and fifteen years Cathy's junior.

She welcomed him with open arms and kissed him as soon as the door was closed.

"How was dinner?" He asked Cathy, kissing her neck and slipping his hands around her waist.

"The usual." Cathy responded. "That boy never smiles anymore."

"That's sad," Christian said distractedly, taking her hand and leading her to the bedroom.

A while later, Cathy lay with her head on Christian's bare chest and played with the dark hair below his belly button.

They had chatted about their day and were now just enjoying the quiet time before she sent him away. Cathy always sent him away.

"Oh, I forgot to tell you," Cathy said suddenly. "Remember that awful trashy girl William dated in high school? She's back in town. William arrested her last night."

"Really," Cristian asked carelessly, running his fingers through her perfectly blow-dried hair.

"Stupid little slut." Cathy said with disgust, "Why couldn't she just stay gone?"

"Hey." Christian said, letting his hand drop to his chest, "They dated years ago. Don't turn this into a big thing."

"You don't know what she was like!" Cathy said with malice in her voice, "That little hussy hooked herself to my son because she had a pretty face and we had money. But she was as bad as her deadbeat father. The first chance a better opportunity came along, she was all over it. She destroyed

Pastor Stan's family, they never got over it. And what his poor wife went through, it's no wonder she killed herself."

"Stop it Cathy." Christian's voice was stern.

"What's your problem?" Cathy asked, sliding her hand further down to tease him.

Christian moved her hand away, "I better get home." He tried to sit up, but Cathy pushed him back down.

"Come on Christian, it's still early."

"I have a long day tomorrow." Christian got out of bed, ignoring her protests and started pulling on his pants.

"Oh, don't tell me that little whore got to you too." Cathy lay on her side, completely naked, watching him.

"Don't call her a whore." Christian said, picking his shirt up off the floor.

"Oh my God, you did sleep with her! How could you?" Cathy got up as well and wrapped a black satin robe around her body.

"I never slept with her." Christian said quietly. He sat down on the bed and started putting his shoes on.

"Then what is your problem? You don't even know her!" Cathy demanded in outrage.

Christian sighed. "Come sit next to me," he said, patting the bed next to him.

Cathy pouted but did as he asked.

"What I'm going to tell you is confidential, so I need you to swear you'll keep it to yourself."

Cathy was taken aback by his serious tone, he was usually so relaxed. "Okay." She agreed.

"When I was still a paramedic, I was on duty when we got the call that Stan was dead, and a girl was injured. I'll never forget that night."

"You were there? Who was driving? Was it her?" Cathy was riveted.

"Cathy, just listen." Christian snapped, "This bullshit about a car accident, I don't even know where it came from. There was no car and there definitely was no accident.

We got called to that old cabin in the woods. That old abandoned one near the lake? There was a cellar under the living room, you never would have even known it was there. When I walked in there, I was so sure she was dead. Stan was lying face up on the ground, there was so much blood, I couldn't see where it was all coming from. He had been dead for a while by the time we got there." Christian wiped his face with his hand as though to get the memory out of his head, "And the smell, oh God, the smell. I can still smell it when I have nightmares about that night."

"Did she kill him?" Cathy sounded vindicated, which only irritated Christian further.

"Just shut up for a minute." He snapped again, "She was lying on the floor next to Stan. One wrist was still shackled with this old iron shackle, but both wrists were raw, almost to the bone on one side. She was so swollen and bruised, I would never have recognised her, I couldn't even tell you what hair colour she had."

"She was his prisoner?" Cathy asked, looking for once, disgusted.

"He had beaten, tortured and brutalised that girl in ways I didn't even think were possible Cathy. I really thought she was dead. When I found a pulse I was shocked.

At first, I thought I had done a good thing, saving her life. But a few weeks later, I was in the staff room at St Joseph's in the city starting my rotation and two of the nurses were talking about her. About how she had spent weeks begging for death, but that the doctors just kept operating on her, kept fixing her.

I went past her room and she was staring at the roof. She looked like a corpse. She didn't respond when I tried to talk to her, but when I explained who I was, tears started pouring down her face.

That was the first time in my medical career that I cried. I have wondered at least once a day if I shouldn't have just let her bleed out on the floor that night."

Christian eyes were tearing up, it was the one case he had never been able to get over. He looked over at Cathy and saw that her expression was thoughtful.

"That's a horrible thing to happen to anyone." She said slowly, "But you have to wonder what she did to set off a man like Stan, he was hardly the type. Maybe they were having an affair and she threatened to out him." Cathy pursed her lips, nodding to herself, "But at least it got her away from William, he was always too good for her."

Christian looked at her in disgust. He walked across the room and started putting on his jacket. "You know I love you Cathy. God knows why, but I do. I have loved you since I was twenty years old and we started this affair.

I have given up everything for you. I came back here after residency, giving up a career in trauma surgery to be with you. I've stayed single all these years, for you! I stayed on the side-lines while your husband beat you and hurt you. When Frank got sick, I cared for him. I took care of your husband every day. And when he died, I was here for you. I waited, day after day for you to be ready to make us public."

Christian opened his wallet and flicked a ring on the bed,

"I've been carrying that since the day after Frank's funeral. Waiting for the day that I could put it on your finger and show the world we belong together.

But you were always too worried about what people would think, how your precious reputation would be affected. But still, I put up with all of it, because I have always loved you and because I thought I alone knew and understood the real you, the one behind the carefully constructed public exterior. I know you can be a bitch, I know that you're a snob, you even seem proud of it some of the time. But I never realised you were truly that cruel. Guess I was the idiot."

Christian had never looked at Cathy with such disappointment and loathing on his face. Without another word, he turned and walked out.

Cathy poured herself a drink in the dining room. Maybe she had been a bit harsh, but really, Christian was overreacting. It would all blow over in a few days. Christian couldn't stay mad with her, he'd never been able to. She knew that if she just carried on as usual, he would come crawling back to her.

Cathy sat on her bed and picked up the ring he had thrown down. It was just her style, eight thin gold bands interlocking, a large sapphire in the middle. She put it on her left hand and admired it for a moment. Silly boy, he knew they could never make their relationship public, her reputation would be ruined. Sighing, Cathy took the ring off and put it into the drawer in her bedside table.

Whatever else, she knew that William had made the better choice when he had settled down with Melanie. She was such a lovely girl, such a sweet person. Sighing sadly again, Cathy picked up her book and laid back on her pillows to read.

Cathy woke up after a fitful sleep. She had been haunted by dreams of Frank, her deceased husband. Frank kept turning into Stan, but Stan wasn't the kind-faced pastor she remembered, instead he had cruelty in his eyes and a sneer on his face. Cathy tried to run in her dream, but found that no matter how hard she tried, she couldn't move. When she realised that she was shackled to the Frank/Stan mutant, she screamed and woke up sweating.

She made herself some coffee and checked her mobile, expecting to find the good morning message Christian sent her every morning. Instead, the screen was blank. She couldn't remember the last time Christian had been angry enough to not send her the message; in fact, she was sure he had never been that angry.

She sighed and sipped her coffee, looking out at her perfectly manicured yard. That stupid little bitch always found a way to get under Cathy's skin.

Cathy sighed again in agitation then put her empty cup In the sink. She had to get ready for the day, she had book club that afternoon and it was her turn to bring snacks. Perhaps a little retail therapy would be in order as well.

# Chapter Eight

Back across town, Emily left the house earlier than she would have preferred, especially after all the wine she had consumed with her houseguests the day before. A fine layer of snow had settled on everything during the night. The view from the front door looked like something out of a Christmas card. Emily saw Sophie attempting to make a snowman with the little bit of snow she could find in her front yard. The little girl waved, bright pink mittens on her hands.

Emily smiled and waved back. Climbing into her car, it took a while for the engine to warm up enough so she could put the car into reverse and make her way to Paige's house.

Casey had apparently agreed to see her, so Paige had sent a text the night before asking Emily to come over in the morning.

Paige let her in when Emily got there and led her through to the kitchen where she was busy making coffee. She handed Emily a cup and took a seat at the kitchen counter. Emily joined her.

"Thanks for coming back Emily."

Emily nodded, "I told you I would try and help Paige. But please don't expect miracles."

"I think the fact that you're sitting in my kitchen is a miracle on its own." Paige smiled at her warmly. "How was your day alone yesterday? Did you explore the town at all?"

Emily shook her head, "No exploring, but I wasn't alone all day. I met my neighbour, Amy something or other."

"Oh yes, she's the art teacher at school, she's lovely. And lots of fun I can imagine." Paige smiled again.

"And Nick from Dusty's came over to return my phone. He stayed for lunch."

"You're kidding?" Paige nearly chocked on her coffee. "He stayed for lunch after getting you arrested?"

Emily shrugged, "I don't think he actually expected me to be arrested for starters. And I was misbehaving so..." Emily trailed off and finished her coffee.

"Is there chemistry between you?" Paige asked curiously.

Emily shrugged and gave Paige a small smile, "I don't do the dating thing Paige, but chemistry, well that's something I'm a little too good at."

Emily stood up, putting an end to the conversation, she could see Paige had more questions about her private life. "Is Casey expecting me?" she asked Paige.

Paige nodded and Emily left her in the kitchen and made her way back up to Casey's room.


She knocked gently on the door. Opening it, she saw Casey was sitting up in bed, still holding her knees as though she hadn't moved since the last time Emily had seen her.

"Hey." Emily said, sliding down the wall to the same spot on the floor as before.

"Hey." Casey said back, looking down at her feet.

"So I see you've been really active since the last time I was here." Emily joked.

Casey didn't even smile. Instead, she turned towards Emily and focused somewhere above her head. "I'm sorry about what I said the other day. My mom said I had the wrong version of events. I'm not usually that mean."

Emily waved her off, "I've heard worse."

"Don't you get angry with people thinking that about you?" Casey asked.

"Not really. I left here so soon after that I never really thought about what people were saying. I was just trying to forget about everything."

"And?"

"And?" Emily echoed.

"Did you manage to forget?" Casey clarified.

Emily's smile was bitter, "I like to tell myself I have sometimes, but the truth is, I don't think it's something anyone can forget. I still have nightmares most nights."

Casey looked back at her feet and Emily wondered if she had said the wrong thing. "Look Casey, I ran from my past and never once tried to work through it. I covered it with drugs and booze and sex, but it's always been there. I've always thought that if I just pretended it never happened, then eventually I'd believe it." Emily shrugged again helplessly, "For the record, that doesn't work so well."

They were silent for a while, both lost in their own thoughts of regret and hurt. Eventually, Casey whispered, "I can't look my parents in the eye. Not my dad especially. How can I when I know what they'll see?"

"What will they see?" Emily asked, "Someone damaged? Or is it more about what you're afraid to see in their eyes? It's the pity isn't it?"

Casey started crying quietly, nodding her head pathetically. "I am the same. Looking your mom in the eye still takes conscious effort. And do you know what I see when I look in her eyes? Ever since I was a kid?" Emily smiled a rueful smile, "I always see hope. Not that her hope ever adds up to much when it comes to me."

Casey cried harder, she pulled her arms tighter around her legs. Emily knew she should go over and comfort her, but it wasn't something she was any good at. Instead, she played with the scar on her left palm, just below her forefinger. Running her right thumb over the scar, she remembered the moment it happened. She had still been trying to fight at that point, early on in her captivity and had bitten Stan's hand as he held it over her mouth. He had punched her and pulled her hand up to his mouth and had slowly and deliberately bitten right through her skin, ripping away the flesh.

Emily shivered and pushed the memory away. She felt sick whenever she had flashbacks of that moment.

Casey had quietened but remained rigid in her bed as though scared to move.

"Sometimes the hope was harder to deal with if I'm totally honest. I always thought if I didn't go back to being the person I was before, she would be disappointed." Emily said quietly, hoping to break through to the girl in front of her.

Casey nodded again, but this time there were no tears, "I worry about the same. What if I'm never the same girl I was before?"

"You won't be." Emily said simply. "That Casey will never come back the same. I guess you just have to find out what kind of Casey you can be now."

"How did you find the Emily you are now?" Casey asked.

Emily shrugged, "Booze, drugs and a lot of sex, although I would recommend none of those things." Emily scratched the back of her neck while talking, "I'm not terribly fond of this Emily."

"How come you never tried to go back to being the Emily you were before?" Casey pushed.

"Because the moment he touched me, some part of me died, I felt it happen and I knew that part of me was never coming back."

There was silence for a while after that statement.

"Do you want to tell me how it started?" Emily asked gently, remembering Paige using the same words so many years before.

"No." Casey whispered, her voice scratchy.

"Want to tell me what you were doing on your trip before all of this?  You were backpacking with friends right? Doing the whole Europe thing?"

Casey sniffed loudly, "We started in Portugal, spent two days there on the coast, drank far too much rum, got horribly sunburnt, and slept a lot. Then we went into Spain, spent one night in Madrid, but we hated it there, it was hot and busy and crowded, so we took a bus to Barcelona. I think we spent a whole week there. Kelly met some Spanish guy named Eduardo and fell hopelessly in love, so it was only when he wanted to get her pregnant so they could have a reason to get married that she started to see sense and we left during the middle of the night." Casey almost smiled at the memory, "Then we went into France, spent a week or so there, travelling around, then spent almost a month in Italy. It was beautiful. I loved exploring the museums, the ruins, the coffee shops. Everything about Italy was amazing. Except the places we stayed. The things they gave us to sleep on couldn't be counted as mattresses, but anyway. Then we went back to France for two nights to go to a concert, I don't think we slept at all on that trip into France. We all fell asleep on the train to Belgium. Melissa got a tattoo of a dragon in Belgium, which was really bad. It was only the next morning that we realised how bad it actually was. I think she had already made an appointment to have laser therapy to have it removed for when she got home. We stopped in Netherlands, but the place we booked, like a backpackers lodge, was overbooked and there were all these weird, sweaty guys from Poland, so after just one night, we left early and went to Germany. We hitchhiked for a few days on our way to Frankfurt and ended up staying on a farm with this really nice old couple for a while and learnt to plow and sow fields. Then we went to Frankfurt." Casey trailed off, any positive emotion from her memories fading with it.

Emily didn't want to push her any further, so she kept silent for a while, lost in her own thoughts. It was only when she noticed how uncomfortable she was that she realised how much time had passed. Looking back at Casey, Emily saw that she had fallen asleep against the headboard behind her.

Emily pushed herself to her feet and stretched quietly before leaving the room and closing the door gently behind her.

Paige was still sitting at the kitchen counter when Emily got downstairs. Paige stood up quickly when she saw Emily making her way towards the kitchen.

"Is everything okay?" Paige asked, "Did she upset you?"

"No," Emily reassured her, "she was fine. We talked more about her than about me." Emily gestured to the kettle, "Can I make some more coffee? I'm freezing."

"I'll do it," Paige waved her to the counter, "You sit. What did she tell you? Do you mind telling me or is it private?"

"We didn't talk about any of the horrible stuff, she was just telling me about her trip until Frankfurt." Emily sat at the counter. "For a moment I saw the Casey you've always described in your emails."

Paige smiled sadly and placed two fresh coffees in front of them. "She was such a happy person. I don't know if she'll ever find her way back to that."

"She won't Paige." Emily put her coffee on the table, "You all need to accept that. That hope that she'll just flip a switch and go back to being the girl she was isn't helping anyone. It's especially not helping her."

"I know," a tear ran down Paige's cheek, but she didn't try to wipe it away.

"I'm so sorry Paige." Emily said quietly. "I can't imagine what this must be like for you."

Paige wiped her face with dishcloth and took a sip of her coffee. "Can I say something?"

Emily nodded, "Of course."

"About your incident, not Casey's."

"Oh." Emily was warier this time. "Okay." She said slowly.

"I remember watching your dad at the hospital a few times." Paige started.

"My dad only ever came once or twice." Emily interrupted.

Paige shook her head, "Your dad was there a lot more than that. He sat with you for hours at the beginning, but once you woke up, he couldn't be in there with you for some reason. He used to stand next to the door and lean against the wall, just outside your room. Eventually the staff put a chair there for him, but I never saw him go back into your room again."

"I didn't know that." Emily said quietly, looking at Paige in surprise.

"I must be honest, at the time, I thought your father was a coward. And I told him as much." Paige wiped another tear. "Now, now I understand. And I feel terrible about what I said to him."

Emily sat unmoving, watching Paige.

"I used to think," Paige continued, "that he didn't want you to survive. That he was just waiting for you to stop breathing. But every time you came close to death, he was the one that insisted they save you. I thought him not being able to look at you meant he was weak, but now... now." She trailed off for a moment then took a shaky breath and continues, "But now I understand. He was mourning the loss of the child he had."

Emily was starting to feel her anger rising. "My father didn't give a shit about me before then."

"He may have not been the best father." Paige offered.

"Oh come on Paige!" Emily snapped. "So long as he had booze he was fine. Why he didn't want me to die was probably so that he had an excuse to miss work and drink."

Emily stood up, pushing her coffee away, "I'm going outside for a cigarette."

Emily leant back on the bonnet of her car and lit a cigarette. It was freezing outside and light snowflakes were falling gently around her. Emily blew a smoke ring into the air, looking up at the light grey sky. She hadn't seen her father since the day she left town, but she could still remember the moment so vividly.

She had packed a small bag of clothes and made her plan to leave after dark. She had walked down the stairs and found him exactly where she had expected to. He was passed out on his recliner, his hand still holding an empty beer bottle by the neck, the bottom of the bottle dangling just off the chipped and faded linoleum floor.

He was snoring loudly, his shirt filthy from a day of labour in the forest and stained with pizza sauce, booze and cigarette ash.

Emily pictured that moment so clearly. Standing on the bottom step and watching her father sleeping, wondering with heart wreaking desperation why it had to be her mom who died instead of him. Or why she should be standing there, alive and in so much pain when she could have been next to her mother, blissfully free of pain or fear.

"Your cigarette's burnt out."

Emily jumped, she hadn't heard Paige join her in the driveway. She looked down at the cigarette in her hand and saw it had burnt out while she was remembering her last day in town. Shrugging, Emily flicked it into the nearby hydrangeas where it bounced off the frosty leaves.

"I'm sorry Emily. It's not my place to bring your father up."

Paige leant against the bonnet next to Emily.

Emily lit another cigarette and drew deeply on it, "It's okay," she replied, "being back here seems to have made me more sensitive than normal."

Paige lit a cigarette of her own and looked towards the distant forest. "He's still here you know." She said quietly.

"And you really shouldn't be smoking Paige. I know you're going through a lot, but you've already had cancer once." Emily responded, ignoring the statement.

"You're right," Paige grimaced, looking at the cigarette in her hand with some disgust, "but we all need a crutch sometimes, don't we?"

"Hmm," Emily murmured, blowing more smoke rings into the air.

"Does your leg hurt often?" Paige asked suddenly.

"My leg?" Emily asked, looking down. She had been subconsciously rubbing her thigh with her left hand while she smoked, "No, not really." She put her hand in her pocket instead.

"I noticed you limped a bit when you arrived and again when you came downstairs. Watching you before I came outside, you were rubbing your leg as though it were sore."

Emily sighed and flicked the butt of the second cigarette away. "I think it's the cold. It's not my leg really, my hip just gets a little stiff." Emily also looked into the distance, watching flakes of snow start to fall gently, "I guess I'm just like those old farmers that know when it's going to rain or snow because my old joints start giving me grief."

Paige smiled but didn't laugh, "You're not old Emily. And I'm sure it must be sore sometimes. Hip injuries like yours never fully heal."

Emily caught a snowflake on her hand and watched it melt almost immediately, "It's fine Paige, really. I'm used to being more active. I run most mornings to prevent stiffness. I just haven't done it here."

Paige flicked her own cigarette away, "I used to run every morning, but I haven't since Casey." Paige paused, "My poor old Charlie must hate being cooped up all day." Charlie was Paige's three-legged bulldog cross. He had just come outside and was sniffing the bushes looking for the butts they had just thrown away.

"Charlie doesn't look like much of a runner," Emily pointed out sceptically.

"You'd be surprised," Paige's smile was genuine this time, "He keeps up with the best of them. Tell you what, if it's not snowing in the morning, why don't we go for a run?"

Emily thought about it. She wasn't sure she wanted to stay in town much longer, and she didn't have any running clothes or shoes, but she was also on top of her work and had nothing waiting for her at home. She also felt that she and Casey still had more to talk about, so it would make sense to hang around for another day or two. She didn't want to push the younger woman unnecessarily.

"Okay, deal."

# Chapter Nine

**E**mily was walking around Berkleys, one of the only clothing stores in town, looking for running shoes. She wouldn't bother looking for clothes until she had found decent trainers. There was no way she was going to go running unless she had comfortable shoes with cushioned bottoms to take the impact off her knee and hip joints. She was trying on a pair of really expensive runners when she heard a sniff. Lifting her head from her rather undignified position, Emily looked up into the unfriendly face of Cathy Richards. The woman hadn't aged at all, and the expression of pure loathing Cathy had on her face was exactly as Emily remembered.

"You're not planning on shoplifting those are you?" Cathy asked in voice that was sickly sweet.

Emily sat up straighter, dropping the shoe she had in her hand back into its box.

"Since I've never been much of a shoplifter, I was considering paying for it." Emily replied in a calm voice, "But then, you never know, do you?"

"Hmmf." Responded Cathy as she walked away from Emily.

"Bitch." Emily muttered under her breath, picking up the box of shoes and going to look for clothes.

Emily threw her purchases into her car, thinking about how hungry she was. Looking up and down the main street, she saw that Molly's was the closest place. It was either that or having to cook again and Emily wasn't in the mood.

Emily entered Molly's and walked down to the far end where she had met Paige for breakfast. Sliding into the booth, Emily picked up the menu and started reading.

She smelt Molly's arrival, the old woman had always smelt like fresh baked biscuits and cinnamon.

"Hey there Sugar," Molly greeted with a huge grin, "I'm glad you haven't skipped town yet."

Emily found herself smiling warmly back at Molly. "Hey Molly, how are you?"

"Always better when I have customers like you." Molly beamed, "What can I get for you on this frosty day?"

"Cheeseburger and fries please." Emily placed the menu back in its holder near the condiments.

"And to drink?" Molly asked.

"Coffee please."

Molly smiled and patted Emily on the shoulder. "I'll get Phillip to bring you your coffee so long."

Emily smiled her thanks and pulled her work mobile out of her pocket and began going through her emails.

Within minutes a cup was placed in front of her by the spotty guy in his early twenties she had seen through the window when she had first arrived in town. He had greasy, unkempt hair and the thick glasses he wore were so filthy, Emily wondered how he could see where he was going.

"One coffee, cream on the side." He said in a strangely deep voice.

"Thanks," Emily said, pouring cream into her coffee.

"I remember you." Phillip said.

Emily jumped slightly, she hadn't noticed he was still there. "Oh?" was all she could think to say in reply.

"Yeah," Phillip was picking an angry spot on his chin thoughtfully, "you were one of the leaders in our Sunday school camps when I was little."

"Oh." Emily said again. She didn't want to get into a discussion about the church in any way.

"You were always nice to me," Phillip went on, not seeming to notice Emily's discomfort. "Not like the other leaders."

Phillip took his glasses off and rubbed the lenses with the end of his t-shirt. Emily looked up at him and for the first time saw his eyes. They were so dark they were almost black. Emily couldn't tell where the pupil began or ended. She gasped involuntarily.

Phillip's sentence drifted off when he realised that Emily wasn't paying attention, "I'll go check on your burger," he told her uneasily then wondered off back to the counter.

Emily watched him walk away, the hairs on her arms standing up uncomfortably.

She gave herself a mental shake, just because the eyes had looked so familiar, it didn't mean anything, Emily told herself harshly. It couldn't be.

Even though she knew she was being unreasonable, Emily couldn't shake the feeling Phillip left her with. She felt dirty. She knew she was being unfair to the kid and had probably freaked him out, but even when he brought over her food, she couldn't bring herself to look at him when she said thanks.

Emily tried to eat, but the food felt flavorless and dry and was getting stuck in her throat and she found herself unable to finish. She had lost her appetite completely and had just paid the bill and left it mostly uneaten. She stood outside Molly's in the cold and shoved her hands in her pockets, suddenly unsure of what she was going to do for the afternoon.

She lit a cigarette and pulled out her mobile to text Paige.

*Hey, are you busy?*

Emily had gotten into her car and turned on the ignition when her mobile pinged.

*At my office at the school, had to do some things. Want to come past?*

Emily sent a thumbs up and pulled out of Molly's parking. Even once she was on the main road, she couldn't shake the feeling that Phillip was watching her drive away.

Edgewood Academy had been founded nearly sixty years ago. Set on a sprawling estate donated by a forestry tycoon, the academy was surrounded in every direction by acres and acres of pine trees.

Because the academy was so far out of the way from any big cities, most of the teachers lived on the property, a separate area from the school and boarding houses. The few teachers that were local lived in the town, like Amy did.

The academy itself was an ancient castle like building that had been revamped and added to over the years. The designers had kept the original designs, extending the building backwards and upwards to house the growing amount of students. The school's high education standard and brilliant scoring meant that it had become one of the most sought after schools in the west. The fees were insanely expensive but every year the school grew bigger.

The only reason Emily had been able to go to Edgewood Academy as a child was because her mother taught there and once her mother had died, the school took pity on Emily and wavered her fees throughout her time there. Emily had often wondered how much of that had to do with the social worker she had at the time.

Emily parked in the visitor's area and climbed out of her car. The school was still an imposing building, even after all these years. The ivy covering the front of the building had thickened in her absence and there was a security guard at the door which was unusual, but otherwise it was exactly as Emily remembered it.

Emily nodded at the security guard as she entered the building and made her way down the brightly lit stone passage towards reception. She suddenly had the uncomfortable feeling that she would be recognised and paused at the reception door before opening it.

She could hear voices on the other side of the door but couldn't hear what was being said. Before Emily had a chance to make up her mind, the door swung open and she found herself face to face with Amy.

The scowl on Amy's face turned to a smile when she saw Emily.

"Hey there. This is a surprise." Amy said.

"Hi." Emily smiled back.

The person Amy had been talking to inside the reception came to the door to see who Amy had greeted.

Emily found herself face to face with Stacey Green.

The blonde woman's face lit up with excitement. "Well, if it isn't Emily Winter! I was beginning to think the rumors were nonsense."

Emily gave the other woman a smile that wasn't genuine. She felt her dislike for Stacey come to the surface immediately.

"Stacey, I wouldn't have recognised you." She replied coolly.

"It's amazing what time and money can do for a person, don't you think?" Stacey touched her blonde, carefully styled hair with manicured fingers. Her smile was sweet but unconvincing. "What brings you to the school?"

"I'm looking for Paige's office." Emily answered.

"Oh? I imagine you're here to talk to her about her poor daughter. How tragic." Stacey's tone let the others know that she didn't have any true interest in Casey other than using her trauma as gossip fodder. "I can't imagine why she would want you of all people though."

Emily swallowed an angry retort, knowing that the other woman was just baiting her.

Amy pushed past Stacey and grabbed Emily by the arm, "Come on," she said cheerfully, "Let me show you the way."

Once they were around the corner, Amy's smile dropped. "What a bitch."

Emily snorted, "No kidding. Thanks for the rescue."

"That woman," Amy said, ignoring the thank you, "She's so bitter and twisted it's disgusting. You should hear the things she says about other people."

"I can imagine." Emily said, "Is that what you were arguing about?"

"No," Amy replied, leading them through a door and down another corridor, "That was about Xavier, she was being unnecessarily hard on him because she doesn't like me."

Before Emily could respond, Amy stopped at a dark wood door and knocked.

Paige sighed as she read over the faded notes in front of her. She had pulled the file out of storage several weeks ago but had been unable to bring herself to open it until now. Turning to another set of stapled pages she had written all those years ago, the memories of that time came flooding back so easily.

Paige had hoped to never have to look through that file again, and she knew that technically she didn't have to do it now. She knew it by heart and the memories of those first meetings after Emily had been found were permanently seared into Paige's memory. She thought about the young girl curled up in her hospital bed, flinching at every sound, terrified of every person that came into the room. The memory still made Paige feel slightly queasy. Knowing Emily before the incident, the drastic change had been heart wrenching to see. Watching her struggle as she did for so long afterwards, Paige had wondered on more than one occasion if it wouldn't have been kinder to let her die the day she had been found.

She sighed again and closed the file. She had always felt bad about that thought, she truly was glad Emily had fought so hard to survive, even with the revelations from the other evening.

There was a knock on the office door, so Paige quickly stuffed the file back into her laptop bag before calling out to whoever was there to enter.

Amy left Emily at the door when Paige had responded to the knock. Emily opened the door and gave Paige a small smile.

"Thanks for letting me come." She said to Paige.

Paige motioned Emily to take a seat and smiled back, "You're always welcome."

Emily sat down on an overstuffed leather armchair and Paige stood up and went to the kettle near her window.

"Do you want some tea?" Paige asked.

"Only if you're making."

"I'm making."

While Paige made the tea, Emily looked around the office. The stone walls were covered in brightly colored posters and positive motivational signs. There were stacks of books on every shelf in no order whatsoever and Paige's desk was covered in files and sheets of paper. It was almost identical to the office Paige had been using when she was still doing social work when Emily was younger, the only difference was that the furniture was more expensive in this office.

Paige gave Emily a cup and sat on the matching armchair opposite.

"Sorry to disturb you at work." Emily said, taking a sip of her coffee and wishing she could light a cigarette.

"No man, as I said, anytime." Paige smiled. "I'm only here today to do some follow-ups. I've been on leave since Casey." Paige's smile faltered a little, she had a sip of her own coffee then smiled once more. "So, what brings you here?"

Emily lost track of what Paige was saying, instead she was looking at the posters on Paige's wall. The one that had caught her attention was a poster of a beautiful sunset on the beach, with a scripture written across it in bold lettering; *"For I know the plans I have for you"* declares the Lord, *"Plans to prosper you and not harm you, plans to give you hope and a future."*

"Emily?" Paige asked kindly.

"Huh?" Emily turned back to Paige, "Sorry, I got distracted."

"I could see that." Paige looked at the poster too, "It's one of my favorite verses. Just so beautiful don't you think?"

Emily shook her head, "Not really. I mean, do you actually believe that?"

"The words?" Paige asked, turning her attention back to Emily, "Yes I do. I take it you don't?"

"No, because His plans have not exactly kept me from harm."

"Those weren't His plans." Paige said quietly.

"He knows our beginning to our end and our end from our beginning, so you can't tell me what is and isn't His plan." Emily said in irritation.

Paige could see Emily was getting angry so she decided not to try and discuss religion with her yet, but she hoped the day would come.

"What was on your mind when you came in?" Paige asked changing the subject with another gentle smile.

Emily was surprised at the sudden change in direction but didn't comment. Instead she shrugged. "I went to get some running shoes and clothes, then went to Molly's for a bite, but." Emily couldn't think of how to explain what was troubling her.

"But?" Paige prompted gently.

"There's a guy working for Molly." Emily began.

"Phillip." Paige guessed, "He's weird, but seems harmless. I know he used to freak Casey out."

"That's the one. He's local right?" She asked then continued when Paige nodded. "Who are his parents?"

"The Downings. They all moved here when he was a baby if I remember correctly. Why the interest?"

"I don't know really," Emily answered, "There's just something about him that really put me on edge. Something about his eyes." Emily shuddered slightly, "But I remember Mr. Downing having really bright green eyes."

"Yes." Paige agreed, slightly confused.

Emily twisted her almost empty cup around in her hands, not looking at Paige. She knew Paige wouldn't push her to say anything, the older woman always waited for the silence in the room to grow until Emily blurted out whatever she was thinking.

As usual, it worked. "I know I should have probably asked about this sooner," Emily began, her eyes still focused on her hands, "But whatever happened to Stan's brother?"

Paige was surprised. "Stan didn't have a brother."

Emily looked up at Paige, confused, "Of course he did."

"I looked into Stan after you were found Emily, he had no siblings." Paige insisted.

"But who was he then?" Emily blurted.

"Who was who?" Paige was looking thoroughly confused.

"Stan's partner. The one who—" Emily trailed off again when she saw the look of horror on Paige's face.

Paige looked aghast, "Emily, are you saying that two men abducted you?"

Emily felt horrified herself. "How could you not know that?"

"How could I possibly know?" Paige asked, looking sickened.

The question brought Emily up short. She had always just assumed Paige knew. Thinking about it now though, she realised the only way anyone would have known about him would have been if she had told them. And Emily refused to speak to anyone after she had been found.

The sudden understanding that the other man had gone free because of her own omission was enough to make Emily nauseous. So nauseous that she bolted to Paige's private bathroom, only just making it to the sink before bringing up the tea she had just finished.

When there was nothing left in her, Emily rinsed her mouth out and splashed her face with icy water.

Paige stood at the door, knowing better than to try comfort the younger woman. Paige herself was in total shock. It had never occurred to her for a moment that Stan hadn't been acting on his own.

She waited until Emily stopped splashing her face. The younger woman had a hand on either side of the sink, her shoulders hunched.

"Emily?"

"Paige, please don't."

"We need to talk about this."

"Maybe. But not today." Emily walked towards the door and Paige stepped back to let her pass. Without another word, Emily picked up her bag and walked out.

Paige stood at her window and watched Emily back her car out of her parking slot and make her way slowly out the school grounds.

Paige sighed. She wasn't sure she was the right person to be dealing with this. Knowing now that there was another man out there capable of such viciousness made her feel positively sick. She thought back to the days after the beaten and bloodied girl had been rescued from that cabin. She was sure she would have remembered the sheriff saying something, anything about a second attacker, but he never said a thing.

It occurred to her that maybe the sheriff hadn't noticed because none of them thought to check. Looking at her watch, Paige went to her desk and scratched through her drawers until she found her old notebook. Turning to the correct page from memory, she picked up the phone on her desk and dialed the number she had scribbled down years ago.

It was answered on the fourth ring. "Hello?" The voice was raspier than Paige remembered, but she knew she had the right man.

"Sheriff Brown?"

The voice on the other end laughed, "No one's called me that for years Paige."

"You remember me?" Paige smiled.

"Of course I remember you. Way too pretty to be doing social work." The old man laughed again. "What can I do for you Paige?"

"I'm sorry to call you out of the blue like this, but I have some questions about Emily Winter."

"Whew, you don't mess around do you?"

"I'm sorry Sheriff, but I didn't know who else to call."

"No problem my dear, what's your question?"

Paige took a steadying breath, knowing she was about to question the man's judgement. "When you did your investigation, did you ever see any sign that there might have been more people involved than just Stan?"

There was silence. It went on so long that Paige thought they may have been cut off, or maybe he had just put the phone down.

"I remember every moment of that case Paige. It's something that still haunts me to this day."

"Me too." Paige replied sadly.

"Worse still as it was my first case as a small-time sheriff. I came to Hawthorne to get away from all the violence." He sighed loudly, "As you'll recall, the girl's father didn't want anything to get out, so I was forced to do everything myself."

"I do remember Sheriff, and please know I'm not questioning your abilities."

"Doesn't sound like it, but anyway." He cleared his throat. "That cabin was used for church retreats for years, then after that, kids used to sneak in there all the time to party. There were plenty signs of multiple people being there, but it was almost impossible to tell when any of those people had been there. The basement that none of us knew existed was another story. There were signs of footprints and obviously massive amounts of evidence pointing to it being a torture chamber, but I was never able to distinguish whether or not the prints belonged to different people or just the same man wearing different shoes. All the prints were size tens. There were no usable fingerprints either"

"Did you do any background checks on Stan himself after?" Paige asked him.

"Of course I did. I did checks on him when I first came to town too, just so you know. Grew up in an orphanage run by a church down south. No family ever came looking for him and he joined the ministry straight out of high school. No criminal record, no prior concerns, even his damn school record was spotless."

"Did he have any siblings that you knew of?"

"No family." He repeated firmly.

"When he was here, did you notice any close friendships he may have had? Visitors from out of town?"

"No, nothing like that. I never saw him have a visitor, and I lived across from him for months. Only ever saw the wife and girls come and go."

Paige knew the retired man must have tortured himself for years for never picking up that he had a monster living forty feet from him.

"None of us had any idea what kind of a man he was Sheriff."

"Hmmf." He grunted, "Anything else?"

"No. Thank you so much for your help." Paige said goodbye and replaced the phone back in the cradle.

She knew she was going to have to talk to Daniel about this. He knew most of the men in the area back then, and there was still a man out there running free after what he did to Emily, it didn't bare thinking about.

Paige thought about her own daughter at home all alone and vulnerable. Paige shivered.

# Chapter Ten

Cathy Richards was sitting in the most comfortable armchair in the living room of Jean's house. She was always given the honor, it was an unspoken understanding of her social status in Hawthorne. She had been paging through the new book they were about to start reading, not paying attention to the ladies around her until she heard Emily's name mentioned.

Looking up suddenly, Cathy started listening in.

"I've never believed that nonsense about a car accident," Stacey Green was saying importantly to the group at large, "my daddy had the only scrapyard in two counties and the only tow trucks, and he never brought in old Stan's car."

"So what do you think really happened?" Jean asked, the older woman's face alight with curiosity.

Stacey used her hand to swing her elegant and expensive blonde hair over her shoulder dramatically, "What my daddy told me was that they found Pastor Stan's car in the forest, near the old church retreat. But it had no damage. His wife came and fetched it but we never saw it or her again so daddy didn't even bring it in. He heard from a friend in the sheriff's department though, there was booze in the car and enough drugs to sink a ship. I think," she paused once more for affect, "That their affair had been going on for a long time and a bad trip made one or both of them lose it."

All of the women shared shocked looks while Cathy smiled to herself. That was a far more rational explanation. Maybe once Christian heard about this he would get over his silly reaction to the girl. She nodded to herself, deciding that when Christian called her again to make up, she would enjoy telling him what she had just overheard. Then she would let him work his way into her good books on her terms.

Feeling vindicated, Cathy placed her book on the table in front of her and joined the conversation that had turned to school rumors.

∞

What little daylight the clouds had allowed through was fading and the wind had picked up. Emily pulled her jacket tightly around her chest as she got out of her car at Dusty's.

The parking lot was deserted except for a beat-up and rusted looking pickup truck near the side of the building.

Emily entered the bar to find it was empty, but there was a fire roaring in the ancient fireplace and the whole room was toasty warm.

Behind the bar was a young woman, she had spiked up short black hair, and her muscular arms were covered in tattoos that went up to her neck. She was wearing a sleeveless black shirt with the faded name of an old rock band stamped across her chest. Emily noticed that the bartender had a nose ring as well as several earrings in each ear. The girl had bright green eyes and without the dark clothing and makeup, she would have been girl-next-door beautiful.

Emily took a seat at the bar and shrugged off her jacket.

"What can I get you?" The bartender asked in way of greeting.

"I'll start with tequila and a beer." Emily told her.

"Ah," the bartender smiled, "You must be tequila girl." She poured the shot and placed it in front of Emily.

"My reputation precedes me." Emily commented dryly, downing the tequila just as her stomach growled loudly.

The bartender took a packet of crisps off the shelf behind her and placed it down next to the empty shot glass, "On the house." She said, winking and walking off to unpack some clean glasses.

Emily opened the bag and ate the crisps quickly, discovering she was famished after all. The queasy feeling from earlier was finally starting to settle a little.

Emily had finished her beer when the bartender returned and set an opened replacement in front of her.

"Thanks," Emily said, "Where's Nick?"

"He closed last night so he's making the most of my visit by leaving me to open." The bartender smiled wryly.

"You don't live here?" Emily asked. She had assumed as much, the only person she had seen in Hawthorne that belonged less than her was the girl in front of her.

"God no." She laughed, "Just came to pay Nick a visit." Emily took a sip of her beer, "Are you together?"

She laughed again and shook her head, "Nick's not my type. He's male for one, and for two, I know him too well."

"You were in the service together?" Emily guessed.

"Yep, five years and three tours." She poured two shots of tequila and slid one across to Emily, "The name's Jax by the way."

"Emily," Emily responded, raising her tot glass in a toast then swallowing the contents.

Emily had spent the early evening playing cards with the old men that arrived shortly after her. They spent their time regaling Emily with old stories and teasing her about her tequila behavior from her previous visit.

Emily had moved on to rum and cokes after her second beer and was sitting close to the fire. It had taken hours but she could finally feel the booze taking the edge of the feelings of anger, confusion and anxiety she had been swallowing since seeing Paige earlier in the day.

She had seen Nick arrive earlier, and had waved, but was concentrating on her poker hand, so hadn't paid much attention to anyone else. Looking around she saw that the bar had filled while she had been distracted.

Excusing herself to go to the bathroom and get another round of drinks, Emily walked past the bar and saw that Jax was gone and Nick was talking to the patrons at the pool table. Looking away and hoping none of the players were the ones she was with the other night, Emily pushed open the bathroom door and stepped inside.

The outer room was small with a basin and a mirror, one cubicle to the side. Standing at the mirror, putting on fresh eyeshadow was Jax.

"Hey." Jax said, looking at Emily's reflection in the mirror. "Do you need me to move?"

"No thanks," Emily replied. Her sudden need for a pee had disappeared as she watched Jax.

Jax turned around and smiled a knowing smile. "Something else you need from me?"

"Just looking." Emily said with a slow smile of her own.

"And? Like what you see?" Jax's voice was low and sultry.

Emily took a step closer to her and placed her hand on Jax's neck, pulling her closer.

Emily felt Jax's hand on her hip as their lips met. The rush she always felt being touched by a stranger was intoxicating.

Emily pushed Jax against the sink, her hands now in Jax's hair, pulling her closer, kissing her intensely.

When Jax pulled away, Emily smiled at her, tipsy from the drinking and breathless from their dalliance.

"I have a place nearby." Emily suggested, running a finger from Jax's shoulder and down her arm.

"If this is what you really, really want, honey, I am in." Jax replied, "But somehow, I'm not sure it is."

Emily pulled her hand away, "I wouldn't have offered if it wasn't."

Jax shook her head and took a step back, "I'm going to hate myself for doing this, but you've had a lot to drink and I'm not taking advantage."

"No one takes advantage of me." Emily snapped, more aggressively than she meant to.

"Maybe not usually, but I don't think tonight is a good idea." Jax said calmly, putting her makeup back into her bag.

Emily felt anger and humiliation rising, she wasn't used to being rejected. "You don't know a damn thing about me."

128

"Maybe not honey, but that look," she pointed at Emily's face, "that look I know all too well."

"What look?" Emily demanded, getting angrier.

Jax sighed. She slung her bag over her shoulder and gently touched Emily's cheek, "The look of someone whose just been forced to face their demons head on and are scared shitless by what they see."

Emily opened her mouth to argue but couldn't think of anything to say.

"I'm not down to be anyone's band aid." Jax said, giving her a sad smile and walking past Emily and out the bathroom.

Emily finished up in the bathroom and noticed her hands were shaking when she washed them. Angry with herself for letting what Jax said get to her, Emily dried her hands furiously then left the bathroom.

Leaving a stack of cash on the bar counter, Emily left the bar before Nick could catch up. She saw him coming out the corner of her eye when she put the money down and didn't feel like talking to him.

Grabbing her jacket off the chair she was sitting on near the fire, she ignored the complaints of the old men about her leaving, gave them a wave and headed out into the freezing night.

Looking around as she lit a cigarette, Emily was pleased to see there were no police cars in sight.

What she really wanted to do was pack her stuff and leave. If she drove through the night, she could be home by morning.

She sighed, opening the driver's door of her car and getting in. As tempting as it was to leave immediately, she knew she shouldn't be driving these backroads after so many drinks. Instead she headed back to the house and promised herself that she would get some sleep, send Paige a message and leave first thing in the morning.

Emily had done what she could for Casey, she didn't really believe that staying would do either of them any good. Emily had never believed that talking about the bad crap in a person's life would make it better, and if the last few days had proven anything, she was right. She had felt out of control ever since she got on that damned plane to Frankfurt.

Emily was sitting on the couch, halfway through a bottle of wine when her mobile beeped.

*Hey, you left in a rush? Everything okay?*

The message was from Nick. Emily looked at her watch and saw it was well after midnight.

*All good. Got cold.* She replied.

*Want someone to keep you warm?* Nick replied with a winking emoji.

Emily thought about saying no, but decided that since she still wasn't tired and it was her last night in town anyway, she might as well take her mind off things.

*Come on over. Bring tequila.*

Suddenly relieved that a lonely night was no longer stretching ahead of her, Emily downed the rest of her glass and went to the bathroom to freshen up.

∞

It had felt as though she had been alone for days. She couldn't keep track of time in the darkness of the basement, no light came through unless the lights were on in the room upstairs and no sound seemed to penetrate the stone walls from outside. Emily wondered if this was their plan, just to leave her down there to starve or die of dehydration.

Between punches and lack of water, Emily's lips were cracked and bleeding, every time she woke up and opened her mouth, she could feel the skin on her lips tearing where the scabs had stuck together while she slept.

She had never been afraid of the dark before, but she was now. She never thought she would wish for them to come back, but she did now. She was so desperate not to be alone in the crushing silence anymore.

The first few days she had screamed herself hoarse, but she had soon learnt that no one was coming to her rescue. Wanting to be away from the monsters that had put her there had been her only wish since those early days that she found herself shocked at how relieved she felt when she finally heard footsteps on the floorboards above her. She knew there would be pain coming now, but she also knew, it was better than being alone.

∞

Emily felt someone shaking her and she yanked her arm away viciously. She fell out of bed, and scrambled backwards in a panic, hitting the back of her head on the cupboard door.

"Shit! Emily, are you okay?" Nick jumped off the bed and rushed to her side.

Emily pushed him away, "I'm fine." She snapped. She rubbed the back of her head where it had connected with the cupboard and could already feel a lump forming.

"You were having a nightmare, I was just trying to wake you." Nick said, backing off. He sat on the edge of the bed looking shaken.

Seeing him sitting there naked and worried irritated Emily. "Why are you still here? I thought we agreed on no overnighters?" She pulled herself up off the floor and walked into the bathroom to splash her face with cold water.

Nick followed her and leant against the bathroom door jamb, his arms crossed. He shrugged carelessly, looking at Emily in the mirror, "It was late, we had a lot to drink and I guess we fell asleep."

Emily dried her face on the towel hanging next to the door and noticed for the first time that she was naked except for her white vest. "Well, we're awake now." She told him, not meeting his eye.

He uncrossed his arms, "Don't worry. I can take a hint."

He was already pulling his jeans on when Emily came back into the room, a towel around her waist.

"I really was just trying to help you know." He told her quietly, pulling his shirt over his head.

"I know." Emily answered, still not meeting his eye, "It's not about you, it's about me."

Nick pulled on his boots in silence and left without another word.

Emily pulled on her pants and a jacket and went to the kitchen and put the kettle on, deciding that trying to sleep again would be pointless. Once her coffee was made, she picked her cigarettes and mobile up off the counter and went outside to sit on her usual spot just outside the door.

Lighting a cigarette, Emily put her coffee next to her on the step and pulled her mobile out of her pocket, she saw it was just after four in the morning but decided to send Paige a text anyway.

*I'm not going to make it for a run this morning. Something's coming up so I'm heading home.*

Emily finished her cigarette and coffee watching moths attempt to get to the light outside the door. Desperate to get to their goal, they were throwing themselves repeatedly against the glass covering the bulb.

Emily was tossing her bag in the backseat of her car when Paige's car pulled into the driveway behind hers. It wasn't Paige behind the wheel though, it was Casey.

"Hey Casey." Emily said, walking up to the open window.

"Could you get in for a minute?" Casey asked in way of greeting.

Emily raised an eyebrow but walked around the car and climbed into the passenger seat, closing the door behind her.

"My mom said you have to leave this morning." Casey said, looking straight ahead and still holding the steering wheel.

"Work stuff, but I've told your mom to give you my mobile number in case you need to talk." Emily told her, also looking ahead in an attempt to make Casey feel more comfortable.

"You said when you were in my room," Casey was fidgeting in her seat, "You said you used sex as one of the ways to get over what happened to you."

"I also said it wasn't the greatest idea." Emily pointed out.

Casey turned to face Emily suddenly. "How? How did you ever allow anyone close enough to you to get naked with them and trust them with your body?"

"First off, I don't trust anyone with my body, but me." Emily told her, "But to answer your question, to be honest, I didn't really care who I was with. I needed to prove to myself that someone would still want me." Emily took a breath, "I also couldn't handle the idea that they be the last ones to touch me. I needed to prove that it didn't bother me."

"Did it help?"

"Sometimes I thought it did, but no, not really."

"Do you think I'll ever have a normal relationship?" Casey whispered sadly.

Emily shrugged, "I don't know Cas, all I know is that I shut myself off from people because it was easier. Using other people came naturally to me, I don't see that happening with you."

"I'm so scared of everyone." Casey said miserably, looking out the windscreen again.

"I know. I am too, but in a different way. I can handle myself physically now, so I'm not worried about that, but I've never had a single relationship afterwards."

"Never?"

"Nope." Emily smiled wryly, "Wouldn't be fair to deal with someone this screwed up." She turned to Casey again, "Which is why it's important you work this through the right way, not like I did."

# Chapter Eleven

## One Month Later

Emily was sitting on her bed, cross legged, surrounded by personnel files from First National, going through all the log on codes and passwords trying to track down the person responsible for a large sum of money disappearing out of several of the bank's call accounts.

She looked at her watch and sighed. It was just after two in the morning, and she had been at this for days but still hadn't come up with a viable suspect. She had a horrible feeling that the system she had so meticulously set up had been hacked by someone outside the bank.

Emily put her hands behind her head and stretched her back. Her back and neck were stiff from sitting in the same position for so long. Her back clicked loudly as she stretched, giving her a feeling of instant relief.

She knew she was going to have to reach out to some contacts in the deep dark web to find out if any of them knew about a hack she hadn't discovered yet. She was loath to go down that road, the dark web always left her with an unpleasant taste in her mouth and one was always taking a risk asking a bunch of hackers for advice, especially when it meant she would have to admit she left a bank open to hacking. Some people would find that too much of a temptation to ignore.

Wondering if she would have any luck texting the one hacker who she almost trusted, Emily got off the bed and went to fetch her mobile from where it was charging on her dresser.

As she picked up her work mobile, she saw the notification light was blinking on her personal one. Picking up both phones she unlocked her personal one and saw a text from an unknown number.

Sitting back on the bed, Emily opened the text.

*Hi, its cas, I'm sorry to bother you in the middle of the night, but I didn't know who else to turn to.*

Emily had left the phone on silent so she hadn't heard the text come through, but she saw on the time stamp that it had been sent less than an hour earlier.

*Its not a bother Cas, I was already up. What's wrong?*

Emily was texting her contact from her work phone when the other one lit up again.

*I really need to talk to someone, I don't know what to do...*

Emily put her work phone on the bed and turned her attention to Casey.

*What's wrong? Do you want me to call you?*

There was no reply for a few minutes so Emily had gone back to work. She had gotten hold of her contact and he had promised to have a look around on Emily's behalf before she had to go delving into the dark side of the internet. They were discussing the price of his assistance when Casey finally replied.

*No, don't worry. I shouldn't have bothered you, please just forget about it.*

Emily frowned at the screen. She was tempted to call the number and make Casey spit out whatever was bothering her, but she knew the girl wouldn't answer.

*I'm here if you change your mind.* She replied instead.

Deciding it was time for coffee, since she would have to wait to see what her hacker friend came up with, Emily left the bedroom and tried to put Casey out of her mind.

Emily woke up to the sound of a phone ringing. She had put her personal mobile ringer back on after the texts from Casey, but she hadn't expected her to actually call. Pulling herself out of a dreamless sleep, Emily groaned and sat up.

It wasn't Casey's number on the screen, it was Paige's.

"Hey Paige." She answered.

"Did I wake you?" Paige asked, sounding concerned.

"Don't worry about it," Emily said, clearing her throat, "I worked late last night because today is Saturday. What's wrong with Casey?"

"How did you know I was calling about Casey?" Paige asked, sounding worried, "Have you spoken to her?"

Emily's brain was clearing from the sleep and she cleared her throat again, "No," she answered carefully, "but since you don't usually call, I guessed."

There was silence on the line, then Paige said, "You're right, I only seem to call you when I need something. I'm so sorry Emily."

"Paige, seriously, I wasn't complaining. You know I'm not a talking on the phone kind of person, and I am well aware of how full your hands are at the moment." Emily crossed her legs on the bed and pulled the blanket up over her lap, "Now, what's the problem?"

"I don't actually know," Paige answered honestly, "She seemed to be doing better these last few weeks. She's been getting out of bed and talking to friends. She even saw her boyfriend Ben a few times. I really thought she was making progress.

But she went to town yesterday to watch a movie with friends and came home and disappeared into her bedroom. She locked the door so I couldn't go in, but I heard her crying."

Emily sighed, feeling bad that she hadn't pushed the issue with Casey last night or at least tried to call.

"I'm sure it's normal for her to have setbacks Paige. There are no quick fixes for this."

"I know you're right, but last night was something else." Paige sounded helpless again, "The crying was different. Something is wrong."

Emily had opened her laptop while they were talking and saw an email from her hacker contact saying he would need a few days to dig around.

"How bad is the snow there?" Emily asked suddenly.

"Um," Paige was taken aback, "it's not too bad, less than two inches I think."

"I'll catch a flight this afternoon." Emily decided, surprising even herself with the statement. "That Amy girl mentioned the airport rents cars now. I'll be there by this evening."

Paige was silent for a moment, also surprised by Emily's sudden decision. "Oh Emily, thank you so much. I can fetch you?"

"No thanks," Emily responded, "I need my own transport. I'll see you later Paige."

Emily had called Glynis soon after she had gotten off the phone to Paige to let her know that she was leaving again and asked Glynis just to check the emails while she was gone and man the phones.

Besides the bank, Emily hadn't taken on any new clients lately, so she knew there wasn't much work she could do in the city. She could have taken on a few new contracts but for some reason hadn't been feeling interested in securing new work.

As the small plane she was on flew past cities and over towns that grew smaller and sparser, Emily had to admit to herself that she was getting to the point where she was going to go on a bender if she had no work to concentrate on. She had been talking to a few people online, preparing to find her next one-night conquest and while she had been careful not to drink every night, she was drinking a lot more on the nights she did drink; waking up with no memory of the previous night, which was something that scared her.

Emily had actually been considering going overseas for a holiday. Whenever she travelled it was for work, and she was considering spending a few weeks in Europe to visit the museums and see the sights.

She knew she was looking for distraction from her own thoughts, she just wasn't sure if going back to Hawthorne was the kind of distraction she needed. If it hadn't been for the texts from Casey, Emily wasn't sure she would be on her way there.

It was late afternoon by the time Emily was led outside the airport by the Avis manager. The wind was bitterly cold, but it hadn't yet started snowing again. Emily looked at the grey purple clouds and knew she didn't have long to get to town before the snow arrived.

The Avis manager helped put her bags into a Ford Explorer SUV and handed Emily the key with a white-toothed smile and hurried back indoors to the warmth of his heated office.

Emily was glad she chose such a large car, especially with the incoming weather. She climbed into the driver's seat and put the heater on as soon as the car started. She was pleased to find seat warmers as well and by the time she was on the main road into town, she was starting to feel pleasantly toasty.

She called Paige as she neared the town center.

Paige answered on the first ring, "Hi Emily, how was your flight?"

"It was fine thanks Paige. I'm almost in town. Must I come straight to your place or do you want to meet somewhere?"

"Would you mind very much if I met you at the cottage you stayed at last time? The key is still under the pot plant where you left it."

"No problem," Emily replied, a little surprised, "I'll see you in a bit."

"Great, I'll bring pizza and wine." Paige said.

Emily stopped at the grocery store and ran in to get a carton of cigarettes, toilet paper, bottled water and fresh milk. She had left everything behind last time so she knew there should be coffee, sugar and maybe even some pasta and biscuits still.

She pulled into the driveway less than ten minutes later and while she was unloading her bags from the back of the SUV, she saw little Sophie from next door waving frantically out the kitchen window. Emily waved and smiled back at the pajama-clad child.

The key was exactly where she had left it, and the house itself was freezing inside. Emily tried to turn the thermostat higher, but it didn't seem to be working at all. She wondered if any of the firewood stacked out back would still be dry enough to bring inside and use.

Emily dumped her bags on the bed and went back to the car to get the groceries. As she closed the boot, Paige pulled up behind her.

Paige was bundled up in a thick woolen trench coat and scarf, but she looked marginally better than the last time Emily had seen her.

As promised, Paige took a large pizza and a packet with clinking wine bottles out the passenger seat and followed Emily inside.

"It's freezing today." She said in way of greeting.

"You're not kidding," Emily replied, taking the packet of wine from Paige.

"Thanks," Paige told her, "How are you?"

"I'm doing fine thanks Paige, how are you?"

Paige put the pizza on the counter and went to the cupboard to take out wine glasses and plates. "It's been a long week." She said wearily, "But I am really happy to see you."

"Where are Daniel and Casey?" Emily asked, avoiding the gratitude she heard in Paige's voice.

"Daniel is at home, catching up on paperwork and Casey is still in her bedroom last time I checked."

Emily poured two hefty glasses of wine while Paige opened the pizza box and put two slices on each plate. They carried their dinner through to the lounge and sat on the couch together.

Paige took a sip of wine before putting her glass down on the coffee table.

"Why did you want to meet here instead of your house?" Emily asked, putting down her own glass and taking a bite of pepperoni pizza.

"To be totally honest, I needed a break," Paige admitted, putting her plate down and picking up her glass again, "the house is so quiet all the time and I feel like I'm walking on eggshells every minute."

Emily swallowed her bite of pizza, "I guess you were so worried about Casey that you didn't take into consideration how much you would be going through."

Paige shrugged, "I knew things would change, I just didn't really consider the extent of it."

Emily nodded and took a sip of her own wine. "What's going on with Casey?"

Paige sighed and pulled her scarf off, "I honestly don't know. She was doing so well. She's even been spending time with Ben again. Not much, but here and there."

"Who's Ben?" Emily asked, taking another bite of pizza.

"Her boyfriend. They've been together since junior year of high school. I honestly thought Casey would break things off after she came home. When we spoke about it, that's what she was planning to do. But Ben's such a sweet guy, he's been so patient and understanding with her since she got back."

"Must be hard for him too." Emily said quietly, thinking about Liam's very different reaction all those years ago.

Paige nodded sadly, "When he first came over and she didn't want to see him, he used to sit in the living room and cry. He was devastated that she had been hurt and he couldn't fix it."

Emily drained her wine glass, "Sounds like a nice kid."

"I just wish she would tell me what's happened. I hate not knowing what's going on."

Emily got up and went to the kitchen to fetch the wine bottle and the box of pizza, "Do you think it has to do with Ben?" she asked, filling up their glasses before sitting down again.

Paige shook her head, "I just don't know. Casey used to tell me everything, now she doesn't tell me anything anymore." Paige took another sip of wine, "For heaven's sake, the kid phoned me an hour after losing her virginity."

Emily snorted, "You must be joking!"

"I am not. She called me from the bathroom because she wanted to tell me. We've always been that close." Paige's smile faded.

"Maybe she just needs time to come to you on her own?" Emily suggested, finishing her third slice of pizza.

"Maybe." Paige agreed vaguely. "I did wonder if someone has said something to her while she was out with Ben or friends."

"Like what?" Emily asked, "Surely she would have said something to you if that was it?"

"I just don't know. I feel like she's carrying all this guilt."

"Guilt for what?" Emily asked incredulously.

"Maybe it's the wine talking, but I feel like she's hiding a lot of shame. Victims always seem to carry the shame with them."

Emily didn't respond. She took a bigger sip than she had planned and promptly choked.

"You okay?" Paige asked her thumping Emily on the back.

Emily nodded, "Just went down the wrong way."

"The wine or the shame comment?"

"Paige, I really don't want to talk about this tonight."

"We don't have to if you don't want to. I just don't want you to feel ashamed of what happened. You did nothing wrong."

Emily put her glass down on the table and pulled her legs under her to get more comfortable. "I don't know what I feel about it."

Paige hadn't expected Emily to answer her at all. She tilted her head to the side. "Do you ever feel like you were to blame?"

Emily got up and went out the kitchen door to fetch some firewood, she found some dry pieces closest to the door. They were both silent as she put the logs into the fireplace and lit the kindling. Emily knelt by the fireplace, coaxing the logs to catch alight. Once the flames were lapping the wood, she took her seat again.

Emily looked at the fireplace. She watched the flames for a while before finally answering Paige, "Not for them taking me maybe, but there are a lot of things." Her voice faded and she continued watching the logs be consumed by flames.

"I can't think of a single thing that happened that was your fault." Paige told her, placing her glass on the table.

"Well you weren't there, so you couldn't possibly know could you?" Emily said tightly.

"But you could tell me if you like."

"No. Not now." Emily got up to put more wood in the fire, more for something to do than because the flames were dying.

"Could you tell me something about the brother?" Paige asked suddenly.

Emily stiffened. She dropped the second piece of wood back on the wood rack and went back to the couch.

"I'm sorry Emily, I shouldn't have asked." Paige said contritely.

"No don't. I was thinking about it a lot today, as much as I would have preferred not to. But I know you have questions, it's only natural. Especially when you have your own daughter to think about."

Paige was surprised by Emily's reaction for the second time that night. "Did you know him before?" She asked.

Emily shook his head. "No, at least, I don't think so."

"You didn't recognise him from church, or town?"

"I never really saw his face Paige."

"Oh." Paige uttered quietly.

"It was always dark and the few times it was light enough to see something, their faces were always in silhouette. The only thing I remember was the smell of his aftershave and they both smelt like whiskey."

Emily swallowed but then picked up her wine glass. "I don't think they make that aftershave anymore. Occasionally someone would wear it when I was working as a temp, but I haven't smelt it in years."

Paige waited to see if Emily would continue without prompting, but the younger woman seemed consumed by her own thoughts.

"Are there any other characteristics you can think of?" Paige asked.

"He had a beard and was a little taller than Stan I think. He was definitely heavier."

Paige felt a little sick. She didn't want to put Emily through this. She didn't want to have to ask her to think about that time and look for details.

"He was meaner too. He enjoyed hurting me." Emily downed the rest of her glass. "He liked to tell me that he wanted to see me bleed." Emily stared at her empty glass for a moment then placed it carefully on the table. She turned to Paige with a slight smile. "I probably should have had a little more to eat before drinking so quickly."

Paige smiled back, "Sometimes it's good to let your hair down."

"Well if you don't mind, I'm going to call it a night." Emily stood up and took the empty glasses and bottle through to the kitchen.

"I don't mind." Paige answered, taking the pizza box and plates through to the kitchen as well, "I'm sorry if I upset you Emily, it wasn't my intention."

Emily shook her head and gave a rueful smile, "You didn't Paige, I've just had less than two hours of sleep and for some reason the wine has gone straight to my head."

"I'll head home now," Paige said, picking up her scarf and winding it around her neck once more, "Hey, if it's not snowing in the morning, are you up for a run?"

"Sure." Emily said, "Provided the roads are dry and I haven't frozen to death in the night."

Paige laughed, "You've been in the city too long. My place at seven?"

Emily nodded, "Why not." She held the door open for Paige.

"Thanks for tonight." Paige said, turning back on the front step.

"Thank you too," Emily replied. She waited until Paige was in her car and had pulled out the driveway before closing the door and locking it.

She thought about going out the back for a cigarette but decided it was too cold. Instead, she sat on the floor near the fireplace and lit a cigarette. Blowing the smoke towards the fire, she hoped Paige wouldn't mind that she was smoking inside.

Emily watched the flames distractedly as they crackled higher. She had never told anyone as much as she had told Paige tonight. She could almost hear his whisper in her ear, wanting to see her bleed.

Emily shivered then flicked her cigarette into the fire.

It wasn't that late, but she was exhausted. Emily went to the bedroom to change, but it was so cold in there that she dragged the blankets off the bed and took them through to the living room. Settling herself on the couch, Emily turned on the television, flicking through the channels until she found an old black and white cowboy movie that had just started.

Emily lay on the couch watching the movie through droopy eyes and soon fell into a fitful sleep.

# Chapter Twelve

Emily was struggling to breathe. There was a weight on top of her, crushing her chest, making it impossible to draw air. When she did manage to inhale some air, it was thick with the smell of his cologne. She turned her head to the side, kicking and struggling as hard as she could.

She felt the cold steel of the blade against her neck and froze. She heard his hoarse whisper in her ear, "Are you going to bleed for me little one?"

∞

Emily woke up thrashing on the floor. She was tangled in her blankets and felt like she was suffocating. Extracting herself with difficulty, she wondered when she had fallen off the couch.

The fire had gone out, there was only a pile of ashes now, and now that the blanket was off, Emily could feel the chill in the air.

She got up and took the blankets back through to the bedroom and saw out the window that while it was cold, the sky outside was bright and clear.

She looked at her watch and realised she would be late to meet Paige if she didn't hurry. Emily took her toiletry bag to the bathroom and brushed her teeth. There was no point showering now when she would have to shower when she got back from the run.

She changed into her running clothes, and pulled on a windbreaker as well as a woolen cap. She put on the shoes she had bought last time she was in town. Thinking of her last meeting with Cathy Richards brought a scowl to Emily's face, she truly hoped she wouldn't bump into the miserable cow on this trip.

Leaving her mobiles and watch on the bed, Emily grabbed her car keys and headed outside, pausing in the kitchen only to grab a bottle of water.

∞

Across town, Cathy was scowling at the thought of Emily Winter. Looking at her blank mobile screen, she felt her anger for the girl rising all over again. She never expected the news she had heard at book club would backfire so badly.

She had waited nearly a week after hearing what Stacey had to say on the matter before calling Christian and asking him to come over. She had hoped that he would have called or at least texted before then, but he hadn't.

When he got there, she was surprised to find he was expecting an apology. When she had told him what she had heard, she had expected him to apologise and drop the subject once and for all.

Instead, he had been furious with her, telling her that blood tests were run on both Emily and Stan. Stan had alcohol and some drugs in him, but Emily had nothing at all in her blood stream. What seemed to make him angrier was the fact that people were talking about Emily when they had no business to.

Cathy had tried to defend herself by telling him she didn't get involved in the conversation, that she had merely been listening at the outside, but Christian refused to hear it. He hated gossip, and she had always known it.

He had stormed out of her home, slamming the door so fiercely behind him that one of the windowpanes had broken.

That was weeks ago and she hadn't heard a word from him since, and she had been too proud to initiate contact again.

She hadn't been eating or sleeping well since the last fight, she was so worried that this was truly the end, a weakness she would never admit to anyone.

Still, every morning, she picked up her mobile and had a moment of hope that there would be a text from him, saying good morning. But as with the last few weeks, her screen was blank.

With a sudden yell of frustration, Cathy threw her phone against the wall with all her might, cursing the day she ever met Emily Winter. The mobile lay in pieces on the floor near the door, and it was only when she saw the shattered screen that Cathy realised what she had done. She sat on her bed, put her face in her hands and sobbed.

∞

Paige was already stretching in the driveway when Emily pulled up, Charlie the three-legged bulldog cross sitting patiently next to his owner.

Emily got out of the car and closed the door, "Are you sure he's going to be able to keep up?" she asked, looking at the mutt dubiously.

Paige laughed, "You said that last time. Give the old boy a chance, he'll give us both a run for our money."

Emily shrugged and started stretching, deciding the dog wasn't her problem anyway.

Emily soon decided she was wrong to make assumptions about Charlie, he kept up with no problem for the first few miles. He even wandered off ahead of them to sniff the bushes for bugs and insects.

As they neared the forest, they slowed down a little on the incline so they could catch their breath and have some of their water.

They passed an overgrown dirt road leading deeper into the forest. A rusted old sign was lying flat on the ground, fallen years before and never removed. It had an arrow and the faded lettering showing the distance to the church retreat.

Paige visibly shivered, "I hate that sign, they should have taken it away years ago. It's an awful reminder."

Emily had slowed to a stop and was staring at the sign, transfixed.

"Emily?" Paige asked cautiously, "I'm sorry, I shouldn't have said anything."

Emily gave herself a mental shake. "Not your fault, just didn't expect to see it is all. Let's keep going."

Without waiting for an answer, Emily started jogging again. The memories of her time at the cabin came to her, not her horrific time there with Stan, but when she was still a carefree teenager. When she was dating Liam and they would sneak down to the cabin with their group of friends to listen to music and make out.

It had been her favorite place in the whole world. Where no one would look down on her for being the poor daughter of the town alcoholic. Liam had told her he loved her in that cabin. They had been sitting on the tiny wooden deck outside to give themselves some privacy, wrapped in a blanket. She still remembered the way he looked at her when he said those three words, and how those words had made her feel.

Then she remembered the look in his eyes the day he came to the hospital to see her and could almost feel the betrayal he had felt.

"Are you okay Emily?" Paige's voice brought Emily back to the present. She realised that Paige was a few steps behind her.

"I'm fine, why?" She replied.

"I was just wondering if there was a reason you want Charlie to drop dead of a heart attack?"

Emily looked at the panting dog with guilt and slowed down to a jogging pace.

"Sorry," Emily herself was panting a little.

"No problem. Want to talk about it?" Paige was relieved the pace had slowed down.

"Not really."

"Want to try anyway?"

"Ha," Emily's laugh was sarcastic, "no thanks."

Emily had a sip of water while they were jogging slowly.

"Was it the sign?" Paige asked kindly.

"No," Emily answered quickly, "well, yes actually, but not in the way you're thinking."

"I'm sure it must bring up some awful thoughts." Paige said.

Emily shook her head, "I was thinking about how we used to sneak out to the cabin when I was, well, before."

"With Stan?" Paige asked in a shocked voice.

"What? No, with Liam and the other kids from school."

"Oh." Paige said with relief. "Hey, I didn't know you used to sneak out there."

Emily laughed again, "That was kind of the point Paige."

"You were so happy when you were with Liam," Paige said, taking a sip of her own water. "And he was happy too. He was always under so much pressure from his parents, but when he was with you, he was like a different person."

Emily didn't comment, she didn't want to hear those words.

They were silent for a few more minutes before Paige spoke again, "How are the nightmares?"

"Getting better." Emily managed a half shrug while keeping pace.

"Happening less often or not bothering you as much?"

"Does it matter?"

"I think so."

"I don't want to talk about this Paige, I told you."

"I know you don't want to, but I still think you need to." Paige told her calmly.

"Why?" Emily snapped.

"Because the second I mentioned it, you started speeding up again. What are you running away from?"

Emily hadn't even noticed that she had changed pace but realised that Paige was right. Emily forced herself to slow down.

"I'm not running from anything." She said more calmly.

"I don't believe you."

"Then don't."

Paige slowed to a stop, forcing Emily to do the same if she didn't want to be alone. They were standing in the shadows of the massive trees.

"What do you want to hear Paige?"

"Do you even know what you're running from Emily?"

"Maybe I just want to exercise without having to have deep, meaningful conversations."

Paige saw a glimpse of the stubborn teenager she once knew shining through.

"I like exercise too, and I've been doing it a lot longer. But this? This isn't for physical exertion." Paige pointed out.

"Maybe you're getting old." Emily said petulantly.

"First of all, fuck you," Paige laughed, "Second of all, you're running away from something Emily. It's not something you can outrun, since it's inside of you."

Emily wanted to shout. She wanted to lash out at the calm woman in front of her. She wanted to scream and cry and yes, she wanted to run. Run away from this conversation, this town, and these people. She was panting even though they had stopped running a while ago.

"You asked me to come here remember?" Emily wiped the sweat off her face, despite the cold around them.

"I know." Paige said, putting up a placating hand, "And I've told you how sorry I am about having brought you into all of this. But we weren't talking about what happened. We were talking about Liam."

"It's the same thing." Emily said, her irritation rising. Her anger seemed to be permanently close to the surface lately.

"It's not the same," Paige insisted, "you were a happy teenager in a happy relationship. Do you let all of your memories get tainted like this?"

"It is the same!" Emily said in frustration.

"How?"

"Because they took everything from me!" Emily shouted hoarsely. "I had nothing left! And when Liam came to see me and he was so disgusted by what he saw, it hurt." Her voice faded away, having never admitted to that before. "It hurt more than anything Stan or his brother did."

"Oh Emily." Paige had tears in her eyes.

"Don't," Emily said bluntly, "I don't want your pity."

"It's not pity." Paige tried to say, but she was cut off.

"Can we just head back now?" Emily asked.

Paige nodded slowly, giving Emily one last penetrating look before turning around and heading back the way they came.

They ran all the way back to Paige's house without another word to one another. Both Paige and Emily were lost in their own thoughts.

When they got back up the driveway, Charlie ran off to his water bowl then flopped next to it in total exhaustion.

"You weren't wrong about the dog." Emily said, breaking the tension.

Paige gave a small smile, "I told you."

Emily opened her car door and threw her now empty bottle of water inside.

"Do you want to come in for coffee?" Paige asked.

"No thanks Paige. I'm going to go have a shower and coffee then will chat to Casey."

"Okay. Thanks Emily."

Emily climbed in her car and waved distractedly to indicate she had heard. She pulled out of the driveway and immediately lit a cigarette. The smoke burnt her chest, but she didn't put it out.

# Chapter Thirteen

**B**y the time Emily had gotten out of the shower and was about to get dressed, she heard a knock at the door. Wrapping her towel tightly around her body, Emily walked through the living room and looked out the window.

Casey was standing outside the front door, bundled in a too-big jacket and looking even gaunter than Emily remembered.

Emily opened the door, "Casey, hey." She greeted in surprise.

"Oh, I'm so sorry, I didn't realise." Casey stammered, taking in the towel.

"Come on in." Emily said, ignoring the apology, "I had to send some work emails before I showered. Let me go get dressed quick."

Casey came in and closed the door behind her. Emily was already walking to the bedroom.

She had lied to Casey. She had been sitting on the floor in the shower, letting the hot water pound her body while she had felt completely broken. She never allowed herself to think of the good memories, and the run had brought up so much for her that she felt as though she were going to break down and sob.

She knew she wouldn't though. The last time Emily had cried had been in the hospital all those years ago. Her tears had dried then and she knew she had nothing left in her now.

When she was dressed in fresh jeans and a thick hoodie, Emily went back into the living room to find Casey had already put the kettle on and had taken two cups out of the cupboard.

"I hope it's okay that I made myself at home?" She said as Emily entered the kitchen.

"Of course." Emily answered, "It's your house anyway."

"That's not what I meant," Casey pointed out, then, "How do you take your coffee?"

"Cream and two sugars." Emily told her.

Casey made the coffee in silence then handed one of the mugs to Emily.

Emily walked to the couch and sat down, where Casey joined her.

"I was going to call you and offer to come over." Emily told her, taking a sip of her coffee and wanting to go outside for a cigarette.

"I needed to get out the house." Casey said, holding her mug in both hands as though trying to draw strength from it.

"I'm glad to see that you're getting out now." Emily commented. "Your mom says you've been seeing some friends?"

Casey nodded, "Just a few of them. And Ben."

"Ben is your boyfriend?"

"He was." Casey sniffed quietly.

"He's not anymore?"

"I don't really know." She replied softly, "I just know that I can't handle anyone even trying to hold my hand now and—" A sob came from Casey. She gripped the mug even tighter in her hands as she tried desperately to stop the tears from pouring.

"It's okay to feel that way Casey, I promise you it won't last forever."

Casey shook her head miserably, "You don't understand."

Emily didn't reply. She once again felt like she should hug the girl or comfort her in some way, but as usual, she found herself frozen to her side of the couch.

"I'm pregnant." Casey whispered wretchedly, the tears now falling freely.

Emily felt frozen, she stared at Casey in horror.

After a moment she asked, "Are you sure?"

Casey nodded, still crying, "I took three tests."

Emily sat back against the couch. "Is there no way it could be Ben's?" she asked.

Casey shook her head again, "No, we were always too careful."

"Didn't they give you anything in the hospital?"

"No, at least, I don't think so. If they did, it didn't work."

Emily was silent for another moment then suddenly stood up. "I need a cigarette. Come on."

Casey got up and followed Emily out the back door and sat next to her on the step. She seemed to have found some courage now that the words were out. She was dry-eyed sitting there, looking out to the forest.

"I take it you haven't told your parents?" Emily took a deep drag of her cigarette and blew the smoke away from Casey.

"No I haven't."

"Can I ask why not?" Emily asked her.

"Because of their stupid faith." Casey answered bluntly.

"Hey, I know they're religious," Emily said, turning to look at the girl, "but this isn't something they would judge you for."

"I know they won't judge me for being pregnant," Casey said, "but they might not want me to get rid of it."

"Firstly, I don't think they would ever pressure you. I honestly think they would support any decision you make, and secondly, is that what you want? To get rid of it?"

"Of course I want to get rid of it." There was a defensive tone in Casey's voice, "Why would I want that reminder every day?"

"I was just asking." Emily said, putting her hands up in surrender. "It's a big decision to make, and you don't know how it will affect you later in life."

"I can't have that evil spawn growing inside of me!" Casey cried, "How could you even say that? Do you know what it's like? Knowing this thing is growing inside of you?"

Emily flicked her cigarette into the nearby shrubbery, not looking at Casey, "I do know actually."

It was Casey's turn to be dumbstruck, she turned and looked at Emily in horror.

Emily swallowed uncomfortably, she had never spoken the words out loud to anyone, not even Paige. She bit her lower lip before continuing. "There was so much physical damage that they didn't think I would be able to carry to the end of the pregnancy anyway." She said, avoiding Casey's eyes and focusing once more on the tree line in the distance.

"So it wasn't your choice?" Casey asked quietly.

"They still asked me." Emily answered, "I didn't hesitate. I told them to cut that thing out of me the second I knew about it."

Casey took a cigarette out of Emily's box without asking and lit it. She inhaled deeply then looked at Emily as though waiting for a comment. Emily said nothing however.

"You regret it." Casey said. It was a statement, not a question.

"Not really," Emily said, lighting another cigarette of her own, "I just think sometimes, usually in the dead of night or when really drunk, that maybe I should have at least thought about it."

"Would you really want to look into the face of a kid that could look like Stan?" Casey asked, blowing smoke rings into the air.

Emily shook her head, "No way. But I did wonder, maybe if I had it and put it up for adoption, it might have had a chance to have a life." Emily sighed, twirling her cigarette between her fingers, "Sometimes I feel like I did this awful thing to get back at him and it was never the kid's fault."

"What if it had grown up to be just like its father?" Casey asked in a quiet voice.

"I don't know." Emily said honestly. "I'm just trying to tell you that it's never going to go away. You shouldn't have to make this decision, this should never have happened to you at all." She sighed heavily again, "But it has happened, and I just want you to think things through. Because there will never be a day where you don't question your decision."

Casey flicked her own cigarette away, "I get what you're saying, but I don't think I have time to wait."

Emily worked it out in her head, it must be three, three and a half months already. She understood what Casey was saying and suddenly felt sick.

"You have to tell your parents." Emily said.

"I know, I just don't know how." Casey looked as though she wanted to cry again, "What if they want the baby?"

Emily looked at Casey, "They'll do whatever they have to do for you. I promise you that."

"It's their grandkid." Casey said sadly.

"And you're their kid." Emily pointed out, "You are their only priority right now."

"I wish I could kill that piece of shit for what he's done to me." Casey said suddenly.

"I understand why you feel that way Cas, but I've got to tell you, that's something that sticks with you forever too. I'm glad you didn't have to kill him."

"How can you even say that?" Casey asked aghast, "I think it's a good thing you killed Stan. Mom told me what happened, and my first thought was that I wish I had the chance to do the same."

"It's a stain that never washes off Cas. I live with it every day and I relive it every night." Emily held up a hand to prevent Casey from interrupting. "Don't get me wrong, I'm glad he's dead, but I really wish sometimes that I wasn't the one with blood on my hands."

"How can you say you're okay with me getting an abortion then?" Casey demanded.

"That's not the same, that's you doing what you need to do for you. Killing Stan wasn't something I was doing for me."

"But it was self-defense?"

"It really wasn't Casey. I really believed I was going to die anyway. I just didn't want him to touch me again."

"Sounds like self-defense to me." Casey said quietly.

They sat once more in silence until it got too cold to stay outside on the step.

Going back inside, Casey picked up her car keys.

"Going to talk to them?" Emily asked her.

"Maybe." Casey said, walking to the door, "Thanks for the talk."

"Anytime."

"Emily?" Casey paused in the open doorway.

"Yeah?"

"Did you ever consider having a kid afterwards?"

"No. When they did some reconstructive surgery later on, for whatever reason, the decision was made and they removed the uterus and an ovary."

Casey looked horrified. "Did you ever ask them why?"

Emily shook her head, "I just wanted everything to be over, I didn't care then."

"Do you care now?"

"Sometimes." Emily gave a small, sad smile, "But it's done. And it was done a long time ago."

Emily had spent the rest of the day answering emails from new perspective clients and going over accounts that Glynis had sent through to her.

She had actually wanted to spend the day on the couch watching crappy movies but was never really able to relax that way, so instead she tried to distract herself in other ways. Work was always her fallback. She decided it was time

164

to take on some new clients to give herself less time with her own traitorous thoughts.

Evening had just started settling when her mobile rang. Seeing Casey's name light up the screen, Emily pushed the answer button.

"Hey Casey."

"You know you're such a filthy hypocrite." Casey said immediately.

"That's not something I didn't know." Emily said after a moment.

"How is okay that you would tell me to think about it when you didn't."

"I'm asking you to think about it because I didn't, not in spite of it." Emily pointed out calmly, trying not to be pulled into an argument when Casey was clearly so angry.

"Tell me the truth Emily. If you could go back and change your mind, would you?"

"I can't go back so what difference does it make? You and I are not the same Casey."

"Just answer the fucking question!" Casey yelled, her voice shaking.

"I would do the same thing a million times over!" Emily snapped back.

"That's what I thought." Casey said, then she cut the call.

Emily sat at the dining table, her hands shaking. She hadn't wanted to get into an argument with Casey, and maybe she shouldn't have snapped back, but her anger had consumed her so quickly, and she knew it wasn't going to go away easily. She tried to tell herself that Casey was lashing out at anyone and everyone, and that Emily shouldn't take it personally. But she also had things to say to Casey that she hadn't gotten a chance to on the phone.

Grabbing an extra jacket and her bag hanging by the door, Emily slammed out of the house and got into her car.

By the time she skidded into the driveway at Casey's house, Emily was less emotional, but still completely determined.

Paige opened the door as Emily got there, but Emily moved past her and up the stairs.

"Emily, what's wrong?" Paige called out in concern.

"Not now Paige." Emily answered not looking back.

Emily entered Casey's room without knocking. Casey was sitting on the bed when Emily entered.

"What are you doing here?" Casey asked, a note of fear in her voice, "Are you going to tell them?"

Emily slammed the door behind her, "No, I'm not going to tell them anything, but I am here to tell you something."

"What, about how you know better than me?"

"No," Emily moved towards the bed, "in all the ways I wish we weren't for your sake, we are the same; you were right about that. But there is one big difference between you and me."

"And what's that?" Casey's defensiveness was back.

"Your parents. I had nobody. I was all alone. I came from a fucked-up family and already had issues understanding love and support. I did the only thing I could do, and yes, I would do it again. Not because of how it got there, but because I couldn't offer it anything.

But don't for one second think it hasn't haunted me every single moment since.

But you have your parents. You have a chance to share your burden and not have to go through any of this shit alone. I suggest you start to appreciate that."

Emily didn't wait for an answer, she turned and left the room again, hurried down the stairs and past a visibly upset Paige and back out the front door.


Emily entered Dusty's less than ten minutes later. Nick looked up from the bar and smiled as she approached.

"You're back." He greeted her.

"I am," she smiled back, taking a seat at the bar.

"What will it be?"

"Rum and coke please."

Nick poured her drink and handed it to her, "On the house as a welcome back." He said grinning.

"Thanks, why don't you join me?"

"Just one then." Nick grabbed a beer out of the fridge behind him, opened it and held up the bottle to her. "Welcome back."

Emily raised her own glass to his but didn't respond to the toast.

"So how long are you here for this time?" He asked after taking a swig of his beer.

"Not long," Emily replied, "At most a couple days."

"Rushing back to work?" He teased.

"No, more like not wanting to spend more time in this shithole than I have to." Emily told him.

"Ouch." Nick pretended to look injured, "You know it's not all bad."

Emily raised an eyebrow at him skeptically and Nick laughed.

"Okay, it's not the big city, but you do have entertainment options available." He winked suggestively and this time Emily laughed.

"Speaking of," she said after a sip of her drink, "What are you doing later?"

"Funny you ask," He answered, swallowing the rest of his beer, "I was just thinking of closing early tonight. Too cold to stay open."

Emily finished her own drink, downing the last half in one go. "Good, I'll get pizza, you bring the booze."

"See you in a bit." He responded with a grin.


Emily stopped at Molly's on her way back to the house and was relieved to see that weird Phillip kid wasn't there. Molly was manning the counter and Emily chatted to her while waiting for her pizza.

"Thought you'd be back," Molly told her with a knowing smile, "this place has a way of getting under your skin."

"You're not wrong," Emily commented with a wry smile of her own, "Just not the under the skin you're thinking of."

"Ha!" The old woman guffawed, "I always loved that sarcastic wit of yours Emily."

Emily accepted the offer of coffee while she was waiting.

"It's an awfully big pizza you've ordered for one person." Molly commented mildly.

"Good thing it's not just for me then." Emily replied just as mildly.

"Paige, Casey, or both?" Molly asked as she handed over the slip for the pizza and coffee.

"None of the above." Emily answered with a smile. She paid the bill, finished her coffee and took the steaming hot pizza

box from the cook who had come through at the same time.
"Thanks Molly."

 "You have a good time now." Molly called after her
knowingly.

# Chapter Fourteen

Emily had just got a fire started and was taking plates out when there was a knock at the front door.

"Come in." She called from the kitchen.

Nick came into the house with three wine bottles cradled in one arm and a jacket slung over the other. Once again he was clad only in jeans and a tight black t-shirt with Dusty's emblazoned across his chest.

"Now as much as I like the view, don't you ever feel the cold?" Emily asked, leaning back against the kitchen counter and watching him walk towards her.

He draped the jacket over the dining chair and put the bottles on the kitchen counter before walking right up to Emily.

"As much as I enjoy watching you take in the view and I wouldn't want to deprive you; no, the cold doesn't bother me. I grew up in the snow. This feels like home to me." He said, placing his hands on her waist and lifting her casually onto the kitchen counter.

He wrapped his left arm around her waist and ran his other hand through her hair, pulling her towards him and kissing her gently.

"I forgot how good you smell." He said, leaning back but still holding her.

"You're not too bad yourself." Emily smiled, wrapping her legs around him to pull him closer.

Before she could get too carried away with the kiss, Nick pulled back again slightly.

"Darlin', I'm going to rock your world in a little while, but right now I need to eat something, build up some stamina."

Emily laughed and pushed him away playfully. She took the plates off the counter and handed them to him, "You take these, I'll get some glasses."

He collected the plates and the pizza box and took everything to the living room instead of the dining table.

Emily joined him with a bottle of chardonnay and two glasses. She poured the wine while he placed two slices on each plate.

She handed him a glass and they clinked gently.

After Nick had taken a sip, he put the glass down on the table and picked up his plate, "This feels like a date."

Emily snorted, "I don't date. And last time I checked, neither do you."

He gave her a wry smile, "While that's true, this still feels a bit like a date."

"Well it's not, so get over yourself."

Nick laughed and took another bite of pizza. When he had swallowed, "So, since this isn't a date and I get to ask whatever I want, what's up with you and Jax?"

Emily choked on the sip of wine she had just taken. She coughed and Nick patted her back.

"I'm not jealous." He assured her.

"I didn't think you were." Emily said breathlessly. She took another sip of wine to clear her throat, "And to answer your question, there's nothing up with me and Jax. Why do you ask?"

Nick sat back against the side of the couch facing Emily. "She's a good person, Jax. She's one of my closest friends and she deserves to be happy. If there's something brewing between you two that has potential, I don't want to stand in the way."

Emily leant on the opposite side of the couch and looked at him carefully. She was touched by his concern for his friend. "There's no potential, because I don't date or do relationships. And she made it clear she's not interested in being a one-night stand."

Nick finished his wine and topped up their glasses, "Are you sure there couldn't be in the future?"

"I'm positive." She nodded, "Are you sure you're not jealous that I made a move on her in the first place?" she asked playfully.

"Only jealous that I didn't get to watch." Nick laughed. He leant forward and pulled Emily over until she was straddling his lap, "How could I be jealous when I'm the one underneath you?"

Emily smiled and took his face in her hands, kissing him deeply, reveling the taste of spicy pizza and chardonnay on his tongue.

Nick slid his hands down her back and under her shirt, but Emily pulled his hands away.

Nick pulled out of the kiss, "Why can't I touch you?"

"Because I asked you not to." Emily whispered playfully, leaning forward for another kiss, but he turned his face away.

Emily pulled back so she was sitting on his thighs. "You don't want this?"

In answer, Nick pulled his shirt over his head and let it fall on the couch beside them. He took Emily's right hand and placed it over his scarred chest. "Does this bother you?" He asked.

Emily shook her head and ran her fingers down his ruined flesh.

"It doesn't bother me either. It's there, but it doesn't change who I am."

Emily looked up from her hand and into his eyes. "It's not the same." She said quietly.

"I don't know what's under there," Nick said just as quietly, "but it shouldn't make you want to hide. Whatever happened, I don't need to know, but I do know that I want to feel your body against mine."

Emily considered climbing off and sending him on his way. Nick could feel her indecision and put his hands on her waist again. "Look, it's not like you're going to hang around. You never have to see me again after this. If you don't like it, you can put the shirt back on. I won't tell anyone." He finished with a wink.

Emily took a deep breath. Everything she had done with Nick so far had been off-script from her usual rules with her lovers. Why should this be any different?

She took the bottom of her shirt in her hands, but Nick stopped her by grabbing both her hands in his own.

"Not like that." He told her, kissing her on the forehead.

He wrapped his strong arms around her tightly and stood up without any effort. She wrapped her arms around his neck and her legs around his waist and he carried her with ease from the living room to the bedroom.

He lay her on the bed then lay down next to her, leaning over to kiss her again. His kiss was tender and intimate, and he held her gently while he explored her mouth with his tongue.

Emily felt completely overwhelmed and found herself feeling close to tears. She wanted to say something to him to make him stop, but couldn't find the words.

Instead, she pushed him on his back and straddled him, feeling more in control.

Nick sat up and kissed her again, his mouth travelling from her lips, down her jawline and along the scar on Emily's neck. She didn't push him away; instead, she tilted her head back and sighed softly.

When Nick started lifting her shirt and vest, she didn't stop him. She held her arms up like a child as he pulled the shirts over her head gently and dropped them on the floor next to the bed.

He looked at her scars with a curious expression on his face but didn't say anything. After a moment, he brought his lips back to her collar bone and ran his tongue down towards her bra.

With a single swift movement he had unclipped her bra and started pulling the straps down her shoulders.

Emily froze suddenly as her breasts were exposed.

Nick looked at her and kissed her gently on the lips once more, then looked down at her breasts. Cradling the disfigured one in his hand, he leant forward and kissed it gently. Emily quivered in his hands and slowly relaxed. No

174

one had ever touched her there with her permission, and it felt exquisite.

He rolled her over onto her back and undid the button on her jeans. He slid them over her thighs and down her legs, pausing to kiss the scar on her inner thigh.

Emily pulled his head away, "Not that one, please." She whispered.

He kissed her stomach instead, and started unbuckling his own jeans. He stood up only long enough to pull them off, then was back on top of her.

Emily shivered, so Nick pulled the comforter off the bottom of the bed and covered them both with it. With his hands on either side of Emily's head, he leant down and kissed her deeply.

Emily reached a hand out from under the covers and removed a condom from the bedside table.

He took it from her and opened it with his teeth, as soon as he had it out the package, he kissed her once more. She felt his hand travelling between their stomachs as he went to slide the condom on.

Gently, he used his knee to spread Emily's legs and as he kissed her deeply as he lowered himself into her slowly.

Emily gasped out loud and grabbed his shoulders.

Nick was still holding himself up but he lowered himself until their bare chests were touching.

Emily felt his warm skin on hers, the scars and the smooth. She put her hands in his hair and pulled him closer.

Nick took his time, every movement and touch, slow and deliberate.

It was only when Emily cried out his name that he increased the speed of his thrusts.

They reached the peak together and Nick buried his face in her hair.

"You are beautiful." He whispered in her ear.

They lay spooning, another rule broken, listening to the crackling of the fire in the other room. Emily wondered again at the feeling of his chest against her bare back. She could feel every breath he took, and it felt comforting and calming.

"What are you thinking about?" He asked her quietly.

"That's a real date question." Emily replied.

He chuckled in her ear, "Maybe you're right, but everything about this feels like a date to me, and it feels right."

She twisted round to look at him and found him watching her with that same curious expression on his face.

"Don't." She whispered.

"I won't, don't worry. But we can pretend for one night? That we don't have all these barriers up?"

Emily sat up and pulled the sheet up to cover her nakedness. "How many women are you sleeping with in this town?"

"Regularly?" He asked, surprised by the sudden change in conversation. "Two. There was another, but she was bat shit crazy."

"Do you ever pretend with them?" She asked him, some bitterness in her tone.

"Look whose jealous now," he said with a laugh, "and no, never."

"And I'm supposed to believe that you don't use that line with all the unavailable women you screw?"

He sat up as well, but did nothing to hide his bare body. "I don't Emily. I've never lied to you and I'm not about to start. I was just enjoying the moment with you."

He touched her shoulder gently, "And if it helps you get more comfortable in your own skin, what's the harm?"

Emily pulled out of his reached and got off the bed, wrapping the sheet around her body, "Are you fucking kidding me?" she asked him furiously.

"What did I say?" He asked back bewildered.

"I am not your fucking charity case!" She snapped in his face.

"I didn't say you were." He tried to argue back, but Emily wasn't listening.

She walked towards the door. "I'm going to shower, when I get out, I want you gone."

She ignored his protests and slammed the bathroom door behind her.

Emily turned the taps on and got into the shower before the water had even heated up. She heard Nick moving around the room, then knocking on the bathroom door, but she didn't respond.

"I didn't mean it like that," he called through the door, "You're nobody's charity case."

When she didn't reply, she heard his footsteps leading away from the door and let out a heavy sigh.

She put her forehead against the wall, none-too gently and stood under the finally warm spray.

This is why she had rules in the first place. This is why she didn't let anyone get close. He said he didn't care about where the scars came from but clearly he made his own mind up and decided she needed a sympathy fuck.

She was so angry with Nick she could punch him, but more than that, she was angry with herself for getting herself into the situation in the first place.

She couldn't understand the feeling of hurt in her chest. She didn't want anything more from Nick, so nothing he said should have bothered her. But it had.

Emily got out of the shower and got dressed, desperately wanting to go to a bar and get shitfaced, but knowing there was no way she was going back to Dusty's, even if it had been open.

She was just pulling on a heavier outer jacket, having decided to go for a walk when she heard a knock at the door.

Hoping it wasn't Nick, Emily pulled the door open and found no one there. Then she looked down and saw Sophie from next door standing on the doorstep, wrapped in a thick pink blanket.

"Sophie? What are you doing here?" Emily asked in surprise.

"I have a letter." Sophie said in a shaky voice, then coughed violently.

"You're sick," Emily said, pulling the girl inside and closing the door behind her.

Emily led the child to the couch and made sure her blanket was wrapped tight. She took the letter from the small hand and went to the fireplace to add more wood.

Opening the folded paper and flattening it, Emily read:

*My mum is sick and I couldn't get hold of Sophie's dad. Please watch her. He will be home at 8.*

A single line, and that was it. Emily felt her anger rising. How can the nanny just leave a child with a total stranger? What kind of person would do that?

Sophie sneezed violently then looked up at Emily, "I was supposed to go to Amy but she wasn't home."

That made more sense, but Emily was still angry that the woman had just left the kid to find an adult to take care of her. What if she hadn't been home either, then what?

Emily stood near the fire awkwardly, painfully aware of the fact that she had no idea how to deal with kids.

"I guess I can't give you coffee, but how about some warm milk and cookies?"

Sophie nodded happily then took the remote off the table and turned the television on, switching to cartoons and settling herself happily on the couch.

Emily warmed a mug of milk and pulled a few cookies out of a box that she had bought during her last stay. Putting the cookies on a saucer, she carried it and the mug of warm milk to the lounge and handed them both to Sophie. Sophie put the saucer on her lap and took a big sip of milk.

She smiled at Emily, revealing a missing front tooth, "Thanks." She said.

"You're welcome." Emily said, flopping down on the couch next to her. "Why is that shark chasing that mermaid around?"

Sophie rolled her eyes, reminding Emily of someone, but she couldn't think who.

"He wants to marry her." Sophie said, turning her attention back to the screen.

"Where's your mom Sophie?" Emily asked her, wondering if maybe she knew Sophie's mom from school.

"She's dead." Sophie said with a careless shrug, nibbling on the side of a cookie and not taking her eyes of the television.

"I'm so sorry." Emily told her, but Sophie didn't seem to hear.

"How did she die?" Emily asked a few minutes later.

"The bad men daddy was chasing came and hurt her. She put me in the cupboard so they wouldn't find me." Sophie told her matter-of-factly.

"Oh my," Emily said, "That must have been so scary for you."

"Nah-uh," Sophie replied, her eyes still glued to the animated shark, "I was just a baby, I don't remember it."

Emily took a cookie off the girl's plate and turned her attention to the television. The fact that Sophie's life had been touched with violence so early on made Emily feel sick. She couldn't imagine what the little girl and her father had been through.

# Chapter Fifteen

**E**mily awoke from a confusing dream to a banging on the front door. It took her a moment to shake off her disorientation. She stood up from the couch that she had fallen asleep on and saw to her relief that Sophie was fast asleep on the other side of the couch.

Emily went to the door and pulled it open to find a furious looking Liam standing in her doorway.

"Liam?" she asked stupidly.

"Where is my daughter?" He asked through clenched teeth. He was as wound up as a caged animal.

"Sophie's yours?" Emily asked incredulously.

"Yes." He spat out angrily, "Where is she?"

Emily took a step back from him and pointed, "She's asleep on the couch."

Liam rushed through to the lounge and looked at his sleeping daughter. Suddenly the recognition of Sophie's eye roll earlier made sense. It wasn't her mother Emily was reminded of, it was her father.

"What did you think you were doing?" Liam whispered angrily, having walked back towards her.

"Liam, what are you talking about?" Emily asked in frustration.

"You took my daughter!"

"I did not!" Emily snapped back. She went to the coffee table and picked up the note, all but throwing it at Liam.

"You should be damn grateful someone was here to take her in, since your nanny buggered off and left her to find Amy on her own. She didn't even check if Amy was there before leaving her."

Liam read the note then crumpled the piece of paper angrily in his fist.

"Or, maybe you should answer your damn phone." Emily added angrily.

Liam seemed to deflate in front of her. All the anger left him and he rubbed his face wearily.

"I'm sorry." He said quietly, "I just got so worried when I couldn't find her." He gazed at his sleeping daughter, not looking at Emily while he spoke. "I saw her scarf in your driveway and just panicked."

Thinking of what Sophie had told her earlier about her mother, Emily could understand why Liam was so upset, but she was also getting tired of being treated so badly by him.

"I get that you were worried, but I'm not the monster you so clearly think I am."

"This wasn't about that. About then." Liam said, finally turning to face Emily.

"Maybe your worry wasn't, but you keep looking at me with such loathing in your eyes and it's not fair." She told him calmly.

"What you did to me wasn't fair!" He whispered furiously, not wanting to wake Sophie.

"What I did to you?" Emily whispered back, just as furiously.

"You broke my heart!" Liam snapped as quietly as possible.

She had finally had enough, she pulled up her jacket, shirt and bra, exposing her scarred stomach and ruined breast, "I

182

broke your heart?" She repeated, louder than she had meant to. "Did you not know me at all Liam? You were the one person I thought would believe me and you stood there in the hospital and called me a whore! I'm not the one that broke your heart Liam, you're the one that broke mine."

Emily took a deep, shaky breath, then in a much quieter voice asked, "Just which one of us had it unfair?"

Liam didn't say anything, he just stared at the scars on Emily's body, his face completely pale. Even from halfway across the room, he could see the damage that had been inflicted on her body.

Emily pulled her clothes down angrily and stepped closer to him, "Take your kid and get the fuck out of this house." She whispered quietly.

Without waiting for an answer, Emily walked through to her bedroom and closed the door. She didn't come out again until she heard the front door close.

Emily was in the kitchen making coffee when there was another knock on the door. Without checking who it was, she pulled the door open furiously, ready to swear at whoever was standing there.

It was Amy. She took a step back seeing the look on Emily's face. "Sorry." She stammered.

"Shit, Amy." Emily said, her angry expression softening. "Sorry, I thought you were someone else. Come on in."

Amy sighed in relief and smiled, "Jeez, I thought you were going to slug me for a second." She walked in and showed Emily the bottle of wine in her hand. "Just wanted to come over and say hi, it's been so boring without you."

"Sorry, really, I didn't mean to give you a fright." Emily said contritely.

"Let me guess. Liam?" Amy asked, walking into the kitchen and opening the bottle.

"How did you know?" Emily asked, joining her in the kitchen.

"Saw him carrying Sophie home. Didn't take you for the babysitting type."

"I'm not," Emily assured her, "Apparently she was supposed to go over to you, but you weren't home."

"Why didn't Bee just call me?" Amy wondered out loud.

Amy handed Emily a glass of wine and they walked through to the lounge. Emily picked up her cigarettes on the way past the dining table and instead of joining Amy on the couch, she sat on the floor next to the fireplace.

"So what did Liam do to make you want to slug him?" Amy asked cheerfully.

Emily lit a cigarette and blew the smoke into the fireplace, "Nothing, at least not now. Our issues go way back."

"Oh, that sounds delightfully intriguing. Tell me more."

Emily laughed, "It's really not. We dated in high-school, it didn't end well. Nothing more exciting than that I'm afraid."

"Did you break his heart?" Amy asked seriously this time.

"He thinks I did. But it was the other way round." Emily answered, staring into the fire.

Amy didn't pry any further. Instead she picked up the pizza box. "Can I warm this? I'm starving."

"Sure." Emily replied.

"The teenager is with his dad tonight so I didn't think about cooking." Amy told her as she went to the kitchen to put the pizza in the oven. "Stacey was in the staff room today talking shit so I didn't go in there for lunch today." Amy picked up their half empty wine bottle and seemed to consider it for a moment. Then, taking one of the other bottles Nick had brought, she brought both bottles back to the couch.

"Was she talking shit about you?" Emily asked, holding her glass out for a top up.

"No, actually, she was talking about you."

"Oh." Emily said darkly, "I can guess what she was saying."

Amy pulled a face, "I don't think anyone believes a word that comes out of her mouth anyway, so I wouldn't worry about it."

Emily flicked her cigarette in the fire and watched the filter catch alight, "I assure you, I couldn't care less what she has to say." Emily stood up and stretched, then moved to the couch across from Amy. She tucked her feet under her, "I'm actually surprised no one has punched her yet."

Amy pulled another face, "She's the deputy head, and she never lets anyone forget it."

The oven pinged, so Amy went to the kitchen to fetch the pizza and bring it back through.

"She's been talking about Casey for weeks like it's the latest hot gossip. It's sick, like she doesn't even realise what the poor girl has been through." Amy continued.

"Staying in a small town like this isn't the best idea for someone like Casey. There's always going to be someone who wants to turn it into gossip." Emily commented, "Although, if I happen to see Stacey again, I'd be happy to slug her on Casey's behalf."

Amy snorted at the comment. "Is that why you left?" Amy asked. There was no joking on her face now, only genuine concern.

"Part of the reason." Emily answered vaguely. She studied Amy for a moment. "So what did Stacey tell you? I'm guessing something about a pastor?"

Amy looked uncomfortable, "Look, I shouldn't pry, it's none of my business."

"Don't worry about it," Emily said kindly. "I know the shit people have been saying around here and I can tell you it's not all true. So if you want to know, ask me."

Emily swallowed the rest of her wine in one go, wondering why she would ever invite an almost stranger to ask her such probing questions.

"Nah," Amy said smiling, "I don't need to know. You don't look like the pastor killing type anyway."

Emily filled her wine glass and looked at Amy, "That part she actually did get right."

Amy choked on her pizza.

"But he deserved it." Emily said calmly.

Amy took a swig of wine then shrugged. "Fair enough." Then took another slice of pizza out the box.

"Hey," she said after she took a bite, "Did I see Nick the bartender leaving here one night on your last trip?"

"That depends," Emily laughed, "Are you one of his regulars?"

"God no!" Amy laughed too. "We had a night of fun, but he's not interested in anything more than casual and I had a feeling he was the type of guy I might want more from, so it was just the one night. I also don't like to share."

"Then yes, it was him." Emily said, leaning over to take a slice of pizza.

"How good is that man at what he does?" Amy asked.

Emily laughed again but refused to comment. "It's a little weird that we've both slept with him." She said instead.

"No it's not," Amy argued, "That boy has made his way through all the single women in this town and most of the married ones. It would be weird if we hadn't both slept with him."

Emily laughed again. "Fair point."

"I was so sure he was messing around with Stacey for a while, but if he did, it must have ended pretty quickly."

"What made you think so?" Emily asked, finishing her pizza and having another sip of wine.

"She was walking around school for a few weeks with that really bitchy, knowing look about her, then all of a sudden, she was in a worse mood than ever. And I've met her husband, I can guarantee he's never put a smile like that on her face."

Emily wondered if Stacey had been the bat-shit crazy woman that Nick had mentioned, then decided it probably was. Thinking that she shared the same man with Stacey wasn't an appetizing thought.

"I think we need to open this other bottle of wine." Emily said.

∞

Emily was walking down the road, close to the forest edge, hiding from the summer sun. She was daydreaming about the upcoming weekend with Liam, they were going to the county fair one town over and she couldn't wait.

A car pulled out from a dusty forest road right in front of her, kicking up dust and giving her a fright. She had been so lost in her thoughts that she hadn't seen it coming. Her school bag fell to the ground, heavy books falling out of the zip she had been unable to close.

The driver was wearing a cap and dark sunglasses, so all she could see was his reddish brown beard.

"You should watch where you're going there girly."

"Sorry." She stammered, trying to gather her books together. Something about the bearded man made her feel uncomfortable.

"You're too juicy to be walking around the big bad roads alone. Someone might want to see you bleed if you're not careful." He leered at her.

She left the books and bag on the floor, backing away, getting ready to run away when the passenger door opened.

She turned and fled, but only managed to get a few yards when she recognised the voice calling her.

"Emily, come back!"

Emily skidded to a stop and looked back at the smiling face of Pastor Stan. She sighed a huge sigh of relief.

Stan walked around the car and bent down to collect Emily's things. He put them carefully into her bag and held it out at arm's length.

"You'll have to excuse my brother," he said smiling as she walked closer, "he means well, but he's not used to being around pretty girls."

Emily stopped walking; even Pastor Stan was making her feel uncomfortable suddenly.

"Come on Emily, I won't bite." He smiled his most compassionate smile, the one he so often used when he was giving a sermon.

Emily knew she was being silly, she had known Pastor Stan for years and she trusted him, he would never hurt her. She closed the gap between them and took the strap of her bag. As she got a grip on it, he jerked the bag towards him, causing her to stumble. Stan punched her viciously in the face, knocking Emily to her knees. She tried to stand up, still holding the bag, but he hit her again. As she fell to the floor, she watched the forest blur and fade to black.

∞

Emily sat up in bed panting. The dream was so vivid, she could smell the pine needles and moss. She was sweating despite the cold. She pulled the blankets off and went to the bathroom to splash cold water on her face.

That wasn't a dream she had had before. She rinsed her face and then was overcome with a wave of nausea and just managed to get to the toilet before throwing up.

She vomited until she was dry-heaving, each spasm making her feel as though her ribs would break.

She sat next to the toilet when she was done and pulled her knees up to her chest.

Toilet, towel, sink, tap, shampoo. Toilet, towel, sink, tap, shampoo. Toilet, towel, sink, tap, shampoo.

She repeated the words like a mantra, waiting for the trembling to stop and her breathing to slow.

When she had calmed down enough to stand up again, Emily rinsed her mouth out and brushed her teeth twice. Then she showered and scrubbed her body until she felt raw.

It was only when she got to the bedroom to change that she looked at her mobile and saw that it was just after three.

She hated this town. She hated so much that she was there, and she was wondering to herself why she still was. She had told Casey what she had to tell her, there was nothing stopping her from going home.

She went to the kitchen to make coffee and knew that there was a little voice in her head, telling her she couldn't go yet. She didn't know why, but she knew she had to be where she was for now.

While Casey may not be her biggest fan at the moment, she was going to need someone outside of her family to get her through what she was about to experience.

She took her coffee to the step outside and pulled her jacket around her tightly.

Lighting a cigarette, she drew deeply as her thoughts turned back to Casey. There was no winning in her situation. Regardless of the decision she made, she would always live with the what-ifs.

Emily always thought it was something she had a reasonably good handle on, that decision she had made so many years before. But having spent time with Sophie, Emily felt that pang that only came when she thought about the fact that she would never have a child to love unconditionally, or one that would love her in the same way.

Emily remembered her own mother, the way she used to hold her hand, and for some reason the moments of her always holding Emily's hand during the hymns in church where she would look at her daughter every now and then with that loving smile came into sharp focus.

The way she would tousle Emily's hair at bedtime and sing terrible country songs as lullabies.

Emily hadn't thought about her mother for years. The memories now brought a pain to her chest so raw if felt as though she had just lost her all over again. She dropped her cigarette and hugged herself as though to pull the ragged pieces inside herself back together.

# Chapter Sixteen

Cathy Richards had spent the night unable to sleep. Instead she had been spring cleaning the house. Everything that Frank had bought without her approval was sitting in a pile in the dining room. She had taken all the photos down and had put them in a separate pile on the table so that she could burn them. The only ones she had kept aside were the ones that included Liam. With those, she intended to cut out the image of Frank and reframe the pictures.

She was sitting cross-legged on the floor, her fourth or fifth dry martini next to her, going through old photo albums. She didn't even bother to open her wedding album, she just flung it to one side.

She took a sip of her martini and looked around the room. The walls looked so bare now that all the pictures had been taken down. The only one she hadn't removed yet was Frank's family crest above the fireplace. She hadn't taken it down purely because it was so high up on the wall and the stepladder was in the store room next to the garage, and she couldn't be bothered to brave the weather in the middle of the night to fetch it.

She wondered if she took Frank's old armchair and put it in front of the fireplace if she wouldn't be able to reach it if she climbed on top of the arms of the armchair.

She hated that family crest more than any picture of Frank, she would love to throw that on the top of the fire pile, knowing how much Frank treasured the hideous thing. Although, she thought to herself, she should probably offer it to Liam first, it was his family crest as well after all.

Cathy pulled herself to her feet with difficulty, she had been sitting in the same position for too long. She bent down to collect her glass off the floor and finish her drink before she started pushing and dragging the ugly armchair to towards the fireplace.

She turned off the gas at the wall so that the fire would go out before pushing the chair into its final position.

Standing back to admire her brilliant idea, she checked the chair was steady and then climbed onto the seat, but she wasn't high enough. So she managed to balance herself with a foot on each arm and reached as high as she could. She was still too short.

Huffing to herself and cursing her bastard of a husband for insisting the bloody thing was placed so high in the first place, she used the wall to balance herself and climbed carefully onto the back of the armchair.

She straightened up and found herself at head height to the crest.

Smiling to herself at the thought of Frank's reaction to what she was doing, Cathy took the heavy wooded crest off the wall.

It happened in a split-second. The old lazy boy started to recline with the added weight on the backrest and Cathy lost her balance and came crashing down, hitting her head on the mantle before landing hard on the floor.

Emily was on her third cup of coffee and going through all the leads her hacker friend had finally sent through for the First National breach. She was surprised she had managed to keep her contract considering how long it was taking her to get to the bottom of it.

She had just recognised one of the IP addresses on the list as that of the assistant bank manager's office computer when there was a knock at the door.

Looking down at her screen, Emily saw it was just before five, the sky outside still dark.

She went to the front door and looked through the window with trepidation.

Liam was standing on the front step, a wrapped-up Sophie in his arms.

Emily opened the door.

"Liam?"

"I'm so sorry to do this so early, I was taking Sophie to Amy's when we saw your light was on and she insisted we came here instead."

Emily opened the door wide and let them in, "Is she okay?" concern in her voice.

"Yeah, she's fine. Well, still sick, but not worse." Liam put his sleepy daughter on the same couch where he had collected her from a few hours earlier. The he walked back over to where Emily was still standing at the front door.

"My mom fell at home and has been taken to the hospital, I need to go." Liam said, "I didn't want to take Sophie when it's still so cold and dark out. I told Soph I have to go to work, I didn't want her to worry unnecessarily."

"No problem," Emily told him, "I'll look after her until you're back."

Liam touched Emily's arm briefly. "Thanks Em."

With that he was gone. Emily touched the place his hand had rested. Liam hadn't called her Em since they had broken up.

She closed the door to keep the cold wind out and went to the couch to check on Sophie.

She seemed to have fallen asleep already, holding onto a ragged looking stuffed bunny. Emily gently wiped some of Sophie's hair out of her face.

"I'm glad Daddy brought me here." Sophie murmured sleepily, then turned her head to the side and was asleep again.

Emily watched her sleeping for a few minutes, thinking how young she looked, how vulnerable.

Giving herself a mental shake, Emily threw another log onto the fire and when back to the dining table to carry on working.

Emily was making scrambled eggs when her cell rang. She looked at the screen before answering.

"Hi Paige."

"Morning Emily, is this a bad time?" Paige responded.

"Of course not. What's up?"

"Can I come over? Or could you meet me at Molly's this morning?"

Emily removed the pan from the heat and dished the eggs onto two plates with toast already waiting. "I can't leave the house right now Paige, I've got Sophie here and she isn't well."

"Sophie? As is Liam's Sophie?"

Emily tucked the phone into her shoulder so she could wash the pan in the sink while talking. "Yes, that Sophie. Thanks for the head's up about the neighbour by the way."

"I did try to warn you, you're first morning in town, but you shut me down, remember?"

"Oh," Emily said, "Sorry. It was just an unexpected surprise."

"If you're babysitting, does that mean you two are on talking terms?" Paige asked.

Emily could hear the smile in the older woman's voice and snorted. "Hardly. But Sophie has taken a liking to me and she's the one that insisted she come here."

"Children are so intuitive." Paige mused. "So, can I come to you?"

"Sure, are you hungry?" Emily asked, wanting to smack herself for already washing the pan.

"No thanks. I'll see you in ten."


Emily put her mobile back on the counter and carried the two plates to the lounge. She gave the smaller one to Sophie who had been awake less than five minutes before announcing that she was about to starve to death.

"Thank you." She said to Emily with a grin.

"No problem kiddo." Emily replied, sitting down with her own food.

Once again the over-infatuated shark was chasing the mermaid all over the ocean on television and Emily ate in silence while they both watched.


Emily was washing the breakfast plates when Paige knocked on the door and came in.

"Hey Paige." Emily called from the kitchen.

"Aunty Paige!" Sophie yelled from the couch, then she started coughing from the exertion of the shout.

Paige went straight over to the couch. "Hello there young lady. I haven't seen you in ages! How are you?"

"I'm fine." Sophie replied.

Emily walked through to the lounge with a glass of water and gave it to Sophie.

"Can't I have juice rather?" Sophie asked, looking at the glass with disappointment.

"Well, I don't think juice while you're coughing is such a good idea for one," Emily told her, "And for two, I don't have any juice. I'll have to stock up if I know you're going to be visiting."

Sophie nodded her agreement and turned her attention back to the television.

Emily gestured for Paige to follow her to the dining table.

Once they were settled, Paige spoke, "You're so good with her."

"Oh please." Emily said with a laugh, "She's only been awake for twenty minutes, I'm sure the novelty will wear off in the next hour."

Paige smiled, but didn't say anything.

"Can I make you some coffee Paige?"

"No thanks Emily, I've been drinking coffee since the early hours of this morning."

Emily saw Paige's eyes were brimming with unshed tears. "She told you." It was a statement, not a question.

Paige nodded and sniffed, trying to keep her composure.

"I'm sorry I didn't tell you Paige, it wasn't my place."

Paige waved her away, "Of course, I understand completely. I'm so grateful she had you to confide in."

Emily was quiet while Paige wiped away a single tear that escaped.

"What did she tell you?" Emily asked quietly, aware of the younger presence in the room.

Paige sniffed again, "That she's terrified mostly. That she wants to end it."

"What did you guys say when she told you that?"

"We told her we would support her no matter what choice she made. But that only seemed to upset her more."

Emily looked surprised. "Why would that have upset her?" she asked.

Paige shook her head and clasped her own hands tightly on the table in front of her. "I don't know. I think it has to do with how much guilt she's feeling."

"She did say she was worried about your religious beliefs." Emily told her quietly.

"I don't think it's our belief that she was worried about. I think it's her own." Paige said quietly.

"What do you mean?" Emily asked.

"She's always been so faithful," Paige said sadly, "She said to Daniel that she's scared she won't be forgiven for killing an innocent child."

Paige started sobbing quietly, her face in her hands.

Emily stood up and went to the couch. Taking the remote, she put the volume up a little louder so that Sophie wouldn't hear the muffled noises across the room.

By the time she got back to the dining room, Paige had calmed herself and was once again wringing her hands together.

Before Emily could take her seat again, there was a knock at the door.

"It's open," she called.

Liam came into the house looking exhausted. His eyes had dark rings under them, and his face was covered in thicker stubble than normal. Emily thought the stubble suited him, but didn't say anything out loud.

Sophie bounded off the couch and ran into her father's arms.

Liam picked her up and hugged her tight. "How are you feeling princess?"

"So much better." Sophie told him, "How was work?"

"Super boring." Liam told her seriously.

Sophie started wiggling in his arms. "Daddy, let me down, I need to pee!"

Liam put his daughter down and she darted off to the bathroom without another word. He walked over to where Emily was still standing near the table and put his hand on Paige's shoulder.

"Hello Paige, how are you?"

Paige managed a smile. "I'm good thanks and you Liam?"

"I'm good thanks."

Emily thought it was silly that they were both looking like crap and lying to one another, but it wasn't her business, so she went over to the couch and started folding up the blanket.

"Thanks for looking after her." Liam said, causing Emily to jump. She hadn't realised he had approached her.

"No problem, she was an easy houseguest." Emily handed Liam the stuffed bunny. "How's your mom?"

"She cut her head open pretty bad, has a bit of a concussion and managed to dislocate her knee."

"What did she do?" Emily asked.

"She was trying to reach something high up and fell off the couch she was standing on. I have a feeling she had been drinking." Liam pulled a face. "But they've stitched her up and got her knee back in. She's on bedrest for a few days until the concussion has time to settle and then she'll be on crutches for a while. They've sent her home though, I think all the nurses are too scared to deal with her."

"Shame man." Emily said as Sophie came back into the room.

"They had to shave part of her head to stich her back up so you can imagine how pleased she is with the doctors." Liam said.

Emily laughed. She knew what a proud woman Cathy was, and could just imagine her reaction to them cutting off her perfect hair.

"Shaved whose head Daddy?" Sophie asked curiously. "Like a mohawk?"

"I'll tell you all about it once we get home. Have you got everything?"

Sophie rolled her eyes, "You've got Benson and the blankets right here Dad."

Emily laughed again, she was so much like Liam.

"What do you say to Emily?" Liam asked.

Instead of saying anything, Sophie hugged Emily tightly around the middle. "Thanks for looking after me."

Emily was surprised at how natural it felt to hug the little girl back. Usually any kind of physical contact that she didn't initiate made her uncomfortable.

"Thanks for keeping me company." Emily told her and without thinking, kissed Sophie gently on the top of the head.

Only after she had walked them to the door and closed it again behind them, did Emily return to the dining table.

"You are good with her, I don't care what you say." Paige told her.

"It's weird. Kids are so innocent with their contact that it doesn't feel wrong."

"Most people are innocent in their contact, but I get what you're saying." Paige said.

"What did Daniel say to Casey?" Emily asked, returning to the subject at hand.

"He wasn't really sure what to say. He told her that God would love her no matter what choices she made."

Emily was quiet for a moment. "Do you honestly believe that?" she asked Paige.

"I do." Paige said, "But I suppose no one can ever truly know the answer to Casey's question until after this life."

Emily picked up a pen and played with it. "This is where I really struggle Paige. And I imagine Casey is going through the same thing right now.

There's this all-loving, all-powerful God that can create an entire universe and knows the number of number of hairs on each of our heads." Emily paused, spinning the pen on the table, "Then this same all-loving, all-powerful God lets things like this happen to people like Casey."

"And to people like you?" Paige asked quietly.

Emily shrugged, "We're talking about Casey now, not me."

"It's the same thing though." Paige pointed out, "And I understand the confusion. There's always the question of why bad things happen to good people.

But Emily, God doesn't let that happen, there is evil in this world. That's the price we paid for our freedom of choice."

Emily stopped spinning the pen and looked at Paige. "The same God that wants you to choose not to sin or do bad things?"

"Yes," Paige said. "That's the choice we have."

"So, Casey is in this situation where none of it is her fault because He decided to allow it to happen, but now she's either got to live with the horrific reminder for the rest of her life or choose to knowingly sin and put her own soul at risk because of a situation that He put her in?"

"He didn't put either of you in that situation."

"He did!" Emily snapped, smacking the table with her hand. "You can't have it both ways Paige. Either He's all-powerful and He's allowing it all to happen, or He isn't, in which case, who gives a fuck what He thinks?"

Paige was shocked by the outburst. She sat in silence watching Emily.

Emily didn't look up, she was once again playing with the scar on her palm, she had surprised even herself with the outburst.

"You have so much anger inside of you Emily." Paige said quietly.

"I wonder why?" Emily answered sarcastically.

"It's completely understandable, I just wish there was something I could do to take your pain away." Paige laid a hand gently on Emily's but Emily pulled hers away. "I know

202

you might not believe this Emily, but God loves you, very much."

"God doesn't give a shit about me." Emily said quietly.

"That's not true, you're His child, he loves you more than you or I could ever understand."

"God loves good people who don't sin." Emily corrected Paige.

"Everyone sins Emily. That's why Jesus gave His life for us."

"Yes," Emily responded, "And all you have to do is believe in Him and repent for your sins and you get to go straight through the pearly gates right?"

"Well, you need to believe it truly, but yes." Paige looked concerned.

"What happens if you don't repent?" Emily asked, suddenly looking at Paige with anguish in her eyes.

"Why wouldn't a person repent if they know their soul can be saved?" Paige replied.

"Why the hell should I repent for an action that came solely from the position He allowed me to be in?"

"I'm not following you." Paige said, trying to understand.

"Do you know there's not a single time in the bible where it's okay to act in self-defense?" Emily asked suddenly. She didn't wait for Paige to answer, "Trust me, I've checked. Taking a person's life is never okay. You're supposed to turn the other cheek and all that."

"Emily, there's no way God would hold your actions against you. You acted in self-defense and did what you had to do to protect yourself from that monster."

"He'll hold it against me if I don't repent of it." Emily stated, "And I can't because I'm not sorry. I'm glad that sick fuck is dead."

"So am I." Paige responded, "And if I could have done it myself to save you the pain of what you went through, I would have done it too."

"Would you have repented after I wonder?" Emily asked her.

"If I was protecting another, I wouldn't need to." Paige pointed out.

"That's not the same then."

"It is the same! Think of how many girls you may have saved."

"Think of all the girls I didn't save because I didn't tell anyone about his brother." Emily countered. She took a breath. "I'm not sorry. Not just because I believe God put me in that position to begin with, but because I didn't do it to save my life. I didn't for a second think I was going to survive that place. I did it because I wanted to hurt him. I wanted to make him feel pain. And dammit, I wanted him to die."

Emily looked as though she may suddenly cry. Saying the words out loud for the first time had torn open yet another old wound she had tried to pretend no longer existed.

"Oh Emily." Paige said, tears running down her own face. I'm so so sorry that I've caused you to live through this pain all over again."

Emily shook her head, the muscles in her jaw tightening. "This isn't about me. Let's get back to Casey."

Emily stood up suddenly and asked Paige again, "Want some coffee?" Then without waiting for an answer, she went through to the kitchen and started making two cups.

When she came back with the coffees, she handed one to Paige. "Can we sit outside? If I have to talk about this, I would at least like to do it while smoking."

"Sure." Paige said, getting up and following Emily to the steps out the back. She wanted to talk through what Emily had just told her, but the switch in the younger woman's personality was startling. Whatever wall Emily put up between herself and her past was firmly back in place and Paige knew this wasn't the time to try take it down again. She sat down heavily on the concrete step and sighed, "You know, I really should get a table and chairs for out here. I never realised how inconvenient it is to not have anywhere to sit."

Emily was already sitting on the step below, a lit cigarette in her fingers. "Guess you haven't spent enough time here to really think about it."

"No, you're right. These last few weeks is probably the most time I've ever spent in this house."

Emily blew smoke rings in the opposite direction to Paige. "What would you want Casey to choose?" she asked.

"It doesn't matter what I want. This is about supporting her decision."

"It doesn't mean you don't get to have an opinion about it. Even if you don't share it with Casey." Emily pointed out.

Paige sighed, her breath coming out in a mist, despite the fact that she wasn't smoking herself. "I would be lying if I didn't say there was a moment where I wanted to raise the baby."

Emily didn't say anything, she sat silently watching her cigarette burn away in her hand while she listened.

"I realise how that wouldn't be possible though." Paige continued. "Casey would probably do it if I asked, but I doubt we'd ever see her again after the baby is born."

"Would you blame her?" Emily asked, not unkindly, "She wouldn't be able to look at the reminder every time she saw you."

"No, I know that," Paige said sadly. "We would never do that to her." She sighed, "I just wonder if it wouldn't be best to give it up for adoption."

"Paige," Emily said gently, "asking her to go through with the pregnancy is a huge ask. And what if it turns out like its father?"

"But what if it didn't? What if this was the only good thing to come out of this whole mess? A chance for a new life to start over?"

"It wouldn't be fair to ask her to do that Paige. And besides, if it gets adopted, you'll never know how its going to turn out."

"I know. I wouldn't ask her to do anything. I will support her choice regardless of what it is."

Emily finished her cigarette and lit a new one. She drank her coffee in silence, not knowing what to say.

"I'm so scared she'll regret this for the rest of her life." Paige said, breaking down and sobbing.

Emily once again felt as though she should comfort her friend, but she couldn't bring herself to move. Instead, she stayed silent, waiting for Paige to cry herself out.

Her coffee and cigarette were long finished when Emily finally spoke, "I know you don't want to hear this, but she is going to regret this decision for as long as she lives. She will always second guess herself. And the truth is, it doesn't matter if she gives it up or aborts it, she will always be haunted by this. There's no pain free way out of it."

Paige sniffed again, "I know." She wiped her face with her hands. "I wish I could take this away from her."

Emily sighed sadly, "I know you do Paige. I do too."

# Chapter Seventeen

The following morning, Emily drove up to Paige's house and parked in the driveway. Instead of getting out, she put her head back against her headrest and closed her eyes.

Casey had asked that Emily be the one to take her to the clinic in the next county. Casey had made her decision, but hadn't wanted either parent to be with her.

Emily sighed. It was going to be an awful day. She opened her door and went into the house.

Casey was sitting on the bottom step of the staircase waiting for Emily. Emily could see she had been crying. The girl's face was splotchy and her eyes red.

"Are you ready?" Emily asked quietly.

Casey nodded and walked out of the house, waiting for Emily to follow before closing the door.

"Where are your parents?" Emily asked, unlocking the car.

"I asked them not to be here." Casey said in a shaky voice.

Emily understood the feeling, so she didn't comment.

They drove in silence for most of the way, Emily hadn't even turned on the radio. She had been concentrating on the slick roads but had also been acutely aware of her silent and rigid passenger.

"Thank you for driving me." Casey said in a scratchy voice.

"It's okay." Emily said, realizing that saying it was her pleasure would have been wrong.

"I really appreciate everything you've done for me." Casey said, looking out the passenger window.

"I know you do." Emily answered simply.

They were entering the neighboring county of Brenton when Emily spoke again. "Are you okay with this?"

"No. But it's the best choice. The only choice." Casey told her.


Emily pulled into the same hospital she had spent so many months in when she was a teenager and parked the car.

Casey got out without saying anything, so Emily followed suit.

Once they got inside, Casey seemed to lose her resolve a little and couldn't walk up to the reception, so Emily did.

"We have an appointment with Dr. Green," Emily told the young receptionist.

Having been shown the direction, Emily and Casey walked down the hall towards the nursery side.

The place looked and smelt exactly how Emily remembered. It was the usual hospital, disinfectant smell, but there was something else as well. The smell of old concrete and treated wood.

The hospital was old, maybe as old as the school back in Hawthorne. It was spotlessly clean though, the walls the same stark white they had always been, although the paint looked newer, and the linoleum floors were faded but spotless.

They passed the window of the nursery and Casey paused. She was looking at two babies that were in a plastic crib near the window. Casey touched the glass with her fingers.

"You okay?" Emily asked quietly.

Casey nodded without looking at Emily and continued walking down the hall to the doctor's office.

They entered the rooms of Dr. Green and Casey went straight to sit down with her head in her hands while Emily approached the nurse. "We're here to see Dr. Green."

The elderly black woman nodded and smiled. "Casey?"

Emily nodded towards Casey. "She's a little apprehensive."

The nurse took a clipboard off the table in front of her and handed it to Emily. "I understand," she said quietly, "her mother explained everything on the phone."

Emily took the clipboard and went to sit with Casey, filling in what she could and only asking Casey to take over for the things Emily didn't know.

The nurse approached them just as Casey was signing the forms.

"Did your mother explain to you what's going to happen now?" She asked Casey kindly.

Casey gave a halfhearted nod but didn't look at the nurse.

The nurse continued, "I'm going to go over it again, just so that you understand everything. Is that alright?"

Casey nodded again.

"First I'm going to take you into that room over there and take a blood sample. Then, I'll ask you to give me a urine sample. After that, the doctor will come in and do an examination and a scan."

"A scan?" Casey asked weakly.

"You don't have to look at the screen." The nurse said in an understanding tone. "We can turn it away if you want. But it is necessary for the doctor to see what's going on before we move onto the next step."

Casey swallowed loudly.

"After that," the nurse said in her soothing voice, "When we know how far along you are, we will give you the necessary medication."

Casey was still swallowing, as though nauseous.

"You need to know," the nurse said, touching her arm gently, "you're in control. If you want to change your mind or wait at any point, then that's what we'll do."

The nurse went back to her desk to drop off the clipboard then looked at Emily expectedly. "Are you going to be with her?"

Emily nodded, "Every moment."

"Alright, let's go."

The nurse led them to an examination room. She asked Casey to pull up her sleeve and put the tourniquet around her upper arm.

She drew three vials of blood then undid the tourniquet and stuck a piece of cotton wool over the puncture hole with medical tape. Then she handed Casey a small specimen bottle and pointed to a door off to the side. "There's a toilet in there. You can leave the sample on the sink, I will collect it when you're done. Then you can come back here, get undressed and put this on," She pointed to a folded hospital gown on the examination bed.

The nurse gave Emily an understanding smile and left the room.

"Casey —" Emily started, but Casey got off the edge of the bed and went into the toilet, closing the door behind her.

Casey was finished quickly in the toilet and came back into the room. She undressed quickly, avoiding looking at Emily and pulled the gown on.

While she was changing, Emily had looked at the pictures on the walls, medical models of women's reproductive organs. It was only when she heard Casey sit on the bed again did she turn around.

Casey was staring straight ahead, not taking anything in. Emily understood the feeling. She knew the young woman was trying to disengage from what was happening and about to happen to her body.

There was a quiet knock on the door and an older woman in a white doctor's coat entered, stethoscope around her neck.

"I'm Dr. Green." She introduced herself, "You must be Casey." The doctor had short, spiky grey hair and the weathered face of an avid runner. Her brown eyes were alert and kind though, and she made Emily feel at ease.

The doctor walked around to the opposite side of the bed and motioned towards a chair. "Why don't you have a seat?" She said to Emily, "You can bring the chair closer if you like."

Emily did as she was told, putting the chair next to the bed. Casey immediately reached out a hand and Emily grasped it tightly.

"You're already passed the twelve-week mark, is that right?" Dr. Green asked.

Casey nodded.

"Okay, then I won't need to do an internal scan for the time being, I can do an abdominal scan instead."

Casey was trembling slightly, but she sighed a sigh of relief at the news.

Dr. Green took the blanket from the bottom of the bed and gestured for Casey to lie down. Once Casey complied, the doctor covered her legs with the blanket and pulled it up just below her waist.

Then she pulled the hospital gown up gently to below Casey's breasts. The doctor noticed the still pink scars on Casey's abdomen but didn't say anything.

"This is going to be cold." She warned Casey, picking up a big tube and pouring see-through gel onto Casey's stomach.

Dr. Green used the ultrasound scanner to spread the gel.

Casey looked pointedly away from the screen, staring at something above Emily's head.

Emily couldn't help looking. The black and grey shadows on the screen made no sense at all to her.

The doctor moved the scanner around then twisted it in her hand.

All of a sudden, Emily could make out the head and arms of the little skeleton. The oversized head looked like it belonged to an alien, but Emily could even see the individual little fingers. The baby was moving around, arms flailing around as though complaining about the sudden invasion of privacy.

The scan moved down the little body, but Emily could only make out a single leg. The doctor pushed a button and the image froze on the screen. She measured the length of the femur then turned the video back on. She measured the head and the spine.

"I need to turn the sound on for a moment." Dr. Green told them.

The next moment the thudding of a very fast heartbeat came out of the machine.

Casey whipped her head around at the sound and stared at the screen. On the monitor, they could clearly see the beating of the tiny heart, the sound like the thrumming of a hummingbird's wings.

Emily felt Casey's hand squeeze her own. Emily couldn't believe her own reaction to what she was seeing. She couldn't look away from the screen. The idea that a tiny, perfect little human was right there was more shocking to Emily than she could have imagined. She had been thinking of the baby as an it, but now she realised she was looking at an actual human being and she felt suddenly ill.

Dr. Green pushed a button and the screen went blank. She wiped the gel off the scanner, then took more paper towel and wiped Casey's stomach, then pulled the gown back down.

When she was done, she turned on her swivel stool to look at the other two. "Right, so we're a little further along than is usually done, but, we can still do the procedure today."

"What happens now?" Emily asked.

"Well, in this case, we will give Casey and injection and a few pills, as well as a few pills to take home. The medication will stop the production of the HCG hormone and within the next twenty four hours, her body will start to reject the fetus."

Casey put her hand over her mouth to stop the sobs that were coming. Emily squeezed her hand tighter.

"I'll give you a few minutes while I get the medications prepared." Dr. Green told them kindly, before leaving the room.

"Casey, are you sure about this?" Emily asked the crying girl carefully.

Casey shook her head, "I'm not sure about anything."

"We can leave right now." Emily told her, "You don't have to do this today."

Casey shook her head again, "If I don't do it today, I never will."

Emily didn't know how to respond. She sat, holding Casey's hand while Casey sobbed miserably on the examination bed.

The nurse entered the room with a tray. There were syringes and a little polystyrene cup with pills inside. There was also a kidney bowl with a few larger white capsules inside.

She placed the tray on the table beside the bed, gave Casey's arm a squeeze and left the room again. Dr. Green entered almost immediately.

"Alright," she said, taking her seat on the stool again, "Do you want me to explain the procedure to you again?"

Casey shook her head, her gaze fixed on the tray behind the doctor.

Dr. Green reached back and picked up one of the syringes. "Are you ready?" she asked Casey kindly.

Casey was trembling all over, but slowly, she nodded.

Dr. Green nodded as well and picked up some sterilizing gauze. She was about to wipe the injection site when Casey suddenly yelled, "Stop!"

Dr. Green put the syringe down. "Do you need some time to think about this?" she asked Casey.

"No," Casey said in a shaky but determined face, "I can't do this. I won't do this."

"Casey, are you sure about this?" Emily asked her.

"I'm not sure about what I'm going to do tomorrow or the next day or the day after that," Casey said, looking at Emily for the first time since they arrived, "But I am sure that I can't do this."

"Okay." Emily said, giving Casey's hand another gentle squeeze.

"In that case," Dr. Green, "I will need to give you some prenatal vitamins to take home with you."

The doctor smiled at Casey and left the room quietly.

Emily was silent, staring after the doctor, her mind blank.

Dr. Green came back into the room with a bottle of prenatal vitamins and handed them to Casey. "If you decide to continue with this pregnancy, you'll need to take one of those every day. No smoking, drinking, caffeine or too much sugar."

Casey nodded and took the bottle of pills silently.

"Oh, and," Dr. Green went around the bed and turned on the ultrasound machine. She pushed a few buttons and waited while the machine printed out a few ultrasound pictures. "These are for you."

Casey took those silently as well.

"I'll let you get dressed. And if I don't see you in the next few days, then I'll see you in ten weeks for a checkup." Dr. Green stopped at the door. "Casey, would you like to know the sex of the baby?"

"I, I don't know." Casey stammered.

"I tell you what." Dr. Green said, "It's not usually so obvious at this stage, but I was able to see quite clearly. I'll write it down and put it in an envelope and leave it with the nurse. That way you can decide when you're ready."

"Thank you." Emily told the doctor, who nodded and left the room.

Casey got off the bed and with shaky hands, changed back into her street clothes.

On the way past the nurse's desk, Emily took the envelope off the counter and returned the nurse's smile.

The silence on the journey back was deafening. Emily couldn't think of anything to say. Casey sat in the passenger seat, staring at the ultrasound images.

It was only when they finally pulled into the driveway of Casey's house did Casey finally speak.

"I can't keep it." She whispered.

"You don't have to," Emily told her quietly, "If you want to have the baby, you can always put it up for adoption. There are so many people out there desperate for a child to love."

Casey swallowed, "Then some stranger would be raising it."

"Casey." Emily said, but Casey suddenly turned around and gripped Emily's hand so tightly that it hurt.

"Would you take it?" Casey asked her.

"What?" Emily gasped.

"Would you take the baby?"

Emily stared blankly at Casey.

"I know it's not what you were thinking and I know the baby of a rapist isn't what you want, but I know it would never grow up to be a monster if you were the one raising it." Casey let go of Emily's hand, "Please just think about it?"

Emily swallowed and nodded.

"Thank you." Casey said, tears in her eyes. She closed the car door and hurried into the house.

# Chapter Eighteen

Emily was sitting at the dining table, the envelope Casey had forgotten in the car clutched in her hand.

It was crazy, something Casey said in a moment of panic. But... But now that the thought was in her head, Emily couldn't stop thinking about it.

She had been so distracted when she got back that she hadn't even closed the front door.

She didn't know how long she had been sitting at the table, holding that envelope when Paige walked in. Emily only really noticed the presence of the other woman when Paige sat down.

"Emily? Are you alright?"

Emily looked at Paige, "Yeah," she answered, "just been a really weird day."

"I can only imagine." Paige said.

"Did Casey tell you?"

"Which part?" Paige asked, "That she didn't go through with it or that she's asked you to adopt the baby?"

Emily sat back and sighed, "It's not even an option Paige."

Paige stood up and went to the grocery cupboard, "Can I open a bottle of wine? I think we've earned it."

"Knock yourself out." Emily said, looking out the window for the first time and seeing how dark it had become.

Paige returned with two glasses of red wine and the bottle tucked under her arm. She handed Emily a glass and sat down again. "You don't want a child?"

"It's never been an option, so I've never thought about it." Emily told her honestly.

"Now that it could be an option if you wanted it to?"

"How would that work Paige?" Emily looked at her oldest friend. "I travel for work all the time, I party way too much, I'm barely able to take care of myself."

Paige took a sip of wine and set the glass down. "Emily, nobody's perfect when they become a parent. I was not interested in giving up my personal time either. I resented having to be pregnant."

"You're the best mother I know." Emily argued.

"I don't know about best. But I love my daughter more than life itself. Having a baby is a huge adjustment, but after a while you start to wonder what you ever liked about a life without them." Paige picked up the discarded envelope, "What's this?"

"Casey forgot it in the car, it's the gender of the baby."

"Wow." Paige was holding the envelope carefully in her hands, "Have you looked?"

Emily shook her head, "That's Casey's choice, not mine."

"Casey and I had a long talk when she got home. About the scan, the heartbeat, why she couldn't go through with it, and then we had a long talk about you."

"Look Paige, she's in shock. She'll wake up tomorrow and realise I'm the worst person to be giving a kid to."

"I don't think she will."

"In what world would I want to raise that monster's baby?"

Paige looked wounded for a moment but gathered herself. "You wouldn't be raising a monster's baby. You'd be raising your baby. How it came to be won't determine who it's going to be."

"You don't know that." Emily argued.

"Well, here's what I do know. You could never raise a child who would grow up to be cruel." Paige held up a hand to prevent Emily from interrupting. "I remember once, when you first started in high school, some of the other girls were giving you a hard time because of your dad. Do you remember what you told me that day?"

Emily shook her head, a skeptical expression on her face.

"You told me that you didn't ask for an alcoholic for a father. You said that just because he fathered you, didn't mean you had anything in common with him."

"It's not exactly the same thing Paige."

"But it's not completely different either."

"I'm really living up to that statement I made huh?" Emily said wryly, holding up her glass of wine and taking a sip before asking, "What would I even tell the kid when it asked about its parents?"

Paige shrugged, "You would tell them whatever you thought was right. That a young girl wanted to give her baby a good life with a loving parent, and that she chose you to be the one to love them."

"Casey would never want to see me again." Emily said quietly, twirling her wine glass in her hand.

"No," Paige agreed, "She probably wouldn't. Just like you couldn't stand to see me for years. You are the person she has needed so desperately these last few months. But your relationship is already so intertwined with what she went through, I think she was always going to distance herself from you when she was ready."

Emily knew Paige was right. Casey would need to live her life without Emily as a constant reminder of her traumatic past.

"What if I screw it up?" Emily asked quieter still.

"Ha!" Paige snorted, giving Emily a fright, "If you're a mother, there's one truth I can absolutely guarantee you, and that is that you will most definitely screw up."

"I don't mean the everyday stuff Paige."

"Neither do I. We all make mistakes as parents, and often those mistakes are big ones, ones that leave a lasting impact on our children. Mistakes that torture us for years after. It's part of being a parent."

"Why are you trying so hard to convince me this is a good idea?" Emily asked while topping up their glasses. "Is it so that you can be in the kid's life?"

Paige sighed, "It's not that I haven't thought about it, but to be honest, I'm not sure I'll ever be able to be a part of the child's life. It would be too hard."

"So why me then?" Emily asked in quiet desperation, "You're asking me to give up our relationship too if that's the case."

"Before all this happened," Paige gestured around the room vaguely, "We never saw each other. Our only communication was the occasional email. Now please don't misunderstand, I have loved having you back in my life, but I think we can still manage something more than what we had before, don't you?"

Paige touched Emily's arm, "But to answer your question, why you? Because you are the most loyal person I have ever met. You put yourself through hell to help me when I asked you to.

And I know you hate the term, but you are a survivor. I think your determination would make you a brilliant mother."

Emily ran her fingers through her hair and bit her lip thoughtfully.

"Obviously you don't have to make a decision now," Paige told her, "I just don't want you to make any decision without giving it some proper thought."

Emily had promised Paige she would give the idea some serious thought and had let her know she would be heading back to the city the next morning to get back to work.

Paige had left some time ago and Emily was busy writing a report on her discoveries for First National when there was a knock at the door.

Emily closed her laptop and went to answer the door.

"Liam, hi." Emily greeted him in surprise.

"Hey Em, I'm sorry to keep doing this to you." Liam said. He was looking more rested, cleanly shaved and far more relaxed in jeans and a sweater than he usually looked in his sheriff's uniform.

"You need me to babysit?" Emily guessed.

"Just for an hour or so. Sophie really isn't feeling great today, but I need to go drop some food off with my mother, then sit with her and make sure she actually eats it."

"Sure. Where is she?" Emily asked.

"She's asleep in her bed, I didn't want to wake her. Would you mind watching her at my place?"

"Let me grab a jacket." Emily said. She took her jacket off the back of the chair she was sitting in then grabbed her mobiles from the table.

Liam was waiting for her outside the front door. They walked together next door.

"Em, I know I owe you so much more than an apology." Liam began.

"Please don't." Emily said curtly, "I really don't mind looking after Sophie, but I don't want to get into that now." Liam nodded stiffly.

"So is your mom not eating?" Emily asked him, trying to cover the awkwardness of the moment.

Liam shook his head, "She's lost so much weight I don't think she's been eating much for a while."

"Is she sick?"

"No, I don't think so. The doctor didn't mention it at least, and he seemed to think she would be okay to go home and rest there." Liam opened his front door and gestured for Emily to enter before him, "I actually think she's been seeing someone the last few years. She would never admit to it, but I have a feeling she's dealing with a broken heart."

"Seeing someone? What about your dad?" Emily asked.

"He passed a few years ago. That's one of the reasons I moved back here."

"Oh, I'm so sorry Liam."

"Don't be," Liam said shortly, "He was a bastard."

Emily was surprised by the vehemence in Liam's words, but she didn't say anything.

Liam walked down the passage to check on Sophie and left Emily in the living room alone. There were a lot of photos above the fireplace, but only two caught Emily's eye. The one was a wedding photo, Liam was standing in a grey morning suit, looking incredibly happy, his arm around a petite blond woman. She was smiling at her groom and even in the photo, Emily could see the absolute adoration on her face.

The other was a picture of the couple in the hospital, a baby bundled up in a hospital receiver. Again, the look of happiness and love on their faces was enough to make Emily's heart ache for Liam's loss.

Liam came through again, looking worried. "She doesn't want me to leave her. I'm sorry Emily, I wasted your time."

"What about your mom?" Emily asked, turning away from the smiling pictures.

"I don't know," Liam ran a hand through his hair, "I'll have to figure something out."

Seeing him looking so worried reminded Emily of a time where she truly cared about his happiness. "Why don't I take the food?" She suggested suddenly, regretting it almost at once.

Liam looked at her in relief, "Would you?"

Oh well, she thought to herself, too late to back out now. "Sure. I'll take it. I'll even sit with her and make sure she eats it if you want."

"Are you sure?" Liam asked her.

"I wouldn't have offered if I wasn't sure." Emily told him. "Does she still live in your old house?"

"Yes," Liam said, "She does. Let me go get the food."

He disappeared for a minute then came back with a small red cooler. "Thanks Emily, I can't tell you what a help this is."

"Don't thank me yet," Emily said, only half-joking, "She might throw the food in my face."

Liam laughed, "I know she didn't approve in high school, but I'm sure she's over that by now."

Emily decided not to tell him about her most recent run in with his mother. Instead, she gave a hollow laugh in return and took the cooler from him.

Emily spent the drive over berating herself for offering to do anything to help Cathy Richards. She should have told him no, or at least tried to talk Sophie into letting her babysit.

Emily pulled into the driveway and turned off the car. The house was exactly how she had remembered it. Ostentatiously large, colonial style. Spotless white walls with black siding. The garden was covered in a fine layer of snow, but Emily knew that there would be perfectly manicured, imported grass underneath.

The rose bushes that lined the walkway were bare now, but Emily remembered that when they bloomed they would be perfectly color coded, starting from the brightest crimson to the softest pink leading to the front door.

The large Blackwood door looked as though it had been recently polished, the ornate brass knocker looked new, even though it was the same one Emily remembered from so many years before.

Emily took a deep breath and knocked. There was no reply. She stamped her feet on the step, trying to keep warm and knocked harder.

A faint voice called her to enter.

Emily opened the door and stepped cautiously inside. The entrance hall looked exactly as she remembered it, except that there were now blank walls as opposed to the obnoxious, posed family portraits that used to hang there. There was only the slightest outline on the stark white walls to show where the pictures had once hung.

"William?" The voice came from down the hall to the right. Emily knew she must be in the master bedroom.

She walked down the passage, feeling like the anxious teenager she had once been, eager to win the approval of her boyfriend's mom.

"William, why did you knock, honestly? Did you think I was coming out to greet you?" The voice grew louder as Emily approached. She felt she should call out, but wasn't sure what to say.

Instead she knocked gently on the bedroom door that was already slightly ajar.

"For heaven's sake William, come—" Cathy didn't finish her sentence, her expression turning from slight exasperation to instant disdain when Emily opened the door.

Emily stopped in the doorway.

"What the hell are you doing here?" Cathy demanded. She was sitting up in bed, the thick down duvet covering her legs. Her head was covered in a bandage that came down over her left ear and left eyebrow. Her left leg was raised under the blanket and a pair of crutches were leaning against the bedside table.

"Sophie isn't well." Emily explained.

"So why are you here?" Cathy asked again bluntly.

"Liam asked me to bring you some food."

"What utter rubbish. I know damn well he arrested you last time you were here, so he would never ask you to do anything on his behalf. Did you think you could come into my home and attack me unprovoked?"

"That's not why I'm here." Emily answered calmly. "Liam asked me to come because I'm staying next door to him, and Sophie wanted him to stay with her."

"You're living next door to my son?" Cathy asked in disgust. "I told him not to live in that slum."

"One, that was rude," Emily said in irritation, "Two, I'm not living there, I'm just staying in the house for a few days."

"Get out!" Cathy suddenly yelled. Then she clenched her jaw in pain.

"No." Emily stated.

"I said —"

"I don't care what you said. Your son asked me to make sure you eat something and that's what I'm going to do." Emily told her calmly. "I am going to the kitchen to warm up your food and then I'm going to bring it back through here. Please don't throw it in my face."

Without waiting for an answer, Emily left the room once more and made her way to the kitchen.

She opened the cooler and took out the container of soup. Opening the lid, she had to admit it smelt delicious. She put it into the microwave to warm. She took a bowl out the cupboard and placed it on the tray that was on the counter.

Adding a spoon, some salt and pepper, Emily poured the now hot soup into the bowl and carried the tray back to the bedroom.

Cathy didn't seem any happier to see her, but Emily made her way into the room and held the tray out for the older woman to take.

Cathy sighed in annoyance but took the tray. "I hope you didn't cook this."

"No I didn't, and I didn't poison it either, in case you were wondering."

"Hmm." Cathy placed the tray next to her on the bed instead of her lap and picked up a book off the bedside table. "You can leave now."

"No, I actually can't." Emily said, "Liam said I need to make sure you eat, so that's what I'm going to do."

"I don't want you here." Cathy said cruelly.

"And I don't want to be here," Emily said mildly, refusing to get into an argument, "So the sooner you eat, the sooner I can leave."

The two women stared at each other with open dislike. But, after a moment, Cathy sighed and put her book aside. She picked up her tray and set it on her lap. Taking the spoon, she had a mouthful and swallowed.

"Happy now?" She asked sarcastically.

"Just twenty more of those and I'm out of here." Emily retorted.

Cathy huffed, but took another spoonful. She ate in silence for a while, pausing only to give Emily dirty looks.

"I suppose you are trying to get back into my son's good graces?" Cathy asked after a while.

"I couldn't care less about your son's opinion of me." Emily answered.

"Then why are you here?" She asked again.

"Because I'm not the awful human being you imagine I am?"

"Please. You can't tell me there's no ulterior motive." Cathy said in disbelief.

"To be honest, I thought I was going to watch Sophie while Liam brought the food. He was so worried about the two of you that I made the offer without thinking."

Cathy raised an eyebrow. "If you say so."

"Should you be here all alone when you're injured and have a concussion?"

"I'm not an invalid!"

"Didn't say you were."

"Bullshit. I don't know what your game is, and I don't care. Here. Take this, I'm done. Don't forget to close the door when you leave."

Emily took the proffered tray and walked to the kitchen. Placing the tray on the counter, she realised that there was no way Cathy could wash dishes with crutches. Sighing in irritation, Emily took the bowl and spoon to the sink to wash it. She looked at the drying rack at the single coffee mug and for a moment found herself feeling sorry for the woman. The cup looked so alone.

Putting the bowl and spoon with the mug to dry, Emily wiped her hands and went back to the bedroom.

"Can I make you some coffee or something before I go?"

Cathy looked up from her book, irritation clear on her face. "I asked you to leave."

"And I will. But it occurred to me that you can't use crutches and carry a mug through at the same time."

"I don't need your help."

Emily bit back a retort. "Look, I'm actually trying to be nice here. I know how frustrating it can be with crutches."

"I'm sure you do." Cathy said flippantly, looking down at her book.

Emily shook her head and turned to leave the room.

"Tea please, one sugar, no milk." Cathy called after her.

"At least she said please." Emily muttered to herself on her way back to the kitchen.

Emily made the tea in the mug from the drying rack and took it back through to the bedroom. Cathy was sitting forward, holding the side of her head above her ear.

"What's the matter?" Emily asked, rushing to the bed and putting the cup on the bedside table. "Must I call an ambulance?"

"No," Cathy shook her head, "I wasn't thinking and scratched my cut under the bandage because it was itchy. I think I popped a stitch or something." She pulled her hand away. There was definitely blood seeping through the bandage, but there didn't seem to be too much of it.

"Here, let me look at it." Emily said, leaning over.

"No, don't."

Emily stood up in frustration, "Stop being so stubborn. I can look at it, or I can call the doctor, your choice."

Cathy huffed, "Fine."

Emily had to get onto the other side of the bed on her knees to get to the wound. She carefully unwound the bandage, pausing to gently extricate the stitches from the material. She noticed Cathy wincing in pain. "I'm sorry, I'm trying to be gentle."

"It's fine, just do what you have to."

It occurred to Emily that Cathy seemed afraid. Not afraid of Emily but afraid of pain.

Pulling off the last strip, Emily lifted the gauze that had shifted. There was a long cut, running from just below the eyebrow until behind Cathy's left ear. Just in front of the ear, the wound gaped open where two stitches had torn through the skin. Blood dribbled freely from the wound now and onto Cathy's expensive silk pajama top.

Emily held the gauze over the wound again. "Yup, you've popped two stiches. Do you have a first aid box?"

"In the bathroom above the cabinet," Cathy pointed to the en-suite bathroom.

"Here, hold this here. Try to put some pressure on it if you can." Emily took the older woman's hand and placed it over the gauze.

She went to the bathroom and found an impressively stocked first aid box where Cathy had told her it would be.

She placed it on the side of the sink and washed her hands thoroughly before drying them on a towel and carrying the kit back through.

"Are you sure you don't want me to get the doctor out? I hear he does house calls. I'm sure he could re-stitch it for you."

Cathy shook her head vehemently, "No, I don't want to bother him. You can just put a plaster on."

"Okay." Emily said skeptically. She took her place on the bed again and pulled out some fresh gauze and antiseptic. "This is probably going to hurt a little."

Cathy exhaled sharply through clenched teeth as Emily wiped the blood away from the wound.

232

Emily placed a fresh piece of gauze over the wound and asked Cathy to hold it. Emily pulled out a few strips of plaster and a pair of scissors.

"I'm going to cut thin strips to pull the skin together, hopefully it won't scar too badly then."

"Okay."

Emily cut the plasters into strips and placed them on Cathy's lap so she could reach them easily.

She pulled the gauze away and using her fingers on her left hand to pull the skin closed, she carefully placed the plaster, strip by strip with her right.

Then she placed another fresh piece of gauze over the wound and wrapped a fresh bandage around Cathy's head.

"All done."

"Thank you Emily." Cathy said quietly.

"You're welcome Cathy."

Emily took the soiled bandage and gauze to the bathroom to throw it away. She washed her hands again then went back through to pack up the first aid box.

Cathy was looking down at her silk top, "This is never going to come out."

"Can I get you a fresh one?" Emily asked.

"In that cupboard." Cathy pointed.

Emily opened the cupboard and pulled out an identical top in a lighter shade of peach.

Cathy unbuttoned the top she was wearing with shaky hands. The slip she was wearing underneath had crept up and Emily could clearly see the scars of what looked like cigarette burns on the other woman's stomach.

Cathy caught her looking and pulled her slip down quickly.

"Like what you see?" Cathy asked nastily.

"No, of course not, I had no ide—"

"It's nothing." Cathy said quickly.

"It's not nothing." Emily argued.

"It's none of your damn business!" Cathy snapped, snatching the top from Emily, "I want you to leave now please."

Emily stood for only a moment, then nodded. "As you wish. I hope you get better soon." She tossed the first aid box onto the bed and walked out.

Emily was in the passage when she heard the other woman call out, "It's none of William's business either!"

"Wasn't going to say anything." Emily called back then left the house, closing the door carefully behind her.

# Chapter Nineteen

## Two Months Later

**E**mily had spent the day in court, waiting for the attorney to call her up to the stand so she could explain to the judge how she had tracked down the IP address of the person stealing money from the customers of First National.

By the time she had been allowed off the stand it was late afternoon and she was hungry and irritable.

Emily hated this side of her job, having her work second guessed by total strangers who didn't know the first thing about what she did.

She was sitting in a cab, stuck in rush hour traffic, so she pulled out her mobile to pass the time. Her phones had been on silent all day. She responded to a few work emails and a text from Glynis before pulling out her personal mobile and checking it.

There was a message from Casey.

*Hey Emily, I know we haven't spoken much lately, but I just wanted to let you know I was at the doctor's today because I haven't been feeling great.*

Emily saw the message had come through hours before.

*Sorry for the late reply, was stuck in a meeting. Are you and the baby okay?*

Emily sat back and looked out the cab window. She hadn't made a decision yet and had told both Casey and Paige as much. She had however, thought about it non-stop since she had made her last trip. She had been dreaming of babies almost as often as she dreamt about Stan.

She had found herself researching online for the best diapers, the best bottles, to have a pacifier or to not have a pacifier. So far, she had realised two things. The internet couldn't make up its mind about any of the products and Emily had no freaking idea what she was doing.

The idea of trying to keep a small, helpless human being alive scared her half to death. The responsibility was so overwhelming that she kept wanting to say no and be done with it.

The problem, though, was that every time she made the decision to say no, it physically hurt her chest. Emily had spent her life trying to avoid any emotion at all, but she had realised that this wasn't a decision her head could make alone.

The idea of a baby lying on her chest and sleeping peacefully was an intoxicating one. One that no matter how much Emily tried to convince herself she neither wanted or needed, wouldn't leave her.

Emily was pulled out of her thoughts by a ping.

*All fine, just a bladder infection. But wanted to know if you wanted the new scans?*

Emily hesitated only a moment.

*Yes please.*

Emily held her breath in anticipation. The taxi driver said something to her, but she didn't hear him.

The images seemed to take forever to download once they came through, but soon she was looking at the most recent sonogram. It took her a moment to figure out what she was looking at, but the first image was a little leg and hip, she could make out the individual toes if she zoomed in. The second image was clearer, the side view of the head. Emily could see the lips and the little button nose.

She ran her finger gently down the face on her screen.


Emily walked into her office and immediately recognised the smell of lavender permeating the room.

"Glyn?" She called out.

"In the kitchen."

Emily walked through, moaning as she went. "I specifically asked you not to buy anything lavender scented."

"And I didn't." Glynis replied as Emily turned the corner into the kitchen.

On the counter was a vase with a large bunch of lavender, wrapped like a flower arrangement.

"What the hell?" Emily asked.

"It came this morning. I didn't want to just throw it out, so I thought I'd wait for you to come read the card." Glynis shrugged, taking a second mug out of the kitchen cabinet to make Emily coffee.

"Whose it from?" Emily asked, looking at the arrangement in distaste.

"No idea, I didn't open the card since it wasn't addressed to me." Glynis responded crisply, handing Emily a cup of coffee. "Here, take the card and I'll put the vase in the hallway for now. I can always take it home with me if you don't want it."

Emily nodded and took the card, "Thanks Glyn. Open some windows too if you don't mind."

The older woman shrugged, "Most people find the smell of lavender relaxing you know." But she picked up the vase and walked to the front door with it.

"I'm not most people." Emily muttered, taking her coffee and the card to her desk.

She pulled the card out of the envelope, wondering which client she had that was weird enough to send her lavender instead of flowers, or how they had found her address.

She stared at the card in horror, goosebumps forming on her arms.

*Come back, I've missed seeing you around town. I never got a chance to make you bleed a little the last time you were here xxx*

Emily threw the card away from herself in disgust.

"Who was it?" Glynis asked from her own desk.

"No one important." Emily managed to say, trying to keep her voice normal.

Emily gave herself a mental shake then picked up the discarded envelope. She looked up the name of the florist on her laptop and checked their website for a contact number.

She had to wait until Glynis left for the day before she quickly dialed the number and hoped they would still be open.

"Lacey's Florist, how can I help you?" The woman that answered sounded young and bored.

"Hi. I received a bunch of lavender today, but the card didn't say who it was from. Would you be able to tell me?"

"I don't think we got a name with that one. It was a weird request, I've never sent out lavender like that before. Hold on a sec."

Emily heard the other woman typing on a computer keyboard. "Nope, it was ordered online. Paid with a money order, so there's no way to see who ordered them."

"Can you see where the order was placed from?"

"Nope, sorry."

"Okay, thanks."

"Enjoy your arrangement."

Emily replaced the receiver, feeling more anxious than before.

Powering up her laptop, Emily decided to do some digging of her own. She managed to hack into the florist's online system in under three minutes. She went through the orders for the last two days until she found the one with her address, but there was nothing there to tell her who placed the order or where they placed it from.

Emily closed her laptop angrily, feeling exposed for the first time in years. Not even Paige knew her home address, how did someone else find it?

She picked up her mobile and phoned Paige.

"Hi Emily, how are you?"

"I'm okay thanks and you?"

"Emily? What's wrong, you don't sound like yourself." Paige's voice was concerned.

"Did you ever get around to asking Daniel about the men that worked in the area years ago that might have been Stan's accomplice?"

"Of course I did. We went through all the people we could think of, but none of them matched your description." Paige paused for a moment and Emily could hear a door close in the background. "Why are you asking now? What's happened?"

"Nothing." Emily answered quickly, "Just had a nightmare last night is all."

"Oh Emily, I'm so sorry. Do you want to talk about it?"

"No." Emily replied shortly.

"Fair enough." Paige replied, "Did Casey send you the scans from this morning?"

"Yes she did." Emily answered. "I'm getting pretty good at figuring these images out."

Paige laughed, "It all looks a bit weird doesn't it? Looking at a skeleton."

"Yeah, a little."

"Have you thought about it at all since you've been home?" Paige's voice was softer now.

"I haven't stopped thinking about it actually."

"And?"

"And? I don't know Paige. One day I'm certain it's not going to happen, the next day I'm looking at cribs online."

Paige was silent for a moment. "Well, at least you're thinking about it."

"How's Casey doing with the whole thing?"

"It's been hard for her," Paige sighed, "She broke up with Ben a few weeks ago and now that she's showing, she's been hiding out at home a lot. She's not sure how to deal with all the attention."

"Shame, I'm sorry she's having a rough time. I'm sure the fact that I haven't made a decision isn't making things any easier."

"Don't push yourself," Paige said, "This is a big decision and I don't want you to make it while feeling pressured."

Emily bit her lip. "What happens if I say no?"

"Well, I suppose we will contact a private adoption agency. There's no shortage of people wanting to start a family."

"I should go." Emily said suddenly.

"Oh, okay, no problem. It was nice to hear from you."

"Bye Paige."

"Wait." Paige said.

"Yeah?"

"Did Casey tell you the sex yet? It was confirmed this morning."

"No, she didn't mention it."

"Do you want to know?"

Emily was silent for a moment. "Yes."

"It's a boy."

"Thanks Paige. Chat soon."

"Bye Emily."

Emily put her mobile down on her desk and swiveled in her chair until she was looking out the window. She put her feet up on the window ledge and watched the sun turn the city golden as it lowered in the distance.

A boy. If Emily was honest with herself, she had been hoping the baby would be a girl. She knew that a girl at least wouldn't be as likely to grow up like its biological father.

Feeling too keyed up to cook, Emily ordered Chinese food and opened a bottle of white wine.

241

She tipped the delivery boy, then made sure her door was securely locked before going through to her bedroom and sitting on the bed. She turned the television on and flicked through the channels, eventually deciding on an old Golden Girls rerun.

It occurred to Emily as she ate that if she did take the baby, she would have to move. There was no room in this apartment for a kid. She had used her living room for an office since she had moved in and the tiny excuse for a spare room had her treadmill and boxing bag. She wasn't even sure she would be able to fit a cot and a set of drawers in the room, let alone any other baby paraphernalia.

She went through to the office to fetch her laptop and once she was settled back on her bed, she started looking at apartments available nearby.

She was surprised to find a three-bedroom executive suite in her building, just a few floors up. She wondered how soon she would be able to look at it.

It was expensive, but still within her range, Emily could either sell her current apartment, lease it to someone, or even keep it as the office. That way, her private life would be even more separate.

But, what if she didn't want to leave the baby with a nanny? Having an office in the apartment would make more sense for the first few months.

Looking at more apartments nearby, Emily realised that her decision had already been made. She couldn't really imagine a future staying in her current apartment with no baby. She wouldn't have been so invested in finding a new place to live if she wasn't truly serious about taking Casey's baby.

Feeling as though the weight she had been carrying for months had suddenly been lifted, Emily actually felt the stirrings of excitement. She picked up her mobile and called Casey.

"Hello?"

"Hey Cas, it's Emily, how are you feeling?"

"I'm okay thanks and you? Feels like my bladder has shrunk to the size of a grape, but otherwise I'm fine."

Emily smiled at the analogy, "Can't be fun."

"It's okay, apparently it will get better once I get rid of the infection." Casey paused. "So, how are you?"

"I'm fine thanks. I've actually spent the evening online looking for bigger apartments."

"Oh cool. Aren't you happy with yours?"

"I love mine, but it's just too small to keep now."

"Does that mean what I think it means?" Casey sounded excited.

"Well, I'm not going to leave the crib in the living room, so the kid will need his own room."

"Oh Emily." Casey was crying so much that her words were coming out in a mumble, "Thank you."

"I'll chat to you soon Cas."

"Okay, bye." Casey sputtered through her tears.


Emily was awake and had already been working for a few hours when Glynis arrived the next morning.

"Morning Boss, did you wet the bed?" Glynis asked cheerfully.

"Ha ha," Emily commented sarcastically, "just wanted to get an early start today."

"And there's no empty bottles in the kitchen!" Glynis went to the coffee machine to pour herself some coffee, "Did you join a cult I should know about?"

Emily snorted, "As if. And for your information, there is half a bottle of wine in the fridge, I just didn't finish it."

Glynis replaced Emily's empty cup with a fresh one. "Still a miracle if you ask me."

Emily took the cup and looked at Glynis, "Do you like your job?"

"Some days." The older woman joked.

"Would you like to keep it?"

"Alright, alright, keep your skirt on. I was just playing."

Emily rolled her eyes at her secretary.

"It's just nice to see you in a good mood is all." Glynis said from her desk across the room.

Emily closed her laptop and leant back with her coffee. "Were you ready to be a mother when your daughter was born?"

"Good God no! I don't think anyone is ever ready for that." Glynis looked up from her own computer suddenly. "Why? Are you pregnant?"

"I wouldn't have had any wine if I were Glyn."

"Well, you never know, some women swear by a glass a day." Glynis shrugged. "Why did you ask about my daughter then?"

Glynis had one child, a daughter named Rose that was killed in a robbery gone wrong seventeen years before, leaving Glynis to raise her granddaughter alone.

"Do you remember my friend Paige?"

"Sure I do. The only person I've ever known you to care about." Glynis answered.

"Hey, I care about you." Emily said defensively.

"That's not what I meant. I meant anyone from your life before I met you. Or anyone after I met you for that matter." She added as an afterthought.

"Anyway, back to the topic." Emily said, not even sure she should continue. "Paige has a daughter, Casey. Casey was attacked in Europe while I was there."

Glynis put her hand over her mouth in horror. "That's why Paige called you. Why she was so frantic."

Emily nodded.

"Emily I had no idea, I'm so sorry. I gave you a hard time about going back the second time."

"You meant well," Emily reassured her. "The thing is, Casey is pregnant from that attack."

The older woman had tears in her eyes. She muttered something in Spanish.

Emily cleared her throat and continued, "She doesn't want to keep the baby for obvious reasons. And while I was there the last time, she and Paige asked me if I would consider adopting the baby."

Glynis burst into tears, holding her face in both hands.

Emily was suddenly very uncomfortable in her own home. She took both her cup and Glynis's to the kitchen to make them a refill.

By the time she put Glynis's fresh cup down, the woman was calmer.

"You really think I would be that bad a mother?" Emily asked casually, dreading the answer.

Glynis shook her head, and said through her tears, "I think you're going to be a wonderful mother. My prayers have been answered."

"You prayed that I would adopt a baby?" Emily asked perplexed.

"No, I prayed that you would find a love you deserve. Someone for you to love dearly and for that person to love you back." Glynis sniffed loudly and pulled a handkerchief out of her sleeve to dry her eyes and blow her nose.

Emily was still standing in front of Glynis's desk. "I didn't know you prayed for me." She told the other woman softly.

"Emily, I have prayed for you every day since we met." She smiled mischievously at her boss, "Sometimes twice a day."

Emily laughed and went back to her own desk.

"You're going to need a bigger place." Glynis commented.

"I know," Emily pulled a face, "and I hate moving. But there's a three bedroom place a few stories up in this building available. I'll go have a look today."

"So you are really serious about this?" Glynis asked her.

Emily nodded. "I am. Only really made up my mind last night, but have been considering it since my last trip."

"That's wonderful. Congratulations." Glynis smiled warmly. "So when is it due?"

"He," Emily corrected with a slight smile, "is due at the end of August."

"A little boy, oh Lord what a miracle."

Emily smiled and shook her head at the older woman. She opened her laptop again to get some work done.

# Chapter Twenty

**L**iam parked his county cruiser in his mother's driveway and sighed. He was exhausted from working overtime the last few weeks. He really needed to hire another deputy, but he just hadn't had time to make any calls.

He took the red cooler off the passenger seat and got out of the car.

At least Bee was back to help with Sophie, although Liam was still upset with her leaving Sophie like she had. Liam hadn't had the choice to fire her though, he didn't trust anyone else with his daughter and he needed someone who could be there on the nights he worked.

The upside of her being back meant that Bee had taken over the cooking once more and the roast chicken he was bringing to his mother had been prepared by Bee that morning.

He opened the front door and called out for his mother.

"In the dining room." Came the reply.

Liam made his way to the dining room. His mother had a crutch under one arm and with the other hand was stuffing old pictures into a dustbin bag.

"Doing some spring cleaning?" Liam asked lightly, putting the cooler on the table.

"Just getting rid of the clutter. Are you sure you don't want this?" She asked, holding up the family crest.

"I'm very sure." Liam said.

His mother was looking better now, the hair that had been shaved had grown in a little and Cathy had been to the hairdresser to have the hair styled over the short side. The scar on her face had healed remarkably well, it was barely noticeable under the foundation she was wearing.

"Can I heat up your dinner?" Liam asked, watching as Cathy tossed the crest into the bag carelessly.

"Honestly Liam, you don't have to stay and watch me eat. I promise I will have it later." Cathy scolded.

"The last two times you said that, you didn't eat at all." Liam pointed out.

"Well this time I will eat it." Cathy told him, throwing some more pictures into the bag.

"How about if I stay for a glass of wine and you can eat your food?" Liam asked, "Then, after I leave you can carry on exorcising the house of its demons."

Cathy sighed and threw a last picture into the bag. "Fine, you open the wine, I'll heat the food."

Cathy used her one crutch to help walk to the cooler then led the way to the kitchen.

Cathy had eaten in a sulky silence and now that she had pushed her plate aside, she looked at her son. "Are you satisfied?"

"Thank you mother. That wasn't so bad was it?"

"Hmmf," Cathy muttered sullenly, "depends on who you ask."

Liam took her plate off the kitchen counter they had been sitting at and went to the sink. "I'm really impressed at how well your face has healed."

"I am too." Cathy replied, topping up her wine glass, "I thought Emily was going to make it much worse, but it's barely there."

Liam looked over his shoulder, "What did Emily have to do with it?"

"That day you sent her over, two of my stitches popped and she cleaned and stuck the wound back together."

"That was nice of her." Liam commented, rinsing the plate.

"I suppose she had a lot of practice with wounds." Cathy commented offhandedly.

Liam wiped his hands on the cloth before hanging it over the drying rack. He turned around and leant against the sink, crossing his arms.

"About that. You know the story you told me when they found her was complete bullshit right?" He asked his mother.

"That was the story I was told." Cathy replied defensively.

"You told me that was what the sheriff told you and you told me it as fact."

"Well, that's what I remember him telling me William."

"It wasn't the true story. It was what you wanted to hear." Liam told her.

"I know that now." Cathy said irritably, "I found out when she came back to town the first time."

"And you didn't think to tell me?" Liam asked angrily.

"Why would I?" Cathy responded tightly, "You were over all that, what was the point of bringing it all up again?"

"I wasn't over it Mother." Liam said quietly, his anger rising, "I wasn't over her."

"What rubbish! You were so much better off without her. And if you hadn't walked away when you did, you never would have met Melanie. Is that what you would have wanted?"

"I wouldn't have wanted to call her a whore!" Liam shouted.

"That was you, not me." Cathy pointed out in her own quiet voice.

"Because of what you told me!" Liam exploded.

"She was never good enough for you!" Cathy screamed back.

Liam stared at his mother in fury, "And when have you ever known what was good for me?"

"What's that supposed to mean?" Cathy demanded, her face reddening.

"You stayed with that monster for years!" Liam shouted, "You didn't care how often he beat me or what he said to me! You stayed with him!"

"You know damn well I tried to get between you as much as possible!" Cathy said angrily, "You wouldn't allow it when you thought you were old enough."

Liam shook his head in disgust. "We could have run. We could have left him and started a new life,"

"With what?" Cathy asked him, "This was all his and we would have been left with nothing."

"It's always about the material shit with you." Liam told her, "Your reputation and your comfort was the most important thing to you."

He walked past her and headed to the door.

"William wait!" she called after him.

Liam stopped at the door and turned to face his mother. "I suggest you call whoever it was you were seeing and beg them to take you back. Because someone else is going to have to bring you food from now on."

Liam slammed the door behind him.


Driving home, Liam felt his anger seep away. He knew he was being unfair on his mother. While he was furious with her for what she had told him all those years ago, he was just as furious at himself.

He pictured Emily's face when she pulled up her shirt and exposed her scars, the pain in her eyes when she had asked if he had ever really known her.

He had known her. And in his heart, he knew she wasn't the person everyone accused her of being.

Looking back now, he had no explanation for his reaction, other than he was young and didn't know how to deal with the situation. But that didn't excuse what he said to her. He felt the guilt and shame of his words building up in his chest like an invisible force, stealing his breath and suffocating him.

The last time he had felt guilt to that degree was when Mel was killed. For years he had woken to the weight on his chest and when he went to bed at night it had only grown heavier. He hated himself for the danger he had put his family in. For the way his wife had suffered because of his work. For always putting his career ahead of her, for being out that night instead of being at home with her when she needed him.

He pulled his cruiser onto the shoulder and slammed on the brakes, kicking up gravel and dust around the cruiser. He held his head in his hands as he sobbed. The only two women he had ever truly loved had both been irrevocably damaged by him.

Liam had been out for drinks with guys from his department that night, he and his partner had gotten a judge to sign off on arrest warrants for a case they had been working on for the last two years. The following morning they were going to make the biggest bust of their career.

He had stayed out later than he had meant to and had missed a call from Mel that had come through while he was in the pub. He knew he should have called back when he saw it, but he decided to buy her some flowers and explain his news in person instead.

He saw her broken body as he had entered their apartment. She was leaning against the wall, her legs splayed and bloody, her beautiful face unrecognizable, her blond hair drenched in blood.

He had held his wife's broken body in his arms for what felt like hours, telling her how sorry he was, crying, demanding that God bring her back, begging Him to bring her back.

It was only when he had heard his daughter's soft cries from the hall closet that he had been able to let Mel's body go. He cradled his infant daughter against his blood soaked chest and wept until the neighbors arrived with the police.

A sharp knocking against his passenger window startled Liam out of his memories of that horrible night.

He hadn't seen a car pull up behind him or the driver walk up to his car, but now Paige Mackenzie was at his window, a look of concern on her face.

Liam used the button on his door to open his passenger window.

"Hey Sheriff, I thought that was you." Paige greeted with a smile.

"Paige." Liam nodded, wiping his face hurriedly on his sleeve.

"You okay Liam?" Paige asked kindly.

"Yeah," Liam said, not meeting her eye, "just been a long week."

Paige nodded understandingly. "Do you want to talk about it?"

Liam shook his head, "No, thanks Paige. I need to get home to Sophie."

"I'm sure Bee wouldn't mind staying an extra hour if it meant you could get some down time." Paige told him gently.

"Maybe some other time." Liam said, still looking ahead.

"Okay Liam, you drive safe." Paige turned and started walking away.

"Hey Paige?" Liam called out suddenly.

Paige turned around and came back to the passenger window. "Yes?"

"You stayed in contact with Emily all these years right?"

Paige nodded, "I have. I didn't always get to see her, but we've remained in contact."

"How's Casey doing?" Liam asked, suddenly embarrassed to be asking about Emily.

Paige smiled sadly, "Some days are better than others, but we just keep taking it one day at a time."

"I heard she's pregnant." Liam blurted without thinking.

"She is." Paige was stamping her feet, "Look Liam, without sounding forward, can I get in for a minute? The wind is chilly out here."

"Of course, sorry." Liam unlocked the door and Paige climbed in.

"That's better." Paige said with a sigh, closing the door behind her. "Yes, Casey is pregnant, and no, she's not planning on keeping the baby."

"Adoption?" Liam asked, staring out his windscreen.

"Yes."

"Found a good family?"

"I think so. It's Emily actually."

Liam turned to look at Paige in surprise. "Really?"

Paige smiled again, "Yes really."

"Huh," Liam muttered, "I didn't think she wanted kids."

"It was never an option for her." Paige explained, "Not after what happened."

Liam was silent for a moment, but the knuckles on his hand was white as he clenched the steering wheel. "Does she hate me?" He asked in a whisper, the muscle in his jaw visibly working to clench his teeth.

"I don't think she does Liam." Paige placed a hand gently on Liam's arm, "She was very hurt at the time, but she has moved on."

Liam swallowed loudly, a tear escaping his eye and running down his face. "I didn't know." He whispered.

"I know." Paige told him kindly, "And so does she."

They sat in silence for a few minutes, Paige waiting for him to open up if he needed to talk.

Finally, Liam released his grip on the steering wheel and turned to face Paige. "Thanks for the chat Paige."

Paige smiled warmly and touched his arm once more, "You're very welcome. Any time you feel like a chat, give me a call."

Paige climbed out the car and closed the door gently. She placed a hand on the window, "Don't be so hard on yourself Liam. You were young, and between you and Emily, you've both suffered the worst life has to offer."

Liam didn't answer but nodded slightly. He waited until Paige was in her car and ready to get onto the road again before he started the cruiser and got ready to pull out.

Liam was sitting on the couch, Sophie asleep with her head in his lap. Normally he made sure she was in bed and had a story before sleep, but tonight she had wanted to cuddle on the couch and watch television and he hadn't had the heart to say no.

He had been scrolling through his social media feed for the last half an hour, not taking in anything he saw when it occurred to him to look for Emily.

There were six Emily Winters, but none were the one he was looking for.

He googled the name instead and found an article about a court case that had just been heard. Cyber security specialist, Emily Winter had been called as an expert witness.

Liam then looked up online security and her name and came up with Winter Consultants. He clicked onto the site and scrolled down to the contact information. There was a landline number and below that, a mobile number for emergencies.

He saved the number into his mobile.

He then carried his sleeping daughter to her room and tucked her into bed, kissing her gently on the forehead. He made sure the nightlight was on before leaving the room and making sure the door was ajar in case she called for him.

Back in the kitchen he grabbed a beer out the fridge and went to sit on the couch, changing the channel from cartoons to the history channel.

Liam put his feet on the coffee table, took a swig of his beer and pulled his mobile out once more.

*I hope this is the right number, I'm looking for Emily that's been in Hawthorne recently.*

He pushed send and turned his attention to the burly men digging for gold on the television.

His mobile pinged a few moments later.

*Who is this?*

Liam looked at his message and realised his mistake.

*Sorry, should have started with that. It's Liam.*

The response was almost immediate: *Did you send a package to my apartment today?*

*No I didn't. Is everything okay?*

*Fine, just trying to find out who send me something.*

*Do you want me to look into it?* Liam asked.

*No thanks, not a big deal.*

Liam tossed the mobile aside, not knowing what to say to her. He had been so involved in finding her number that he didn't consider what he would do if he actually got hold of her.

The show he was watching had just come to an end when his mobile pinged.

*Liam? Why did you text me?*

He sighed, wondering if he should say the Sophie was asking about her or if he should just be honest.

*I'm not sure. You've just been on my mind a lot lately and I wanted to talk. Wasn't sure what to say though.*

He put his empty beer bottle on the table.

*Oh, ok. Goodnight Liam.*

*Goodnight Emily.*

Liam felt like such an idiot. He never should have sent her a text at all.

He took his empty bottle to the bin in the kitchen and washed the supper dishes before turning out the lights and going to his bedroom.

He undressed and got into bed in his underwear, grateful that winter had finally released its icy grip on Hawthorne. He had just picked up the book on his bedside table when his mobile pinged.

Emily had sent a phone number through. He was considering asking her what the number was for when a second text came through.

*This is my private number... For next time you're not sure what to say but want to talk anyway.*

Liam smiled to himself. Maybe he wasn't such an idiot after all.

# Chapter Twenty-One

Emily was sitting on her own bed, wondering at the random contact from Liam. She wished she had been able to see his face, it was too easy to misread the context in messages.

She found herself imagining what he was doing at that moment and whether or not he was going to reply. She couldn't decide if she wanted him to or not.

She could almost hear Paige telling her that closure was a good thing and the more issues Emily worked through the happier she would be.

Emily wasn't sure she agreed, but she had to admit that having more people in her life hadn't been as terrible as she had imagined it would be. She enjoyed her time with Amy, Paige, and even Casey. Having people to care about and share things with had been more rewarding than she could have imagined.

I'm getting nostalgic, she thought to herself, picking up the parenting book Glynis had given her that morning. She was reading about what to expect during the baby's first three months of life and was for the first time quite grateful that she was a chronic insomniac, the lack of sleep sounded rather terrifying.

She had also realised that morning that neither of her vehicles were suitable for baby seats, so she would have to go shopping for a new car too. She didn't want to get rid of her Mustang, so she just hoped the new apartment came with an extra parking slot.

Her mobile pinged as she was reading about reflux.

*Sophie is going to be spending Friday and Saturday night with her grandparents in the city, so I'm checking into a hotel nearby. Would I be able to buy you coffee or dinner?*

Emily's first reaction was to say no. She wasn't the coffee type. But then, ever since she started going back to Hawthorne, she had been doing many things that weren't normal for her.

*Sure. Let me know where and when and I will meet you.*

Deciding her life was getting way too weird for her own good, Emily closed the baby book and decided she had earned a glass of wine.

When she got back to the bedroom she saw the little notification light flashing.

*Great, I'm really looking forward to it.*

Emily smiled at her screen but didn't reply.


An hour later she still couldn't get Liam out of her head. Emily didn't like feeling like this, as though someone else's attention was needed for validation. This was why she stayed away from any sort of connection. It made her think of that night with Nick, where she felt close to someone for the first time in years, only to be a pity case.

She was so irritated with herself for opening up to Nick the way she had, that she decided it was time for bed. She must have been exhausted, within minutes she was fast asleep.


∞


259

"The smell in here is getting unbearable." The man commented, dipping his head slightly to avoid hitting the low ceiling in the basement.

Emily remained silent, too tired and sore to talk.

"I brought you a present though." The man told her as he approached. He had what looked like a pillowcase in his hand. He opened it and pulled out a single piece of lavender.

"There's definitely some kind of infection going on, you smell like shit." He told her, dropping the lavender near her head. He pulled out more by the handful and dropped them all around her. "This should help keep away any nosy animals." He chuckled, "We wouldn't want them to have their turn with you before we're done now would we?"

Emily knew what he was talking about. Recently she had heard the scrabbling of claws against the cement floor in the darkness. She tried to make noises or thump her feet on the floor to scare them away, but she had felt sharp teeth tearing into the skin of her calf more than once.

"When will you let me die?" she whispered in a croaky voice.

The man had removed his shirt and was folding it carefully, placing it carefully on a three legged stool. He was taking his pants off and smiled at her, she could see his teeth in the darkness.

"You only throw away your toys when you can't play with them anymore." He lay down beside her, placing his hand gently on her lower stomach. "And I'm not done with you yet."

The touch of his skin on hers repulsed her, but she knew fighting him off would only make him punish her more.

260

"Besides," he whispered in her ear, his hand travelling down her stomach and between her legs. He gently caressed her, finding the most sensitive areas and rubbing them softly, almost lovingly, "you can't pretend you don't like it when I touch you like this."

Against her will and with a feeling of disgust, Emily felt the tension growing in her stomach as she opened her legs. Emily whimpered, begging him to stop.

"You love this you little slut."

∞

Emily sat up in bed trembling. The sheet was knotted around her legs, and she was covered in a thin sheen of sweat.

She pulled the sheet off her legs and tossed it aside in irritation.

She went to the bathroom to rinse her face. She had an awful taste in her mouth. After rinsing her mouth out with mouthwash, Emily turned on the shower.

She was disgusted to find her underwear was damp after the nightmare, but not surprised. It sometimes happened even with the worst nightmares.

She threw her panties into the laundry basket and got into the shower.

Emily stood under the spray for a long time, letting the water pound her head and shoulders. She was still trembling.

Dreams like this one were the worst, they left her feeling sickened and dirty. She would rather have the violent dreams any day.

Emily dried herself off, but instead of getting back into bed, she dressed in jeans and a tight black, sleeveless shirt. She pulled on her riding boots and took her riding jacket off its hook behind her door.

Grabbing her personal mobile off her dresser, and her bike helmet off the chair, Emily left her bedroom and headed out of her apartment.

It was after one in the morning, but Emily knew most of the bars in the city would still be pumping. She decided to go to the business district, knowing she would be able to find professionals out for good time. The drinks would be expensive but the bar would be clean compared to the grungier places she occasionally trolled looking for a lay.

Emily parked her bike outside of a bohemian themed pub and made her way inside, giving her jacket and helmet to the bouncer at the door. She went to the bar and ordered a tequila. The barman had just slid the glass in front of her when a man sat on the stool next to her.

"That's quite a drink." He said in way of greeting.

"It's been quite a day." Emily replied casually.

"In that case," he smiled, "let me get you another one."

Emily looked at him for the first time. He was wearing an expensive charcoal suit, his silk tie loosened slightly and the top button his shirt was undone. He was handsome in a bland way, his dark hair carefully slicked to the side.

She shrugged, "Sure, why not."

Seven tequilas and less than an hour later they were in a cramped bathroom stall. Emily was bent, both hands flat against the flimsy toilet divider wall, her jeans pulled down just far enough for access. The blandly handsome man had only pulled his zip down and had been thrusting himself into Emily roughly for ten minutes.

"You could be more enthusiastic." He grunted.

Emily had both hands above her head, holding on to the divider wall. She dropped her right hand to his hair and pulled roughly, jerking his head towards her.

"Better?" she asked.

"Much," he said, putting on hand on her throat from behind and squeezing.

Emily scratched the back of his neck as he fucked her harder.

He pulled her hand away, "Don't, my wife won't be impressed."

Emily froze for a second then pushed the man away, causing him to stumble backwards into the opposite wall.

"What the fuck?" He sputtered, "I was almost there."

"You're married!" Emily said, pulling on her jeans in that cramped space.

"So what? You never asked."

Emily stood up and faced him. "I don't fuck married men."

"Oh please!" He spat at her, "you sluts are all the same. You're nothing but a cock-tease."

"I may be a slut." She told him angrily, "But I'm not a bitch."

He tried to grab her arm, but Emily pulled away. He slammed his fist into the divider wall next to her head. He then grabbed the front of Emily's shirt but before he could do anything else, Emily brought her knee up between his legs.

He grunted in pain and doubled over, releasing his grip on Emily's shirt.

Emily slammed her way out of the stall, causing a man at the urinal to spin around in shock and pee a perfect crescent on the floor.

Emily ignored the torrent of swearing from the man she had just had inside her and stormed out the bar, stopping only to get her helmet and jacket from the bouncer.

Glynis opened the front door and almost immediately tripped over one of Emily's riding boots.

"Oh dear." She said out loud, taking in the mess.

Emily's riding jacket and boots were strewn across the rug, the helmet and bike keys were on the floor next to the sofa, and papers littered the coffee table, desks and floor as though the files had been thrown around in rage.

Glynis sighed, she hadn't seen anything this bad since shortly after the Germany trip. She picked up the discarded pieces of clothing as she made her way through the apartment.

Glynis wondered what could have set Emily off so badly. She prayed that it had nothing to do with the baby, and that the little one was still okay.

Glynis dumped the clothes into the basket in the laundry room next to the kitchen, then went to the fridge to look for an energy drink.

That was the first time Glynis noticed the blood. There was a smear on the freezer compartment door and when she looked around, there were droplets all over the floor. Not enough for her to panic and call the police, but enough to make her worry.

The bed was empty when Glynis entered the room, the blankets twisted on the floor. Glynis didn't see any blood on the sheets and made her way around to the curtains to let some light in.

Emily was curled up in the fetal on the floor in her panties and undershirt, her arms over head as though protecting herself. A dishcloth was clumsily wrapped around the one hand, the material soaked through with dried blood.

"Emily?" Glynis called gently, not wanting to frighten her. "Emily, wake up."

Emily didn't move.

Glynis leaned a little closer, "Emily!" she said in a louder voice.

Emily pulled herself into a smaller ball.

"Emily wake up, you're bleeding."

"What?" Emily mumbled, unmoving.

"You are bleeding! You need to wake up."

"Okay, geez, stop shouting." Emily sat up groggily, looking around in confusion. "Where's the bed?" she asked stupidly.

"Right where you left it." Glynis told her, "Now get up and come to the bathroom, I need to look at your hand."

Emily held up her right hand and moved her fingers, seeming surprised to find the dishcloth wrapped around it.

Glynis left Emily on the floor and went into the bathroom, her shoes crunching on broken glass. The large bathroom mirror was smashed, glass everywhere. In the center of the mirror there was a splatter of blood that had run down in a stream and dried. The sink and floor was also smeared with the black-brown blood.

"Emily, come to the kitchen rather." Glynis called out, leaving the bathroom and closing the door behind her. That was a mess that could be tackled later.

Emily was sitting on the edge of her bed, her head in her good hand.

"Emily?" Glynis called.

"I'm coming." Emily said in a raspy voice, "Just a little nauseous."

"I'm not surprised." Glynis commented in a snarky tone.

By the time Emily managed to drag herself to the kitchen, Glynis had already unpacked the first aid kit and had a bowl of hot water and some towels folded on the counter.

"Up." She ordered Emily.

Emily grumbled as she lifted herself onto the counter with her good hand.

Glynis put a towel on Emily's lap, then took the injured hand and held it over the towel, gently unwrapping the dishcloth.

"What did you do?" Glynis asked Emily as fresh blood stained the cloth.

Emily shrugged. "I don't remember."

Glynis shook her head, "You can't keep doing this to yourself."

Emily didn't comment, she watched in nauseous fascination as the dishcloth came away, revealing bruised and bloody knuckles, as well as two long, deep gashes. One between her middle and ring fingers the other slicing through the fleshy part between her thumb and index finger. Emily held her hand up and flexed, causing blood to dribble out of the wounds.

"Stop that." Glynis chastised.

"I was just trying to see if anything was broken." Emily defended.

"You need stitches."

"No I don't," Emily said, "I'll just strap it up, it will be fine."

"No it won't!" Glynis argued.

"How do you know?"

"Because I can see bone, that's why!"

Emily twisted her hand around so that she could look at her knuckles from the front. The gash was gaping open, revealing the stark white of her knuckle bone and the tendons holding it together.

"Oh." Was all Emily said in response.

"I'm going to sweep up the glass in the bathroom while you have some coffee, then you're going to shower and I will drive you to the emergency room."

Emily didn't bother to argue, she didn't have the stomach for it.

Glynis carefully wrapped a bandage around Emily's hand and down to her wrist. "That will have to hold everything together until you can be seen to."

"Thanks Glyn."

"Don't thank me." Glynis said shortly before walking away.

Emily climbed off the counter and turned on the coffee machine with her left hand. She hadn't felt anything when she had first woken up, but now her hand was throbbing painfully from the tips of her fingers to halfway up her arm and she felt sore and swollen.

She hadn't been exactly truthful with Glynis, she vaguely remembered coming home and showering and for some reason had looked at her reflection in the mirror and had lost it completely, hitting the glass until there was no reflection left to look at.

Emily wasn't sure if it was her scars or her disgust with herself for screwing a married man that set her off, she just remembered not being able to stand the sight of herself.

The machine pinged and Emily clumsily poured two cups of coffee with her left hand.

She left Glynis's on the counter and carried her own through to her bedroom.

"I can clean the mess Glyn." She called out.

Glynis opened the bathroom door and came out carrying the bin and the sweeper and scoop. "It's done. Not well, but well enough for you to shower."

Emily walked past the older woman feeling sheepish. She closed herself in the bathroom and took in the damage. She had really gone to town on the mirror.

Emily turned on the shower and used her left hand to pull her clothes off. She couldn't remember the last time she had done something so self-destructive. She was so ashamed of her lack of self-control.

She showered as quickly as she could with one hand and brushed her teeth before getting out the shower and drying herself off.

She managed to pull on her underwear and a pair of jeans with difficulty, but then realised she wasn't going to manage to clip her bra.

Swallowing her pride, she called Glynis.

Glynis came into the room wearing cleaning gloves. "Yes?"

Emily swallowed, feeling embarrassed. "I can't clip my bra."

Glynis pulled off the gloves and put them on the dresser.

Emily had her left arm covering her breasts but had to move it away so she could put her arms through the bra straps Glynis was holding out.

Glynis saw Emily's scars for the first time and gasped out loud. "Jesus, Mary and Joseph, you poor, poor child."

Emily shut her eyes tightly, not wanting to hear the pity in the older woman's voice. "Don't." She said through clenched teeth.

Glynis deftly clipped the bra then straightened the straps over Emily's shoulders.

"Thanks." Emily murmured.

"No problem." Glynis replied in a much kinder tone than before. "I'll be waiting by the door. Keep your hand up, it's starting to leak."

Fresh blood was indeed seeping through the dressing and starting to drip onto the hardwood floor. Emily did as she was told and held her hand up to her shoulder.

"With all the alcohol in your system, it's a wonder you didn't bleed to death." Glynis commented as she walked away.

"Chance would be a fine thing." Emily muttered to herself while she dug in her drawers for an undershirt.

What a pathetic way to go though, she thought. Drunk and dead from a fight with her own reflection.

Emily pulled on the shirt with difficulty and then pulled a plain black t-shirt over it.

She pulled on her running trainers with her good hand and went to meet Glynis by the door.

Nine frustrating hours later, Emily opened her front door. She had dropped Glynis at home on their way back from the hospital, insisting she could drive herself. Glynis was butchering Emily's stick shift in her mustang and it was more painful than her hand.

X-rays had shown several hairline fractures to the carpels in Emily's wrist and hand, but the doctor had been happy to stitch her up and put her in a high tech hand and wrist brace. He didn't feel surgery would be necessary unless Emily misbehaved.

Thirty-seven stitches later and Emily's hand was back in one piece. She had told the ER doctor that she had slipped and her hand when through the glass shower door. Glynis had shot her a look but hadn't called her out on the lie.

Emily put her keys and bag down on the kitchen counter and tried to wiggle her fingers. She could feel the stitches pulling at the skin uncomfortably, so she stopped. Her hand was aching terribly, but she didn't want to take any pain killers. Instead, she wanted to take the bottle of tequila out of her freezer and drink until she couldn't remember why she started.

She pulled the bottle out of her freezer with her left hand and went to her bedroom.

# Chapter Twenty-Two

**F**riday had been chaos from the moment Liam had opened his eyes. He had overslept after the night shift, so had woken up later than expected. He had run around the house, barking orders at Bee who seemed completely uninterested in helping him pack.

By the time Liam managed to get to the airport, he and Sophie had missed their flight. The only good thing to come out of the day was the fact that Fridays and Saturdays were the only days of the week that had two flights into the city. The downside was that the next flight was only six hours later.

So Liam had taken Sophie back into town for lunch and then they had gone back home to watch movies while they waited.

Sophie had been so excited about the flight that she had barely slept the night before and was agitated all day waiting for the second flight.

She had been so excited in fact, that she had fallen asleep ten minutes after takeoff and slept the entire flight, waking up grumpy and irritable.

The airport in the city had been busy and crowded, people were jostling them about so badly that he had put Sophie on his back so that they didn't get separated.

Finding a cab to take them to their destination was a separate headache, they waited in a queue for nearly an hour before finally settling into the backseat of a beat up old taxi.

Fortunately, the city lights had cheered Sophie up greatly, so by the time they arrived at her grandparent's penthouse, her excitement and good humor had returned.

Liam greeted his in-laws politely and had received a stiff, formal greeting in response. Richard Myles, his father-in-law had barely shaken his hand before turning his attention to his beloved only grandchild.

Rita Myles had given Liam a dutiful air-kiss then relieved him of Sophie's bag.

"Daddy, why can't you stay here with me? There's lots of rooms." Sophie asked her father.

Liam knelt down and pulled his daughter into a hug. "I get you all the time, and Granny and Grandpa just want to spend some time with you." He explained. "You're going to have the best weekend."

"But I want you to stay with me!" Sophie complained loudly.

"I'm sure your father has his own weekend planned out." Rita Myles told her granddaughter firmly.

"I'll see you on Sunday kiddo." Liam told Sophie, ignoring Rita's comment. "And I'll phone you every morning."

"And every night?" Sophie asked in a small voice.

"Every night." Liam promised, giving her a last kiss on the forehead before straightening up.

"You have my mobile number?" He asked Rita who nodded.

"Have a good weekend." Liam said politely before turning and leaving.

At least he had made it passed the entrance hall this time. His relationship with his in-laws had always been strained, but since Mel's death they could barely stand to look at him. Not that he blamed them, he didn't think they could possibly hate him more than he had hated himself.

Mel's parents were incredibly wealthy and had thought their daughter had married beneath her just to get back at them for wanting her to live a different life.

When Mel had been killed, her parents had fought tooth and nail for custody of baby Sophie. It had taken all of Liam's savings and a year of his life to win custody of his child.

Still, he knew they loved their grandchild and made sure that she spent at least two weekends with them every year. Some trips he didn't even make it to the penthouse. Richard would greet him in the lobby and take Sophie off his hands. But the last year or so, Sophie had insisted he come inside. Liam was sure she was hoping one of these trips he would stay and they would be one big happy family, and he hadn't had the heart to tell her why that was never going to happen.

Liam breathed a sigh of relief as he left the lobby of the exclusive apartment building. As much as he would miss Sophie, he was glad to be out of that oppressive atmosphere. He found a newer looking cab quickly and climbed in, giving the driver the address of his hotel.

He pulled out his mobile to check if Emily had sent him a text. She hadn't. It was already after nine, he wasn't sure if she would still be willing to meet him or if they would have to arrange something for tomorrow.

*Hey, we missed our first flight but are finally in the city. Can I buy you dinner tomorrow?*

He wondered if he should have included an option to meet for drinks tonight, but decided it would seem too desperate if he did.

*Why don't you come over now?*

The reply came through with an address. Liam asked the driver which address was closer and he was a few blocks closer to Emily than he was to his hotel, so he gave the driver the new address and sat back in his seat, smiling to himself.

*I'll see you in 5* ☺

Emily looked at her mobile screen in horror. She had never given anyone her address before.

She had been drinking steadily since she had woken up that morning. She had only gotten out of bed at noon and had chosen booze over painkillers, deciding then already that she wasn't going to see Liam at all.

Now he was five minutes away and she had just invited him to her apartment. She looked around to see if anything needed to be tidied up, but she hadn't eaten anything all day, so it was just the empty vodka bottle on the counter and the half empty tequila she had ordered earlier. Throwing the vodka bottle out, Emily poured herself another shot of tequila.

If Liam wanted to see her, then he was going to see the real her. This is who she was and she didn't have to pretend to be anyone else, she told herself fiercely.

The doorman buzzed up a few minutes later. "There's a Mr. Richards here to see you."

Emily pushed the intercom button, "Send him up."

"Will do Ms. Winter."

Emily ran her fingers through her hair in a last minute attempt to make herself presentable, then waited for the knock on the front door.

She opened the door before Liam had had a chance to knock twice. "Hey you." She smiled at him, "Come on in."

"Hey." Liam said, looking a little surprised, "You been to a party or something?"

Emily laughed, swaying slightly, "I had a choice between painkillers and tequila," she told him, pointing at her arm, "guess which one I chose?"

"Tequila?" Liam asked with a raised eyebrow.

"Clever boy." Emily said, "Come inside before the nosy neighbors come to see who's here."

Liam walked in and Emily closed and locked the door behind him.

"Were you planning on a slumber party?" Emily asked, eyeing out Liam's overnight bag.

"No, just your place was closer than my hotel. Figured I'd save on taxi fare if I went there later," he explained. "What did you do to your arm?"

"I had a run in with my shower." Emily said breezily. "Can I get you a drink? Looks like you have some catching up to do."

"Sure, but I'm not much of a spirits man. Have you got any beer?"

Emily shook her head and hiccupped. "No beer here. There's wine though?"

"Wine would be good thanks. Why don't you tell me where it is and I'll open it for us?"

"I'll show you." Emily led the way to the kitchen and took a bottle of red wine out the cupboard. She handed the bottle to Liam, then went to the drawer to get a bottle opener.

"You have a nice place." Liam commented, looking at the desks in the living room.

"Very intimate hey?" Emily said sardonically.

Liam took the proffered opener, "Are you okay Emily?"

Emily leant back against the kitchen counter, "Why wouldn't I be?"

"I don't know. You just seem like you have a lot going on." Liam answered carefully.

"I'm fine. I've had a long week and I'm just unwinding. It's not like I knew you were going to come over so late at night." Emily defended.

Liam passed her a glass of wine, "You don't want a cup of coffee rather?"

"No, I don't." Emily responded quickly.

Liam shrugged and picked up his own glass.

They stood awkwardly in the kitchen for a moment before Emily remembered her manners. "Let's go sit on the only sofa I own."

She went back to the living room/office and took a seat, putting her feet up on the coffee table.

"So you work from home?" Liam asked.

Emily nodded, "Since I moved in here about eight years ago."

"You must end up with a lot of people coming and going, clients and whatnot."

Emily shook her head, "Clients aren't allowed here. The only person besides my assistant to ever enter this apartment is you."

Liam was taken aback, "Seriously?"

"You may not have noticed this," Emily leant forward and whispered conspiratorially, "but I don't really like people that much."

"You used to love people." Liam pointed out.

"That was until..." she paused, thinking better of saying Stan's name out loud, "Until I didn't like people anymore."

Liam put his glass on the table, "This isn't the way I wanted to do this, but I really need to say something to you."

"Liam," Emily put her hand up, "I'm in a good mood and don't feel like getting into a deep conversation right now, so can you just drop it?"

"Just let me say this please." Liam insisted. "I am so, so sorry about the way I behaved back then. You deserved so much more from me."

Emily rested her head against the back of the couch and stared at the ceiling. "I really did you know."

"I know, and I feel terrible about it. And I would do anything to take it back." He told her earnestly.

Emily shrugged, then smiled, "I guess you'll have to find some way to make it up to me." Emily leant over and tried to unbutton Liam's shirt with her swollen right hand. She shifted closer to kiss his neck.

Liam took her hand in his and pulled it gently away from his chest. "Not like this." He whispered to her.

"Come on Liam, it's just a little fun." She kissed his neck again but he leaned away from her.

"Emily, please."

Emily sat back abruptly, spilling the wine in her left hand. "What's your problem?" she asked him.

"I don't have a problem," Liam told her, still holding her right hand in his, "I just don't want to take advantage of you." He sat up straighter, "Look, why don't I make us something to eat and we can carry on talking."

Emily snatched her hand away from him, "I don't need your pity!" She almost spat in his face.

"Woah, what pity?" Liam asked, holding his hands up in surrender, "I just thought you could use something to eat. I'm also hungry."

"No." Emily said angrily.

"No?" Liam asked uncertainly.

"You don't care if I eat." Emily snapped, "You just don't want me."

"That's not true." Liam said quickly.

"I'm too fucking damaged for you aren't I Liam?" Emily shouted suddenly, getting off the couch. "Who wants to fuck a whore that's this broken?"

"Emily please." Liam was standing now as well, stepping back.

"Get out!" She screeched at him, pointing her braced hand towards the door. "Now!"

Liam held his hands up once more, "Okay, okay." He walked to the door, "I'm sorry Emily, I didn't mean to upset you."

"Out!" Emily screamed, throwing her wineglass at his head. It missed and shattered against the door, spraying Liam's grey shirt with burgundy wine.

Liam left without another word.

∞

Emily felt hands tighten around her throat, she struggled to pull the hands away, her body frozen in panic.

"You're a little whore, look at what you've done." The man said to her calmly. He hadn't taken off his shirt and now there was a smear of blood on it from Emily's face. His face was serene behind the beard, as though he were having a simple conversation.

"Please." Emily whimpered pathetically. Whether she was begging him to stop or to carry on until she died, she wasn't sure. She would have taken either at that point.

"Look at what you've done!" He screamed into her face, tightening his grip on her throat. "LOOK!"

∞

Emily sat up in bed, covered in sweat. She lifted her hand to her throat where she could still feel the pressure of his fingers against her skin.

"Emily?" A voice called out quietly from outside her bedroom.

"Whose there?" She called out in a panic, jumping out of bed.

"It's Liam. Can I come in?"

Emily walked over to her bedroom door and wrenched the door open. "What are you doing here?" She demanded.

She was suddenly very aware that her jeans were no longer on her body, she was dressed in only her underwear and t-shirt. "What did we do?" She asked him in a quietly horrified voice.

"Nothing I swear." Liam said quickly. "I forgot my bag here last night when you threw me out so I came back to ask for it. Your front door was unlocked and you were passed out on the couch. I helped you to bed then tried to leave but couldn't find the keys to your front door so wasn't sure I could lock it." Liam shrugged helplessly, "I couldn't leave you here with an unlocked door so I slept on the couch. Nothing happened." He repeated.

Emily felt suddenly embarrassed. "Liam, I'm so sorry about..."

Liam shook his head, "Don't worry about it. Can I make some coffee?"

"Um, sure." Emily said uncertainly.

"Do you want some?" He asked.

"Thanks." Emily closed the bedroom door and rushed to her bathroom to shower and brush her teeth.

When she got to the kitchen after throwing on some fresh clothes, she found a bagel and a cup of coffee on the kitchen counter, along with a note.

*Enjoy your breakfast – Liam.*

"Liam?" She called out, but she knew he wasn't there.

She took her coffee into the living room to lock the front door and saw that the broken wine glass from the night before had been cleaned up and he had tried to get the stain out the carpet.

Emily looked around the empty room and felt a lump in the pit of her stomach.

She picked her mobile up off her desk and sent a text to Paige.

*I think I really screwed up this time.*

Her phone rang as she lit a cigarette.

"Emily? Are you okay?"

"Yes Paige, I'm fine. I meant more in a personal way." Emily opened the window behind her desk.

"What happened?" Paige asked, her concern clear in her voice.

"I don't even know what to say. I've been on a major bender the last few days."

"Drinking or drugs?" Paige asked carefully.

"Relax Paige, only booze. But Liam was here last night."

"Liam, Liam? Liam from Hawthorne Liam?" Paige asked.

"Yes, that Liam. Sophie is with her grandparents and he asked to come around. He tried to apologise to me and I flew off the handle. I threw a wine glass at his head."

"Oh Emily."

Emily took a deep drag of her cigarette, "Paige, I don't think I'm cut out to be a mother."

The line was quiet for so long that Emily thought they may have been cut off.

"Is that what set off the bender?" Paige asked, "The idea of being a parent?"

"No." Emily said, "Yes. Hell, I don't know, maybe." Emily stubbed her cigarette out angrily, "So much has changed in such a short amount of time Paige, I don't know how to deal with it all."

"You know I think that's the first time you've ever admitted to struggling." Paige told her.

"Great, I made a breakthrough." Emily responded sarcastically.

"You may not feel that way now, but I honestly think you have Emily."

There was silence again.

"Emily, why did you text me?" Paige asked.

"I don't really know." Emily answered truthfully.

"Are you very busy at work at the moment?" Paige asked.

"No, not at the moment. Why?"

"Why don't you come through to Hawthorne for a few days and decompress?"

"I don't know if that's such a good idea Paige."

"Just a few days. I know Casey would be happy to see you. So would I."

"How is Casey?" Emily asked, changing the subject.

"Ben has a new girlfriend and some local kids spray-painted some unpleasant things on the side of the house, so she's had a rough few days."

"Spray-painted what?" Emily asked, her anger rising on Casey's behalf.

"Whore." Paige admitted quietly.

"Paige, I'm so sorry."

"It's not your fault." Paige said quickly, "And I really was thinking the trip could be good for you."

"Yeah, maybe you're right. I'll come out this week."

"See you soon. Oh, and Emily?"

"Yeah?"

"Don't be so hard on yourself. Change can be a good thing. Maybe you just need to stop fighting the idea that you deserve some good in your life."

Emily didn't know what to say to that. She swallowed uncomfortably, feeling as though she wanted to cry, "Bye Paige."

"Bye Emily."

Liam was sitting on his bed in his hotel room, wondering if he had made the right decision to leave Emily's apartment without saying goodbye. No, he shouldn't have stayed, the whole situation was awkward enough.

He sighed loudly, taking a sip of the cheap coffee he had bought in the lobby.

He knew she was damaged, he had expected it. But had he expected that? No, he hadn't, not to that extent.

Liam had told Emily the truth about the night before, but he had left out some details.

When he had gotten back to her apartment after realising he had forgotten his bag, Emily had been passed out on the floor, leaning against the sofa.

He had picked her up and she had wrapped her arms around his neck so tightly, and in her sleep, she had begged him not to hurt her.

She was the one who insisted her jeans come off, he had helped her only when he realised she wasn't able to bend her fingers on her right hand.

When he had pulled her jeans down and had seen the scar on her inner thigh and what looked like cigarette burns up and down both legs, he had pictured what she had been through and had felt nauseous at the thought.

After covering Emily, Liam had used her bathroom. He had seen the shattered mirror, what was left of it, and had guessed it was the reason her hand and wrist were strapped up. The mirror had shattered outward from each impact, and Liam could make out at least four separate points of impact. Someone had wiped the blood away and picked off the loose pieces of glass, but Liam could still see dried blood in the cracks and on the drywall behind the glass.

He didn't know Emily well anymore, but he couldn't believe this was something she did regularly. She didn't seem the type to lose control.

He thought about the first time he saw her in Hawthorne, outside Dusty's and wondered if she was an alcoholic. He hadn't smelt booze on her when he had collected or dropped Sophie, but then maybe he just wasn't paying attention.

He could just picture his mother telling him I-told-you-so, but he couldn't believe that Emily was beyond saving. She couldn't have gotten this far in life without being able to put her past aside and move forward. He was certain that she was displaying some form of PTSD. Probably brought on by her recent visits to Hawthorne and her relationship with Casey and Paige.

Liam was pulled from his thoughts by a text message.

*I want to apologise for last night, my behavior was inexcusable. I promise you that is not a side of me I wanted you, or anyone for that matter, to see. For the last few months I've been dealing with demons I thought I had killed. Turns out I had just pretended they were never there to begin with. I clearly have a lot of stuff in my own head to deal with, so I don't think it would be a good idea for us to see each other anytime soon. Thanks for staying the night, and for cleaning up. I'm really sorry about the wineglass by the way, I'm glad I missed.*

Liam spent the next twenty minutes trying to think of a reply, but every time he typed one out, it looked stupid. He wanted to tell her that he had been broken when Mel died, that he still had nightmares about it, so he understood to a degree how she felt. He wanted to tell her that he didn't care about her scars or how damaged she thought she was, because when he looked at her, all he saw was a survivor who still had enough compassion to look after a stranger's child. He wanted to tell her that she didn't have to fight her demons alone, that he could stand beside her. But he said none of those things.

 He finished his coffee and deleted the most recent text he had typed. Instead, he sent a single line.

*I wish you well Emily.*

# Chapter Twenty-Three

Liam had been sitting at his desk for the last hour going over staff wages and the incident reports for the weekend. Only two things happened while he was away. One was a fender bender near the dentist. Neither driver felt the damage was worth claiming for, so the police report was a waste of time. The other crime committed seemed to be vandalism. Someone had spray-painted graffiti on the McKenzie house. Liam put the file aside so he could follow up on that one himself.

He and Sophie had arrived home the previous evening. Sophie had been over excited the whole trip home, after her grandparents had spoilt her ridiculously over the weekend. Liam had ended up putting his own clothes in a packet so that his daughter's new dolls and toys could ride in his bag.

He had battled to keep his enthusiasm up during the flight home though. He couldn't keep his mind off the silent mobile in his pocket. There had been no response to his message, and he had been tempted to text or call a hundred times already that day.

He was sure she had taken his message to mean whatever was happening between them was over. And maybe in some way, that is what he was trying to convey at the time. He had to put Sophie first, always. He couldn't justify getting involved with someone who needed more than he could give, even if he desperately wanted to be the one to give it.

But ever since he had sent that text, he had regretted it. The only reason he hadn't texted her was because she said she didn't want to see him in her previous message, and he was trying to respect her by giving her space.

He had a horrible feeling though, that he had ruined any chances of them having any sort of friendship.

He looked up from the paperwork he was trying to read and saw a large black Ford drive past. He could have sworn that Emily was in the driver's seat.

Maybe she was back to see Casey, he thought to himself.

He wondered if he should go past later and say hello, but decided once more to respect her wishes.

He wished for a moment that Pastor Stan had never died. He wanted so badly to beat that man to death with his own two hands. He didn't know the details of what happened, but he knew Stan deserved to spend an eternity burning in hell for what he had done to Emily.

Getting off his chair suddenly, it occurred to Liam that he could find out the details without ever having to ask Emily. He walked downstairs to the basement where all the records were kept. There were thousands of files down there, most of them nothing more important than the weekend's bumper bashing, but still meticulously filed away in boxes, carefully labeled by year.

It still took Liam nearly an hour to track down the year in question. It had been tucked away in the wrong decade. When he finally pulled out the file on Emily and Stan, he found it was almost empty, and what papers that was there had been redacted with a black marker.

Liam slammed the file down in frustration, causing several other files he had taken out of the box to fall to the floor and lose their paperwork.

"Shit." He muttered to himself, bending down and shoving papers back into files.

Back in his office, Liam closed his door and sat at his desk. He took the post-it note off his computer monitor that had been there since the day he started and dialed the number written on it.

"Hello?"

"I'm looking for Sheriff Brown?" Liam said.

"You found him."

"My name's Liam Richards, I've taken over as sheriff here in Hawthorne."

"Oh yes, we've never officially met, but I've heard good things about you Liam."

"Thank you Sheriff."

"Please, call me Dave."

"Dave then. I'm wondering if you can help me with some information about an old investigation."

It sounded like the old sheriff was scratching his beard, "Sure, but I don't remember having any unsolved cases."

"It's actually a solved case," Liam explained. "The incident with Stan Whitley."

Dave sighed in irritation, "Let me guess, Paige McKenzie wants you to re-open the case and find the mystery accomplice."

"I'm sorry what?" Liam said.

"Yeah, she called a few months ago asking if I knew anything about a second perp. And I'll tell you now what I told her then. There was plenty of evidence that a lot of people had been in and out of that cabin, but in the basement, the only thing in that chamber of horrors were shoe prints. All of which were size tens."

"The cabin in the woods used for church retreats years ago?" Liam asked.

"Yeah that one. I tell you what kid, I kept the files with me at the family's request, but I'll ship them out to you today." There was the scratching noise again. "I did my job Sheriff."

"I'm sure you did. I wasn't calling about an accomplice. I didn't even know about it."

"Oh." The old sheriff said then coughed violently for a few moments, "Why were you calling then?"

"To be honest, I wanted to know where he kept the victim and how he died."

"Can I ask why the sudden interest?"

"Would you still send the files if I told you it was personal?" Liam asked.

"Yeah, okay. You let me know if you find anything else huh?"

"I will do. Thank you Dave."

The old man disconnected the line without saying goodbye.

Liam sat back in his office chair, wondering why on earth he hadn't looked this information up before now. He knew it was because he had been too quick to believe his mother's version of events.

Making a sudden decision, Liam stood up and grabbed his sheriff's jacket off its hook behind his office door.

Liam arrived at the McKenzie residence five minutes later. Before he had a chance to knock on the door, Paige came around the side of the house, bucket of soapy water in one hand and a sponge in the other.

"Sheriff. Hi, have you come to see the damage? I told the deputy I was going to wash it and he said it was fine because he had photos."

"I just came by to ask you what happened and see how you were doing." Liam answered politely.

"Well, come around back and see for yourself." Paige said, turning and heading back the way she had just come.

Liam followed her around the side of the house, coming to a stop a few feet behind her. Scrawled on the wall with black spray paint was the word 'whore'. It was about six feet long and three feet high.

"Jesus." Liam whispered.

"I've tried to wash it off, and I sprayed it down with thinners, but I think we're just going to have to paint over it." Paige told him.

The house was completely face-brick, in order to paint over the words they would have to plaster then paint the entire house.

Liam shook his head in disgust, then noticed a plastic bag near Paige's feet. "What's in the bag?"

"It's the strangest thing." Paige said, picking up the packet and handing it to Liam. "Whoever did this, also threw a whole lot of lavender stalks everywhere. There's three other packets in the garage. I picked them up with gloves and was going to drop it by the station. Not that I imagine you can do anything with it."

Liam opened the bag, getting a strong whiff of lavender. "That's strange." He said more to himself than to Paige.

"I thought so." Paige agreed.

Liam closed the bag again and held it shut in his hand. "Is this why Emily is back?" He asked gesturing towards the wall.

"Yes and no." Paige answered carefully. "I was hoping she could get away from the pressure of city living for a few days."

"Paige, can I ask why you recently contacted my predecessor?"

Paige put her hand to her mouth in surprise, "Did he call to complain?"

Liam shook his head, "No, I called him about something and he mentioned it. He asked if you had come to me about re-opening the case and finding an accomplice."

"Ah," Paige said, looking abashed, "I suppose that is something I should have come to you with immediately."

"Would have been nice." Liam agreed putting his hands on his hips. "Why didn't you?"

"I actually don't know. I suppose because I didn't think anything would come of it."

"What made you think that there might have been a second person involved after all these years?"

"Emily told me there was." Paige answered.

"When?"

"A few months ago."

"And that's the first you ever heard about it?" Liam asked disbelievingly.

"Yes Liam," Paige said firmly. "When she was first in the hospital, her jaw was wired shut because it had been broken so badly and she refused to communicate with anyone through writing. Once she healed, she always refused to talk about what happened. It never occurred to any of us that he wasn't working alone."

Liam felt his irritation ebb away. "I'm sorry Paige, I didn't mean to question your integrity."

"It's alright Liam, I understand."

"Could you tell me anything about what happened?" He asked her now.

Paige shook her head, "No, I'm sorry. That's not my story to tell and there's nothing I can tell you that would help with the investigation. I'm afraid if you want the details about what happened, you're going to have to ask Emily yourself."

"Fair enough." Liam answered. "I'll follow up at the station about all this." He held up the bag of lavender, "I'm sorry about your wall Paige."

"Thank you."


Liam threw the packet of lavender into his cruiser then pulled out of the McKenzie driveway and headed towards the forest roads.

He found the turnoff from memory alone, although he almost missed it completely at first. His cruiser crunched over fallen pine needles and dry leaves as he drove down the overgrown dirt road.

A tree had fallen across the road, making it impossible for Liam to get past in his cruiser, but he could see the cabin in the distance, so it was close enough for him to walk.

He took his flashlight and made sure his gun was in his holster before getting out of his car and heading towards the cabin. The forest had taken back its land, growing dense and thick. There was a canopy of tall trees above, letting in little sunlight to the pine covered ground Liam walked on. He could hear the birds chirping above, moving from branch to branch, complaining about the intruder in their forest.

The roof of the cabin had collapsed on one side, rotten-looking timber and thatch sticking out at unnatural angles, moss and ivy had taken over all the walls, making the cabin look for all the world as though it belonged in one of the bedtime stories he read to Sophie. He half expected to hear the shrill laugh of the evil witch coming from inside.

Liam walked gingerly up the stairs to the porch, worried he was going to fall through the rotting wood. He looked at the corner of the porch, remembering the day he and Emily had sat there together as teenagers, wrapped up in a blanket, feeling as though they were the only people in the world that mattered.

Liam shook the memory away as he reached the door. It had been padlocked years ago, probably by Sheriff Dave, but it looked as though the lock had been broken off. The pieces were rusting on the floor, so Liam knew it hadn't been done recently.

The door creaked loudly as Liam tried to push it open. He had to ram it with his shoulder to get the swollen wood to move enough for him to enter.

The room was covered in dust and cobwebs, faint sunlight coming through the hole in the ceiling. Liam could hear the rustling of bugs or mice in the corners of the dark room, but he couldn't see any of them. Most of the furniture was still there, the armchair was flipped over, its material torn and chewed through, moldy sponge lay scattered around it. The wooden table and chairs were still there, but looked as though a simple breeze would knock them down. Old straw from the thatch roof littered the table and floor.

Liam turned on his flashlight and looked around. His boots were leaving large footprints in the thick dust. He looked into the corners and around the floor but didn't seem to find anything. When he got to the fireplace, however, he could make out some stains under the dust. Using his foot to wipe away the dust, Liam found old blood stains on the wooden floor. There wasn't a lot of blood, but a few spatters here and there. Looking to the right of the fireplace, Liam finally found what he was looking for. The handle for the trapdoor was up against the wall, blending into the background so well that it was almost invisible.

With a huge effort and a grunt, Liam managed to pull the trapdoor open.

He shined his flashlight down the hatch. There were wooden steps leading down into the darkness.

Liam walked down the stairs carefully, painfully aware of the cracking sound they made every time he placed his weight on one.

When he reached the bottom step, Liam shone his flashlight around. The cellar was about the same size as the cabin above. It was musty and damp, some of the stone walls had rivulets of water running down them. Liam walked deeper into the room and shined his light into the corner. Rats scattered, scurrying in all directions to get away from the sudden invasion of light and noise.

"Shit!" Liam yelled as a rat across his foot. "I hate rats!"

In the corner where the rats were nesting Liam saw what looked like a metal shackle. He bent down to have a better look, moving away the thick cobwebs that had been built over the years. It was an old school iron shackle bolted into a large stone in the wall.

There was a rustling next to him. Scraps of what looked like an old blanket had been turned into nests by the rats. Tiny, blind, hairless baby rats were wriggling around in the dark, climbing over one another, searching for the safety and warmth of their mother.

There was a wooden stool nearby, knocked on its side, but it offered Liam no information.

He brushed some of the dust aside with his hand. The rough cement floor he was standing on was stained with old blood. A lot of it. He took a step back, using his boot to wipe away more dust. He could see what looked like the outline of a body, the blood seemed to have pooled on either side. There were also a few dried twigs on the floor, scattered all over, but Liam couldn't tell what they might have been at some point.

On the wall above the shackles were more bloody marks, some looked like handprints. Looking closer, Liam saw something sticking out in the mortar between two of the stones. He pulled it out with his fingers. It was a broken fingernail. It looked like it had been ripped from the nailbed. Liam dropped it on the floor, not caring that he had touched evidence with his bare hands.

He could picture Emily fighting desperately, shackled to the wall like an animal. So desperate to get away that she clawed at the walls until her nails were ripped out.

Liam couldn't look around anymore. He bolted up the stairs, taking them two at a time and rushed out of the cabin, barely making it down the steps before throwing up into the bushes.

He had been to many awful crime scenes over the years, but none of them affected him like this one had. When he was down there it was as though he could hear the echoes of her screams of terror. Her voice as she begged him not to hurt her when he carried her through to bed was haunting him as though she were whispering in his ear that very moment.

Liam straighten out and spat into the bushes, trying to get the taste of bile out of his mouth. Whatever he thought he was going to find wasn't there. He wasn't sure what he was looking for to begin with, and after all these years, any evidence had been ruined or stolen by the rodents that had taken over.

Liam walked back to his cruiser and took a bottle of water out of the driver's door. He rinsed his mouth out and spat some more water onto the ground before taking a sip and swallowing.

He hauled himself up into his cruiser and slowly reversed the way he had come. There was no place for him to turn around so it took him a good ten minutes to get back to the main road.

He was still feeling sick to his stomach as he made his way slowly back to the station.

# Chapter Twenty-Four

**E**mily had stopped at the store before going to the house, she unpacked the fresh milk and bread into the fridge, adding the wine she had bought.

Emily had told Paige she would only be in town in the afternoon, there was something she wanted to do first, and she had wanted to do it alone. She knew if she told Paige, Paige would offer to come with her, and Emily didn't want to be tempted to say yes.

It was much warmer in Hawthorne now, which Emily was grateful for, she wasn't sure she wanted to spend another night in the small cottage with a non-functioning thermostat.

Emily put her bags in the bedroom and took her toiletries to the bathroom. Her hand had been giving her trouble since she had gotten off the plane. It was sore and seemed more swollen than the night before. She took some painkillers out of her toiletry bag then went through to the kitchen to pour some water.

Emily had left her handbag in the car, so once she had taken the painkillers she left the house and locked it behind her before getting back into the rented SUV and reversing out the driveway.

Hawthorne cemetery was on the outskirts of town, past the forest road and past the old church cabin. Emily parked in the parking lot and took a deep breath. She hadn't been here since before Stan had taken her.

She remembered the way though, through the gate, down past the first lot of headstones, left at the Griffen family crypt, towards the slight hill. A large oak tree stood watch over this side of the graveyard, a silent guardian of the lost and forgotten.

Claire Winter didn't have a headstone. When Emily's mother had died, her father had been too broke to afford a marble headstone. Instead there was a small block of concrete where the headstone should stand.

Emily got onto her knees and cleaned away some of the grass that had covered her mother's name. There was a small cup next to the slab, dead flowers drooping miserably from the side. Emily hadn't even thought to bring flowers.

She pulled out the dead flowers as well and lay them aside, then sat back with her feet under her.

Emily ran her fingers over the engraving, CLAIRE WINTER – BELOVED MOTHER. They hadn't even been able to afford the dates, but the statement was something that her father had insisted on. Emily for the first time felt truly grateful for that gesture.

"Hi mom." Emily said quietly. She didn't know what else to say, so instead she sat there quietly, listening to the wind rustle through the leaves above her and the birds chirping nearby.

She stared at her mother's name until her vision became blurred. Hot tears filled up in her eyes, threatening to overwhelm her.

"Emily?"

Emily spun around so quickly she fell onto the side of her butt.

She could only see the silhouette of the man in front of her, but she knew immediately who it was.

"Hi Dad."

"I, I can't believe you're here." Mitchell Winter stepped closer to his daughter. His head was almost bald on top, only a thin layer of grey above his ears. His face was deeply lined, but Emily would have recognised him anywhere.

In his right hand he held a fresh bunch of posies.

"Why aren't you working?" Emily asked stupidly, not knowing what to say. She clambered to her feet, not wanting to feel at a disadvantage.

"I had the day off." His voice was the deep, hoarse smoker's voice she remembered so well. "What are you doing here?" He asked.

"I just wanted to see her." Emily said quietly.

"You been in town a few times before, did you come then?"

Emily was surprised he knew about her previous trips, but then realised that with Hawthorne being so small, she shouldn't be. "I haven't been before, no."

"Why not?"

"I wasn't ready." She answered simply.

"May I?" Mitchell Winter held up the posies.

Emily took a step back so he could bend down and place the fresh flowers in the cup.

"How often do you come here?" Emily asked him.

"Every week since the day she passed. Sometimes more often if I can."

Emily looked around at the nearby headstones and noticed they were all more overgrown and worn than her mother's plot.

"I was thinking maybe I could replace her name slab with a proper headstone." Emily, wanting to break the silence.

Mitchell shook his head, "No."

"I'd pay for it, it wouldn't cost you anything."

"This is what she asked for. Nothing more. She didn't want no fancy headstone."

"Oh." Emily said quietly.

"You don't remember that time but this is what she wanted."

"I remember more than you think." Emily argued.

"Maybe you do," Mitchell shrugged, "but then, maybe you don't. But I'm not having you come in here and ignore her wishes so that you can feel better about yourself."

He touched his wife's name gently with his calloused fingers then straightened.

"I just thought she deserved better." Emily said quietly.

"She did deserve better, but no piece of marble is going to give it to her." He looked at his daughter sadly, "You grew up good." He said to Emily. He nodded as though to himself then turned and walked away, leaving Emily alone with the dead.

Emily knelt down again, but couldn't settle. Her father's appearance and shattered whatever moment she had been having. She sighed and made her way back to the car. She opened the driver's window and lit a cigarette, drawing deeply before putting the car into gear and reversing out the parking spot.

As she was about to put the car back into drive, there was a rap on her window, causing her to jump.

Phillip, the weird guy from Molly's was standing outside her window. Emily opened the window slightly.

"Hey, Emily right?" His hands were in his pockets and his shoulders hunched and he was wearing a thick jacket despite the warm weather.

"Yeah. Hi."

"Could you give me a lift? I rode here on my bike but it's a long ride back."

"Uh, I wasn't planning on going straight back to town." Emily said carefully.

"I don't mind waiting in the car. Please?"

Emily shifted in her seat uncomfortably, "Yeah, okay sure."

Phillip grinned at her, "Great. Can you pop the trunk so I can put my bike in?"

Emily did as he asked but stayed in her seat instead of helping him. Phillip had to lower the back seats to fit his mountain bike into the boot, but soon he closed the boot and climbed into the passenger seat.

"Thanks for the lift, I almost never see anyone out here."

"No problem." Emily said, putting the car into gear and pulling out.

"Who were you visiting?" Phillip asked, as though they had been somewhere more pleasant than a cemetery.

"My mother." Emily answered, not wanting to get into a deep conversation with Phillip, but also not wanting to be rude.

"I was visiting my dad." Phillip offered.

"Oh, I didn't know Mr. Downing had passed, I'm sorry."

"No, he's alive still. I meant my birth father."

"Oh. I thought you were from out of town."

"My birth mother had me two counties over, but my dad was from here." Phillip was picking at an angry spot on his chin, "My dad was murdered."

"I'm sorry to hear that." Emily said awkwardly.

"Yeah, his girlfriend killed him. Stabbed him to death."

"That's awful." Emily pulled the car into Molly's parking.

"Oh, I thought you weren't coming into town?" Phillip asked, as though only noticing where they had been going now that they had stopped.

"Don't worry about it, Molly's wasn't far out of my way. I'll go now."

"Thanks for the lift." Phillip opened the door but didn't get out, "Hey, would you like to grab some dinner sometime?"

"Goodbye Phillip." Emily said firmly.

"Bye then." He shrugged and got out of the car and went to the back to off load his bike.

Emily had to stop herself from shuddering. There was something so off about that guy, she just couldn't put her finger on it.


Emily arrived at Paige's a few minutes later. Paige was standing in the driveway with Daniel, their heads bent together in discussion.

"Emily! Hi." Paige walked to Emily's car to greet her. "How was your trip?"

"Hey Paige, it was fine thanks, how are you?" Emily closed her car door. "Hi Daniel."

"It's good to see you Emily." Daniel smiled warmly.

"I'm good thanks, happy to see you." Paige told her, then she turned back to her husband, "I don't think we have any other choice, so we might as well bite the bullet."

Daniel nodded in agreement, "I'll call the contractor now." He walked away, leaving the women in the driveway.

"You doing house repairs?" Emily asked.

"Come look at this." Paige said, leading the way around the house to the wall that had been painted.

"What the hell?" Emily gasped when she saw it. "Who would do something like this?"

Paige shrugged helplessly, "Who knows, they police don't have any suspects. But we can't get it off so we're going to have to plaster over the bricks and paint."

"Wow, I'm so sorry Paige, this is horrible." Emily looked at the word sprayed onto the side of the house and felt suddenly anxious, the same way she felt when she woke up from her nightmares.

"It is horrible, but at least none of us were hurt. Come on inside, I'll make us some coffee and we can catch up." Paige said.

Emily followed Paige into the house and through to the kitchen. "Where's Casey?"

"She's having a nap. She's been battling to sleep at night so I try to make sure she has a nap in the days now."

"How's she doing?" Emily asked, taking a seat at the kitchen table.

"She has good days and bad," Paige said, while preparing the coffee. "It seems the bigger she's getting, the more bad days she has."

"Must be awful to have that reminder all the time." Emily said quietly.

Paige held the two cups of coffee, "Why don't we go sit outside, then you can smoke and we can talk."

Emily got up again and followed Paige through the spacious living room and out the glass doors onto the stone patio.

They sat down on wicker chairs, and Paige put the coffees down on the small glass top table between them.

"Let me fetch you an ashtray quick." Paige got up again and went to a storage cupboard under the window, taking out an ornate looking glass ashtray and bringing it back to where they were sitting.

"Thanks," Emily said, taking her cigarettes out of her pocket. "Do you want one?"

Paige shook her head and smiled, "I've managed to find other ways to cope."

Emily lit a cigarette and smiled through the smoke, "I'm glad to hear that."

Paige sat back and crossed her legs, "Are you planning on quitting anytime soon?"

Emily looked at the cigarette in her hand, "I suppose I'll have to, won't I?"

"Well, there isn't a law saying you have to, but it would be the healthier option for you and the baby."

"Mmm." Emily murmured, taking a sip of coffee.

"Have you changed your mind about the baby?" Paige asked gently.

"I want to be a good mother, I'm just so scared I won't be." Emily told her.

"What makes you think you won't be? The bender you went on?"

"I don't know Paige, I don't even know what set me off." Emily said honestly, "One minute I'm looking at a bigger apartment and a baby-safe car, then I'm chatting to Liam of all people, and the next moment I'm out looking to get laid and black-out drunk."

"Well it kind of makes sense don't you think?" Paige asked with a small smile.

"Um, no. Do you want to explain it to me so we both understand?"

Paige put her cup down on the table and leant forward. "There is a side of you that's going to have to change drastically. And that side is fighting back, not wanting things to change. Like men going to a strip club for their bachelor's party. One last walk on the wild side before settling down."

"But what happens if I go on benders when I've got a baby to look after."

"You won't." Paige said simply.

"You don't know that."

"I do. You won't ever put your child in jeopardy. You won't be the most important thing in your life anymore, you'll see. Your priorities will change so much. And," Paige added as an afterthought, "there's nothing wrong with going out from time to time and letting your hair down. Even moms need a night off from time to time. That's why babysitters were invented."

Emily stubbed out her cigarette, "So you're saying I should still do this?"

"Only if you want to." Paige said, "I told you, I would never force you. If you change your mind at the last second, I won't hold it against you."

"Thanks Paige, I appreciate that."

"What do you think about when you think of taking the baby home with you?" Paige asked her.

"Depends I guess. But the one idea I can't get out of my head is sitting back in bed, reading a book with the baby asleep on my chest."

Paige smiled, "That is one of the best feelings in the world."

"And at least I have a few months left to get my shit together." Emily mused with a half-smile of her own.

Paige laughed, "That's the spirit."


Casey walked outside a few minutes later. She was dressed in loose sweatpants and a baggy t-shirt. The bulge was clearly visible under the shirt.

"Hey Emily, I thought I heard your voice."

"Hey you, I hope we didn't wake you."

Casey grimaced, "Nah that was your kid."

My kid, Emily thought, smiling to herself.

"Emily, won't you join us for an early dinner? Daniel is going to grill some steaks just now."

"Oh yes, you have to stay." Casey agreed, sitting down next to Emily, "Dad makes the best steaks."

"Sure, why not?"

"Oof," Casey moaned, rubbing her stomach.

"You okay?" Emily asked, looking at Casey.

"Yeah, he's just kicking. Want to feel?"

Emily looked at Paige uncertainly, but Paige nodded with a smile.

"Here, give me your hand." Casey said. She took Emily's good hand and placed it to the left of her belly button. "Now just wait a moment."

"Okay." Emily said. As she spoke, she felt something move under her hand. "Oh, wow."

"I think he likes the sound of your voice." Casey said, moving Emily's hand more to the left.

There was another little thump under Emily's hand. "Hey there little guy." This comment was met with two stronger little thumps.

Emily laughed, she never imagined feeling a baby kick would feel like this. She looked up and saw Casey and Paige smiling at one another.

Emily and Paige shared a bottle of wine while Daniel grilled the steaks.

"I need to go make the salad before this wine makes me too lazy." Paige said, getting up.

"I'll come help." Emily stood up as well.

"I'll come and watch you two work." Casey joked, getting off the chair with a little difficulty.

In the kitchen Paige handed Emily a cucumber on a cutting board and a sharp knife. Then she handed Casey a head of lettuce.

Casey started tearing strips of lettuce off and putting it into a large salad bowl.

Emily took the plastic off the cucumber and started slicing it.

Paige was cutting baby tomatoes in half and throwing them in the bowl with the lettuce.

"Did you finish filling in all your forms?" Paige asked Casey.

"Yup," Casey said, stealing a slice of cucumber from Emily's cutting board.

"What forms?" Emily asked, using the knife to scrape the sliced cucumber into the bowl.

"I want to go back to college and get my masters." Casey told her, stealing another piece of cucumber, "Since your kid should arrive before September, I was thinking I could still make it back for the first semester."

"Oh wow, okay." Emily said, taking a slice of cucumber for herself, "You ready to go back?"

Casey shrugged, "I don't know. But I can't stay in this town forever. I need to start living my life again."

"Good for you." Emily told her.

"Casey's going to stay with her cousin off campus for the first semester, just to see how she settles back into college life." Paige said, breaking pieces of feta into the salad.

"That's probably a good idea. Do you get on with your cousin?"

"Oh yeah, she's great. And she's lesbian so I don't have to worry about her bringing strange frat boys home."

Daniel called inside that the steaks were ready.

"You take the salad out, I'll get the plates and cutlery." Paige told Emily.

Emily grabbed the bowl and made her way back to the patio, walking with Casey.

"Wait." Casey said quietly, putting her hand on Emily's arm.

"What's wrong?"

"Nothing." Casey tried to smile but didn't seem to manage, "I just wanted to thank you again for what you're doing. It's made this whole thing," she gestured to the bump, "so much easier to deal with. I can tell myself I'm carrying your child and it helps me sleep at night."

Emily swallowed, feeling emotional. "It's me that should be thanking you."

"Wait til he doesn't sleep and night and then tell me how grateful you are." Casey joked, breaking the tension. "Come on, let's get outside before mom finds us here and wants to know what we're talking about."

After dinner, Casey complained about heartburn and asked Emily if she would go on a walk with her. Emily agreed and they left Casey's parents to do the washing up as they went out the living room doors and headed out into the massive back yard. They didn't go very far, once they were behind a thicket of bushes, Casey sat on the ground and crossed her legs with difficulty. Emily sat next to her, leaning on her hands and stretching her legs out in front of her.

"I heard Ben has a new girlfriend." Emily said after it became clear Casey wasn't sure what to say.

"Steph was a friend of mine in high school. I always thought she had a thing for him." Casey pulled a face. She was tugging single pieces of grass out with her fingers and flicking them into the air, watching them float back down to earth.

"Want me to find them and punch them?" Emily asked.

Casey snorted but shook her head. "Thanks for the offer, but he deserves someone like her."

"You mean someone not like you?"

Casey shrugged, "No one wants to be with a victim."

"Who says you're a victim?" Emily asked, pulling out a blade of grass as well.

"I do." Casey said simply. "How do you know when you're not a victim anymore, when you're suddenly a survivor?"

Emily lay back on the grass and stared at the evening sky. "Have you ever been pulled out to sea by a rip current?" She asked Casey.

Casey shook her head.

"One second you're just swimming around having fun and the next second a wave dumps you under and a violent current grabs you and tosses you around until you don't know which direction the surface is.

You kick and you thrash, but you only seem to get more and more disorientated and you can't breathe and you're terrified.

Then you finally break the surface and take in a lungful of air and you become a survivor, and everyone thinks you've done it, that everything's going to be okay now. But you haven't. You're still in the sea, desperately trying to stay afloat, the shore never quite within reach. Sometimes the undertow pulls you back under, and even when the water's calmer, you're having to kick and swim non-stop just to breathe. The water's still all around you, threatening to swallow you back in and take you under. Survival is just about trying to breathe. It's not living, it's just being alive and there's a difference."

"Well fuck." Casey said, "I don't think I want to be a survivor either."

"Sorry, I probably could have worded that better." Emily said contritely.

"Is that how you feel after all this time?" Casey asked.

"Some days." Emily admitted, "But I've got to tell you something. These last few months I've connected with more people than I have for years. And this baby is coming and I think I've found another stage I want to get to."

"What stage is that?" Casey asked, looking at Emily.

"Living on purpose. Not surviving because my lungs continue to inhale and exhale, but living because I want to, because I have something to live for. I'm finally learning that that is the best revenge I can have."

"Is it working?" Casey asked, raising an eyebrow.

Emily snorted, "Not every day, and especially not lately, but I don't think I've been trying very hard."

"Maybe we can try together?" Casey suggested.

"Now that's a deal." Emily grinned at her.

# Chapter Twenty-Five

Emily left just after sunset. She could see Casey was exhausted and she was looking forward to some peace and quiet. Not that she hadn't enjoyed her time with the McKenzies, they were great hosts and Emily really had a really pleasant afternoon. But she wasn't used to socializing so much and was ready for some alone time on the couch with the television or a book.

She pulled into the driveway and immediately noticed something on the welcome mat by the front door. She couldn't see what it was from inside the car, so she took her bag and climbed out, locking the car behind her.

She walked up to the front door and bent down. It was three sprigs of lavender, tied together with twine. With it was a little card – *Welcome home my little whore.*

Emily froze, the card and lavender in her hand.

"Emily, you okay over there?"

Emily spun round, Liam was jogging over from his house.

"Sorry, I know you wanted space." Liam began, but Emily cut him off.

"It's fine Liam, what do need?"

Liam looked taken aback. "Nothing, just saw you look worried when you got out of your car. Hey, did Paige give you that?" He asked, pointing at the lavender in Emily's hand.

"What? Oh, no, she didn't." Emily stuffed the lavender and card into her bag, "Why would Paige give me lavender?"

"The vandal that messed up the side of their house left lavender all over the place."

Emily froze for the second time in two minutes. "What?"

"Yeah, it was the weirdest thing." Liam scratched the back of his head, "Wait, was that waiting for you when you got home?"

"Liam, I think you need to get a deputy to stay at the McKenzie house." Emily said urgently.

"Right now I'm more worried about you." Liam said, looking around. "Can I go into the house before you and check it out?"

"No, its fine, just promise me you'll make sure someone is watching Paige and Casey."

"Emily, what aren't you telling me?" Liam asked.

"Nothing." Emily said stubbornly.

"Bullshit!" Liam snapped, "I might be a small town sheriff, but I am still the sheriff and more than that, I know you and I know you're lying to me."

Emily thought for a moment, biting her lip. "Okay. Where's Sophie?"

"She's home, Bee's staying over tonight because I might have to go to work later."

"Come in." Emily said, unlocking the front door. "I guess we better talk."


Emily dumped her bag on the dining table then went to the kitchen to make coffee while Liam went from room to room checking windows and cupboards.

"Do you want coffee?" Emily called out.

"Yes please." Came the reply from the empty second bedroom.

Emily took two cups down from the cupboard and noticed with annoyance that her hands were trembling slightly.

She made the coffee quickly but clumsily, her right hand being more of a hindrance than a help. She was hoping Liam wouldn't notice her hands when he returned from his search.

"It's all clear." Liam said, coming back through.

"I didn't think it wouldn't be." Emily commented, handing him his coffee.

"Thanks."

"I'm hoping you still drink your coffee the same way you did as a teenager." Emily said, gesturing towards to the coffee.

Liam took a sip and nodded, "I'm surprised you remember after all these years."

Emily shrugged and walked to the little dining table, sitting down. "It's the same way I have it."

Liam sat down as well and placed his coffee on the table.

"Now, tell me what's going on." Liam said. "Does all this lavender have to do with the mystery accomplice?"

"How did you – Oh, Paige."

"Again, I am the sheriff, something you both seem to keep forgetting."

"Look Liam, I don't know. It could just be someone playing a prank."

"Seems like a pretty specific prank." Liam pointed out. He took a sip of coffee then put the mug down again. "When I texted you, you asked me if I sent you a package. What was in the package?"

Emily swallowed uncomfortably. "More lavender." She admitted.

"And?" He pressed.

"A note and before you ask, no I don't have it."

"What did it say?"

"It said something about me coming back to Hawthorne soon."

"And tonight's? Was there a note?"

Emily sighed loudly and pulled her bag towards her. She took the lavender and note out and put it on the table.

"This could be considered a threat." Liam said, reading the note, his expression darkening.

"It could be considered a lot of things Liam."

"Do you think it's the accomplice?" Liam asked her, still holding the note.

"I don't know! I told you."

"What can you tell me about him?"

Emily shook her head and shut her eyes. "Nothing, I don't know anything useful."

"Tell me what you know and I'll decide if it's useful or not. How tall was he?"

Emily shrugged, "Maybe a little taller than Stan."

"Hair?" Liam asked.

"Dark I think."

"You think?" He repeated.

"Yes Liam I think. I didn't get much chance to see him in the light!" Emily snapped.

Liam cleared his throat, "I'm sorry. I didn't mean to push."

"He had a reddish beard and he drank whiskey and smoked cigars I think." Emily said, ignoring the apology. "He smelt like grease sometimes, like engine grease but slightly different."

Liam nodded, waiting for her to continue.

"He spoke well, but I got the impression he wasn't a pastor like Stan. He had a weird obsession with God, but not the same." Emily shut her eyes tightly again.

"Can you remember how old he was?" Liam asked gently.

"Maybe Stan's age, maybe a little older? I'm not sure."

"Okay." Liam said, "That's fine." He had a sip of coffee, "It doesn't sound like anyone I've ever seen around here."

"I definitely hadn't seen him before that." Emily said.

"Where does this come in?" Liam asked, holding up the sprigs of lavender.

"He, uh, he used to bring it with him. He said it was to mask the smell." Emily was pale, she felt so ashamed of admitting these things to Liam.

Liam thought about the little twigs he had found in the cabin and suddenly understood. "I'm so sorry Em, I am so, so sorry."

Emily looked down at her lap and shook her head, "Please don't Liam."

"I want you to get your bag, you'll stay at my place tonight."

"What?" Emily looked up suddenly, "No, I'm not going to hide."

"Well, it's either that or I'm going to have to go wake my sleeping daughter and bring her here, because I am not leaving you alone tonight."

Emily swallowed the last of her coffee and put the cup down with a little more force than necessary. "I don't need a bodyguard!"

"This is not an option." Liam said calmly.

Emily stood up and took her cup through to the kitchen.

Liam followed her, "Emily please, I won't sleep knowing you're here alone."

Emily sighed again, "Fine, but just for tonight. And only if you swear you'll send someone to keep an eye on Paige and Casey."

Liam smiled, "I swear. As soon as we get back to my place I'll call the station. You can even listen."


Emily collected her bag and her toiletries then met Liam at the door. He insisted on taking the bags from her so she could lock the door.

They walked the short distance between the houses in silence. Liam opened his front door and ushered Emily in. "Let me show you to the main bedroom. I'll sleep on the couch."

"I'll be fine on the couch." Emily argued.

"The sooner I show you where it is, the sooner I can call the office." Liam said, walking down the passage without waiting for an answer.

As they got to the door of the bedroom, the door opposite opened and Bee stuck her head out.

"Bee, my friend is staying with us tonight. I'll be on the couch."

Bee lifted an eyebrow knowingly. "No problem. I'm going to have my earphones on tonight so I can listen to my radio talk show, so don't worry about making noise." She winked and them and closed the door again.

Liam shook his head ruefully, "That woman."

He walked into the main bedroom and put the bags on the double bed. The room was bigger than the one Emily was staying in, but sparsely furnished. Behind the bed was a headboard that connected to two bedside tables each holding a matching lamp. On the one table was a picture of

Sophie, grinning at the camera, showing off a missing front tooth. On the other side was a candid picture of Liam's wife.

Liam noticed Emily looking at the photo. "That's the last picture I ever took of her. We were on a picnic for our anniversary."

"I'm sorry you lost her." Emily said quietly. She felt like she was invading the other woman's space.

"Thanks." Liam answered awkwardly. "So, are you tired or do you want some more coffee or maybe some hot chocolate?"

"I'm okay for drinks, but I'm not really tired yet."

"Do you want to watch a movie?"

"Can you make that phone call first?" Emily asked first.

"Fair enough. Phone call then movie?"

"Sure, why not?" Emily followed Liam back through to the living room and sat down on the couch feeling even more awkward than before. Their last text conversation was still fresh in her mind. As was the wine glass throwing, screaming banshee moment that preceded the texts.

Liam took his mobile out his pocket and pressed a button. It was answered quickly. "Sam, hey it's me. I need you to take a cruiser out to the McKenzie place." Liam paused while he listened, "I want patrols the whole night. Any activity is reported straight to me. Gary will manage just fine at the desk alone." He paused again. "Great, thanks Sam, I'll have someone relieve you at six."

Liam disconnected and turned to Emily, "Happy?"

Emily nodded, "Thanks Liam."

"I would have done it anyway, I don't want you to think for a moment that I'm not taking this threat incredibly seriously."

"I know that, and I appreciate it."

"Now, what kind of movie are you in the mood for?" Liam asked.

"I'm not fussy. Something brainless." Emily said, wanting to say something to alleviate the tension but not having the courage to open her mouth.

"I recorded just the thing then." Liam grinned at her, reminding her of the boy he had once been.

Within moments the opening credits of a cheesy horror film was on the screen.

"You weren't kidding." Emily laughed, "I can't believe you still watch these!"

"Of course, they're my favorite." Liam told her with a grin.

When they had dated in high school, one of their regular dates had been finding the cheesiest horror movie they could at the video store and taking it to one of their houses to watch, usually Emily's house since Cathy hadn't approved of the relationship and since her father was usually at work, it meant they had plenty of time to make out. They would take turns to mock the acting, the story line, the effects, or anything else they could find. They preferred cheesy horrors over any other genre.

Emily hadn't watched one in years. She usually stuck to old black and white movies that would play in the background or documentaries. She was finally beginning to understand that she seemed to have lost the piece of herself that did things for the pure enjoyment of it.

"Did you watch cheesy horrors with your wife?" Emily asked, regretting the question as soon as it left her lips.

Liam shook his head with a half-smile, "Mel hated them. She thought they were the biggest waste of time. She was more of a rom-com girl." Liam looked at the screen and shrugged slightly, "I will say it's definitely lonelier mocking everything on my own."

"That doesn't sound like much fun." Emily grimaced in agreement.

"Hey, I know what we need." Liam exclaimed suddenly, jumping off the couch. "Here, pause it, I'll be back now."

He tossed the remote to Emily and hurried towards the kitchen. Emily pressed pause as instructed then put the remote on the coffee table.

It felt so strange to be here, sitting companionably with Liam and acting as though they were teenagers again when less than an hour ago she was reading that note and finding out that Paige or Casey might be in danger.

As much as it was Liam's job to protect the people in the town, Emily was still personally grateful to him for making sure there was a cop standing by all night at the McKenzies. Emily smelt the popcorn before she heard the kernels popping. She smiled to herself wistfully. No cheesy horror was ever fully appreciated without butter smothered popcorn. She had forgotten how carefree they had once been. How the only disagreement had been who stole the more buttery pieces and whose legs were going to go on whose lap.

Liam came back into the living room holding a large bowl of popcorn and looking triumphant. "Now we're ready to really enjoy this work of artistic brilliance."

Emily laughed, "Couldn't possibly have appreciated it without the appropriate snacks."

"Damn right!" Liam agreed, flopping down on the couch again and putting the bowl between them.

The longer the movie went on, the less Emily was aware of what was happening on the screen and the more she became aware of the man sitting next to her. They had made a few comments at the beginning of the movie, but it had felt a little forced, so they had both given up. Emily wished they could have been more comfortable around one another, but knew it was partly because she just didn't know how to let her guard down. And more than likely, their last meeting in the city was playing on both their minds. By the time she had gotten used to the smell of the popcorn, Emily had been able to smell Liam's aftershave from her spot on the couch, it was a woody, natural smell that seemed perfect for him. She noticed the way his eyes crinkled up when he laughed, and while it showed his age a little more, it suited him. He was so relaxed, his long legs stretched out in front of him, one arm resting on the arm of the couch, his other hand on his right thigh.

Emily realised that Liam had been watching her watching him and blushed furiously. She hadn't noticed him turn to face her while she had been looking at his hand.

"You okay?" He asked with a slight smile.

"Yeah, I'm fine thanks." Emily said, turning her attention back to the movie.

"Emily?"

"Mmm?" Emily said, not turning to face him.

"I'm sorry this feels awkward, I really wish it didn't."

Emily did look at him this time, she could feel his earnest gaze was searching her face.

"It's not your fault Liam." She told him, "I'm just not good with people anymore."

"You're good with Soph, she adores you."

"She's different. She's little, she doesn't expect anything from me."

"What do you think I expect from you?" Liam asked, completely ignoring the screen where the heroine's boyfriend was being bludgeoned to death with a toaster.

"That's not what I meant," Emily said, "kids are so innocent, they never have ulterior motives."

"I get what you're saying, but you should know, I don't have any ulterior motives either." Liam told her.

"I know. It's not you, it's me." Emily muttered.

Liam was quiet for a while, looking down at his own hand, "Don't you get lonely? Living like this? Not letting anyone close?"

Emily shrugged, "I'm used to it. I've been alone more than half my life. It's all I know."

"I feel like that's partially my fault." Liam said quietly.

Emily shook her head, "It's really not Liam."

"I hurt you." He insisted.

"Maybe you did. But after what I had been through, there's no way I would have been able to have a relationship with anyone for a very long time. I would have ended up hurting you far worse." Emily said, surprised at how frank they were able to be with one another.

"Have you been in many relationships?" He asked.

Emily shook her head, "I don't date."

Liam raised an eyebrow, "Not ever?"

Emily shook her head.

"Not even with the local barmen?"

Emily looked at him sharply, "What did Nick say?"

"Nothing, I just saw him leaving your place early one morning."

Emily looked embarrassed again, "I meant it when I said I don't date. I have never been in another relationship after you."

"Sorry, it's none of my business." Liam said, looking abashed.

Emily looked towards the movie once more.

"I wish I could take away any pain I caused you." Liam said suddenly.

"Don't worry about it." Emily said, refusing to meet his gaze.

"I've only dated two women in my life and I hurt them both so unforgivably."

Emily turned back to him when she heard his voice crack. Liam had his head in his hands.

"Liam?"

He didn't answer.

"Liam." Emily said a little louder, "you need to stop blaming yourself for me. I was pretty fucked up without your help." When he still didn't respond, Emily took his wrist in her hand and pulled it away from his face.

"I should have known the truth, it shouldn't have even been a question. I should have known from the moment I heard you were gone that you wouldn't leave me like that. That you could never do something like that."

"It doesn't matter Liam, we can't change the past."

"I should have known better. For both of you. I was so stupid and it cost you both so much." Liam said wretchedly.

"I think it's fair to say that Stan and his brother cost me a lot more than you ever could." Emily told him sternly, "And

I don't know what happened with your wife, but I know you loved her. I can see it all over this house and all over your face."

"I should have been home the night she died." Liam said, his face crumpling, "She hated the work I did. She begged me to change departments when she got pregnant and I ignored her."

Emily still held his wrist, but they were both frozen in place. "Liam, you couldn't have known."

Liam shook his head as though to stop Emily's words from coming.

"Liam, look at me." Emily said, tugging on his arm.

Slowly Liam turned to face her, agony etched on his handsome face. "I'm so sorry I hurt you Em, I'm so sorry I hurt both of you."

Emily moved closer to him and took his face in both her hands. "Liam, look at me properly."

With tears in his eyes, he raised his gaze, devastated blue eyes met intense green.

"Your wife loved you, and you loved her. That's all that matters. You have a beautiful little girl that you will teach all about her mother and what a wonderful woman she was and how much she loved her family. That she gave her life to protect her child's." Emily used her thumb of her good hand to wipe a tear off Liam's cheek. "And let me make this very clear Liam Richards. I forgive you."

Liam searched her face in desperation, as though to confirm the truth of her words.

"I forgive you Liam." Emily repeated, her eyes staring intently into his.

As they looked into each other's eyes, a million things were said without a single word being uttered. Emily leant forward slowly and Liam met her half way, his lips touching hers incredibly gently.

Slowly, as though he was trying not to scare her away, Liam lifted his hand to her face and touched her cheek gently with his fingertips.

The kiss deepened, their lips opening slightly, their tongues touching. The space between their bodies grew smaller as Emily placed her own hand on the side of his neck.

She had never felt a kiss so intense, so intimate. She wanted so desperately to pull him closer, but she was scared it would break the spell.

"Daddy? That's gross."

Liam and Emily shot apart as though they had received an electric shock.

"Soph, why are you up baby?" Liam asked, getting off the couch.

Sophie was standing near the coffee table, her entrance had gone unnoticed by either of them.

"I heard a noise." Sophie said, rubbing her eyes with her fist.

"Where did you hear a noise?" Liam asked her, kneeling down in front of her.

"Outside my window."

"Okay, you stay here with Emily, I'll go have a look."

Sophie walked over to Emily and climbed onto the couch, immediately putting her head on Emily shoulder.

Emily looked up at Liam, who looked worried. She wrapped her arm protectively around the little girl.

Liam disappeared down the hall.

"Emily?" Sophie asked in a sleepy voice. "Are you going to marry my dad?"

Emily coughed uncomfortably, "No sweet girl, your dad and I are just friends."

"Oh." Sophie said, her eyelids already drooping.

Liam came back a few moments later, "There's nothing there." He whispered to Emily.

Sophie's eyes popped open suddenly. "I did hear a noise Daddy."

"I know you did, but I think it was just a cat or a bird, nothing to worry about." He heaved his daughter into his arms. "Let's get you back to bed."

"Daddy, can Emily come with us to the fair?"

Liam paused for a moment. "That would be up to Emily. But you can ask her if you want to."

Sophie looked over her father's shoulder, "Emily, will you come with us to the county fair on Friday night?"

Emily smiled at the little girl. "I'd love to. Go get some sleep now and you can tell me all about it tomorrow."

Sophie smiled widely at Emily as Liam carried her away.

Emily sat on the couch, her left leg tucked under her right. Her left elbow was resting on the back of the couch and she was biting the back of her left thumb unconsciously.

This was a bad idea. She shouldn't have agreed to come over and she definitely shouldn't have kissed him. She felt the desperate urge to flee back to her own space, but the keys were in her bag and her bag was in Liam's bedroom. She knew Liam would just follow her if she tried to leave and insist she came back.

She rubbed her face in irritation.

"You okay?" Liam asked, returning to the room.

"Yes, just a bit tired, it's been a long day." Emily lied.

"Oh, well why don't you go off to bed?"

"I really don't feel comfortable taking your bed." Emily insisted.

Liam gave her a look, "Seriously, I'm not giving you a choice here."

Emily sighed in resignation and stood up. "Do you mind if I use your shower quickly?"

"Of course, help yourself. There are towels on the shelf behind the bath."

Emily tried to walk past, but Liam took her injured right hand gently in his own. "Em, about what just happened..."

Emily pulled her hand away slowly, "Please don't Liam, that was a mistake."

Liam's jaw tightened, but his expression didn't change. Instead he nodded, "You're right. Goodnight Emily."

Emily hurried away before she did something stupid. She was tempted to kiss him again. She wanted to feel his arms around her, his skin against hers. She wanted to take him to the bedroom and have him inside of her. But she knew it would be a mistake. She didn't want a relationship and too much had happened between them in the past. It wouldn't be anything like her one night stands, and she couldn't pretend it could be.

She had never met a man so intrinsically decent, Liam was good to the core. Emily wasn't even sure how to be a good person anymore. She had spent so much of her life trying to protect herself that she had become the most selfish person she knew. She had spent so many years ignoring her own feelings that she forgot how to treat other people without hurting theirs.

Liam deserved so much more than she had to offer. Turning him down now was the only way to protect him from more unnecessary hurt.

# Chapter Twenty-Six

"Please, please just let me die." Emily whispered into the darkness, praying to a God that didn't care. She didn't know how long they had been gone this time but she knew it wasn't long. She could feel fresh blood oozing between her legs so she knew she couldn't have been unconscious for long.

Tears filled her eyes and spilled over, burning the fresh graze on the side of her face. She was in so much pain she wanted to vomit, but there was nothing left inside her to bring up. She choked on a sob and it sent a spasm of pain through her chest. She was pretty sure another rib or two were broken. She had upset the scary one by crying earlier and he had become enraged, kicking her furiously until he was panting from exertion. Emily had pretended to pass out from the kicking, but he wasn't buying it. He was all over her, rubbing himself against her, trying to get a reaction.

When Emily had stayed completely still, he had taken her left nipple into his mouth and bitten down. Emily bit her lip and clenched her fists, trying not to react, tears pouring from her closed eyes. That seemed only to make him angrier, so he bit down again, this time so hard she could feel his teeth tearing through her flesh.

She screamed as he pulled his head away, hot blood spurting onto her chest.

∞

"Emily!"

Emily sat up suddenly and put her arms in front of her face protectively. "Please don't."

"Emily, it's me."

Emily lowered her arms and saw Liam standing in the light of the doorway, his gun drawn. He walked into the room and pulled the curtains open. The window was still closed tightly.

He turned away from the window and lowered the gun. "Are you alright?"

Emily swallowed uncomfortably. "It was just a nightmare."

Liam was wearing only a pair of boxer briefs and his hair was tousled from sleep.

"I'm sorry, I didn't mean to startle anyone." Emily said quietly, embarrassment and shame evident in her voice.

Liam put his gun down on the bedside table and sat on the foot of the bed, facing Emily. "Do you have a lot of nightmares like that or is it because of what's happened here in the last few days?"

Emily pulled her knees up and wrapped her arms around her legs tightly, looking down at the blanket at her feet. "I have them anyway. I can't say they're worse or not. They all suck."

Liam was quiet for a while, looking at the wall above Emily's head, then he said quietly, "I used to have really bad nightmares about Mel. It got so bad that I was too scared to sleep, knowing I was going to have to relive that night over and over again."

Emily looked up from the blanket. "I used to be too scared to sleep too, but it didn't stop them, so I just try to sleep while I can." She tried to smile wryly, "Booze helps... Did yours stop?"

Liam nodded slightly. "I still have them sometimes, but not often anymore."

"How did you get them to stop?" Emily asked.

"I had to go to the police therapist for months. The first few sessions I didn't say a word, I didn't want to be there and I thought the whole therapy idea was total bullshit. I would take the paper in with me and read the sports section for my allotted hour." Liam grimaced, "Eventually though my therapist started breaking through; I started talking and once I did, I couldn't stop. Once my mandated time with the therapist was over, I kept going. I saw my therapist for over a year and he really did help me."

"I'm glad you got the help you needed." Emily said quietly.

"Have you ever spoken to anyone about what happened?" He asked, looking at her now.

Emily shook her head, "No, not really. I mean, sometimes I speak to Paige, more now than ever before, but never on a professional level."

"Can I ask why not?" Liam asked.

Emily shrugged, "I remember someone talking to my dad or the doctor outside my hospital room, I can't even remember who it was, but I think it was the hospital shrink they had assigned me. He was telling whoever was outside my door that he wasn't equipped to deal with that level of trauma. I remember lying there, staring at the ceiling and thinking there probably wasn't anyone on earth equipped to deal with what happened to me. People like me shouldn't be allowed to live."

"Shouldn't be allowed to live? What do you mean?" Liam frowned, "Like the doctors should have killed you, or the men that took you?"

"I didn't mean it like that," Emily sighed, "But doctors do their job, they operate and cut open and sew back together; trying to fix a person, never once pausing to consider whether or not they should. They think if they can get the body to act right again, then they've done a good job, that they're the hero."

"And they're not?" Liam guessed.

"They mean well, but people don't ever really survive something like that."

"That's not true," Liam said, "you're a survivor."

Emily pulled a face, "I hate that saying."

"But you are." He insisted.

"There's nothing about being a survivor to be proud of."

"Of course there is."

"Liam, being a survivor means just that. You survive. Your life continues because your heart keeps beating and your lungs keep drawing air. You go through the motions, you eat to survive, do what you have to. But most of the time, you're doing just what's necessary to stay alive. You don't feel truly alive. Your body does what's expected of it and sometimes you managed to break out of that feeling for a while, but soon enough, there's a nightmare or a smell or a memory that puts you back in that place. So you drink or you take drugs or you screw anyone that will have you, just for that moment when you can feel like you're actually just living.

It's not living, it's just being alive." Emily looked towards her feet again, "The person who went into that cabin died, only the doctors didn't let her heart stop when it should have. So what was left was – I don't know what was left."

"My God Emily, is that how you truly feel?" Liam's voice cracked.

"It's how it is." Emily said sadly, refusing to look at him, "I read somewhere once that women who survive sexual assault are victims who never get to leave the crime scene, and that struck me in its honesty. I had never thought about it that way before, but it's true. People move out of houses they get attacked in, they move cities after being in a bank robbery or hold up or whatever, but where can I go? These scars are with me. Their marks are always with me, their personal brand of torture is permanently etched on every part of me. I can't escape their handiwork."

Liam didn't know how to respond to that. He clasped his hands and stared at them.

"I don't know what's wrong with me tonight," Emily tried to make light of her words, "I don't usually get so dark and twisted. It's not all that bad."

"I never thought about it like that." Liam said, "When I was still a beat cop, I remember dealing with women who had been raped but never —"

Emily shut her eyes tightly and grimaced, "Please don't say that word."

Liam looked up in surprise, "What word?"

Emily shook her head, "It doesn't matter, forget it."

"I won't forget it, what word? Rape?"

"Yes, please stop saying it." Emily repeated pathetically.

"I'm sorry, I won't say it again." Liam told her, "But you just said it?"

"I said sexual assault." Emily pointed out.

"It's the same thing though isn't it?"

"I know it's stupid." Emily said.

"It's not stupid. I don't think you should let a word hold so much power over you, but I can understand why it does."

Liam reached out and placed a hand on Emily's knee. "It's ridiculously early, but I don't see myself going back to sleep.

336

I need to head to the precinct early anyway, so why don't I make us some coffee?"

If anyone else had touched her like that, Emily would have pushed their hand away, but with Liam, she didn't feel uncomfortable with the touch.

"Coffee sounds great, but only if I can go outside for a smoke."

"Deal, come on."


Emily went through to the kitchen while Liam was pulling on pants and a t-shirt. She turned on the kettle, placing two cups on the counter she had found on the drying rack.

Liam came through, running a hand through his hair, making it even more tousled than it had been earlier. Again, Emily was reminded of the teenager he had once been.

He took over at the counter, pulling coffee out the cupboard. "Can you get the milk out the fridge?" he asked her.

Emily opened the fridge and took the milk out. The whole front of the fridge was covered in hand drawn pictures, all displaying Sophie's name scrawled at the bottom of the page. Emily smiled at the pictures before taking the milk to Liam.

"Thanks." He said, absentmindedly, putting sugar into the cups.


They took their coffee out the back door. Liam had a small round table and four chairs outside the door, so for a change Emily didn't have to sit on the step. She had brought her cigarettes through from the bedroom, so she sat down and immediately lit one.

"So, are you seriously considering coming to the fair with us?" Liam asked, taking a sip of his coffee and looking at Emily over the side of his cup.

"I believe I was invited as Sophie's plus one, not yours." Emily joked.

"Well, maybe you would be kind enough to let me chaperone you then." Liam laughed.

"I think I could be okay with that." Emily laughed too. "Is the fair the same as it was when we were kids?"

"Oh yeah, most of the rides are even the same ones, so you can feel nice and comfortable knowing the equipment holding you up in the air is older than dirt itself."

Emily laughed again, "That definitely sounds comforting."

"It's not all bad, lots of junk food and games and children running around high on cotton candy."

"I haven't had cotton candy in years," Emily mused, "not since the last fair I went to here probably."

"That's criminal." Liam stated deadpan, "We definitely need to rectify that situation on Friday night." He took another sip of coffee, "Were you planning on staying in town for the weekend?"

Emily shrugged, "I think so. I'll go see Casey today and spend some time with her, see how she's doing. Maybe I can even convince her to come to the fair with us tomorrow night. I need to talk to Paige as well, she has no idea about the lavender, and I need to make sure she's warned."

"Maybe I should come with you to speak to Paige, let her know that I've got someone watching the house."

Emily nodded in agreement.

"I'm also going to get a few deputies from surrounding counties to work the fair tomorrow night."

"Is that really necessary?" Emily asked.

"We usually have a couple here to make sure the teenagers behave, and I'll only add a few. I have a job to do and there is a serious threat out there."

"Maybe I should go home," Emily said thoughtfully, "Take the target off Paige and Casey."

Liam shook his head, "If anything, I think it will make the situation worse. The graffiti happened before you got here."

He had a point.

"We need to find the person responsible." Liam continued, "If you get anything else, please don't touch it, I want to send it to the lab."

Emily nodded contritely, "Sorry, I should have thought of that when I saw it."

"It's a natural instinct to pick it up and look at what it is." Liam reassured her. "What about that other delivery you had back home? Did the note have the florist's name on it?"

Emily nodded, "Yes, but I hacked into their online ordering system and the order was placed online and paid with a money order. There was no way to track it. I even tried to track the IP address of the computer the order came from, but it wasn't logged onto the florist's system."

Liam lifted an eyebrow, "Did you just tell a cop that you illegally hacked into a corporate online system?"

He sounded impressed.

"Are you going to arrest me again?" Emily asked, smiling over her cup of coffee.

"I could you know." Liam teased, "Actually, it would make this whole protection thing a lot easier if you were in a cell." He added thoughtfully.

"I don't need your protection Liam." Emily said, lighting another cigarette.

Liam's brow furrowed in irritation, but he didn't say anything. He looked towards the little house Emily had been staying in, keeping his thoughts to himself.

Emily's second cigarette was almost finished by the time Liam looked at her and spoke once more.

"I know you can take care of yourself, but you have to realise this asshole has been running around for nearly twenty years without justice being done. On top of that, you're already worried about Paige and Casey, what happens when the baby comes? How will you feel then?"

"You know I'm taking the baby?" Emily asked in surprise.

Liam nodded, "I wasn't prying, I was asking Paige how Casey was doing and she mentioned that you were considering adopting it."

"Him." Emily corrected. "And to be honest, I don't know how I would feel about it after he was born. I've always had this selfish thought that so long as he stayed away from me, I didn't care what happened to the other nameless, faceless girls out there."

"You didn't want him to be punished?" Liam asked.

"I wanted him to burn in hell," Emily corrected vehemently, "I wanted to be the one to send him there. But, I also didn't want to have to deal with it. If I did, I would have told the authorities back then about him." Emily's expression hardened, "I know it was cowardly, and I don't care."

Liam put his hand across the table as though to reach for Emily's, but he stopped short, "If there's one word I would never equate with you, it's cowardly." He told her, "You were a teenager who had been through hell, I can't imagine what you must have been feeling but I can definitely understand you not wanting to go through the process of trying to press charges."

"Even if it meant he went off and did it to others?" Emily asked quietly, revealing one of her deepest fears, "Every girl he hurt after me was my fault."

"Anyone he hurt after you was his fault." Liam insisted, "That's not on you."

"But I could have stopped him!" Emily insisted back.

Liam shrugged, "Maybe, but probably not. How would you have even been able to identify him back then?"

Emily stopped short. She hadn't considered that. "I don't know, the sound of his voice maybe?"

"Em, I've been a cop for a pretty long time, and now fortunately, things have changed a lot. But back then? It would have been impossible to prove with no evidence and chances are, even if they found the guy, he wouldn't have gone to jail. The system was fucked up back then. Abuse on women wasn't taken very seriously."

The truth in Liam's words sunk in. Emily felt as though the incredible weight of guilt she had been carrying around since she found out no one else knew about Stan's brother was starting to lessen. She bit her lip and stared at the stars, not knowing what to say.

Liam took his last sip of coffee, "So, a little boy huh? You thought of any names?"

Emily looked away from the stars and back at Liam, "I haven't even thought about it to be honest. I was kind of hoping it would be a girl, then I would have named her Claire."

"After your mom."

"Yeah." Emily bit her lip, "But a boy? I don't know. I guess I'll have to get one of those name books or something."

"Are you excited about becoming a mom?" Liam asked, watching her biting her lip and remembering the many times he had seen that habit when they were younger.

"Excited? Maybe. Terrified? Definitely."

Liam laughed, "Well, then you're about as ready as you're going to be. And if it helps, that feeling never goes away."

"I already feel sorry for the poor kid." Emily said, only half joking.

# Chapter Twenty-Seven

Emily arrived at Paige's home wishing she had gone back to sleep for an hour or two that morning. Instead, when Liam had left for work, she had taken her bags back to the little house of Paige's, had a shower and done some work on her laptop. She hadn't felt tired at the time, but now as she pulled into the driveway, her eyes were burning and felt scratchy.

She parked behind Liam's cruiser, relieved to know he had gotten there first and she didn't have to try speak to them alone.

She opened the car door and climbed out, feeling her hip click painfully as she did so. "Shit!" She muttered to herself, slamming the door a little harder than necessary.

"Emily? Are you alright?" Liam asked, coming around from the side of his police cruiser.

Emily hadn't seen him there, she turned to face him. "I'm fine, just stepped out the car funny."

Emily limped a few steps before the pain subsided enough for her to walk normally. Not limping was usually a conscious effort for her every single day, but when her hip clicked like that, the muscles would spasm, forcing her to limp until they loosened up again.

Paige opened the front door and smiled warmly at the two of them. "Good morning. Liam, this is a surprise."

"Morning Paige." Liam nodded, a tired smile of his own, "Would you mind if I joined Emily to have a quick word with you?"

"Of course not. Come on in." Paige said, "Does this have anything to do with the police officer who seemed to find himself glued to my driveway last night?"

"Yeah, there's some things we need to discuss." Emily told Paige as she entered the house. "Where's Casey and Daniel? I think they should hear this too."

Paige closed the door behind them, "Daniel's at work, but Casey's upstairs. I'll go call her, then I'll meet you in the kitchen."

Emily nodded at Paige, then gestured to Liam to follow her through to the kitchen.

Emily sat down on a stool at the kitchen table while Liam stood at the end of the table. Neither of them spoke as they waited for Paige and Casey to join them.

Casey entered the kitchen in her pajamas, her hair unkempt and messy. Her skin had broken out, her face covered in angry red spots.

"Hey Emily," she yawned as she approached, "Morning Sheriff, please excuse the PJs, not much else fits at the moment."

"No problem Casey," Liam replied, "How are you doing?"

"I'm okay thanks." Casey answered nonchalantly, taking a seat next to Emily.

"Hey Cas." Emily said.

"Your kid isn't letting me sleep at night." Casey complained, "I had such heartburn last night I wanted to cry."

"Sorry Cas, I promise to ground him the moment he's born. No walking or talking for at least seven months." Emily told her with a grin.

Casey laughed at her.

Paige walked past the table to the kettle. "Is everyone having coffee?"

"Tea please mom." Casey asked.

"Emily and Liam?" Paige asked, opening the cupboard to remove cups.

"Coffee please." The said in unison.


Liam waited until the coffee was served and Paige was sitting opposite Emily and Casey before speaking.

"As you already noticed, I placed a car on your property last night."

"So do you know who messed up the side of our house?" Casey asked, more alert.

Liam sighed, "Yes and no, we've got a pretty good idea of who's responsible, but unfortunately we don't know who that person is."

Casey pulled a face and looked at her mother in confusion, "What the hell does that mean?"

Emily cleared her throat. "When I first found out about the graffiti, I didn't really think twice about connections until Liam told me there was lavender found everywhere."

"What does lavender have to do with anything?" Paige asked, also looking confused.

"I've been receiving lavender back home and last night when I got back to the cottage after our dinner." Emily took a breath, "It's something that Stan's accomplice used to do when he came. He always brought lavender with him and threw it all around whenever he left."

Paige put a hand to her mouth in shock. "Do you think it's him?"

Liam answered, "We're not sure. As far as I understand, Emily never told anyone about the lavender or the second perpetrator. There was nothing written about it in the files I have on Stan. I'm still waiting for more files from the previous sheriff to arrive so I can look for any leads of a second person."

Casey seemed frozen in shock since Emily had spoken.

"Casey, I'm so sorry, I never wanted you to get involved." Emily told her, but Casey didn't respond.

"So what do we do now?" Paige asked worriedly.

Liam's gaze had been focused on Casey, but when Paige spoke he turned his attention to her. "You will have someone watching the house permanently until we can figure out who the perpetrator is. We'll keep you all safe, don't worry."

Paige nodded slowly, "And what about Emily? Is she being watched as well? Especially if they've reached her here and in the city."

"I'll make sure all of you are safe." Liam assured her.

Paige looked relieved at Liam's words, but Casey still seemed to be in shock.

"Casey?" Liam asked gently.

Casey looked up at him as though surprised to see him there. "Yeah?"

"I'm going to make sure you're all safe, I promise you."

Tears glistened in Casey's eyes, "You don't get it. He knows what happened to us. He knows what we've been through. He gets off on the idea of what's been done to us. We're marked with it and we'll always be targets. Monsters like him can smell it on us.

We'll never be safe, not me, not Emily and not my baby."

Emily was shocked by Casey's words. "That's not true Cas, you'll be okay, I promise. This isn't about you. I should never have come back here. You being involved is my fault."

Casey turned to Emily, her expression blank, "Yes, this is your fault, and now we all have to pay."

Without another word, Casey stood up and left the lounge, leaving the others in shocked silence.

"I think I'm going to head back to the city." Emily said quietly to the others after a while.

"I don't think that's a good idea— " Liam began, but Emily stood up, interrupting him.

"I think you should go ahead and phone that adoption agency Paige." Emily's voice was shaky, "I'm really sorry you all got dragged into this."

"Emily wait!" Paige called out, but it was too late, Emily had already rushed out of the kitchen, down the passage and out the front door.

By the time Liam got to the door to follow her, Emily was already reversing out of the driveway. She didn't look back towards the house as she turned into the street.

Emily screeched into the driveway of the cottage, gravel from the driveway spraying onto the grass. She had just put the key into the front door when Liam's cruiser made an equally violent stop in front of the cottage, parking the rented SUV in.

Liam got out of the cruiser just as Emily got the door open. She stepped inside but turned around and stood in the doorway, one hand on the door, ready to slam it at a moment's notice.

"Whatever you're here to say Liam, I don't want to hear it." Emily said bluntly.

"Please just wait a minute, before you make any decisions." Liam said, hurrying up the drive to get to the door before Emily closed it.

"What for? I have no reason to stay." Emily said stubbornly.

"Actually there's a few reasons to stay." Liam replied, relieved that she hadn't moved from the door.

"Such as?"

"I was hoping you would help me go through the files on Stan when they arrive, you might have insight no one else will have."

Emily glared at him, "So let me get this straight, you want me to go over the official record of what that sick fuck did to me so that you can do your job?"

Liam stopped short. "I, I didn't think about it like that."

"You cops are real understanding of a victim's mental wellbeing." Emily said sarcastically.

"Look, I know it's a big ask," Liam said, trying to calm her down, "but I could really use your help. I want to stop this monster as badly as you do. Preferably before he hurts someone we care about."

Emily seemed to deflate. She leant against the door frame. "That's not fair you know." She told him quietly.

"I know," he replied just as quietly, "but even if there's the smallest chance you'll find something the rest of us would miss, don't you think it's worth a shot?"

Emily sighed irritably.

"Besides," Liam said, smiling slightly, "You promised my daughter a date to the fair tomorrow night."

Emily shook her head, "Fine, I'll stay until Saturday morning, but that's it. If your files aren't here by then, I'm leaving anyway."

"Fair enough." Liam agreed, relieved that she was going to stay.

Emily straightened up, "If you don't mind, I'm going to go inside and get some sleep now."

"Of course. If you need anything at all, you have my mobile number." Liam looked at her with a tender expression, "Casey's just scared and hormonal, you know she didn't mean what she said right?"

"Whether she meant it or not, I think she was right. I'm not the kind of person that should be raising a kid. It should have been a sign when I lost the ability to have my own."

"I'm sorry, but I don't believe that. I've seen a lot of shitty parents, especially when I was still in the city. Those people should never have had kids, but they did. You wouldn't be a shitty parent."

"You couldn't know that." Emily protested.

"I've seen you with my kid." Liam said, "I've seen the way you deal with her and the way she looks at you. Kids know when someone is inherently good and trustworthy. So I do know."

Emily looked away from Liam, too embarrassed by his words to face him.

Liam touched her shoulder, "You get some rest now, I'll come past later if you don't mind and see how you are."

"See you Liam." Emily said, going inside and closing the door behind her.

Emily thought about making something to eat, but decided lying down was a better idea. She went through to her bedroom, kicked off her boots and flopped onto the bed, fully clothed.

Lying on her back Emily clasped her hands and put them behind her head. She sighed heavily, unsure if the sinking feeling in her stomach was because of exhaustion, the threat of some sicko hanging over their heads or Casey's earlier outburst. Probably all three she decided, closing her eyes and trying to ignore the feeling of impending doom.

Ten minutes later, Emily sat up in frustration. She couldn't shut her mind off, thoughts of Casey and the baby kept swirling through her mind. She was worried about their safety, but she was also worried that her chance to be a mother had just been snatched away from her.

Even though she had been so undecided about the baby, knowing that Casey no longer wanted her to have the baby left a hole in her chest that Emily hadn't felt since her mother had died.

What she wouldn't do to be able to talk to her mother about all this. Emily had spent most of her life alone, but never before this moment had she felt so desperately lonely.

Emily pulled her boots back on, making a split-second decision. She knew she should probably let Liam know where she was going but she didn't want to be followed or asked if she were okay.

She arrived at the cemetery ten minutes later and parked her car in the same spot she used the last time.

Emily left her mobile in the car and walked over to her mother's grave.

Sitting down on the ground next to the grave marker, Emily ran her fingers across the name engraved on the concrete.

She tried to imagine what her mother would tell her in this situation, what insight she would have into Emily's emotions. Emily knew her mother would probably know just what to say, but she couldn't imagine what that could be. The problems she had had as a small child were so insignificant compared to now. Her mother had always taken Emily's problems or worries very seriously though and would sit with her for as long as it took to talk it through and find a solution.

This situation wasn't as simple as Bobby Radler pulling Emily's hair in preschool though, there was no easy remedy this time.

Emily knew her mother would have encouraged her to have a baby, even if it wasn't Casey's baby. Claire had loved babies and children and had often told Emily she hoped to teach her grandkids the same things she taught Emily.

Knowing that her mother missed out on so much was painful. That she never got the chance to be a grandmother was cruel and unfair.

Emily heard a twig snap nearby and looked towards the source.

"You're here twice in one week." Her father said in way of greeting.

"So are you." Emily replied, turning back to her mother's grave.

"I got the morning off." Mitchell Winter told her gruffly. He knelt down and carefully removed a dead flower from the cup, flicking it towards the tree.

Emily didn't have a response to that, so they were silent while he moved the better flowers to the front.

"I loved her you know." He told Emily in a gruff voice, "I know the older you got, the less you thought I loved your mother, but I loved her more than anything."

"You don't need to convince me." Emily replied quietly, surprised her father noticed her feelings when she was younger at all.

"I wasn't a good father, I know that." He continued as though Emily hadn't spoken. "Your mom was so good with you that I was never needed. Fathers didn't get involved so much back then, and I was worse than most."

"Listen..."

"No, you listen," he said, still looking at his wife's tiny grave marker, "when I lost her, I lost everything. I didn't know what I was doing with you and I just wanted her back. You looked so much like her that it hurt just to look at you."

"I don't think I look like her." Emily stated.

"Maybe not the hair, and you got my chin, but your eyes, the way you look through people, that was just like her. She could look into my eyes and I swear she was staring into my soul. You used to do that to me too." Mitchell shook his head sadly, "Only, when she looked at me, I saw love in her eyes. When you looked at me, there was only disgust."

352

"What did you expect?" Emily asked him, feeling attacked, "I lost the only person who took care of me. You loved the bottle way more than you ever loved me!"

"Aren't you listening girl?" Mitchell growled, "I couldn't stand to look at you."

"I was a child!" Emily almost yelled.

He stood up and looked at his daughter. "You were, and I had no idea how much I was hurting you. I was selfish, and damn right I drank too much. I was so wrapped up in my own pain that I didn't have space to deal with yours. That's no excuse, it is what it is. I know I let you down Emily, I tried later, when you were in the hospital, but you didn't want anything to do with me."

"I never saw you at the hospital, Paige said you just sat outside, what part of that is trying?"

"I was a coward! Is that what you want to hear? I was so scared I was going to lose you too. I knew I should be sitting in that room with you. But the one time I was in there you threw something at me. I didn't think you wanted me in there with you. And seeing you like that? It was too hard. Your mother would have been devastated."

Emily vaguely remembered throwing a jelly or custard cup at her father at one point, but couldn't remember why.

"What do you want from me?" Emily asked warily, not rising to the bait. Telling her how her mother would have felt wasn't what she wanted to hear.

"I wouldn't ask anything of you. I lost my chance to have a daughter a long time ago." Mitchell shook his head, "You should know though, I've been sober since the night you ran off. But by the stories going around town, you got more from me than just my chin."

"You don't get to judge me." Emily said stubbornly.

"I'm not judging." Mitchell sighed, looking older than he should. "Just concern from an old man who doesn't want to see you follow in his footsteps."

Mitchell dusted off his hands and started walking away. He was two rows away when he turned back and called, "I loved you too, I know you don't believe that, but I did. I still do, always will."

Emily had turned away from him when he had walked away and she didn't turn to look at him when he spoke. She heard his words, clearly carried by the breeze, but she had no response to them. She had no idea what she was feeling. She had so many emotions tearing her up inside that she didn't have space for more.

Life was certainly easier when she had denied any and all emotions.

Emily placed her hand gently on her mother's name before standing up and brushing herself off. Her hip clicked loudly again as she was getting to her feet. Emily grunted in pain, furious with her leg for letting her down twice in one day.

Deciding it was time to get well and truly drunk, Emily made her way back to her car, not bothering to hide the limp, intending to spend the rest of the day drinking and watching movies.

She stopped at the bottle store and was walking the aisles, deciding what to buy when the bell above the door jingled. Cathy Richards had entered the shop, leaning heavily on a cane. She was looking as thin as the last time Emily had seen her and her makeup wasn't done. Emily didn't think she had ever seen the woman out in public without makeup. Even her hair was tied back in a messy bun as opposed to the normally perfectly blow dried style she had used for the last few decades. Emily considered greeting her, but decided after their last encounter that avoiding her would be the better option.

Emily took two bottles of tequila and a bottle of gin to the counter to pay. She handed her credit card to the old man at the register, packed her own bottles into a paper bag to speed up the process and left the shop as soon as he handed her the receipt and her card.

Emily had barely opened the driver's door when the door swung open again and Cathy limped towards her.

"I really thought you couldn't sink any lower." Cathy said to Emily in an eerily friendly voice.

"Excuse me?" Emily asked, throwing the paper bag on the driver's seat and slamming the door shut. Her anger had reached boiling point and she was ready for a fight, she didn't care who it was with.

"Why did you have to come back here?" Cathy wailed miserably, ignoring Emily's question. "Things were good without you here."

Realizing the woman was close to being hysterical and more than a little drunk, Emily decided this wasn't the fight she needed after all, her anger dissipated as quickly as it had risen. She shook her head, "I don't have time for this." She said calmly, turning back towards her car.

"I was happy!" Cathy screeched, causing the cashier to look out the window of the bottle store curiously.

"And I'm the one that made you unhappy?" Emily asked her incredulously.

"If you hadn't come back here, we wouldn't have talked about you and he would still love me." Cathy said loudly, not seeming to care that people were starting to stare.

"Whatever your issues are with Liam," Emily said patiently, "They're between the two of you, I don't want anything to do with it."

"I'm not talking about William!" Cathy spat in irritation.

"So who are you talking about then?" Emily was confused now. She took a few steps closer to Cathy, in hopes that the older woman would lower her voice.

"Why would I tell you?" Cathy scoffed, "So you can steal him away like you do with every other man you want?"

"Don't." Emily warned.

"First my son, then Stan, I wouldn't trust you around anyone."

Emily closed the gap between them, itching to slap the woman. She lent in close and said quietly. "You know damn well I didn't want anything to do with Stan."

"He wanted you though." Cathy laughed then hiccupped, her breath smelling of vermouth.

"That wasn't my choice!" Emily snarled at her. "And since we're throwing accusations around, staying with your abusive piece of shit husband was your choice. Allowing him to hurt your son the way he did, over and over? That was also your choice."

Cathy went pale.

"Yeah, I knew about it. I was the only one he could talk to because his own mother let it happen."

"Damn you to hell girl." Cathy said in a quiet, quivery voice. "Everything I ever did was for William's own good."

"Bullshit, do you know how broken Liam was when we met?" Emily said in disbelief.

"Of course I knew," Cathy said dismissively, "I was doing everything I could to give him a good life."

"Letting your husband brutalise your son was for his own good?" Emily asked in disbelief.

"Don't you judge me girl." Cathy pointed her finger in Emily's face, "I got between them every chance I could. I protected him every time I got."

"Leaving that monster would have been better." Emily snarled. "And judging by his scars, you didn't protect him much."

"I stayed for William!" Cathy spat, "I was miserable and terrified most of my adult life. But we couldn't leave. We would have had nothing. Frank would have left us penniless. How would I have put him through a good school and college huh?"

Emily swallowed. She didn't have any response to that. Cathy lowered her hand and straightened up, the old pride coming back. "Everything I have ever done has been for my son, whether you believe it or not."

Emily looked at the older woman's hands, so tightly clasped in front of her, clutching the cane. She knew Cathy was trying to hold it together in front of her.

"Why didn't you leave when Liam was in college then?" She asked quietly.

"I was going to, but there was no way a young man would have wanted his mother with him in college." She gave weary smile, "Frank and I had been together so long I wouldn't know how to be alone anymore. I stayed because it's all I know. And because he would have killed me eventually, no matter how far I ran. He would have found me and he would have killed me."

Cathy turned and hobbled off towards her car, leaving Emily to stare after her. Emily gave herself a mental shake and went back to her own car. She put the key in the ignition but didn't start the car. She was wondering what it must feel like to spend your whole life scared of being hurt by the person you live with. Emily knew she had been through something incredibly traumatic, but at least it hadn't been for so many decades in her own home. Her home was her refuge, her safe place. She couldn't imagine being afraid for herself in her own home all the time, let alone afraid for her own kid.

Emily looked out the passenger window and saw that Cathy was still parked next to her. The other woman seemed to be yelling at her steering wheel.

Emily told herself it wasn't her problem. She turned on the ignition and put the car in reverse, but didn't take her foot of the brake. She was still watching Cathy, who seemed to be trying to start her own car with no luck.

Emily sighed and put her car back into park. Turning off the motor, she climbed out of the rented SUV and went round to Cathy's driver's window and knocked on the glass now.

Cathy opened the window slightly and said in irritation. "What do you want now?"

"Won't it start?" Emily asked.

"What do you think?" Cathy asked sarcastically, turning the key to no effect.

"Did you leave the lights on or something?"

"No I didn't." Cathy snapped. She slammed her hand against the steering wheel. "I'm going to have to call a tow."

"Leave the key with the shop manager," Emily suggested, pointing towards the bottle store, "I'll give you a ride home."

"I'll wait thank you." Cathy said crisply.

"Cathy, it's getting cloudy, it's going to rain. It's just a lift. Standing around in the cold waiting for a tow won't help your knee."

"I don't need your help."

"I know you don't, but I'm offering anyway. You don't want to be out here when all the schools get out and all the local mothers are in town gossiping."

She had hit the mark. Cathy sighed loudly but collected her handbag, her walking stick and the packet of booze she had just bought. Getting out the car, she handed the keys to Emily. "Take the keys to the teller, I'll call Freddy to come get it. Please." She added as an afterthought.

Emily raised an eyebrow at the order but took the keys to the teller as instructed. By the time she got back, Cathy was already in the passenger seat of the car, on her mobile.

She ended the call as Emily climbed into the driver's seat. Cathy sniffed disapprovingly, "This car stinks of cigarette smoke."

"It's allowed," Emily said carelessly as she put the car in reverse again and started pulling out of the parking, "I checked."

"Kindly don't smoke while I'm in here with you."

"Wasn't planning to." Emily said in the same breezy tone.

They rode in silence while Emily navigated the main road, but once they got onto the outskirts heading towards

Cathy's house, Cathy looked out the window but spoke. "You don't have children, do you?"

"No, I don't." Emily replied.

"I know you may not think I'm a good mother and I know you don't believe I did what was best for my son, but let me tell you something. The instant I found out that I was carrying a child, I knew that there would never be a moment of my life from then on that I didn't put that child's needs in front of my own. You won't understand it until you have children of your own, but everything I ever did was so that he could have the best life I could offer him, even if he never saw it that way."

Emily drummed her fingers on the steering wheel. "Why did you treat me like shit all the time when we were dating then? Was that also for his own good?"

"What would have happened to Liam if you stayed with him?"

"Um, we would have carried on seeing each other?" Emily asked, not understanding the question.

"I saw the way he looked at you. He would have sacrificed his future for you. He would have refused to go to college if it meant leaving you. He would have ended up in this small town with no future."

"What makes you think I wasn't going to college?" Emily asked, stung by the insult.

"Where could you have afforded to go besides some community college?" Cathy said dismissively, waving a hand, "Liam went to one of the most prestigious schools in the country."

"Just for your information, I had every intention of going to college. My GPA was high enough that I would have had my choice of Ivy League schools. The guidance counsellor confirmed I would have been given a full ride to any school of my choice."

"Well I didn't know that, did I?" Cathy said. "I was so sure you were going to get yourself pregnant the first chance you got to make sure you had him trapped. You knew he was the kind of boy to stick with you."

"Okay, that's really insulting. And for your second revelation of the day, Liam and I never slept together."

"Rubbish!" Cathy scoffed, "I saw you two often enough, you couldn't keep your hands off each other."

"That doesn't mean we were having sex!" Emily shook her head, "Believe it, don't believe it, but we made a promise to wait until college when we were both old enough to know what we were doing."

"Well how was I supposed to know that?"

"You could have asked!" Emily exploded, "You could have given me the slightest bit of credit and bothered to try find out what sort of person I was, rather than making assumptions because of my family's financial status!"

They were approaching Cathy's driveway. Cathy turned to Emily with an almost regretful look on her face, "I never bothered to get to know you because you were never going to be good enough for William, and we both know that."

Emily pulled the car to a stop and unlocked the doors. "That's true, I won't argue that, but that wasn't your choice to make was it? I thought you wanted him to be happy."

"Of course I wanted him to be happy." Cathy said, collecting her belongings.

"Just so long as it was your idea of happiness and not his." Emily commented.

# Chapter Twenty-Eight

**L**iam slammed the phone down in frustration. He had been trying to get hold of his predecessor for the last few hours but the phone just rang and rang.

"Problem boss?" Muriel stuck her head in the door. She had been running the daytime front desk shift for the last few years.

"Do we have a forwarding address on file for Sheriff Brown?" Liam asked.

"Probably. Want me to go find it?"

"Please Muriel."

"Okay dokes. I'm going to bring you some lemonade first though, you look like you could use a glass."

"Thanks." Liam said. He ran his fingers through his hair irritably. He needed those files. He felt like he was playing a game of chess, but his opponent was always five moves ahead of him.

Liam didn't know where else to look. No one involved remembered ever seeing a man fitting Emily's description.

Liam had gone through all the arrest reports two years prior to the incident and the two years following, hoping to find something, anything that might tell him who the man was. He had hoped to find a speeding ticket or some minor misdemeanor at least, but there was nothing.

The only explanation that Liam could think of was that the man was from out of town and had come through purely to do what he did with Stan then left again.

His last hope now was the rest of the files that were supposed to be on their way to him. Liam wondered why the previous sheriff had removed the files in the first place. Regardless of Emily's father's wishes, it was against protocol, and from what Liam had seen, in all other respects, Sheriff Brown had been a stickler for the rules.

Emily was sitting on the couch, a bottle of tequila resting between her knees. Instead of watching the comedy playing on the television, Emily was replaying her encounter with Cathy over in her mind. She had been so insulted by the woman's assumptions of her that Emily had wanted to pull over and kick her out of the car. The ironic thing is that Emily had turned out just as Cathy had expected, no college, a bad influence and a very bad choice for Liam. Ironically too that Liam had done exactly what Cathy had wanted and here he was, still living the small-town life. She wondered how Cathy felt about that and about how she must have treated her daughter-in-law. Emily couldn't imagine Liam allowing Cathy to treat his wife with any disrespect.

Emily knew she wasn't good enough for Liam, she knew it then, just as she knew it now, but it didn't stop Cathy's words from stinging. As for the revelations of her life with her husband and why she stayed for all those years, Emily found she couldn't stay angry with the woman for what had been thought about her. In a lot of ways, she just felt sorry for Cathy.

Emily wondered how much Liam knew. Cathy had demanded that Emily never say a word to Liam about their conversation that afternoon, she said she had kept her son out of it for a reason, but surely he would want to know? She wondered if it would make a difference now.

Did her own father's confessions she had heard that day make a difference? Emily wasn't sure. She didn't have place in her thoughts to dwell on it. It wouldn't do any good now anyway, there was no chance of them ever having a father-daughter relationship. She didn't even want one.

And as for him commenting on her drinking, what a cheek. She pictured him passed out in his chair all those years ago when she had run away and scoffed to herself.

Picking up the bottle, Emily took another swig, wanting to make her thoughts fuzzy and less depressing.

∞

She heard the footsteps above her and wondered whose turn it was now. She watched as Stan's shiny dress shoes made their way down the rickety wooden steps and sighed with relief. At least he wasn't always vicious. Stan was still better than his brother.

"Hello my dear."

"Hello." Emily croaked, desperately hoping the tin cup in his hand had water for her.

"Are you thirsty little one?" He knelt down beside her.

Emily nodded, too scared to speak in case he took the water away again. He didn't. He helped her hold her head up enough for two meagre sips then took the cup away from her and placed it beside him.

Emily could see he was in one of his gentler moods and tried to make use of it. "My arms really hurt, please can you rub them?"

Stan studied her for a moment then did as she asked, his hands spending little time on her arms before roaming down her shoulders and stopping at her breasts. He tugged at the remaining nipple and smiled when it hardened under his fingertips. He ran his other hand down her belly and dipped his fingers between her legs. "Tell me how much you love me little one. Tell me how much you want me."

Emily tried desperately to stop her body from reacting, but against her will she could feel his fingers slipping into wetness. "I love you." She whispered, "Please unlock me."

Stan pulled his hand away and used his left hand to squeeze her breast painfully, "You're playing with me."

"I'm not!" Emily protested, shaking her head, "Please."

"You think I'm stupid?" He yelled, unbuttoning his shirt while he continued to squeeze her sensitive skin, "I'll show you games."

"No! Please!"

∞

Loud pounding on the front door woke Emily from the disjointed nightmare. She had fallen asleep on the couch without meaning to. She sat up, kicking the empty tequila bottle on the floor by accident.

"Emily!" Liam's frantic yell could be heard through the door.

"I'm coming!" Emily yelled back groggily. She heaved herself off the couch and walked unsteadily to the front door.

"Why the hell didn't you answer your damn phone?" Liam demanded as soon as the door opened.

"I was asleep." Emily muttered irritably, leaning against the door frame for support.

"I was worried sick! I nearly broke the door down." Liam was exasperated.

"I don't think Paige would have appreciated that." Emily giggled, struggling with the words.

"Are you drunk?" Liam asked.

"Why yes officer, I am. And since I'm not driving or in public," She emphasised the word 'public', "you can't arrest me this time."

"I wasn't going to arrest you, Jesus Emily. Are you alright?"

"I'm here aren't I?" Emily gestured wildly around her, "You didn't want me to go home, so I stayed, just like you ordered."

"Can I come in?" Liam asked.

Emily swung the door open wider with a flourish, "Come on in. If you're really good I'll let you frisk me."

Liam closed the door behind him and locked it. Walking into the living room he saw the empty bottle on the floor. "You can drink an entire bottle and stay standing?" He asked Emily in amazement.

"Correction, I could probably drink two or three. And for your information, I was sleeping, not standing when you arrived."

Emily flopped back onto the couch, feeling suddenly dizzy.

"Why don't I make us some coffee?" Liam suggested.

"Why don't you bring the other bottle of tequila off the counter and we can play a drinking game?" Emily countered.

"I think coffee might be a better idea for now." Liam said reasonably.

"Fine," Emily waved a hand dismissively in his direction, "make yourself coffee and bring back the tequila for me."

Liam returned from the kitchen a few minutes later with two coffees and a bottle water tucked under his arm.

"That's not tequila." Emily pouted.

"No it's not," Liam agreed, putting a coffee and the water on the table in front of her, "careful, the coffee's really hot and really strong." He couldn't help but smile at her expression, she looked like a child whose trip to Disney World had just been cut short.

Emily grumbled incoherently, but picked up her coffee and took a sip. "Shit!" she exclaimed, burning her tongue.

Liam said down next to her with his own cup, "I told you it was hot."

Emily put the coffee down and picked up the water instead, "Yes, thanks for that." She said sarcastically. She took a long drink of water then looked over at Liam quizzically. "Why are you here? Have you got the files of misery you want me to go through?"

Liam took a sip of his coffee before placing his cup next to Emily's. "No, they haven't arrived yet. I was coming over to check on you."

"I'm fine." Emily insisted.

"I know that, but there is some creep out there trying to mess with you remember?"

"Bleh," Emily said, "let him come. I don't care."

"Well I do care." Liam said, "And while you might not care about yourself, I do know you care about Paige and Casey. And your baby."

"Not my baby." Emily corrected, "Some random stranger's baby. Definitely a good thing too, what kind of a role model would this be?" she pointing towards herself and pulling a face.

"Did something happen today? Did you get another package?"

"Nope," Emily said, "I told you I would give it to you if I did. I just had one too many heart to hearts today."

"You mean the thing with Casey?"

"Nuh-uh. I mean with my dear father and then with your dear mother."

Liam looked surprised.

"Did you know your mama stuck it out with your shithead father so she could afford to send you to college?"

"Maybe we should discuss this in the morning." Liam said carefully, taking his cup to have a sip before putting his coffee back on the table.

"She told me that if she had left him, you would have been broke."

"It's always been about money and comfort for that woman." Liam said, picking up his coffee again.

"Nope, she wanted to leave him while you were in college, but she was too scared he was going to kill her." Emily said, trying to take another sip of water but missing her mouth. "He probably would have too." She added as an afterthought.

"Let's talk about something else." Liam said, feeling uncomfortable.

"Okay." Emily agreed, wiping her wet shirt half-heartedly. She leant over until she was resting her head on Liam's shoulder. "Or we could just fuck instead." She suggested sleepily.

"Maybe that's also something we can talk about tomorrow." Liam responded.

"You think I'm ugly and broken." Emily whispered, not moving.

"I think you're beautiful." Liam whispered back, kissing the top of Emily's head.

In moments Emily was snoring softly.

∞

Emily felt a burning sensation on her thigh, it started slowly but built up until it felt as though someone were holding a blowtorch against her flesh. She moaned, too weak to scream out.

"Shh." Stan said in the muted light of a lantern, "This infection looks really bad, I'm trying to clean it."

The burning intensified, but now that Emily was awake, she could smell the sharp scent of disinfectant.

"Please, please just let me die." She whispered to the man she once admired and trusted.

"We can't do that." Stan chided, "You are mine and I am yours, it's my duty to take care of you."

"You're not mine." Emily said, trying once more to get on his good side as she had been doing the last few days, "And I can't be yours because you're not the only one who has me."

"Ah my little one," Stan said, moving the soiled gauze he was using to her still-seeping breast, "but I'm the only one that loves you."

While the bigger man was more violent, Stan scared Emily more with the way he spoke. Air hissed through her teeth as the disinfectant touched her open wound.

"You're not mine." Emily said again, moaning as Stan swabbed roughly.

"Of course I am." Stan said, smiling. Not the reassuring smile he used in church, but a maniacal smile that twisted his whole face into something gross and unnatural.

"How can I be?" Emily asked carefully, "When I'm never allowed to touch you?" She pulled pathetically on the shackles with her right wrist, since her left arm was still useless.

"That's because I can't trust you little girl." Stand told her.

"Please, let me touch you." Emily begged, disgusting herself.

Stan sat back on his heels and looked at her thoughtfully. "I have longed for your touch for so long. Since you were a little girl and you used to look at me with those wanton eyes." He said, nodding to himself, "Perhaps just the one hand then. Then we can finally be one, the way it was written."

Emily tried not to look too relieved as Stan went to the other side of the room to take the key off its hook on the wall.

When he returned, he kneeled beside her and kissed her on the mouth. Emily knew if she turned away, he would change his mind, so she kissed him back, fighting the urge to bite off the tongue that was violating her mouth.

Finally, he took the key and unlocked the ancient shackle around her raw and bloody right wrist. Emily's arm had been above her head for so long that she didn't have the strength to bring it down next to her body, she had to wait like a small child for Stan to do it for her.

By the time he was done cleaning and dressing her wounds though, Emily had started to get a little feeling back in her fingers.

Stan climbed on top of her, leaning down for another kiss. Emily wrapped her weakened arm around his neck as tightly as possible and moved her mouth the moment his face was close enough, biting down on flesh on his jaw as hard as she could.

Stan roared in pain and pulled back, grabbing his bleeding jawline with one hand and bringing the other fist down against Emily's face.

∞

Emily opened her eyes groggily, she looked around feeling disoriented. The last thing she remembered was sitting on the couch with Liam, but now she was in bed, under the covers. The room was dark, the curtains drawn. Emily reached over to turn on the bedside lamp. Next to the lamp sat both her mobiles, a bottle of water, two aspirin, a can of soda and a note. Emily sat up, wincing as pain shot through her head and picked up the note.

*Soda is my go-to for hangovers. Take two aspirin and call me when you wake up, I'll bring you greasy food. I took your spare key so I could lock when I left, I will return it later. Feel better ~ Liam.*

Emily swallowed the two aspirin, drinking almost the entire bottle of water before opening the soda and sitting back against the headboard with her mobile.

She found a text from Paige, *Please can we meet before you leave? Just quickly if you're in a hurry. I can come to the cottage.*

Emily saw the text had come through earlier in the afternoon. She quickly typed out a reply, *I'll be here until Saturday morning, Liam wants me to go through some files with him. Is it ok if I stay at the cottage until then?*

Emily took another sip of the sweet soda and put the can aside.

*You're welcome to call it home for as long as you need. Can I come over? I'll bring burgers and wine.*

Emily's stomach growled loudly, *Sounds good. See you soon.*

It was already dark outside, Emily went to the bathroom to brush her teeth and straighten up a little. She made herself some coffee in the kitchen and texted Liam, *Hey, I'm up and only slightly mortified. I have to stop doing that around you... Paige is coming over for dinner, so I'll chat to you later.*

Emily took her coffee out the back and sat on the step to have a cigarette. She had been smoking less lately, but there didn't seem much point in quitting now.

Lighting one and drawing deeply, Emily tried to remember everything she said to Liam earlier. She still felt a little drunk so she was battling to get her thoughts together. Suddenly she remembered telling him about his mother. Shit, she thought to herself. She was going to have to talk to him about that. It wasn't fair of her to say what she said without explaining herself. More than that, she had decided, Liam had a right to know, even if Cathy disagreed.

Propositioning him she remembered all too clearly and was so humiliated. She kept doing that to him when she was drunk, he must truly think she is a whore. Even if she wasn't when they were younger, she certainly behaved like one now. Emily groaned at her own stupidity. All she was doing was pushing him away.

She knew they couldn't have a relationship. She lived in the city and he was in Hawthorne, neither of them would be willing to move. And Sophie needed a better role model than Emily could offer. Not to mention, Emily knew she would screw up the relationship sooner or later, hurting both Liam and Sophie.

She snorted to herself, thinking that Liam would even consider a relationship with her in the first place was ridiculous. They had kissed once and it was only because he was wracked with guilt and she took advantage. Men like Liam didn't want women like her. Liam was too good. He needed some one more like his late wife, not a borderline alcoholic who had slept with more people than she could count.

Emily rubbed her face with her hands. She was tired and angry with herself. The tequila had left an awful taste in her mouth, even after brushing her teeth and she couldn't shake the faint feeling of nausea she had woken up with.

Emily swallowed the last of her coffee and lit another cigarette. Her mobile buzzed in her pocket.

*Arranging a patrol outside the cottage and the McKenzies. If you're still awake when I get home I'll come past.*

Emily wasn't sure she wanted him to come over, she was too embarrassed to face him, but at the same time, she knew she needed to tell him about her conversation with his mother. Helping Cathy in some small way was the least Emily could do before she left. Maybe something good could come out of her trip to town after all.

Thinking of Liam and Cathy's relationship made Emily think of her father again and what he had said that day. She wasn't sure why he thought it was so important that she knew he loved Claire. Looking back, Emily didn't really remember much of her parents' relationship. There were a few family dinners and maybe a few times that Emily had crept down the stairs at night to see them cuddling on the couch, but she couldn't remember any real conversations between them.

He was right in his assumption about her own beliefs though, Emily thought, she had never believed that her father loved her mother very much. The older she got, the more certain she was that Mitchell didn't care about anyone but himself and his next drink.

Why he bothered to try and defend himself as a father, Emily didn't know. What did he care now? He already admitted he lost his chance to be a father, so why did he even bother to tell Emily? She already knew he was a coward and that he couldn't step up when she had needed a parent, he didn't need to remind her of that. Was he looking for forgiveness? Emily wasn't sure. It's not like he even apologised, just made excuses.

Thinking of her father reminded her of why she chose to mainline tequila earlier. Emily flicked her cigarette into the darkness and went back into the house, being careful to lock the door behind her.

Cathy Richards was sitting in her living room, staring at the blank wall wondering how things had fallen so spectacularly apart in such a short space of time. She swirled the clear liquid in her glass around slowly, not drinking any.

She knew it was her fault. She knew she had treated that girl terribly. Years before and now again. She also knew that if she were going to have any sort of relationship with her son and grandchild, she was going to have to swallow her pride and apologise to her. And hope to hell Emily told William about it. Christian was another matter. He still wasn't taking her calls or responding to messages. She had a feeling that even if she did apologise to both him and Emily, it would still be too late.

Everything he had said that night so many months ago had been true. She was selfish and far too proud. She had taken him for granted and he was the one man on earth who had treated her with love and consideration. She didn't deserve him. Christian deserved to be with the type of woman who would be proud to be his wife, one that would bore him beautiful children that would have the same kind, thoughtful heart that he had.

Silent tears ran down Cathy's face as she sat alone. She had made so many mistakes in her life and she was finally paying the price.

# Chapter Twenty-Nine

Emily opened the front door of the cottage when she heard Paige's car pull up to the drive. She met her at the car, taking the takeout bag from her so that Paige could get her bag and a bottle of wine off the passenger seat.

"Thanks for letting me come." Paige said, climbing out the car and locking it.

"You brought food, I wasn't going to say no." Emily replied flippantly. She was actually nervous about having Paige come over. She wasn't sure she wanted to hear what Paige had to say. She waved to the middle-aged policeman sitting in the cruiser across the road.

"I brought wine too. Don't forget the wine." Paige smiled, holding up the bottle.

"That's true," Emily said, walking into the cottage, "But I must be honest, I think I already boozed myself out for the day."

"More for me then." Paige said cheerfully, putting the bottle on the kitchen table, then going back to close and lock the front door.

Emily took plates out and the bottle opener, while Paige took two glasses down from the cupboard.

"Are you going to have one glass at least?" Paige asked, opening the bottle.

"Sure, why not." Emily shrugged, "But if I pass out or get messy drunk, don't hold it against me."

Paige laughed, "Fair enough. Let's sit at the table shall we?"

Emily took the food and plates to the little dining table and sat down. When Paige joined her, she took a glass from Paige and handed the other woman a plate.

"So, about this morning." Paige said cautiously, pouring the open wine into the two glasses. "Firstly, I want to apologise, you must have been very hurt by what Casey said."

"I wasn't hurt," Emily said, suddenly losing her appetite, "She was telling the truth. None of this would have happened if I hadn't come back to this place."

"Well if you want to play the blame game like that, then it's my fault that all of this happened. I'm the one that asked you to come." Paige pointed out.

"You didn't start this Paige."

"Neither did you! The only person to blame here is the one painting houses and leaving threats."

"If I had just spoken up about him back then..." Emily drifted off.

"If I had just not taken you to that church when you were a child," Paige countered, "if I had just said no when Casey wanted to go backpacking around Europe. If-only's and what-if's aren't going to get us anywhere. You were a child that had been traumatised in ways that are unimaginable. I consider it a win that you ever opened your mouth again after that."

"Thanks. I think." Emily took a bite of her burger, chewing it slowly.

"The point is, placing blame on anyone besides the culprit is a waste of energy."

Emily swallowed with difficulty then took a sip of wine, "But since we have no idea who the culprit is, I think the best thing for me to do is get as far away from you, your family and this place as I can."

"If that's how you truly feel, then I won't stop you. But for the record, I don't think it will stop him either."

Paige downed the last half of her wine and topped up her glass. "Have you given any thought to how he found your address in the city?"

Emily shook her head, "I tried to track him through the florist that sent the lavender, but I didn't have any luck. None of our letterheads or cards have the physical address on them because I don't want clients going there."

"Then maybe it's someone that works with the telephone- or gas company," Paige suggested, "there must be a way people like that can find that sort of information."

"Anything's possible. If I've learnt anything in my business is that there's usually a way to get the information you want, you just need to be willing to dig."

Suddenly it occurred to Emily to ask her dark web connection to see if he might be able to find out who had been tracking her information. It would mean giving a virtual stranger her private information, but it was worth the risk. Emily had already decided that baby or no baby, she was going to move apartments. She didn't want to stay in a place that could be reached. She would open another company under a pseudonym and buy a new place under the company name. It might even be time to change cities. She wondered if Glynis would follow her.

Emily remembered how upset she was when Glynis had showed up at her apartment unannounced, she couldn't believe anyone had been able to find her. Glynis had told her that she had picked up the address from the invoices

Emily had sent to the company Glynis had been working for. After that incident, Emily made sure that all correspondence from her office would only have a postal address, a move which she had assumed would prevent anyone else from finding her in the future.

"Emily?"

Emily looked up at Paige, "Yeah?"

"Have you heard a word I've been saying?"

Emily shook her head, "No, sorry, I got lost in thought for a minute. What were you saying?"

"I was saying that Casey feels awful about what happened this morning."

Emily took a sip of her wine, "She shouldn't, I don't blame her. She's doing the right thing not wanting me to have the baby."

"She never said that." Paige said quietly.

"No, but she said her baby would never be safe if he were with me. He needs to go to a family that will take care of him. A couple that's not fucked up and can actually handle a kid."

"Did you feel that way this morning when you were joking about grounding him?" Paige asked.

"Doesn't matter what I felt this morning. It's time to be practical here. I'm not going to be any good for that kid and Casey will never have peace of mind if I'm the one that takes him. So let's just drop it."

"Casey is in a really bad place at the moment, she's lashing out at everyone and everything. I thought she was doing better, but it's normal for her to be taking a few steps back. She's scared right now, hell, I'm scared right now."

"I'm sorry that I've made you afraid in your own home Paige."

"I'm scared for you Emily. I don't think this person is actually going to do anything to us, I think he's doing these things to bait you. I'm worried about Casey's wellbeing of course, but right now, I'm most afraid for you. You don't seem to have that self-preservation streak most people have and if there was ever a time to use that streak, now would be it."

Emily thought for a while, "It's hard to suddenly be careful of everything because the boogeyman might be around the corner. I spent a lot of years trying to stop living that way, I don't want him to make me live like that again."

Paige put a hand on Emily's arm, "I know you don't, but right now, you need to make your safety a priority. Just until this psycho is caught."

"And what if he isn't Paige? Am I supposed to spend the rest of my life looking over my shoulder? Too scared to leave my home in case he's waiting?"

"I don't know how to answer that." Paige shrugged helplessly. "Maybe you'll find something in the files the old sheriff is sending over. Maybe we'll find him before you even go home."

Emily looked skeptical.

"In the meantime, I'm very grateful that there's an officer outside keeping an eye on things. Both here and at my house. Daniel installed a few cameras outside the house that work on motion detectors, so anyone that comes into our property, we'll know about it." Paige finished her second glass of wine, "If you would like us to set some up here too, we'd be happy to."

Emily shook her head, "I'm not planning to stay around much longer. As soon as I've done what I told Liam I would do, I'll be taking the first flight out of here."

"That's fair." Paige said, taking a bite of pizza and chewing it thoughtfully. "I take it asking you to speak to Casey would be out of the question?"

"I think we've said everything we need to each other." Emily replied, downing her glass of wine. "Just do me a favor?"

"Anything." Paige promised.

"Make sure he gets a really good family."

Paige's eyes brimmed with tears but she nodded, "I will."

"Thanks Paige."

"Will you do me a favor in return?" Paige asked, sniffing.

Emily lifted her eyebrow in response.

"Please take care of yourself, be careful." Paige asked, "Even if you can't do it for yourself, I'm asking you to do it for me."

"I'll try." Emily promised.


Emily took a shower after Paige left, wanting to try and clear her mind a little. She sat on the bed in her towel for ages, staring at the wall, unable to find the motivation to get up. Getting irritated with herself, Emily pulled out her running clothes from her suitcase and got dressed.

She tied her shoelaces before going to the kitchen and drinking two big glasses of water. She knew it probably wasn't a good idea to go running when she had spent the better part of the day drinking, but she needed to feel the slap of tarmac under her feet. To pound the road until her lungs felt like they would burst and she wouldn't be able to think about Casey, or the baby, or the lavender, or anything else that had happened since the day she went to Frankfurt.

Emily left her mobiles on the kitchen counter, went outside and locked the front door behind her. She slipped the key into the little pocket on her running shirt and zipped it closed.

It was dark outside, but the moon was shining brightly, giving Emily enough confidence to run on the county roads without a torch. She would avoid the forest and other dark areas tonight.

Emily waved at the patrol car but didn't stop when he called out the window. She didn't bother stretching either, instead starting with a jog down the driveway and turned left at the bottom to pass Amy's house then headed towards the main street in town, knowing she would feel more comfortable running on the well-lit roads.

She wondered how long it would take her babysitter to contact Liam and let him know she had left the cottage.

By the time she had run the first mile, her chest was indeed burning, but not in the way she was hoping. Without warning, nausea rose and Emily had to sidestep into the bushes to throw up. All the water she had drunk before she left the cottage came out of her into the bush, as well as the burger and wine she had consumed with Paige.

Emily finally straightened, feeling totally wretched when there was a rustle in the bushes to her right. Emily's head came up sharply, her nausea forgotten. The understanding of how stupid it was to go running in the middle of the night with no way to contact anyone was a sudden reality. Emily cursed softly, she had promised Paige she would try and be more careful, and there was nothing more risky then being alone on the roads at night.

There was another rustle. Emily fought the immediate reaction to bolt, knowing she was too unsteady on her feet after throwing up to get very far. The bush was only waist height, so it occurred to her that whatever was moving around in there, probably wasn't very big.

She leant over to look into the bushes and jumped back in surprise when she came face to face with a furry nose. A scrawny, mangy looking dog came out of the bushes and walked towards Emily carefully. Emily could see scars all over his body, places where the wiry hair had stopped growing. He was skinny, but came up to the height of her knee.

"There's got to be more polite ways to greet someone." Emily grumbled at the stray.

His stumpy, hairless tail wagged slowly. It looked as though he had lost half of it recently, the tip of his tail was still pink where the new scar tissue was growing.

Emily looked at the pathetic animal. She stood with her hands on her hips and cocked her head to one side then laughed when the dog cocked his head too.

"You look starving," Emily told him, "but I haven't got anything for you to eat. You better beat it."

Emily decided one scare was more than enough for one night and started walking back towards the cottage. She had walked only a few feet when the scruffy mutt fell in step beside her. Emily stamped her foot, giving the dog a fright, "Go on! Get out of here." She hissed.

The dog merely wagged his stump again and continued following her a few steps behind.

Emily thought about throwing something at the dog to chase it away, but didn't want to be unnecessarily mean to it. She shrugged and started jogging slowly, wishing the unpleasant ache in her head would subside.

It took her longer to get back to the cottage than she expected. She found the officer watching the cottage leaning against his car. He looked relieved that she was back.

"Evening." Emily said, slightly abashed, knowing he must think she's an idiot.

"Ma'am." He nodded his head towards her, "I know it's not my place to say, but you sure would make my job a lot easier if you let me know where you're going when you leave."

Emily nodded, "I'm really sorry, that wasn't a smart thing to do." She unzipped the little pocket to take the house key out. "Hey, do you know who the mutt belongs to?" She asked the deputy.

"Seen him around from time to time. Just a stray. I know the sheriff and a few other people have tried to catch him before to take him into the pound, but he usually bolts at the sight of people." The deputy shrugged, "I never seen him follow anyone before. Sure looks like he could use a vet though."

Emily looked down at the dog, now sitting patiently next to her leg. Why would a dog who doesn't like people decide to follow her? The dog was watching her with eyes the color of molten honey, his stumpy tail wagging slowly against the ground. There was something in the look he gave her that reminded Emily what it felt like to be so alone and scared.

"Come on dog." She told him, walking towards the house.

The dog hesitated for only a moment before bounding after her.

Emily closed and locked the front door behind them then went to the kitchen to pour herself some water. The dog followed her again, sitting on the kitchen floor and watching her drink curiously.

Emily took a plastic bowl out the cupboard and filled it with water. "Here," she said, placing the bowl on the floor.

The dog drank thirstily, his silly tail going into overdrive.

"I don't have dog food, so you're going to have to have some pizza tonight." Emily told him.

He stopped drinking, water dribbling out both sides of his mouth and he cocked his head at her again.

After he wolfed down two slices of cold, left-over pizza, the dog settled down at Emily's feet where she was sitting on the couch. He rested his head on one of her feet and sighed contentedly.

"You're easy to please." Emily commented, drinking a cup of coffee and watching the news.

When she climbed into bed an hour later, the dog jumped onto the bed with her. "Oh no," Emily told him, "This isn't going to work, you smell like shit." She tried vainly to push the dog off the bed, but he just looked at her with those eyes of his and lay still.

"Argh." Emily complained after realizing he wasn't going to move. "Come on, you need a shower then."

Emily went to the bathroom and turned on the taps. Once the water was warm, she gestured for the dog to get in. He cocked his head to one side again, looking at her curiously.

"If you bite me, this friendship is over." Emily told him sternly, pulling off the running clothes she was still wearing and getting into the shower in her underwear.

The dog watched her calling him for a few moments before cautiously putting a paw into the shower. The spray hit him in the face and he jumped back in fright, slipping onto his butt.

Emily laughed at the bewildered mutt. She knelt down so she was the same height as him, the shower spray bouncing off her shoulders. "Come on." She coaxed.

The dog took another furtive step into the shower. He was shaking in fear. Emily gave him a pat for the first time. First the dog pulled his head away as though scared, but when he realised Emily wasn't hurting him, he pushed his head under her hand.

Emily rubbed his head and neck with both hands. "You're not used to affection are you ugly boy?"

He allowed Emily to soap him up with her expensive shampoo and conditioner, sitting patiently in the water. Emily didn't think too many dogs would be this well behaved in the shower and told him so. Telling him he was such a good boy while she scrubbed his ears.

Feeling proud of herself, Emily got out of the shower and wrapped a towel around her body before picking up another towel for the dog. "Come on." She told him, gesturing at the towel.

The dog got out of the shower and immediately shook his whole body, spraying the bathroom, and Emily with water.

"Gross." Emily protested. She tried to drop the towel on the dog to stop the shaking but he bolted out the bathroom, skidding into the passage wall and running to the living room, his tail wagging frantically.

Emily chased him around the cottage for ten minutes in her wet underwear before thinking about bribing him with food.

Once he had another slice of pizza in front of him, Emily was able to dry him as best she could. Fortunately, his wiry fur seemed to dry quickly. His tail thumped against her as he ate.

"Glad one of us is now clean and dry." Emily grumbled at him.

Emily took off her wet underwear in the bedroom and considered trying to shower again, but decided she was too tired. Dressing in cotton pajama pants and an old t-shirt, Emily climbed back into bed.

The dog jumped up and curled into a ball near her feet, sighed once and fell asleep.

# Chapter Thirty

Emily vaguely remembered being woken from a nightmare during the night by a whiskery face nuzzling her neck, but after that, both she and the dog had slept soundly all night.

She got out of bed, leaving the dog asleep on her pillow. Emily had a shower and got dressed before going to make herself a cup of coffee.

She was sitting on the step outside with her coffee and a cigarette when the dog came padding outside. He nuzzled Emily briefly before investigating all the bushes next to the house, eventually lifting his leg against one.

"At least you're house trained." Emily told him when he returned to the step and flopped down beside her.

Emily was making toast for herself and her furry houseguest when Liam arrived. She let him in with a smile. "Hey."

Liam smiled back, "Hey to you too. Woah, what the hell?" Liam took a step back when a blur of fur came running up to him.

"That's Mutt." Emily introduced casually, patting her leg to get the dog to come to her.

"You adopted the county mutt?" Liam asked in disbelief, putting his hand out to let the dog sniff it.

Emily shrugged, "He adopted me, I didn't have a say in the matter. Want some toast and coffee?"

Mutt seemed to realise Liam wasn't a threat and went back to the kitchen with Emily to wait for his breakfast.

"That would be great thanks." Liam said, following the two of them into the kitchen. "Did you enjoy your run last night?" He asked casually.

Emily buttered a piece of toast and gave it to Mutt. "I know it was stupid Liam, you don't need to come and moan at me."

Liam watched the dog eating the toast for a moment before looking up, "You promised to be more careful."

"I know, I don't know what I was thinking." Emily said, buttering another piece of toast and handing this one to Liam, "But at least I had a guard dog with me on the way home."

"You know he can't live on toast right?" Liam said, gesturing with his own toast toward the dog.

"He had pizza last night." Emily said in defense. "I'll go get some proper dog food today."

"Are you going to keep him?" Liam asked, starting to prepare the coffee.

Emily shrugged, "I have no idea. He wouldn't leave last night. I thought the least I could do is feed him up and take him to the vet to get checked out. Then maybe I'll take him to the pound."

Mutt seemed to be listening to their conversation, he leant his head against Emily's thigh and she patted him distractedly.

"He seems to have other ideas." Liam said, "I've tried to catch him a few times, so has the pound, but he always gets away. I've never seen him go to anyone before."

"That's what the deputy said last night," Emily replied, taking her coffee. "I don't know why he's taken such a liking to me."

They went to sit on the couch, Mutt lying at Emily's feet.

"You can't seriously be naming him Mutt." Liam said, dusting the toast crumbs off his hands.

Emily shrugged again, "I don't want to get attached if I send him to the pound." She took a sip of coffee, holding the mug in both hands. "Have the files arrived yet?"

Liam shook his head frustrated, "No, and I can't get hold of my predecessor."

Emily was secretly relieved. "I think after tonight's fair, I'm going to head back to the city tomorrow morning."

Liam nodded, "I thought you might."

"I don't have much reason to stay." Emily pointed out.

"I know, I just don't like the idea of you alone in the city." Liam said, scratching Mutt with the tip of his boot.

Emily avoided the comment, "Once again I owe you an apology." She told Liam.

Liam waved her off, "Don't worry about it, you have a lot going on."

"It's not that, when I'm around you, I don't seem to have much control of my mouth."

"That and the tequila probably helped." Liam said wryly.

"That too," Emily said, blushing slightly, "But I shouldn't have told you about the argument with your mother." Emily put her cup down, "And for the record, she really did seem to think she stayed with your father to give you a better life."

Liam cleared his throat, "My issues with my mother at the moment have less to do with my father than with other issues."

"Oh." Emily said, standing up to take the coffee mugs through to the kitchen.

Liam followed her, "What are your plans for the day?"

"Vet, if I can get an appointment at such short notice and then the shop for dog food I guess." Emily answered, rinsing the mugs and putting them on the drying rack. "Then I'll probably come back here and work on my laptop until it's time to go to the fair." Emily paused, "Assuming you still want me to come."

"Of course." Liam said easily, handing her a dishcloth to dry her hands, "I believe I still have to right the wrong of life without cotton candy."

Emily laughed. "Are dogs allowed at the fair?"

"Yes, but they need to be people friendly and on a leash at all times." Liam looked over at Mutt who was now stretched out on his back on the couch, "I think you're already too attached to give him up."

"I just don't want him destroying Paige's house while I'm out." Emily defended. "But I think it will be easier to leave him behind and hope for the best."

"Uhuh," Liam muttered, unconvinced, "Just text me please if you're planning on any detours today."

"I will." Emily promised.

"Thanks. I'm going to head to the office now and see if I can track down that evidence box or the old sheriff."

Emily walked him to the front door, "Oh, and Liam?"

"Yeah?"

"Your mom was definitely seeing someone."

Liam smiled, "Oh I knew. I also knew she didn't want me to know, so I played along. My mother forgets, like most of the women in this town, that I'm actually a pretty good detective."

Liam gave Emily a smile before heading towards his cruiser.


The vet was able to see Mutt on short notice, although he wasn't impressed about it. Mutt, however, was even less impressed with the vet and tried to bite him repeatedly until the vet insisted on putting on a muzzle.

"Sorry Mutt." Emily said quietly, smoothing the scruffy fur on his head.

"I always figured this one would get run over or poisoned before he let anyone come near him." The vet was a wizened old man with more white hair growing from his ears than on his head, "Waste of medication if you ask me. He's going to run off the first chance he gets."

"I'm willing to take the gamble." Emily said lightly, she found the vet unpleasant and would have left if there was another one in town to take Mutt too.

"He's mostly healthy, has a bit of mange which I'll give you shampoo for and he's probably got worms, so you'll need to give him meds for that. His ribs feel broken, but healed, could be they're still healing, so he's sensitive on that side, but I don't see a need to do anything with it. Other than that, I can give him his shots and he's good to go."

"Thank you." Emily told him.

After paying what she was sure was far more than she was supposed to, Emily took the muzzle off Mutt and led him out to the car, where he jumped in happily and settled himself on the passenger seat.

Emily had to leave Mutt in the car while she ran into the shop to get dog food, a bowl, a leash and collar set and when she got to the counter, she couldn't resist buying a few chew toys as well.

Once they were back at the cottage, Emily began the task of showering him again with his new shampoo, but this time she was smart enough to close the bathroom door so he wouldn't escape while he was still wet. He still managed to shake water everywhere, even spraying the ceiling, drenching Emily in the process.

By the time Mutt was clean and dry, Emily needed another shower of her own, having discovered that wet dogs really do smell as bad as people say they do.

When Liam and Sophie arrived to fetch Emily, Mutt was fast asleep on Emily's bed having just finished a big bowl of dog food.

"Hi Emily!" Sophie greeted enthusiastically.

"Hey you." Emily greeted back, giving the little girl a tight hug. "Hey to you too." She said to Liam.

Liam smiled, "Are you girls ready for the best night ever?"

"Yes!" Sophie yelled, jumping up and down.

"Believe it or not, she actually hasn't had any sugar yet." Liam told Emily conspiratorially as they walked towards his police cruiser.

"Is the cruiser really necessary?" Emily asked, "We can go in my rental?"

"No way, this baby means we can park wherever we like." Liam said with a grin.

"Fine, just don't put me in the back seat, people might think you're arresting me again."

Liam laughed but opened the passenger door for Emily then helped Sophie into her booster seat in the back.

"Daddy, you arrested Emily?" Sophie asked, scandalised.

The fair was as noisy and crowded as Emily remembered from her youth. The lights blinked furiously on the Ferris Wheel in the middle of the fair, kids were running here and there, yelling loudly, hyped up on excitement and cotton candy.

Sophie walked between Emily and Liam, holding hands with both grownups as they made a loop around the games and rides before deciding where to start.

Having decided that she was in desperate need of a corndog, Sophie dragged the other two to the food court.

Liam ordered three corndogs and three sodas while Emily and Sophie went to find an open seat at the tables under the gazebo.

Amy spotted them and waved them over to where she was sitting alone at a table for four.

"Come and join me." She called.

Sophie gave Amy a hug then took her seat.

"Are you here alone?" Emily asked, taking the seat opposite Amy.

"No, I'm here with Xavier, but heaven forbid a teenager be seen in public with his mother." Amy rolled her eyes, "He took off the minute we got here. So I'm drinking these terrible, warm beers and people-watching."

Liam came over with the corndogs and drinks on a tray. "Hey Amy, would you like a corndog?"

Amy helped herself. "Thanks Liam."

"I'll go and get some more." Liam said to the table and disappeared once more into the crowd.

"You and the sheriff have made up then?" Amy asked with a wicked grin.

"They were making out the other night." Sophie piped up, causing Emily to choke on her soda.

Amy howled with laughter, then went around the table to slap Emily on the back to help with the choking.

The four of them chatted while they ate, fortunately without Sophie mentioning anything more about the kiss. When they were done, Sophie was ready to go on the rollercoaster, something she had been too short to do the previous year.

"Are you coming?" Liam asked Emily.

"I think I'll skip the rollercoaster if you don't mind. I've just eaten."

"Come on Soph," Liam said, taking his daughter's hand, "let's leave these chickens here while we go have fun."

Sophie waved at the two women happily while her father led her to the rollercoaster queue.

"So," Amy started as soon as the other two were out of earshot, "I take it things are better between the two of you?"

Emily blushed slightly, "There's nothing going on."

"Oh sure, I regularly make out with people I have no interest in." Amy agreed cheerfully, taking a sip of her beer.

"That was a mistake, one that will not be repeated." Emily said, tearing off a piece of dough from a left-over corndog and rolling it between her fingers.

"Why not? As far as I know he hasn't shown the slightest bit of inclination towards anyone since his wife died. Maybe it's time to rekindle that high school love?"

"For one, I don't live here remember?" Emily flicked the ball of dough towards her empty soda cup but missed, "And for two, it would never work, we're way too different now."

"I don't know Emily, the way that man looks at you? I wouldn't have left Erik if he still looked at me that way."

"Is Erik still dating the boss's niece?" Emily asked, changing the subject.

"Oh yes, they're as happy as can be those two." Amy answered, flicking the same ball of dough towards the cup.

Emily couldn't help but notice both of them were sitting there, talking about men they wanted but no longer had. She had no doubt that Amy missed her ex-husband, even though she joked about it so often.

"Oh look." Amy whispered loudly, pointing towards a grumpy looking older man and his daughter, "That's Stacey's husband. Money up the wazoo and an arrogant bastard too. See what I meant about not being impressive?"

Emily snorted, "I see your point."

"At least I still have a husband."

They both whipped round to find Stacey standing behind them with a haughty expression on her face. "Tell me Amy, is it true that Erik has proposed to that lovely girlfriend of his?"

Amy shrugged carelessly, "You'd probably know more than me, aren't the two of you friends?"

"Yes we are." Stacey smiled, "But I'm glad to see you've finally found yourself a friend Amy. It's good that you outsiders can stick together."

Emily lifted an eyebrow, "I'm rather proud of being considered an outsider as opposed to a small-minded, small-town hick. What about you Amy?"

Amy laughed and nodded.

"It's just as well you no longer have a husband, otherwise Emily might make a grab for him." Stacey smiled sweetly at both of them, "Oh, and I know my husband is older and that's right up your street Emily... You've always had a thing for older men haven't you? Some real daddy issues."

"Walk away before I punch you in the smug face you cold-hearted bitch!"

Emily was shocked at Amy's threat towards Stacey but was secretly pleased her friend had stood up for her. Emily hadn't even been given a chance to react when Amy stood up and towered over Stacey.

"As if you would." Stacey said, although she was already backing away. "Enjoy your date ladies."

Amy sat back down and glared at Stacey. "What a colossal bitch."

"That," Emily said, picking up her glass and raising it towards Amy, "was freaking hilarious. She backed off so quickly I'm surprised there aren't skid-marks."

Amy laughed and picked up her own glass to tap it against Emily's.

Emily had gone on most of the other rides with Sophie and Liam, laughing and joking with them. She actually felt truly at ease for the first time in months. Liam bought them all a big stick of cotton candy to eat and they walked around the fair watching other people play the games while they ate.

"Is it as good as you remember?" Liam asked Emily.

"Mmm," She replied, savoring a piece, "I forgot how good it is... And how sticky." Emily had a piece stuck to her finger, which she playfully stuck to Liam's cheek.

"Oh it's war!" Liam laughed, taking some of his own and flicking it towards Emily.

Sophie squealed with delight, taking a handful of cotton candy and attempting to reach her father's face. Emily heaved the little girl up from behind and rushed towards Liam, allowing Sophie to put the whole gooey blob in Liam's hair.

Emily was laughing so much she had to put Sophie back down and doubled over.

"Hello Nana." Sophie said, looking over Emily's shoulder.

Emily stopped mid-laugh and spun around.

"Hello love." Cathy said to Sophie. Her hair and makeup was once again flawless, though she was still walking with her cane. She smiled stiffly at her son, "Hello William."

"Mother." Liam greeted as stiffly, not even trying to smooth his messy and sticky hair.

"Emily, I wonder if I could have a word with you?" Cathy asked politely.

"Uh, yeah, sure." Emily said uneasily, "Soph, can you hold my cotton candy and make sure your dad doesn't steal any?"

Sophie nodded and took the stick from Emily with a solemn expression on her face. "I'll look after it." She promised.

As Emily started towards Cathy, Liam caught her arm and leaned in to whisper, "You don't need to do this, you don't owe her anything."

"Don't worry, she doesn't look like she wants to fight." Emily whispered back, "but if she does, I think I can take her." She added with a wink.

Cathy took a few steps away from her son and granddaughter and waited for Emily to join her.

"Look Cathy, I'm not playing games with Liam, we're just friends, so before you get on your high horse and—"

"Oh shush." Cathy interrupted. "I didn't even know you would be here with him. Now please just let me say what I need to say without interruption." She took a deep steadying breath, "I know a simple sorry won't do it justice, but I came here tonight, hoping you would be here so that I could at least apologise face to face.

You were right, I should have taken William and run when he was a baby, but the truth is, I'm a coward, I had never had to work before and I was scared I wouldn't be able to provide for him the way Frank could. I didn't want to spend my life looking over my shoulder, which is silly I suppose because I had to face it every day instead.

I was weak and you were young and I took all my anger and judgement of myself out on you. My behavior towards you has been atrocious all these years and for that, I am truly, truly sorry.

You lost your mother and the one time you could have truly used support, I turned my son against you. I knew the rumors couldn't be true, but I listened anyway. You know when someone of authority tells you something, you assume it's the truth. Anyway," Cathy sighed again, less nervous this time and more sad. "I have lost everything, but the fault of that lies where it always has. Squarely at my own feet. Apologising to you won't fix the relationships in my life that I've destroyed, but it's still something I should have done a long time ago. I'm sorry Emily."

A single tear ran down Cathy Richard's face and it was the tear more than anything she said that made Emily close the gap between them and envelope the older woman in a hug.

Emily wasn't sure who was more shocked by the gesture, Cathy or herself. Cathy froze for a second, then returned the hug fiercely, holding tightly, as though Emily were the only thing holding her to the earth.

"So that looked super weird." Amy was telling Emily.

The two were once more sitting in the food tent, both drinking a beer. Emily had sent Liam off with Sophie, claiming that her feet hurt and she needed a breather.

The truth was, she needed to gather her thoughts away from Liam, who was naturally curious about what his mother had said. Emily would tell him later when they were in the car or back at the cottage.

"It felt a little weird." Emily admitted.

"I've seen the famous Cathy around but have never been high enough in the upper echelon to speak to her." Amy pulled a face suddenly, "I'm pretty sure she's in a book club with Stacey and Lorraine."

"Who's Lorraine?" Emily asked curiously.

"The boss's niece. She's far too little-house-on-the-prairie to work, so when she's not cooking and cleaning for Erik, she lunches with the ladies."

Emily snorted, "That sounds awful."

"Speak of the devil." Amy said, straightening up suddenly.

A tall man with dark hair, pointed nose and friendly green eyes walked up to the table.

"Hello there. I was looking for our son, I told him I would meet him here and challenge him to a game of air hockey."

"If you're thinking he'll be anywhere near his mother when there are girls around, you are very much mistaken." Amy responded. "Erik, this is my friend, Emily. Emily, this is Erik."

Emily shook hands with him.

"Where's Lorraine?" Amy asked with forced politeness.

"She's at home, fairs aren't her kind of thing."

"No, I don't imagine they are." Amy said under her breath, but loud enough for Emily to hear.

"Since Xavier is otherwise occupied, would you care to have this dance?" Erik gestured towards the live band, bowed dramatically and offered her a hand.

Amy laughed and took his hand. "Why not?"

Next to the food court area they were sitting in was a stage with a live band singing old country ballads. In front of the stage was a dancefloor, which was made up of some slabs of plywood dumped on the floor.

As Amy and her ex-husband got onto the dance floor, the band started playing an old country love song.

Emily watched the two of them dance with the ease and comfort of a couple who had been together a lifetime.

She knew Amy regretted that Erik was no longer her husband, but Emily wondered if Amy saw the way Erik looked at her. She didn't think Amy was the only one living with regret.

# Chapter Thirty-One

Sophie had fallen asleep before the cruiser had left the fair ground.

"The only good thing about a sugar rush," Liam told Emily quietly as they drove back home, "Is that after the rush, comes the crash. She's going to sleep like a baby tonight and maybe even let me sleep in a little tomorrow."

"She's a really good kid." Emily said in a quiet voice, not wanting to wake Sophie.

Liam's smile could be seen illuminated by a passing car, "She really is." He agreed.

Liam pulled the cruiser into his driveway. "Are you coming in for coffee?"

"I don't think that's such a good idea Liam."

"It's just coffee." Liam turned to look at her, "I don't have any ulterior motives."

"I know you don't, you're not the one I'm worried about." Emily said wryly.

Liam chuckled quietly, "Well, since fair beer has nothing on a bottle of tequila, I feel fairly safe in your presence tonight." He reached out cautiously and laid a hand over hers, "Just coffee. And maybe another cinematic masterpiece."

"One coffee then." Emily smiled, feeling suddenly shy.

Half an hour later their empty coffee cups sat on the coffee table while they joked about the lead character in the cheesy horror Liam had recorded the night before.

"Surely she must be top heavy with implants like that." Liam said as the heroine ran through the forest and inevitably fell over a root.

"At least she had a padded fall." Emily commented, causing Liam to snort with laughter.

They were quiet for a while longer, watching the heroine be dragged unconscious into the killer's cave.

"Hey Em?"

"Mmm?"

"What did my mother say to you tonight that made you hug her?"

Emily took the remote from between them and paused the movie. She turned sideways on the couch and pulled her legs up so that she was sitting cross-legged facing Liam. "She apologised." Emily told him. "She apologised to me for every bit of petty meanness she's thrown at me over the years." Emily gave a half-smile, "But I don't think that apology was meant only for me though. I think I was the person she was least afraid to apologise to."

"What do you mean?"

Emily shrugged, "If I threw it back in her face, the consequences wouldn't be enormous, but if you or someone else close to her didn't want to hear the apology, I think it would break her."

"I don't think you realise how tough my mother is."

"No Liam, I don't think you realise how fragile your mother is under that tough exterior. She didn't have to say anything to me, but I could see she's really unhappy and is trying to make amends the best she can."

Liam looked down at his hands for a while before looking back at Emily. "Are you saying I should be a better son?"

Emily shrugged, "I'm not saying you should be anything. I'm certainly not one to talk, considering I can barely stand to look at my own father. You asked me a question and I answered it the best I can."

Emily unlocked her front door and waved to Liam who was standing in his yard watching her go inside. He had wanted to go with her, but Emily told him not to leave Sophie alone.

They had finished watching the movie before Emily had gotten ready to leave. When she got to Liam's door there was a moment she was sure he was going to kiss her, but then the moment passed and he just wished her a goodnight. She felt silly now, thinking it was just her imagination.

Mutt greeted her enthusiastically, jumping up against her, his tail wagging crazily.

"All right, all right, just let me get inside." Emily moaned at him, locking the door behind her. She dropped her bag on the floor instead of trying to make it to the kitchen counter and crouched down to give the dog some attention.

"Are you hungry big guy?" Emily asked him, rubbing his soft ears. "Come on, let's get you some food then I'll let you out for a bit."

Emily walked to the kitchen and saw the notification light on her personal mobile was blinking. Thinking it might be Paige or Casey, she picked it up on the way to the dog food and unlocked the screen.

An unknown number had sent her pictures. Emily clicked to download them then put the phone on the counter and put some dog pellets into a bowl for Mutt.

Once Mutt was happily munching his food, Emily turned back to her phone.

The first picture was of her, Liam and Sophie, laughing and eating corndogs at the fair. The next picture was a side shot of Emily sitting alone watching Amy and Erik dance in the background. The third picture was taken from outside Liam's living room, the two of them gesturing at the television. The fourth picture was of Paige sitting curled up on her outside sofa, her hair tied up in a messy bun, a book in her hands. The fifth was a picture of Casey napping inside the living room, lying in the fetal position, a thin blanket covering her bottom half.

Emily felt faint. She reached across the counter automatically for her work mobile and dialed Liam's number.

"Hello."

"Liam, I need you to get over here now. But bring Sophie, don't leave her there."

"Emily? What's happened?" There was urgency in his voice.

"Just hurry please."


There was a knock at the door less than a minute later. Both Liam and the cop from outside were at the door. Sophie was asleep on her dad's shoulder.

"What's going on?" Liam asked in way of greeting.

"He's been following us all night." Emily said, opening the door and gesturing them all inside.

"Matt, do a perimeter and keep close." Liam told the deputy, who nodded and pulled out his weapon immediately.

"Emily, lock the door then come sit with Sophie in the living room while I check the bedrooms."

Emily did as she was told and settled Sophie on the couch, pulling a blanket over her. She saw Liam take a gun out of the waist of his jeans as he went through to the bedrooms.

He was back within minutes and motioned Emily through to the kitchen.

"What makes you think he's been following you?" He asked in a tense whisper.

"Us," Emily corrected and handed Liam the phone. "And Paige and Casey."

Liam paled as he flicked through the pictures on the screen. "Call Paige and tell her to stay inside the house with the doors locked, I'm going to send another deputy out there immediately. He must have climbed over the back wall or something. Ask her to have the security tapes ready for review."

Emily took her work mobile again and dialed Paige. The conversation was brief. Emily promised to fill her in properly when they had more information.

Liam was ending his own call when Emily finished with Paige.

"We can ask the labs in the next county to trace the number, but they will only open again on Monday." Liam said, rubbing his face in frustration.

"I might be able to do it a little faster." Emily told him, "I just need my laptop."

"This isn't exactly legal." Emily warned Liam as she booted up her laptop.

"Just find this asshole so I can kill him." Liam said darkly.

Emily used every back door and trick she knew, but it was just a regular burner phone, bouncing of the only two towers in town, meaning that while he was in town somewhere, they had no idea where to look because she couldn't triangulate the location.

"I might have a contact that could hack the number and get into the info on the actual device if it's connected to the internet." Emily suggested helplessly.

"Do it." Liam said, looking over at his sleeping daughter.

Emily reached out to her dark web friend and was relieved to find that he was online. She didn't give him much information, just the number and a promise to pay double if he found anything out.

He said he was happy to help and would get right on it, though he warned Emily that it might take a while.


Emily made them both coffee while Liam paced the living room in agitation.

"Liam, please come sit down, you're making me nervous." Emily said, taking a seat at the dining table.

Liam sat down heavily next to her. "Thanks for the coffee."

"Why don't I send the number a text?" Emily asked, toying with the cable for her laptop.

"You could. What are you going to say? I don't think he's going to tell you anything useful."

"Maybe I can rile him up enough to make a mistake?" Emily suggested.

Instead of texting, Emily dialed the number from her work mobile and put the call on speaker. The number rang twice before being disconnected.

Then she tried from her personal phone, and it was disconnected before the first ring could finish.

*What do you want?* Emily texted from her personal phone.

*The same thing I always wanted... I want to see you bleed.*

Liam snatched the mobile from Emily and dialed the number again, but this time it was dead, going straight into an automated voicemail. "Son of a bitch!" Liam roared in anger, looking like he was about to throw the phone at the wall.

Sophie groaned and mumbled something in her sleep, causing Liam to calm down enough to put the phone back on the table.

"Liam," Emily started cautiously, "I want to go home."

Liam shook his head, "We've discussed this, I can't keep you safe there."

"No, but you and Sophie will be safer if I'm not around you. I'm the one making everyone else a target."

Liam was still shaking his head, but Emily pressed on, "You've seen the locks on my apartment. The doorman never lets anyone through without permission from the tenant, I'd be safe there."

Liam slammed his coffee cup down, coffee spilling over the edge and splashing on the table, "And then what? You're going to hide in your apartment indefinitely?"

"If I have to. It will give you time to track this bastard down, without him knowing you're still looking for him."

"And what happens when you have too much to drink and decide that you don't want to be careful and you go out partying?"

"Well," Emily said, slightly stung, but knowing he was telling the truth, "then it wouldn't be your responsibility anymore."

"I won't let this fucker hurt you!" Liam snarled at her.

Emily leant back in her chair and Liam immediately backed down. "I'm sorry Em, I didn't mean to go off on you, I'm just trying to keep you safe."

"I know that Liam, but I'm trying to keep everyone I care about safe. How do you expect me to live with myself if Sophie, or Paige, or Casey, or you got hurt because of me?"

"I don't know Em," Liam said, a look of desperate pain in his eyes, "But I've lost someone because of something I did. I can't lose you too."

Emily wasn't misreading the situation this time, it was too obvious on his face. She wrapped her arms around herself as though she were cold. "Liam, this could never work." She said quietly, not wanting to look at him.

"Why not?" Liam reached across to try take one of her hands, but Emily pulled away.

"You live here and I live there."

"So what? One of us will move." Liam said with confidence.

"Come on Liam, you don't want to raise Sophie in the city, and I could never move back to this place."

"Then we find somewhere else to go." Liam said.

Emily shook her head, "This is your home, it just isn't mine."

"Home is where the people I love are." Liam told her firmly.

"Liam, do you have any idea how many people I've slept with?" Emily was exasperated, trying to get him to see sense.

"So?"

"So, you deserve better."

"Bullshit," Liam snapped, making Emily jump again. He took a breath before continuing, "In college I screwed around a lot. And after Mel died, I spiraled. I lost count of how many one night stands I had. I was so desperate to get away from my pain and guilt that I tried to screw it out of my system.

It doesn't matter to me Em. I still feel the way I did about you in high school. I can't help it. The idea of someone trying to hurt you or take you away from me sends me into a blind rage."

"Now's not the time to think about this, there's too much going on."

"Now's the best time to think about it, to talk about it. You want to run from this, from me."

"I told you! I'm doing this for you!" Emily hissed, aware that the blanket covering Sophie was moving around. Mutt leant against her thigh as though sensing she was upset and needed comfort. She rubbed his ears distractedly to reassure him.

"Please don't leave." Liam pleaded quietly.

Emily looked into his eyes and knew that he meant what he said. That he truly wanted her, no matter how damaged she was. She thought about the little girl sleeping soundly a few feet away and about the unborn baby she would never get to hold. The reasons she would never get to hold him. She wouldn't do that to Liam or his little girl.

"What happens when I've had too much to drink and I decide I don't want to be the little woman and go out partying?" She threw his words back at him with as much venom as she could muster.

Liam looked startled, "I didn't, I wouldn't —"

Emily interrupted him, "No. I don't want that life. I don't want this! I am taking the first flight home tomorrow."

Emily saw the pain in his eyes and felt terrible for being the cause of it, but she knew it was for the best. She pushed her chair back and stood. "I think you should go home now, or sleep in the other room or the sofa or wherever. I'm going to bed."

Emily was almost to the little passage near the bedrooms when Liam grabbed her arm and spun her around. Holding on to both of her arms he looked her in the eye. "Tell me then. Tell me you feel nothing for me."

"Liam, it doesn't matter what I feel."

"God dammit Emily, look at me and tell me you don't feel something. You think I don't know the reason you keep pushing me away? Why you only seem at ease with me when you've been drinking? Because you're scared shitless of feeling something for someone else.

I know you think you're doing this for me, but taking yourself away from me is the cruelest thing you could do to me."

Emily didn't think about the man threatening her, she didn't think about the cop standing outside the front door or the child asleep on the couch, she couldn't think of a single thing other than the man in front of her. In his eyes she saw the same desperate need she felt in herself.

She put her hand to his cheek and it was all Liam needed. His lips met hers fiercely, his arms wrapping around her, crushing her body against his own.

Emily could feel his heartbeat thudding against her own chest. She wrapped her arms around his neck and kissed him back with more passion than she ever knew existed.

His hands roamed her back, pulling her closer as though trying to pull her body into his. Emily gasped as his mouth left hers and made its way down her jaw towards her neck, his lips searing her skin.

"Wait." She gasped out, trying to push him away.

"Not this time." He said back breathlessly.

"Not like this." Emily begged. She lifted his face with her hands so she was looking once more into his blue eyes which seemed to crackle with electricity. "Not here." She took him by the hand and led him through to the bedroom.

She barely got the door closed when he pulled her into his arms again, kissing her deeply, stealing her breath. Emily pulled his shirt upwards, and he paused long enough to pull it over his head before crushing her to him once more. His hands slid down her back to her hips, he slipped his thumbs into her jeans and started tugging them down. Emily undid the button on the front of her jeans with frantic fingers, then started unbuckling Liam's belt. The lost their balance and toppled onto the bed, both their jeans around their ankles. Emily lay on top of Liam and kicked off her shoes and jeans while he did the same. In one deft movement, Liam had spun her onto her back and was on top of her. He leant over her, his lips almost touching hers, but didn't kiss her.

"What's wrong?" Emily breathed.

"Nothing," Liam answered, "I want to savor this. I want to remember this moment." He bent his head down and his lips touched hers more gently now, his kiss softer but somehow more intense than before. He pulled her over again so that he was sitting on the bed and she was straddling his lap. He dug his hand into her hair and kissed the scar on her neck, causing Emily to shudder.

He was slow to take her shirt off, pulling it over her shoulders gently then over her head. He undid her bra just as slowly, sliding the straps down her arms with a caressing touch.

He held her face in his hands. "Emily." Was all he whispered.

Liam lay her back against the bed, kissing her slowly, gently. The feeling of their naked skin against one another was more incredible than either of them expected. When he entered her, he did so slowly, whispering her name again.

Emily finally understood the phrase 'making love'. Nothing she had ever experienced came close to this. They took their time, savoring each other's bodies, tasting one another's skin and when they reached the peak of ecstasy, they reached it together, Emily sighing Liam's name over and over.

Afterwards, no words were said. Liam lay behind her holding her close to his chest, their breathing the only noise in the silence. Emily entwined her fingers through his and marveled at how happy she could feel in that moment. It was as though no world existed outside of the bed, that they were the only two people who mattered. She wanted it to last forever, too scared to sleep in case the spell was broken. Instead, she focused on the feeling of his arms around her and drifted unknowingly into a contented sleep.

# Chapter Thirty-Two

**P**aige had been unable to sleep at all. She had been sitting with Daniel in the living room all night, both silent in their worry. She went out only to give the policemen both coffee at around two in the morning and had waited until one of them was near the front door before unlocking it and calling him.

The new security system had shown nothing on the videos, so whoever it was either knew where they were or was using a long distance lens. Liam seemed to think the pictures were probably taken from the same phone that the pictures were sent on.

By the time the sun had risen, Paige had a splitting headache. Daniel had gone to shower while she went to the kitchen to make coffee.

They had discussed a trip last night. The three of them packing up and flying off somewhere for a while. They had both decided it was the best thing to do, they were desperate to keep their daughter safe. Daniel had said he would go to the office that morning and make the arrangements from there. Paige just had to make sure they were packed and ready to go by the time he got back.

The kettle whistled, giving Paige a fright. She poured the boiling water into the cups and looked around her kitchen. She loved this kitchen. She loved this house. She and Daniel had lived their entire married lives in this house. They had renovated every room over the years until it was exactly how they wanted it. She dreaded the idea of leaving, even if it wasn't forever. Paige hated the idea that they were being forced to run and hide.

She wanted so badly to call Emily and see how she was doing, but knew that it would only add more stress to Emily's plate. She knew Emily well enough to know that she was blaming herself for everything that was happening.

Paige looked out the window towards the driveway, lost in thought. Casey entered the room, making her mother jump for the second time in ten minutes.

"Sorry mom." Casey said, walking towards the fridge, scratching the underside of her swollen belly.

"I didn't realise you were awake." Paige said, turning back to the coffees.

"Couldn't sleep. I need to try see if Emily will talk to me. I wanted to send her a text last night, but I think I should go past the cottage today if she's still there."

"I think she's leaving this morning," Paige said, turning back to her daughter, "and I need to talk to you. Your father and I think its best that we all take an extended vacation."

"Does this sudden vacation have anything to do with your late-night call last night?" Casey asked, taking the orange juice out of the fridge and putting it on the counter.

"Yes and no. We would just rather we're all out of the area for a while until things settle down."

"Is that why Emily's leaving? Because she thinks this is her fault?"

Paige shrugged helplessly. "She was never going to stay here. She hates this town. The only reason she stepped foot here again is because I asked her to. But yes, I think she's leaving because she thinks it will protect us."

"This isn't her fault." Casey said, tears in her eyes. "This is all my fault mom. I did this. I'm the reason she's got this maniac chasing her and the reason we have to leave."

Paige went to her daughter and enveloped her in a tight hug. "It's not your fault my love. I brought her here. She came here. We both did what we did because we love you. This isn't your fault. It's the sicko out there that's to blame. No one else."

Casey sniffed, wiping her eyes with her pajama sleeve, the way she used to as a small child. "Do you think if he's caught, Emily might still want to take the baby or have I have I ruined the chance?"

"Do you still want Emily to be the mother of this child?" Paige asked her, rubbing her arms gently.

"She's doing everything she can to protect us when I was so cruel to her." Casey shrugged, "What more could a kid ask for in a mother?"

"Then we'll speak to her. But let's first get through this."


Casey had gone upstairs to pack, and Daniel had left for the office, promising to be back as soon as he could.

Paige went upstairs to change and decided she would drive over to Emily and see if she had left yet. She didn't want to leave or have Emily leave without saying goodbye. Paige knew she would never be able to express the true depth of her gratitude to the young woman she had come to love as her own daughter, and she definitely didn't want Emily to think she was the reason Paige and her family were going away. She was hoping if Emily was still there, Paige would be able also to gauge the situation and see if Emily might still want the baby. She knew in her heart Emily would be a good mother, her first choice if someone else was going to raise her grandson.

Throwing her mobile into her bag, she yelled to Casey that she was going to the shop quickly and that Casey shouldn't leave the house, then headed outside to her car.

Paige waved to the officer standing near her gate as she pulled out of her driveway. She truly hoped Emily would still be there. She knew there were two flights on Saturdays, but she was sure the first one wasn't due for a few hours yet.

Paige was so distracted she didn't see the man getting up from his hidden position in her back seat. She slowed to a stop at the stop street and saw too late the gloved hand swinging out from the back seat.

Everything went black.

∞

"You'll have to stay down here til that heals." The bigger man was telling Stan in an angry voice. "People are already asking questions. That drunk for a father and that bitch of a social worker are both up in arms about her running away, you can't go walking around town looking like that." The man kicked the small stool across the room, "I told you we should have ended this days ago Stanley, she's costing too much now."

"I'm not ready." Stan said miserably, holding a cloth to his torn and bloody face.

Emily had woken when they had first started talking, but she had been careful to keep still, scared of the repercussions of her actions. She had been hoping to get the key off Stan during the quick attack, but hadn't gotten the chance.

Her right wrist was still unshackled, but her left wrist was still in the irons, and she could see the key was back on its hook near the trapdoor.

"This is not going to end any other way, you knew that." The bigger man's voice seemed almost kind to Stan, "We'll get you another girl. We always do."

"But she's mine. He told me that she would be mine forever."

"Til death do you part." The bigger man corrected, "It's just that the time of her death has come now."

∞

Emily woke up to a wet lick, starting at her chin and finishing in her hair. "Gross Mutt, off!" She squealed, covering her head with the blanket. She heard laughter from the doorway and pulled the blanket down again.

Liam was leaning against the door frame, dressed in fresh jeans and a dark blue button up, a cup of coffee in his each of his hands.

"I really don't think it's fair that you name that poor mongrel Mutt." Liam smiled and walked into the room, handing her a cup of coffee. "And if I didn't know better, I'd say he was jealous someone else got to share your bed last night."

Emily blushed, feeling suddenly awkward. The dream she had been having was drifting in and out of focus, making her feel dirty and ashamed.

Liam leant down and kissed her on the mouth, "Good morning." He smiled at her.

"Go away, I haven't brushed my teeth." Emily said, pushing him away good naturedly, hoping he wouldn't pick up on her feelings.

"I'm making breakfast. Sophie's been up for an hour and is apparently starving to death." Liam rolled his eyes, "So go shower and come through."

He kissed her once more on the top of her head and left the room.

Mutt took his chance and jumped onto the bed, flopping down next to her and looking at her with a forlorn expression on his face.

"What?" Emily asked him, pulling the blanket up to cover herself before giving Mutt a rub behind the ears.

After showering and dressing in jeans and a t-shirt, Emily joined Sophie and Liam at the dining table for some French toast and fruit juice. Sophie had poured syrup on her own toast and was feeding Mutt the crusts with sticky fingers.

"Looks like I'm going to have competition for his affection now." Emily said mildly, watching Mutt take the toast gently between his front teeth, careful not to touch Sophie's hand.

"I like him Daddy." Sophie said happily.

"I can see that." Liam told her, "But then, you'd like anyone that ate the crusts so that you didn't have to."

Emily took a bite of toast and watched Mutt eating his share under the table. "What are your plans for this morning?" She asked Liam. Now that the morning had come, the fears and dangers from last night were forefront in her mind.

"I'm heading to the station now to go over Paige's surveillance tapes in case they may have missed something and will follow up with the night shift. Then," Liam shrugged in frustration, "then I don't know. Stay near you girls."

"I still think I should head back today." Emily told him.

"I thought we discussed that last night." Liam said, placing his coffee carefully on the table.

"Yes we did," Emily said gently, "and I want to go for all the reasons I had last night. Only more so now."

"Did I do something wrong?" Liam asked, looking at her with concern on his handsome face.

"Liam, never has anyone ever done anything so right." Emily smiled at him across the table. "And if you're in, then so am I." Emily held up a hand when he started to smile, "But, only when this mess is over."

Liam grumbled something incoherent then stood up to take the empty plates through to the kitchen.

"Why didn't we just sleep at our house last night Daddy?" Sophie asked, now licking her own fingers and making Emily grimace.

"We thought it would be fun to have a sleepover." Liam told her over his shoulder. "Bring me your empty glass please so I can wash it, then I need to take you to Bee for a little bit."

Emily took the empty glass from Sophie, "You cooked, I'll wash up. You go and do what you have to do."

Liam turned to face her, wiping his hands on a dishcloth, "And what are you going to do?"

"I won't bolt without saying goodbye." Emily reassured him. The expression on Liam's face told her that's exactly what he thought she was going to do.

422

"Relax Liam, the morning plane is leaving too soon and I would have to find out if they would let me take Mutt. I suppose I'd have to go get one of those pet crate things from the pet shop first, so I'm not going anywhere yet."

Liam put the cloth down on the counter and walked to Emily, wrapping his arms around her waist. "Were you serious when you said you were in?" He asked, searching her face.

Emily put her own arms around his neck. "I'm probably going to make a huge mess of it, and you're probably going to end up hating me. But yes, I meant it."

Liam kissed her gently.

"Gross Daddy!" Sophie was back from washing her hands in the bathroom, Mutt trailing along behind her. "Sheesh, I thought you weren't getting married." The little girl rolled her eyes so much like her father that Emily laughed.

"No one said anything about marriage." Liam told her, keeping on arm around Emily's waist, "But we did think it might be nice to have Emily around more often. What do you think?"

Sophie shrugged, "I think it's awesome. And if the dog stays with Emily, then I'll be able to play with him whenever."

Liam smiled at his daughter, then gave Emily a quick kiss on the cheek. "I'll see you in a bit."

"Bye." Emily watched them leave and close the door behind them.

"Come on Mutt, we've got to hurry." Emily went through to the bathroom to collect the toiletries she had already packed after her shower, then went through to the bedroom to pack the last of her clothes into her suitcase.

She hadn't wanted to argue with Liam, but she had to leave. For him, Sophie, Paige and for Casey, she knew she was doing the right thing. Emily had already booked a ticket online for the morning flight and she had also arranged a rental pet carrier through the airline for Mutt.

Emily looked around the room, collecting her laptop bag, mobile chargers and her suitcase, taking them through to the front door.

She wasn't sure how she was going to get past the deputy stationed outside. She just had to hope that she would be able to get to the airport before Liam tried to stop her.

Emily took her suitcase out to the car with a bowl of dog pellets and another empty bowl for water, intending to go back into the house for her laptop and handbag. Mutt joined her outside and leapt gleefully into the backseat, eager for another road trip. Emily went to the boot and threw her bag and the bowls inside.

Reaching into her pocket, Emily pulled out her personal mobile to send Paige a text and let her know she was leaving.

Emily unlocked the screen to find another photo had been sent. She opened it warily, hoping the sicko hadn't had a chance to take photos of her and Liam in bed last night.

The picture loaded and it took a full minute for Emily to realise what she was seeing. Paige, her hands tied behind her back, her feet had been hogtied to her hands and she was gagged. Emily could make out blood on Paige's hairline.

"Oh God." She whispered, her hand to her mouth.

*Like what you see?*

The text came through, quickly followed by another one: *It's not a party without you little one. So why don't you join us?*

Emily tried to type back with shaky fingers, *Please don't hurt her.*

*That's up to you. I'm tracking your mobiles, so don't call your boyfriend or attempt to contact anyone else. I'm going to send you directions. Once you're on the road, I'll send more. And hurry, your darling friend doesn't look so good.* ☺

Emily swallowed, feeling sick. Mutt stuck his head through the open window and tried to lick Emily's face, but she didn't notice. Her hands were still shaking when the text with directions came through. She knew she didn't have a choice, there was no way she could run now.

Emily climbed into the driver's seat and started the engine. She didn't have time to think. She quickly typed a response: *On my way*

*That's a good girl*

The reply made her skin crawl, but Emily put the mobile in the cup holder of the center console and put on her seatbelt.

She had just put the car into reverse and put the handbrake down when there was a knock on the driver's window made her jump with fright. The deputy was standing outside her window, a polite smile on his face.

Emily opened the driver's window while telling herself to act calm.

"Heading out?" He asked her cheerfully.

"Yeah, I just need to get some milk, Sophie drank all of mine." Emily said in the friendliest voice she could manage.

"I should come with you." He said, tucking his thumbs into his belt.

"I'd rather you stayed here and made sure that sicko doesn't get in. Especially with all the pictures he's been taking." Emily said carefully, trying not to look rushed.

"Maybe you should wait for Liam to come back? He said he wouldn't take long."

"Listen, I'm not a very nice person without my morning coffee and if I don't get some soon, Liam's issue isn't going to be with the freak following me." Emily said impatiently. "I'll be back in five minutes." She took her foot off the brake, hoping she came across as bossy instead of hysterical.

Emily drove out of the driveway, careful to head towards town and made sure the deputy hadn't started his car. He was standing in the driveway looking after her in bewilderment.

Once around the corner, Emily picked up her mobile to check the directions. She was to go through the forest, and past the cemetery, heading out of town. After that, she had no idea. She put the mobile back in the cup holder next to her and drove as fast as she dared, not wanting to draw attention to herself.

# Chapter Thirty-Three

Liam had just driven into the station parking when his cruiser radio crackled to life.

"Sheriff?"

It was Sam, the day shift deputy watching Emily.

"What is it Sam?" Liam asked hurriedly, wanting to get inside and go through the meagre evidence he had from Emily's case.

"Yeah, I thought I should let you know that your lady friend went tearing out of here."

"What?" Liam yelled into the radio handset. "Where did she go? Did you follow her?"

"She told me not to Sir, she said she was just going to get milk and that I should watch the cottage."

"Goddammit." Liam muttered, slamming down the radio. She promised him she wouldn't leave.

He pulled out his mobile and called Emily's number, unsurprised to find it was cut off at the first ring.

"Dammit!" He said again, hitting his dashboard in frustration.

He rushed into the station, calling to Muriel as soon as he was inside.

"What's up Boss?"

"Call the airport," Liam instructed, "find out if they have any tickets booked under the name Emily Winter."

"Sure thing Boss." Muriel said cheerfully, picking up the handset on her desk.

Liam rushed through to his office to collect the post-it note on his screen. If he was right and Emily was heading for the airport, he didn't have time to try call the old sheriff again now.

He went back to the front desk and handed Muriel the post-it.

"She's booked on the flight leaving in the next twenty minutes. She should be boarding any second." Muriel informed him, taking the number from him. "Want me to tell them to ground the plane?"

"No." Liam said, shaking his head, "You just keep dialing that number until someone answers it and gives me some damn answers."

Liam was out the station and back in his cruiser before Muriel had even been able to respond. He put on his sirens for the first time in his position as sheriff and tore out of the parking lot.

He knew he was cutting it fine, he wasn't sure if he was even going to make it to the airport on time. The only thing he kept thinking is that she must be running late as well. She couldn't have made it there already, at most she probably had a ten minute head start. If Liam was lucky, the plane would take off without her, but if not, he hoped he could still make it there before it took off.

As he drove at high speed through the winding, narrow roads, Liam asked himself why he was bothering to chase her at all. It was obvious she wanted to leave.

He didn't know what was driving his desperate urge to get to her before she left, but he had a sickening feeling that if he was too late, something terrible was going to happen and he wouldn't be able to stop it.

Liam skidded to a stop at the small airport just as the plane began to taxi down the runway. Hoping she might have been too late, Liam ignored his mobile when he saw it was Daniel McKenzie's number flashing on the screen. He didn't have time to update the man now. He bolted into the airport and ran to the flight desk, scaring the janitor as he shot past.

"Did Emily Winter get on that plane?" He asked breathlessly.

The woman behind the counter lifted her eyebrow in surprise, but answered, "No Sheriff, she did not. She booked a seat for herself and for a canine, but we've been calling her for the last half an hour with no response. We didn't have a choice but to bump her to the later flight."

Liam sighed with relief. "Thank you." He told her, "If she gets here, I want you to contact me immediately. Do not let her board a plane." Liam handed her his card.

"Is she dangerous?" The woman asked in concern.

Liam shook his head, "Unpaid parking ticket." He said simply before turning and rushing back out of the airport.

It was only when he got to his cruiser that it occurred to him that Emily should have been on the road in front of him then. He had passed only two cars on the way and neither of them were her rental.

He got back into his cruiser, pulling out his mobile to call her number again, only to have it start ringing in his hand. It was Daniel again. He pushed the answer button.

"What is it Daniel?" He asked sharply.

"It's Paige. She told Casey she was going to the shop over an hour ago and she hasn't been back. She was supposed to be packing for us to leave, not shopping. Now her phone is off and no one in town has seen her or the car."

"Fuck!" Liam exclaimed. "I'm on my way."

He dropped the mobile on the seat next to him, turned his siren on and screeched back onto the main road, a sickening feeling threatening to engulf him.

Daniel and two deputies were waiting in the driveway when Liam pulled up.

"Any word?" Liam asked, getting out of his cruiser and rushing up to the trio.

Daniel shook his head with a worried expression. "She never would have gone off without telling me where and she never leaves her phone off. Especially since Casey."

"Where is Casey?" Liam asked urgently.

"Upstairs in her room."

Liam turned to one of the deputies, "You don't let that girl out of your sight, if she needs to pee, you stand in the room and face the wall. Got it?"

"Yes Sir." The young deputy said, rushing off towards the house.

"Where did she say she was going?" Liam asked, turning back to Daniel.

"She told Casey she had to get some things at the shop, which is strange in itself, because we didn't need anything.

I was planning on taking my family on a vacation, starting this morning, and staying away until you sorted things out here."

Liam ran a hand over his face in frustration. "Is there anywhere, anywhere at all that she may have gone?"

Daniel shook his head again. "Casey thought she might have gone past Emily at the cottage to say goodbye, but your deputy radioed the man on guard and he said no one had been there."

"You stay here with the deputy," Liam told Daniel, trying to keep his own panic down, "let me know immediately if there's any contact at all."

"Where are you going?" Daniel asked him as Liam started walking back to his cruiser.

"To the cottage to see if I can find any sign of either of them."

"Emily's also missing?" Daniel asked, horror stuck.

"I'll keep you informed." Liam called, not answering the question.

Liam arrived at the cottage a few minutes later. Sam the deputy was standing near the front door.

"It's not locked." He told Liam as Liam was pulling the spare key out of his pocket. "I did a sweep of the inside as soon as I got off the radio with you."

Liam walked up to the door and opened it. He stepped into the cottage properly and saw Emily's handbag and laptop case dumped near the doorway. "She didn't take her handbag." Liam said, more to himself than to Sam. He picked up the bag and looked inside, hoping to find something, anything that would give him an indication of where she had gone.

"What exactly did she say to you?" Liam asked Sam.

"Just that she needed her morning coffee or you were going to have to deal with her and that she would be back in five minutes."

"How did she seem?"

"Pretty hyped up actually. Couldn't tell if she was furious about the milk or something else, but she was real on edge. Nearly jumped out of her skin when I tapped on her window."

"And you didn't think to follow her?" Liam asked in anger.

"No Sir, she made that damn clear. Said I needed to watch the house because of the perp taking pics from outside."

Liam wanted to punch a wall, but knew it wouldn't do any good. Instead he opened Emily's handbag again, riffling through her purse, looking for clues.

Leaving the bag open and the old till slips he had tossed strewn all over the floor, Liam moved onto the laptop case. He pulled the laptop out and powered it up, thinking that maybe there was something in her emails, or maybe her mobile was linked to her laptop and he might be able to track her.

An instant message popped up as soon as the laptop had powered on. Someone Emily listed as Deep Dark Man.

*I don't have a name, but I did manage to get a pic of someone from the phone's media files. There were a lot more that were deleted and I couldn't get them back. Let me know if you need more. Ned*

Liam clicked on the attachment, realizing this was the contact Emily had enlisted the night before to track the mobile.

The picture wasn't very clear, and it only showed the top right-hand side of a face, taken selfie style, but Liam recognised the glasses immediately.

"Get deputies out to the Downings place. Have them break down the door if they have to. I want that little fucker Phillip in custody immediately. Confiscate any and all electronics you find."

"Without a warrant Sir?" Sam asked timidly.

"Now, Goddammit, we have plenty probable cause. Go!"

Liam headed for his cruiser, he knew it was a long shot, but he wanted to check the cabin. Maybe Phillip was stupid enough to take them there.

"Sam!" Liam called out as he started his cruiser.

"Sir?" Sam asked, pulling his head from the patrol car, where he was using the radio.

"Do not, for one second, take your eyes off my daughter. You get me?"

Sam nodded, "I got you Sir."

Liam pulled the cruiser to a stop in front of the fallen tree where he had stopped on his previous trip to the cabin. He pulled out his gun and made sure the safety was off before heading quietly towards the cottage.

How had Phillip gotten involved? Liam asked himself for the twentieth time. His father definitely didn't fit the profile of the second perpetrator, but Phillip was too young to have been the accomplice.

Liam had called Muriel from the car and asked her to pull up everything she could find on the Downings and their son. Liam had a vague memory of someone mentioning that

Phillip was adopted, but he knew it couldn't have been a local adoption.

The cabin door seemed the same as Liam had left it, but still, he entered the darkened room with his weapon drawn and his torch on, listening for sounds that would give away any sign that he wasn't alone.

The main room was as empty as it was before, but Liam noticed new footprints in the thick layer of dust on the floor. It looked as though someone had tried to stand in his own footprints from his previous visit, but had miss-stepped a few times.

Liam held his breath as he started down the rickety stairs to the cellar, but found it empty as soon as he was able to duck down and look inside. He walked to the end of the room, trying to see what was different from his last visit and now.

The rats were scurrying around, trying to get away from the thin beam of light from Liam's torch. He shone it around the room and settled it on the wall next to the pile of rags in the corner. That's when he saw it. There was a hole in the wall where the shackles were once bolted.

The shackles were gone.

# Chapter Thirty-Four

**E**mily pulled her car to a stop on the side of the dirt road, taking out her mobile to check the instructions. She was heading further into the wilder forests than she had ever gone before. She looked into her review mirror. Mutt's face was between the headrests, his tongue lolling out happily. She didn't want him to be in danger, she had brought enough people into her horror story as it is. Emily got out the car and called Mutt who followed her happily. He immediately started sniffing the bushes nearest the car, but when he realised Emily was getting back into the car, he ran back to her. She got out again, "Go on! Get!" She yelled at him. Mutt cocked his head in confusion, then tried to take another step towards the car.

"Go on you stupid mutt! Get out of here, go back to town where it's safe." When he didn't turn away, Emily picked up a handful of gravel and started throwing it at him.

Mutt yelped when a piece hit him in the face and backed off a little with a growl.

"Please just go." Emily begged him, hating the look of confusion on his furry face. She threw another handful before Mutt turned around and bolted into the forest to her left.

Emily sighed sadly, she hadn't even given the poor dog any thought when she had left. She should have left him with the deputy. She climbed back into the idling car and put it back into drive and took the small, overgrown road to the left as instructed. As promised, about a mile down the road she came to a dead end. She parked the car as close to the bush as possible and got out, finding the camouflaged tarp exactly where the text had said it would be. With difficulty, Emily managed to haul the tarp over the car and pull it into place until the car was covered as instructed. Standing back, she realised that no one would see the car from the road, not even if they were looking for it.

A chill ran down her spine, the forest was wild out here, nothing like the pine trees from town. She knew somewhere, waiting nearby was a monster, wanting to hurt her. And she was heading straight towards him.
Emily felt her mobile vibrate in her pocket and pulled it out. Reading the new set of instructions, Emily memorised where she was heading then put the phone on the floor and crushed it beneath her boot. Knowing she was probably being watched, she didn't want to skip a single step, not wanting to put Paige in anymore danger than she was already in, Emily took her work mobile out her back pocket, she held it up in the air before putting it next to her personal one and crushing it as well. She had no way of calling for help now.

Emily took a deep breath and headed deeper into the wild tangle of brush and trees. It grew darker the deeper she went, her footsteps muted by the layer of fallen and soggy leaves. Every crackle of twigs snapping or leaves crunching sent Emily's heart into her throat, she didn't think she had ever been so truly afraid. She walked carefully, counting her steps, ninety four, ninety five, ninety six. When she got to one hundred and fifty, she looked for a small foot path to her right, heading up a steep incline. She found it a few feet ahead of where she had stopped and started climbing. The ground beneath her feet was slick and muddy, Emily found herself on her hands and knees more than once, having to haul herself back up repeatedly, holding an exposed root or low-hanging branch. Her hands and knees were already grazed and her hip was throbbing painfully at the steep climb, but Emily pushed on, ignoring the pain, ignoring the terror welling up inside her.

When she finally reached the top of the steep slope, Emily came to a small clearing. She could hear water flowing somewhere in the distance, the sounds of birds and insects chirping all around. Up ahead she saw a small cottage. It looked like an old, abandoned hunter's lodge. Built from roughly cut wooden poles with a thatched roof, it had an unpleasant similarity to the cottage that had been Emily's prison so many years before. Emily took a careful step into the clearing, almost crouching, hyper aware of everything around her. The small window of the cabin was boarded over, so there was no way for her to see if anyone was inside.

The sudden silence of the creatures around her brought Emily up short, but before she could do anything but take a breath, she felt a sharp pain in the back of her neck and upper back and fell to the ground, white explosions bursting in front of her eyes. Emily felt her body jerk, then nothing.

∞

Liam parked his car back at the station and hurried inside. "Have they found anything at the Downing's place?" He barked at Muriel as soon as he got in the door.

"The Downings left on a Mediterranean cruise three days ago Sheriff." Muriel told him, handing him the notes she had written down. "It was believed that Phillip had gone with them, but when I called the booking agents that the Downings used, there were only two tickets reserved. Molly said the boy had taken leave because he was going on the cruise, so he must have been hiding out somewhere."

Liam had never in his life felt so helpless. "Did they find anything in the house that could connect him to anything?"

Muriel shook her head. "Not a thing. There were no computers, laptops or mobile phones in the house. Wherever he is, he must have them with them. Molly told me he has a laptop he always keeps with him and that she's forever telling him to get off his mobile while he's at work. She's real shook up Sheriff."

Liam rubbed his eyes roughly as he listened.

"Does old man Downing have any other properties in the area?"

"No sir, he doesn't even own the house they live in now, it's a forestry house."

"Dammit!" Liam snarled, slamming his fist down on the counter. "What about Dave Brown, have you gotten hold of him yet?"

"I'm really sorry to tell you this, I didn't want to tell you over the radio and have the older guys hearing either. The phone was eventually answered by a housekeeper. She said he left to go to his nephew for a few days but was killed in

438

a car accident on his way there. His nephew identified the body. The car was destroyed. She didn't know anything about any packages that were supposed to be sent out before he left. But that doesn't mean it's not on its way still. Could be he posted it using snail mail before he left."

"Goddammit!" Liam yelled, slamming his fist on the counter again. "Maybe Phillip intercepted it from the post office if Brown had sent it before the accident. It would explain how he knew enough about the case to do what he's done so far." Liam was talking more to himself than to Muriel, but she was nodding along with everything he said. "If he has a connection in the post office, it could explain how he managed to get Emily's address in the city." Liam continued this train of thought.

Liam went back to the cruiser to get Emily's laptop from the front seat. He took it into his office and opened it. He clicked on the instant message that Emily's contact had sent the photo from.

*Is there anything else you can find from the number? Any new movements? Also track these please. I'll pay whatever.* Liam added both of Emily's numbers and Paige's mobile number to the message, hoping he would have a better time tracing them.

Liam was looking through the files hoping that Emily might have the Find-my-Phone app, but if she did, he couldn't find it.

*Who is this? I know it's not EW.*

"Shit." Liam cursed loudly, then typed. *No, but I am a friend. She's been taken by the guy in the first picture and I need to get her back.*

The police line rang in the front and Muriel answered it quickly. Moments later she called out, "Sir, there's someone on the phone for you. He's insisting he speak to the sheriff and no one else."

Liam picked up the extension. "Hello?"

"Yeah, someone's gotten hold of a friend's laptop, I think she might be in trouble. I'm not sure of her name, but I know she's there in town."

"Ned?" Liam asked.

"Who is this?"

"This is Sheriff William Richards, I'm the one with the laptop. Our friend was taken hours ago and I have no other way to track her."

"Sheeet," The voice on the other end of the line said, "Ya'll gonna bang me up if I help you?"

"I don't care what it takes or how many laws you have to break. You get busted, I'll deal with it." Liam promised.

"Yeah, alright, let me see what I can dig up man."

"Thanks."

Liam gave Ned his own mobile number and thanked him before putting the phone back in its cradle.

"Hey Boss?" Muriel was standing at the door. "I know it's not my place to ask, but don't you think it's time to bring the feds in?"

Liam looked at the receptionist. "Yeah it is, but I don't have time to sit around waiting for them to get here and then taking them through what we have and don't have." Liam said.

"Policy dictates they need to be brought in." Muriel pointed out gently.

440

Liam nodded, "Make the call. Tell them I'm busy unless they have something useful to add."

"Will do Boss." Muriel turned away.

Liam put his face in his hands and tried to steady his breathing. He had no idea what to do next. He was scared and worried sick. Every time he thought about Emily might be going through, it felt as though an icy sword was being thrust through his heart. He had to save her, he just didn't know how. He kept picturing Mel's bloodied face and broken body, then picturing Emily in her place, beaten to death and it made him sick to his stomach.

Getting out of his chair again, he yelled to Muriel that he was going to the Downing's house to look around for himself.

∞

Casey sat on the sofa in the living room staring at the wall. She hadn't moved in what felt like hours. She was in shock, she knew, but she couldn't bring herself out of it. Her father had been pacing the room talking to one of the deputies for ages, but Casey didn't hear a word of what they were saying. She was picturing her mother going through the things that Casey had gone through months before and no matter how hard she tried, Casey couldn't get the pictures out of her head. The flashbacks kept warping in her mind, one second it was her being held down and brutalised, the next second it was her mother, screaming for mercy. Casey put her hands over her ears as though to block out the screams and rocked on the sofa. Her father sat beside her and took her in his arms.

"It's going to be okay." He told her, holding her tight.

"It's not Dad, it's not." Casey wailed, she knew she was becoming hysterical.

"Maybe I should call the doctor?" The deputy asked, shifting uncomfortably from one foot to another. He was the oldest of nine kids and he did not want to ever have to witness childbirth up close again.

"Please." Daniel said, "Ask him to get here as soon as he can. Liam told us not to leave the house."

"You got it." The deputy left the room, relief obvious on his ruddy face.

∞

Liam had come up empty at the Downing's. He had pulled Phillip's room apart, piece by piece but hadn't found anything that would help him. He was heading back to his cruiser when one of the deputies followed him out. "Sir." He called out.

Liam stopped and turned.

"I don't know if this will help, but I found it in the back of an old photo album in the dining room." The deputy held out an old manila envelope to Liam.

Liam pulled out the papers inside. They were adoption papers. On the second page was the name of Phillip Downing's birth mother. "Thanks." Liam said, getting into his cruiser and pulling out his mobile. He called Muriel and asked her to do a check on the name of the birth mother and get back to him as soon as possible.

Liam drove out of the Downing house and headed towards the McKenzie house, wanting to go around the yard again in case they had missed something earlier.

∞

"Emily!" A voice hissed through the cloudy fog of Emily's thoughts. "Emily, are you okay?" Emily turned her head to one side, feeling the sudden onslaught of pain in her head. She tried to sit up but couldn't. She didn't know if she was in a nightmare or not. She couldn't remember where she was or what she had been doing. Emily tried to lift a hand to the back her head to see if there was blood but her hands didn't seem to want to respond. She tugged he right hand again, feeling confused and suddenly wanting to vomit.

"Emily, can you hear me?" The shrill whisper came again. Emily tried to open her eyes but the light hurt so badly she shut them again.

"Emily!"

"What?" She moaned loudly in response.

"Shh, he might hear you."

Emily recognised Paige's voice now through the pain fogging her mind. In seconds, the past several hours caught up with Emily's conscious thoughts. She twisted her body sharply towards the voice. "Paige? Are you okay?"

"Please Emily shh, yes I'm fine, but you need to whisper. Are you alright?"

Emily tried to open her eyes again, blinking against the light. If she turned her head to the side, she was able to move away from it slightly.

They were in a dark, square room from what Emily could make out. There was a single bright spotlight shining onto her face, so it was hard to see anything behind it. The floor beneath Emily's hands felt like and smelt like freshly compressed earth, not wood or tiling. With a sinking feeling of dread, Emily realised they were underground, in what was probably another hidden basement under the old hunting cabin.

Emily was lying on her side, her hands restrained behind her back and her feet tied together at the ankles. She tried again to get herself into a sitting position but it was impossible. There was a length of rope tying her hands to her ankles, leaving her effectively hog-tied.

Paige was in a similar position to Emily's right, just in the shadow of the spotlight. Emily could see the older woman's hair was matted with blood.

"How badly are you hurt?" Emily whispered to her.

"Not too badly, I haven't felt fresh blood for a while." Paige answered. "What about you? He was laughing about tasing you and how high he had set the taser."

That explains the headache, Emily thought, but then suddenly, she realised something else. "Who is it? Who took you?" She asked in an urgent voice.

"Phillip Downing." Paige whispered back in disgust.

The image of Phillip's spotty face swam in Emily's mind. "I'm going to kill that little fucker with my bare hands."

"Get in line." Paige commented dryly. "Except for the fact that we're at his mercy at the moment."

Emily struggled with her restraints, pulling against them, chaffing her wrists raw. Pain exploded in her head from the exertion, making her roll back to the side to throw up. She coughed and choked, unable to get herself into a better position.

"Emily!" Paige called her, terror in her voice, "Are you alright?"

Emily spat out the bile that was in her mouth. "Yeah, I think I've got a concussion or something." She managed to mumble.

She took a deep breath then tried once more to pull on the restraints. She was desperately reaching for her boots.

"What are you doing? You're going to hurt yourself." Paige whispered.

"I love these boots." Emily said, wiggling her body against the wall so that she could reach her feet easier.

Paige didn't understand what was going on, "We have to get you to a hospital."

Emily twisted one last time, finally able to get hold of the heel of her left boot. "Ha!" She said a little too loudly.

Above their heads, they could hear the sound of footsteps. "He's coming back!" Even through her whisper, the terror in Paige's voice was evident.

"I'm not crazy, I promise." Emily whispered back calmly, "I've got a secret weapon."

# Chapter Thirty-Five

Liam pulled his cruiser in behind the local doctor's SUV and got out, meeting the man in the driveway.

Christian Stone had paused on his way to the door and waited for Liam to join him.

"Is it true?" He asked Liam as they made their way towards the house, "Emily Winter has been taken as well as Paige?"

Liam nodded curtly, not trusting himself to speak.

"Do you have any idea who may be responsible?" Christian asked, feeling as helpless as the sheriff beside him. Christian could still see the moment he first realised Emily was alive so vividly that there were times that he swore he could smell the coppery scent of blood when he thought about it.

"We know who it is, but we can't find him. Why are you here?" Liam asked, knocking on the front door and finding it ajar.

"Your deputy said that Casey wasn't coping well, he thought she was close to hysteria. Daniel requested I come and see what I can do for her."

Liam stopped listening as he pushed the door open. On the floor, near the stairs leading to the second floor was a neatly tied sprig of lavender.

"Doctor, get outside, now!" Liam ordered, pulling his weapon from its holster and making his way cautiously into the house.

Liam didn't bother to check if the doctor had listened or not, he did a quick sweep of the entrance hall before moving into the kitchen. He saw the shiny black boot of a deputy uniform sticking out from behind the center island. After making sure the corners were clear, Liam rushed round and found his deputy lying face down in a puddle of blood. Feeling for a pulse, Liam found one, although it was weak and thready. Liam rolled the deputy into the recovery position and took off his jacket to place under the other man's bloody head.

Standing up, Liam went quickly and quietly into the living room, adrenalin taking over. He dreaded what he might find, but his instincts took over and he swept into the living room at a crouch, clearing the room with his eyes. Daniel McKenzie lay on his side near the coffee table. Liam approached him and was relieved to find a strong pulse. There were burn marks on Daniel's neck, the tell-tale marks of a stun-gun.

A broken coffee mug was near the sofa, next to the blanket that was usually on the back of the sofa. It was scrunched up as though it had been hurriedly thrown aside. A lamp near the fireplace lay broken on its side, Liam could follow the track of the occupants leaving the house. It was clear that Casey had put up a fight. The sliding door was open to the back yard and in the distance, the forest stood dark and quiet.

Liam took the stairs two at a time to the second floor and searched every room, but Casey was nowhere to be found. The main bedroom window was wide open, the breeze making the curtains billow out into the room.

As soon as he was sure the house was clear, Liam yelled out for the doctor to come inside.

Christian followed the sound of Liam's voice and found him in the kitchen, holding a cloth to the head of the bleeding deputy.

Christian immediately knelt beside them and opened his case.

"Casey and Daniel?" He asked Liam while manipulating the loose skin around the head wound and finding fractures in the deputy's skull.

"Daniel is in the living room, I think he took a taser to the neck, but his pulse is strong."

"Casey?" Christian asked as he felt the back of the deputy's neck, his deft fingers probing the vertebrae beneath the skin.

Liam shook his head, "She's not here."

"Call an ambulance, this man is going to need immediate surgery." Christian told him. "Then go find this monster, I'll wait here."

Liam nodded, getting to his feet and pulling his mobile out again, not even noticing the blood on his hands or soaking through the knees of his trousers.

∞

A trap door opened somewhere behind the spotlight, Emily could hear the hinges creaking but couldn't see anything behind the light. She could only hear the sound of something solid hitting the earth and then heard the sound of shoes on metal stairs.

"Well, well, well. I was beginning to think I used too much juice on you." Phillip walked towards Emily, a sickeningly arrogant grin on his face. "Nice to have you back with us." Phillip took hold of the stand the spotlight was on and pulled it back towards the opposite side of the room, bringing the rest of the room into the light. "It's not much, I know, but it will have to do." Emily could see Paige clearly now, although the other woman was lying silent and still. The room was bigger than Emily had originally thought, past Paige was a bare mattress, up against the wall, where she could see now, shackles had been bolted to the wall. Bile rose in her throat.

"You like?" Phillip asked, watching Emily as she looked around.

"Why are you doing this?" Emily asked him, managing to stop her voice from trembling.

"Why do you think?" Phillip asked her, crouching down near her as though they were having a friendly chat.

"Because you're a sick little pervert?" Emily asked with as much sarcasm as she could muster.

"I AM NOT A PERVERT!" Phillip screamed suddenly, his shrill voice echoing and bouncing off the rough walls.

"Then why?" Emily yelled back, refusing to be scared of him.

"You're the pervert!" Phillip said, his crazy grin back in place. "This is what you wanted."

"What the hell are you talking about?"

"You did this to yourself!" Phillip continued, waving his arms around, "You did this to me!"

"I never did anything to you!" Emily yelled at him.

"You killed my father!" Phillip yelled back.

"What?" Emily asked, shocked into silence.

"My pathetic birth mother was one of the first I was told. But you, you were supposed to be special. My father loved you. He worshipped the ground you walked on." Phillip's voice was quiet now, taking on a younger tone. "He said you would bring the new world order. He would be the Father and you would be his Mary."

"Stan was your father?" Emily asked, feeling nauseous again.

"My mother wasn't Mary, so when she was taken care of, my uncle took her to the hospital, pretending he found her. He waited there until I was born and she was declared dead before leaving. My father came to find me not long after, to tell me who I was and who I would one day become." Phillip licked the sweat off his upper lip, "But then you came along and killed him! Murderous little slut."

"You're crazy." Emily said, struggling to comprehend was she was hearing.

"You were supposed to love and honor my father! You were his and he was yours! Do you have any idea what kind of a gift he gave you?"

"Gift?" Emily choked out a laugh, "He was a sick fuck who enjoyed torturing and killing teenage girls. He was a monster!"

"He was searching!" Phillip told her, his eyes wide and wild behind his filthy glasses. "And when he thought he had finally found Mary, she was just another little whore who couldn't close her legs."

"Phillip." Paige said quietly from the other side of the room, "Listen to what you're saying."

450

Phillip rounded on Paige, his face contorted with rage, pulling a large hunting knife from his belt. "You shut up! Or I'll cut your tongue out! Demon whore!"

"What about your uncle?" Emily asked, desperate to get his attention off Paige.

"What about him?"

"He also raped me." Emily said. It was the first time she had every used the word out loud and it felt wrong. It made her feel weak and dirty.

"He wouldn't. He knew you were my father's. He looked after both of you. He kept your relationship a secret."

Emily shook her head vigorously, "No, that's not true Phillip. He and Stan took turns raping me over and over again."

"LIAR!" Phillip rushed at her with the knife, and Emily was certain he was about to plunge it into her face.

He stopped just short of her, cocking his head to the side as though he were studying an interesting piece of art. Slowly, deliberately, he placed the tip of the blade on Emily's jaw and pushed the tip into the skin slowly. Emily cried out in pain as the blade pierced her skin and he pulled it down toward her chin.

"Phillip stop!" Paige screamed from across the room.

Phillip pulled the knife away then lifted it above his head and brought the handle down viciously, the ivory handle slamming into Emily's temple.

∞

Liam called Muriel as soon as he had finished calling for an ambulance.

"What do you need Boss?"

"Did you call in the big guns?" Liam asked her.

"Yes, they said they would be sending someone out and asked for all the info I had."

"Okay, good. I think there's a second accomplice helping Phillip."

"Good Lord! How many sickos can we have in one town?"

"Call the mill and find out if any of the men didn't show for work today, then work your way down any of the other businesses you can think of. Then call Brad, he was supposed to be doing rounds at the McKenzie place, but he's not here. Kenny Steeple has been injured, Dr. Stone is with him now, waiting for an ambulance, you better call his mom and sister, they can meet them at the hospital."

"Yes sir. Poor boy, is he going to be okay?"

"I don't know." Liam answered honestly.

Getting into his car, Liam heard a ping and looked at his mobile to see he had been sent a message from Ned, Emily's dark web connection.

*Call me.*

Liam called the number, waiting anxiously while it rang.

"Yoh, cop man."

"Did you find something?"

"Yeah, your friends' numbers are all no longer connected to the service, but our friend was smart enough to leave her location on until the mobile was disconnected."

"Have you got a location?"

"I can tell you she was moving towards the east side of town, she got a ping from one of the towers the next town over, is there anywhere there you can think of?"

"There's only one heading out of town to Brexton and another up the mountain to the hiking trails. Anything else?"

"Nah man, that's all I got."

"Thanks." Liam disconnected the call then called the precinct again. "Muriel, find out if Phillip has any friends or family out in Brexton, maybe old school friends or something."

"Will do. I already called the school to see if there was anyone he was friendly with at school, but they haven't gotten back to me with the list yet."

"Let me know."

∞

Emily felt something cold on her head and tried to pull away. "Stop that." Phillip ordered, putting the cold compress back on Emily's temple where he had hit her.

Emily's face contorted in pain. Her vision was blurry, she was sure if she didn't have a concussion before, she had one now.

"I shouldn't have hit you so hard, I just got angry. It was your fault." Phillip sounded like a petulant child. "But I'm making it better now."

Emily was struggling to get her thoughts into a coherent pattern. "Where's Paige?" She mumbled quietly, "Please don't hurt her."

"I don't want to hurt her." Phillip told Emily, he wiped the hair out of Emily's face gently. "She was needed to get you here. Of course, I don't think we'll let her go, that just wouldn't be a good idea."

"Please let her go." Emily begged, her voice gaining a little strength.

"Think about it Emily, if we let her go, she'll know everything."

Emily looked at him out of the corner of her eye, "Who's we?"

Phillip dropped the compress and backed away. "Not your concern yet. You'll find out soon enough."

Phillip moved the spotlight closer to Emily, shining it directly on her face, making her head throb painfully again. Then he climbed back out the trapdoor, pulled a ladder up and shut the door again. Emily could hear a padlock being closed above and knew they were properly trapped.

"I'm so sorry Paige." Emily said quietly, looking towards the silhouette of her friend, "I'm so so sorry this has happened to you."

"This isn't your fault." Paige said, ever the caregiver. "This is his fault, and it's not over yet. Casey and Daniel would have let Liam know that I'm gone by now and you can be damn sure he's been looking for you since you left the cottage."

"They won't find us though. We're somewhere up Hawley's Peak, in some sort of hunter or poacher cabin."

"They'll find us, we have to have faith." Paige said, although her voice was no longer as steady.

"Faith won't get us out of this Paige." Emily said, trying again to reach her shoe. It was easier this time.

"God will come through."

"Oh yeah? Like He did last time?" Emily grunted as she tried to twist the heel of her boot with her good left hand. Phillip must have removed the brace off her right hand, and it was aching painfully. There was no way she could try use that hand to undo the heel.

"You're still here. He helped you then."

"He didn't help me, I helped me." Emily said, her head pounding from the exertion of trying to loosen the heel of her boot, "And I'm going to help us again." She said triumphantly as the heel twisted away and something metal clinked on the floor behind her.

"What are you doing?" Paige was keeping her voice as low as possible.

"I told you, I love these boots. Had them specially made a few years ago." Emily felt behind her, her bound hands brushing the dirt beneath her before her fingers closed around the metal object that had fallen out of the secret compartment of her heel.

Emily opened the small pen knife and started desperately sawing at the rope holding her feet and hands together. Her back, thighs and shoulder muscles were screaming from being in the same position for such a long time.

Emily had to take several breaks, allowing her body to relax as much as it could while restrained. Her hip was competing with her head as to which was causing more pain.

"Emily, what are you doing?" Paige asked again.

"Trying to cut the ropes." Emily hissed across the room. With a satisfied grunt, the rope gave way and Emily was able to stretch her legs and back straight. She allowed herself only a moment to enjoy the feeling before getting herself into a sitting position and with difficulty and starting on her wrists.

She had to hold the knife awkwardly in her fingers as she sawed the blade with as much pressure as she could. She couldn't see what she was doing since her hands were still behind her, but Emily knew she wasn't flexible enough to get her hands to the front of her body. Every few moments the blade slipped and would slice into the skin on the sides of her wrists and hands. The still healing bones in her hand were protesting painfully with each movement.

"This could take a while." Emily whispered in frustration. Looking over at Paige, Emily closed the penknife, held it tightly in her fist and scooted towards Paige with her butt and feet.

Paige turned to her side to give Emily as much access to her own bounds as possible. Emily backed up to her friend and started cutting into the ropes between Paige's hands.

Within minutes, Paige's right hand was free. She immediately started pulling at the ropes on her left wrist, freeing both hands then twisting around to start on her ankles.

"If I forget to tell you at some point," Paige panted while she pulled on the knots, "You're a genius."

"A genius wouldn't be in this situation," Emily remarked dryly, "Here's the knife, cut me loose."

Paige took the knife and started cutting through the bonds holding Emily's hands together. Once her own hands were free, Emily started on her own ankles, untying the knots with shaking fingers.

"Now what?" Paige whispered.

Before Emily could answer, they heard footsteps above them. "Quick, lie down like you were, hide the ropes."

Emily hurried back to her own spot near the wall, grasping the knife tightly in her fist and laying back down with her back to the wall so Phillip wouldn't see what they had done.

The ladder slid through the trapdoor and landed on the floor with a thud. Phillip walked towards Emily carrying a bottle of water in one hand and the hunting knife in the other. He sat down on a small stool behind the spotlight.

"I want you to tell me about my father." He said conversationally.

Emily couldn't see where he was so she wasn't willing to make a move yet, she had to wait for the right moment.

"What do you want to know?" She asked, keeping her voice shaky.

"He treated you like a queen. He loved his congregation, he loved his daughters, and he loved me. But for some reason, he loved you even more. What did it feel like to have that level of devotion from someone so incredible?"

Emily swallowed, "It was... overwhelming." She said.

"Is that why you hurt him?"

Emily shook her head, not knowing what he wanted her to say.

"Why did you hurt him?" Phillip asked, sounding as though he were crying.

"I just wanted to be free." Emily told him semi-truthfully.

"You had the Father, you didn't need anything more." Phillip whined. "You didn't have to take him from me!"

"I was scared." Emily said.

Phillip leaned forward, so that Emily could see his profile in the shadow of the spotlight. "Scared of what? Scared that he was too good for you? Scared of being his Mary?" Phillip sounded hopeful.

"Scared of everything I guess. I was just a kid Phillip, it was too much."

"He was going to bring about the new world, with you at his side. You were going to bring the Son into the world, through your loins. You didn't give him a chance to conceive a child with you."

"Actually I was carrying his child." Emily whispered, hoping he would have to come closer to listen to her.

"No you weren't, don't lie to me!" Phillip was shouting again, spittle flying out of his mouth and reflecting in the light before spattering on the dirt in front of Emily. He seemed to have totally lost his grip on reality.

"It's the truth." Emily said.

"There was no baby!" Phillip argued, "You never had a child, I would know."

"No," Emily agreed, "I didn't have the baby. I had them cut out of me the moment I knew he was there."

Phillip howled, the animalistic sound echoing off the walls. "I'll kill you!" He lunged, knocking the stool backwards and rushing at Emily. Emily barely got the knife in front of her when Phillip collapsed on top of her.

Emily lay in shock for a moment.

"Come on, let's get out of here." Paige hissed. She was standing over Phillip, the stool she used to knock Phillip out still in her hands.

Emily shoved Phillip's motionless body off her with a grunt and stood up. "Let's go." She rifled through Phillip's pockets while Paige made her way to the metal ladder Phillip had put through the trapdoor. Emily was hoping to find Phillip's mobile but he didn't have it on him. "Dammit." She muttered, getting up and following Paige up the ladder.

The door of the cabin was locked, Paige was pulling on it when Emily joined her in the room. "What now?" Paige asked Emily.

"The window." Emily said, rushing over and trying to pull the boards off with her hands.

Paige grabbed a walking stick from near the door and went to Emily to help, jamming the walking stick between the window and the boards and started pulling back on it, levering the walking stick against the frame to pry the boards off.

Once the first board was off, the others came off more easily and they were able to make a gap big enough to climb out. Emily helped Paige climb through then followed her out the window, landing on the ground with a thud.

"Come on, let's go." Paige urged, pulling Emily to her feet.

They ran around the front of the house, past the door when Emily skidded to a stop.

"Emily, come on, we have to go." Paige begged again, tugging on Emily's arm.

"Paige, the door is locked from the outside." Emily said, pointing at the large, old-fashioned padlock on the door of the cabin.

# Chapter Thirty-Six

**P**aige tugged on Emily's arm again, "All the more reason to get the hell out of here."

Emily allowed herself to be pulled away from the door, breaking into a run behind the older woman.

The tree line was only a few yards ahead of them when Emily was tackled to the ground. She landed hard, the wind getting knocked out of her. She twisted around, trying to get away, but Phillip had already wrapped both hands around her throat and was squeezing. Emily choked, blood dripping off Phillip's face and onto Emily's.

Paige tackled Phillip from the side, throwing him off Emily. They wrestled to the floor, Phillip landing a vicious punch to the side of Paige's head.

Emily got up and kicked Phillip as hard as she could in the ribs. Phillip grunted in pain, rolled away from Paige and landed hard on his side. Emily jumped over Paige and kicked him in the ribs again, she drew back her leg and kicked Phillip in the head.

When she tried to kick him again, Phillip grabbed her by the ankle and pulled her down to the ground, elbowing her in the face.

Emily felt the cut on her jaw open, warm blood spilling down her neck. "You bitch!" Phillip yelled in her face, "I'm going to cut your throat open."

Emily brought her knee up between Phillip's legs, causing him to yell in pain.

Paige sat up, stunned from the blow she had taken. She watched the other two wrestle on the ground, both swinging and kicking. She watched as Phillip pulled the penknife out of his pocket. "Emily!" Paige screamed as she scrambled to her feet, rushing towards the tangled duo.

Phillip managed to grab Emily's right hand, pushing it down to the ground. Emily fought, trying to get her arm loose. Phillip slammed the knife down, trying to stab Emily in the face. Emily managed to pull her head to the side as the knife came down. Phillip yelled in frustration, swinging down instead. The knife went deep into the inside of Emily's right thigh. Emily screamed, trying again to roll away. Phillip pulled the knife out and raised his arm for another go at her face.

Suddenly there was a vicious growl from the bushes and Mutt launched himself through the air, landing hard against Phillip's shoulder and snapping at his throat. Phillip fell next to Emily, his arms up in defense against the attack from Mutt. Mutt got hold of Phillip's left hand and Emily saw what was about to happen before It did. WIth hIs rIght hand, Phillip plunged the blade of the knife into Mutt's ribcage. Emily yelled, Mutt howled and backed off immediately.

Emily used the moment of surprise to elbow Phillip as hard as she could in the nose. He fell back and she climbed over him, straddling him, wrapping her hands around his neck.

A gunshot went off, stopping them all in a moment.

"Oh thank God!" Paige cried, spinning around and seeing who was there. She immediately headed towards the man with the gun.

Both Emily and Phillip froze and looked at the man who had stepped out of the forest, tall and grim, a hunting rifle in his hands.

"No, Paige run!" Emily yelled, forgetting about Phillip underneath her.

"I can't believe you're here." Paige sobbed in relief, "How did you find us?"

"No!" Emily screamed, trying to get loose from the hold Phillip now had around her waist to get to Paige. Paige turned to see what Emily was yelling about so she didn't see the man raise his rifle again and take aim.

∞

With nothing else he could think to do, Liam headed toward the hospital to see if Daniel was conscious yet. He might be their best chance of knowing if it were Phillip or an accomplice. He had asked Christian to let him know if Daniel had regained consciousness, but it was possible that Christian was still busy dealing with Kenny and didn't have an update.

Liam had pulled into the main road, driving past the police station when a man ran into the road in front of his cruiser. Liam slammed on the brakes, his seatbelt protesting as he brought the cruiser to a sudden stop.

Mitchell Winter was standing in front of Liam's cruiser looking furious. Liam opened his door, "Are you out of your Goddamned mind?" He yelled at Mitchell.

Mitchell walked towards Liam, his face thunderous. He shoved Liam back against the back door of his cruiser, "My daughter is missing again, taken by that sick fucker and you don't bother to let me know? I had to hear it at the gas station!"

Liam straightened up, it actually hadn't occurred to him to contact Mitchell at all. As far as he knew, there was no relationship between Emily and her father.

"It's an ongoing investigation." Liam said, rubbing his chest.

"Ongoing my ass! Every dog and his mother knows about it. What are you doing to find her?" Mitchell shouted.

"Everything I can!" Liam yelled back. "I'm doing everything."

Mitchell punched the side of the cruiser in anger.

Liam saw a father who was as distraught as a man could be. Breathing deeply to calm himself down, something occurred to him. "Mitchell, when you asked the sheriff to take all the files from Stan's case, did you see any of them?"

"What?"

"The files! The police files, did you see any of them?"

"Boy, I don't know what you're talking about. I never saw no police files, and I never spoke to the sheriff about anything. I dealt with a deputy."

"You didn't ask the sheriff to personally keep the files?" Liam asked urgently.

"Are you deaf boy? I didn't speak to him. I only ever spoke to the deputy that came to try get Emily's statement at the hospital."

"I have to go!" Liam said suddenly, leaving his cruiser idling in the street, he ran into the station at top speed.

"Get me everything you have on Dave Brown!" He yelled at Muriel and he burst through the reception and went into the staff break room.

On the wall hung a photo of his predecessor. Dark hair and eyes, beard, bigger and slightly older than Stan. The reality hit Liam like a kick to the face.

"Looks like Kenny's going to be okay." Muriel said, walking into the break room.

Liam looked at her blankly before realizing she was talking about the deputy that was injured. "Good. What about the files on Brown?"

"We don't have any." Muriel shrugged, "The only thing we had was his numbers and the address for his place upstate. But I did find something interesting on the Downing boy's birth mother when Brenton PD sent through the records."

"What?" Liam asked urgently.

"She was near death when a local cop found her on the side of an old dirt road. He took her to the hospital and stayed with her until the boy was born and the mother was dead. Want to know who that cop was?"

"Brown." Liam said darkly.

"One and the same."

"Nothing else? What about his service record?"

"Can't find it, if we had it, it's gone now." Muriel told him. "The only thing I know about him is that he used to own an old hunter's cabin back in the day on Hawley's Peak, and I only thought about that now. My hubby tried to buy it when the sheriff retired."

Liam grabbed Muriel by the shoulders. "Where exactly is the cabin?"

∞

Emily was still trying to pull herself loose from Phillip when the gun went off a second time. Paige staggered in place, her shocked eyes focusing on Emily for a brief moment before she looked down. Blood was staining her shirt, just below her ribs on the left. She looked at Emily again and collapsed.

"No!" Emily screamed. She became enraged, kicking and clawing at Phillip until he let her go. She got up and made for man with the rifle.

"Stop!" He yelled, pointing the rifle at Paige again. "She's not dead, but I can change that."

Emily skidded to a stop a few feet away from him, watching him carefully. She took a few steps sideways and knelt at Paige's side. Paige lay on her left side, her eyes closed, but she seemed to be breathing. Dark blood stained her shirt, and the stain was expanding, the bullet had pierced her lower back and gone straight through.

"Get away from her." The man ordered.

"She needs help." Emily said, trying to staunch the blood pumping out of the wound.

"You get away from her or the next shot will be to your little incubator whore."

Emily looked up at the man. His rifle was no longer pointed at Paige or herself, but at a third woman, bound tightly to a tree five feet from where he was standing.

Casey's eyes were wild and terrified. She had been gagged and tied to the tree by her shoulders and waist, completely unable to move. Her eyes kept darting from her mother to the man with the gun. One eye was swollen shut and the whole side of her face was purple and black.

Phillip had gotten to his feet and had limped over to where Emily was kneeling. "Meet my uncle, Sheriff Dave Brown."

Emily looked into the face of the man that had tortured and brutalised her so many times. The man responsible for so many of the scars she so hated on her body.

"Sheriff." She whispered in disbelief.

"You were my first case." He grinned at her, "The tragic death of the local pastor at the hands of his teenage lover."

"You told people it was a car accident." Emily realised.

"Took the pressure off you see. Stanley wouldn't have minded. Boy!" He barked, looking at Phillip, "Get that one downstairs and secured. Try not to fuck it up."

"Yes Uncle." Phillip said quickly rushing to Casey and working on the knots holding her to the tree. Once she was loose, with only her hands bound in front of her, Phillip pulled her towards the cabin. Casey looked at Emily in terror as she was lead past, her bound hands trying to hold her swollen belly protectively.

"Now you." Dave said, pointing his rifle once more at Emily, "Help your friend inside."

"We shouldn't move her."

"Now, or I end her here!"

Emily looked at Paige's deathly pale face, worried that she was bleeding to death as she lay there. She pulled the shirt she was wearing over her vest and rolled Paige so that she was lying on it. Then she took the sleeves and tied the knot over the exit wound on Paige's stomach as tightly as she could. Paige groaned in pain, her eyes fluttering open.

466

"Get her inside or we can leave her out here, I don't really care." Dave said.

"Sorry Paige." Emily whispered, pulling Paige into a sitting position, causing the injured woman to moan in pain again. "Please try get up." Emily put her hands under Paige's arms and pulled her into a standing position. Paige was conscious enough to try to help. Emily put Paige's arm around her shoulder and together they shuffled slowly towards the cabin, Paige grimacing in pain with each small step she took. "I'm so sorry Paige." Emily told her again as she struggled to help Paige through the door while limping with her injured thigh.

"Not your fault." Paige whispered back, her voice sounding stronger than Emily expected.


Getting Paige down the ladder through the trapdoor was the most difficult part. Phillip was standing at the bottom, holding the ladder impatiently. Paige had only made a few of the rungs when Phillip grabbed her by the ankle and pulled her roughly down. Paige landed with a sickening thud at the bottom of the ladder, but she had enough strength to pull herself into a semi sitting position against the wall next to the ladder.

Emily followed Paige down, her hands so slick with sweat and Paige's blood that they slipped off the ladder repeatedly.

"Tie her up." Dave barked from above as he started making his way down, rifle in hand.

"Yes Uncle." Phillip had his hunting knife in his hand again, holding it above Casey's head. Casey had been put on the mattress in the corner, her legs now tightly bound as well.

"Just try something," He sneered at Emily, "and your other little slut loses her pretty face."

Emily swallowed her fear and stood at the bottom of the ladder unmoving.

"Walk over here." Phillip instructed. He had blood streaked down his face from his broken nose and above his eyebrow, but he appeared not to notice. He seemed to be enjoying the level of power he was wielding over Emily.

Emily walked slowly towards Phillip, keeping her hands in sight, worried that he was jumpy enough to hurt Casey by accident. She prayed desperately for God to get Casey out of this. "Even if you never cared enough to rescue me, I'm begging You, get Casey and the baby out of here safely." She prayed silently in her head, over and over.

As she got closer to him, Phillip swung back and punched her in the face. Emily fell backwards, stunned by the force of the blow. Before she could react, he had grabbed her and forced her face down into the dirt, both arms pulled behind her. She heard what sounded like zip-ties being closed around her wrists, the sharp plastic digging into her already raw skin. She felt Phillip put his full weight on her back as he rubbed himself against her. "Now I get to see what all the fuss is about." He whispered into her ear.

Emily could feel his excitement growing against her and tried to struggle, but he was too heavy. The feeling of him rubbing himself against her made her sick to her stomach. She couldn't go through this again, she would rather die.

His hands started pulling on her jeans, his fingers digging into the flesh of her hips. Emily let out a muffled scream and kicked her legs, trying to get away from him.

With a loud, sudden groan, Phillip's weight was off her. He landed next to Emily, clutching his side.

Dave had kicked his nephew off Emily with brutal accuracy. "I told you boy, this one is mine."

"She killed my father." Phillip whined pathetically, "I also want to make her pay."

"She's mine. I've waited too long for this." Dave looked down at his nephew with distaste. "You've royally fucked this up, you know that?"

"How was I supposed to know she hid a knife?" Phillip said in the same whiny voice.

"Not for letting them escape, for taunting them in the first place. They're bringing in the feds you fucking idiot. They know it's you."

"I was careful!"

"Not careful enough! I don't know how you expect me to get you out of this mess."

"I'm sorry Uncle." Phillip said sulkily, still rubbing his ribs. "I just wanted her to suffer like my father suffered."

"And she will, but that's my place, not yours."

Emily was trying to get herself onto her knees or at least off her back into a more dignified position when Dave brought the rifle butt down against the back of her neck. Darkness was a welcome relief.

# Chapter Thirty-Seven

Emily woke to the sound of Stan praying, as she had done the last few times she had gone to sleep. He seemed to spend his time stuck in the festering darkness with her either on his knees or pounding himself inside her. He had never re-shackled her right hand, he seemed to get a kick from holding it down above her head when he was on top of her. The last few times he had been as brutal as the other man, Emily was so sore all over that she couldn't tell which part of her body hurt worse. She was sure now that she was dying. They may not kill her outright, but she could feel her body dying. She was conscious for less and less time now, the blissful darkness taking over without her noticing anymore. Her memory of the last few days was sketchy at best. Some of the time, she didn't feel any pain at all. She couldn't feel the iron digging into her skin, nor could she feel the blankets under her or the rough earth beneath them. Instead, it felt as though she were floating, suspended somewhere between life and death.

The more often the darkness came over her, the more Emily welcomed it. She had thought at first that she would see Jesus, or maybe her mother in those dark moments, waiting to take her away from the dank and disgusting cellar, but they hadn't come. She wasn't scared of the darkness anymore, as she had been in the beginning. If darkness is all there was after this, it was still more peaceful. Anything would be better than this hell.

"You ruined everything you know." Stan said. He had stopped praying but was still on his knees. "You're going to take everything from me, and I would have allowed it to happen, because you are mine and I am yours. But what am I supposed to do now?"

Stan was weeping into his hand, the other was clenched around the neck of an almost empty whiskey bottle.

"You could just let me go." Emily said to him, "I'll never tell anyone."

"It's too late for that," Stan sobbed, his words were slurring badly, "people in town are all saying we ran away together. My wife is distraught."

"We can think of something." Emily insisted, then coughed because her throat was so dry from lack of use and water.

"It's too late." Stan said again.

"What if we blamed your brother, we can tell them that he was the one that did this to us." Emily pleaded, hoping, praying that for once she could talk him into something.

"No one would believe that."

"No one would belleve that you would hurt me either." Emily said quietly, staring at the ceiling.

"I would never hurt you." Stan said in surprise, "You are mine, you are my Mary."

"You hurt me all the time." Emily told him.

"Never!" Stan was shaking his head as though to block out her words.

"I know you wouldn't mean to, you didn't have a choice. He made you do it." Emily said in a pleading voice.

"STOP IT!" Stan screamed, getting to his feet, "Stop it! Stop trying to turn me against him!"

"It's true, you know it's true."

"Liar!" Stan threw the whiskey bottle at Emily. It shattered on the wall above her head, splinters of glass and splatters of whiskey hitting her in the face. The whiskey burnt her eyes, so she squeezed them shut, not seeing him come towards her.

"I'll show you pain!" He was on top of her, his left hand grabbing her right wrist and squeezing it tightly against the floor, his right hand pulling at her, squeezing her breast painfully, then digging his nails into the flesh of her thigh, shouting incoherently about being cleansed.

He was using his knee to force her legs open, kneeing her wound on her thigh repeatedly. Emily lay back, trying weakly to keep her legs together, wishing for the darkness to come. She prayed as she hadn't prayed for a long time that the darkness would take her before he was inside her again.

Instead of the darkness, Emily felt a sharp pain in the back of her hand as he pushed her arm higher above her head. The broken shards of whiskey bottle were cutting into her hand. She could feel individual slivers piercing her skin and tried desperately to concentrate on that pain instead of the pain that was going to come.

In his drunken state, Stan kept trying to undo his belt buckle, but his fingers weren't able to grasp the buckle properly. He took his left hand away from Emily's right, lifted himself into a kneeling position to get his belt off and his zip undone.

Without thinking, Emily grasped around, grabbing the first piece of glass she could find. When Stan lowered himself onto her again, she thrust the piece of glass up with as much strength as she had left in her.

The bottle piece pierced Stan's throat, just under his jaw, to the left of his chin. His eyes opened wide in shock and reflexively he grabbed Emily's hand tightly in his own and pulled the hand away with the glass.

Hot blood gushed out, squirting everywhere, covering Emily's face, burning her eyes and pouring into her nose and mouth making her choke. Still squeezing her hand so tightly that the glass cut into her palm, Stan collapsed on top of her, his left arm and Emily's right trapped between them.

Emily's eyes burnt so badly that she was sure she was blind, but as she blinked the blood away, she saw Stan move his head to look at her one final time, his lips moving noiselessly. She watched the life leaving his eyes as he stared at her. His head dropped onto her shoulder and he was still.

Emily felt the warm blood continue to trickle out of his body and onto her own chest. His weight was suffocating her. Emily tried vainly to roll him off, but with her only useful hand pinned between them, she was helpless. The more she struggled, the more breathless she became, the weight his body making each breath more and more difficult. Emily saw the edges of her vision clouding over and gratefully waited for the blackness to come, knowing that he would never be inside her again.

∞

Emily came round slowly, feeling groggy and drunk. She knew something bad was happening, but she couldn't wrap her mind around what. She heard voices somewhere in the distance, angry male voices, but she couldn't hear what they were saying. She moved her jaw around to test if it was broken and felt something hard in her mouth. Spitting it out in front of her, she discovered it was one of her back molars. She felt around her mouth with her tongue, feeling the jagged edges of what was left of the tooth. Emily looked around and saw Casey on the mattress crying, her mouth was still gagged, but even from the other side of the room, Emily could see the girl's heaving sobs.

Emily swallowed, not wanting to look to where she knew Paige had been last, not wanting to see. She didn't want to know.

Flashbacks of then and now were blending together, confusing Emily, keeping her thoughts from clearing or making sense. She forced herself back into the now, concentrating on the pain in her thigh and looked up. Paige was sitting against the wall where she had been when she had been pulled down the stairs. She didn't appear to be moving at all. Emily tried to get up to go to her, only to find that her ankles had been restrained by handcuffs and the chain between them had been fed through a bolt that had been hammered deeply into the floor.

"Paige!" Emily called in a hoarse whisper. "Paige!" But there was no response. Paige's body was completely motionless, her head resting on her shoulder, looking for all the world as though she were asleep, except for the chalky pallor of her skin. Emily choked on a sob of her own, "Oh God Paige, please no."

Out of the corner of her eye, Emily saw Casey double over in grief, unable to voice her cries through the gag.

Emily felt numb. She sat back and leant against the wall, her mind going completely blank. Emily began rocking herself backwards and forwards, relishing the pain it caused her. Her ribs and hip reacted painfully as she rocked. Without thinking, Emily started kicking at the bolt in the floor, just with one foot, over and over again, not expecting it to do anything. She just wanted to distract herself from the body across the room.

The voices above them got louder and angrier, followed by a slamming door. Emily was surprised to feel the bolt give a little under her boot. She kicked it again, feeling it move a little again. She pulled both her legs sharply towards her body, pulling at the bolt then kicked it again. She heard footsteps above her, heading towards the trapdoor, so she kicked it only once more, as hard as she could before she saw shoes stepping onto the ladder.

Phillip stepped off the ladder and cocked his head slightly as he looked at Paige, as though curious to see death up close. Then he shrugged carelessly and moved towards Emily.

"While my uncle is out sorting out my mess as he calls it, I'm going to find out what you did to my father. I know you killed him. I want to know how." He knelt in front of Emily, his hunting knife swinging loosely between his thumb and forefinger. "How did you do it?" He asked, that same curious expression on his face.

Emily refused to look at him or answer him. He leant forward and stuck his thumb into the wound on her thigh, making her cry out in pain. Heat travelled up her leg and into her body as though she were burning from the inside out.

"Answer me!"

Emily looked at him with loathing on her face but said nothing.

"Fine, if making you bleed doesn't work, then I'll make her bleed." He jerked the knife towards Casey in the corner and started standing up.

"No! I'll tell you." Emily cried out, "Please, I'll tell you."

"Tell me then." Phillip said with a satisfied smile, going down on his haunches again.

"I sliced his throat open with a piece of broken bottle." Emily told him.

"Why?" Phillip's mouth was pulled into an ugly grimace. "Tell me why!"

"Because I fucking hated him! I wanted to make him bleed. I wanted to watch the life drain out of his eyes for what he did to me!" Emily yelled. "I didn't want him inside me again."

"So you mutilated him with glass?" Phillip had that same insane look on his face she had seen so many times with Stan.

"Clichéd isn't it?" Emily asked with a sarcastic snort. "And you want to know something else?"

His jaw was moving, but Phillip didn't say anything.

"I did it because I wanted to." Emily continued, "I didn't care if I lived or died, I just wanted to make sure that he never took another breath on this earth. It was never self-defense, I did it because I wanted to make him pay!"

Phillip roared like something unnatural and launched himself at Emily, shoving her over. He punched her again and again, his knife fallen forgotten where he had been hunched down. "I'm going to kill you!" He was screaming, over and over as he pummeled her body with his fists. Emily had no way of defending herself, her hands were still trapped behind her body. In his rage, he threw her over onto her stomach, once more pulling at her pants, screaming into her ear that he was going to make her pay.

Emily held onto the back of her pants, infuriating him even more. She had hooked her fingers through the belt loops of her jeans, making it almost impossible for him to get her hands away. Viciously he ripped her arms upwards and Emily felt the sickening pop as her left arm dislocated once again from her shoulder. He forced her arms above her head, her now loose arm giving way so her right arm could move. She screamed in pain, and started jerking her body, trying to throw him off. He grabbed her useless shoulder and flipped her back onto her back.

"I'd rather see your face." He told her, his voice now calm as he reached down to undo his pants. He knelt on either side of her legs, tugging at her pants, this time able to pull them down.

Suddenly, blood gushed out of Phillip's head as Mutt leapt onto him from the side, grabbing Phillip's ear and ripping it from the side of his head. Phillip roared in pain, jumping up and kicking Mutt in the head. Mutt yelped and collapsed next to Emily, where Phillip kicked him again and again, until the dog was still.

"No!" Emily whimpered, unable to help.

Phillip was breathing hard, he held a hand to his head to stem the blood but looked at Emily with a sickening grin. Without looking at the dog again, he knelt down again, forcing Emily's pants down lower.

"When I'm done with you, I'm going to go have fun with that little whore over there. Then I'm going to cut that demon out of her the way you cut my brother out of you."

"No!" Emily yelled, forcing her right arm to pull her left in front of her and reaching down for her pants as though to pull them up.

"Then I'm going to find that little Sophie. She's a tasty little piece. I'll let her know that you're the one that sent me when I tear her up inside."

"No!" Emily screamed again. Her pants were down by her knees already, but she wasn't thinking about that. She twisted her body around suddenly, grabbing the handle of the knife still embedded in Mutt's side and yanked it out. In one swift movement, she twisted it around and slammed it into his left eye. His right eye looked at her in utter bewilderment. She twisted the blade in her hand more, "No," she said again, "you fucking won't."

His body began to spasm, jerking and kicking, he collapsed on top of Emily, gave two more shudders then was still.

Emily lay under him for a minute, winded. Then with all her might she rolled to the side, shoving his body off hers. "Get off!" She yelled at the dead man before she rolled onto her knees, looking down at the Phillip's face, barely able to believe that she had taken another life. Fluid and blood were bubbling around the blade in his eye. Emily felt disgusted at the sight, once more feeling as though she were about to be sick.

She heard the door above open again and tried desperately to pull on the bolt in the ground again. It was looser, but it still wouldn't give way completely. She was still tugging and kicking it when Dave got to the bottom of the ladder. Seeing his nephew's lifeless body on the floor, he stopped in his tracks, his rifle falling out of his hand.

"What have you done?" He asked Emily in shock. "He was all I had left, what have you done?"

Emily tried to scoot back away from him, but she could only back up against the wall again, her feet still securely trapped.

He stepped towards her, pausing only to pick up the discarded hunting knife. "You took my family from me. You took my brother and now you've taken my only son! My son! Mine and Stan's." He said, tears pouring down his face. He knelt in front of her, lifting the knife above his head.

Emily closed her eyes, asking God to get Casey out of there. Even if He didn't care about Emily, she begged him to save the girl across the room. She heard the swoosh of his arm coming down and shut her eyes tighter.

# Chapter Thirty-Eight

The bang was deafening in the confined space. Emily's eyes shot open to see the right-hand side of Dave's face explode in front of her. Slivers of skull and bits of brain matter splattered the wall above her head. His body landed in a crumpled heap at Emily's feet. Looking up in total confusion, Emily saw Paige half-lying / half-crouching on the floor, the rifle in her hands. Her pale face was drenched with sweat from the effort of moving, but her eyes were bright and determined.

More yelling could be heard above, followed by several sets of heavy footsteps. Emily wondered what could possibly happen next when Liam landed on the ground behind Paige, followed closely by her father. Liam made towards Emily, but she shook her head, "Help Paige! She's been shot."

Liam knelt next to the once more unconscious Paige and yelled through the trapdoor for help. Mitchell Winter rushed to his daughter. He pulled a knife out of his belt and cut through the zip-ties. Then he pushed both hands down on the wound on Emily's leg, trying to staunch the bleeding. It didn't hurt, in fact, she couldn't feel any pain at all.

Emily tried to smile at him and she had the strangest urge to laugh. Things were feeling fuzzy again, although this time it was a far more pleasant kind of fuzziness.

"There's too much blood." She heard Mitchell saying but she couldn't understand why he was so worried. She looked over to see another deputy had untied Casey and the young woman had rushed to her mother and knelt beside her, holding Paige's hand and crying.

Emily felt a feeling of total peace, knowing that Casey was going to be okay. "Okay." She said to God, or at least tried to say, she didn't know whether or not her mouth was moving, "I get it, You do care. Thank you for saving her."

The blissful darkness was coming and Emily slipped peacefully away into its comforting embrace.

# Four Weeks Later

Casey walked into her mother's hospital room, her belly announcing her arrival before the rest of her entered. Paige looked up from the crossword she had been doing and smiled.

Paige's hair was very grey now and her face still gaunt from the weight she had lost over the last few weeks, but her smile was the same, warm and kind.

"Hey Mom."

"Hello my love, how are you doing today? How was the checkup?"

"It was pretty good actually. Doctor says this little man can enter the world in the next month quite safely and I can have my bladder back."

"That's good to hear." Paige said, sitting up more in her bed and making space near her feet for Casey to sit down. Paige held her daughter's hand, "I have to tell you this, I'm just so proud of you. The way you've handled everything."

"I'm proud of you too." Casey said, "Thank you for not giving up."

Paige wiped a tear away, "I wasn't done yet."

Paige had lost so much blood by the time she had gotten to the hospital that the surgeons told Casey and Daniel that she had very little chance of making it. But Paige had kept on fighting. After less than a week on a ventilator she began breathing on her own. Now, four weeks after being shot, Paige was walking up and down the hospital aisles with the help of a walker.

Casey looked around the hospital room, which was, as usual, filled with flowers and cards. "You know, I think I might actually miss this room when you get out of here."

"I won't." Paige said bluntly, making her daughter laugh.

Casey picked up one of the framed photos next to the bed, a picture of teenage Emily standing with Paige at a school dance. Casey smiled sadly and squeezed her mom's hand. "I'm always going to miss her aren't I?"

Paige's smile saddened too. "Every day I hope."

Casey nodded and put the picture back down, too emotional to speak. She rubbed her belly gently. "Let me go. I need to get some stuff on the way home, I can't let dad cook anymore."

Paige laughed, wiping a tear from her face. "I'll be home soon to take over."

Casey kissed her mother's thin cheek and headed back out of the hospital room.

Casey pulled out of the hospital parking lot and made a split-second decision. She called her father to let him know what she was doing but didn't bother to go home and pack. Instead, she headed straight for the airport, hoping desperately that they would allow her on the plane in her late stage of pregnancy.

Three hours later she was banging on an apartment door loudly. She had gotten the address from Liam on her way over from the airport.

The door opened and an older Spanish woman looked at Casey curiously. "Can I help you?"

"I need to see her." Casey said, pushing past the woman and into the apartment.

Glynis watched the pregnant young lady walk through the living room and smiled. She could see why Emily felt the way she did about the girl.


Casey burst into the bedroom without knocking. "How could you just run away from us like that?" She demanded.

Emily looked up from the book she was reading. She put the book aside and rubbed Mutt's head gently. Mutt had started growling as soon as the bedroom door had opened. He had become incredibly protective of his human since he had recovered. He had lost his right ear from the vicious kicking he had received and he had taken two weeks in the vet's before his punctured lung and fractured skull had begun to recover enough for the vet to tell Emily he would survive.

"I wasn't running Casey. Come and sit down." Emily patted the bed.

Emily too had lost a huge amount of blood. No one had realised at first that the stab wound in her leg had sliced open the femoral artery in her thigh. If it hadn't been for her father's quick reaction, Emily may not have made it to the hospital at all.

Emily got out of the hospital before Paige, but because of the broken ribs she had, she had been forced to spend most of her time in bed or on the couch.

Casey sat on the edge of the bed but still looked angry.

"Did you fly here in your state?" Emily asked curiously.

"It was a short flight." Casey said defensively. She looked very young all of a sudden, her lip trembled as she tried desperately not to cry. "Why did you leave like that?"

Emily had been released from hospital after sixteen days and had caught the first flight back to the city with Mutt, needing to get out of Hawthorne as quickly as possible. She hadn't said goodbye to anyone at the time, she couldn't. She just needed to go so that she could sort out her own thoughts.

"I wasn't running." Emily repeated softly, "Not really. You have to remember I have a whole life here too Cas, and with everything that happened, I wanted to recover in my own home, where I feel safe. Can you understand that?"

Casey nodded but looked as though she wanted to argue.

"And as for the reason I didn't say goodbye," Emily sighed, "I felt so responsible for what happened to you and your mom that I wasn't sure I could face you. I wasn't sure I could be around you, knowing that your little boy would be held by some other woman, and loved by her."

"But we never—" Casey said.

"No, we never." Emily agreed. "I've spoken to your mom since then and she assured me that you still wanted me to take the baby."

"Of course I do! No one else in the world would protect him like you could."

"And I was going to come back and see you, but I must be honest, I've needed some time to recover. Not just physically, but this time I needed to take the time to process what we went through and deal with it properly."

"And?" Casey asked, "Have you processed it yet?"

Emily laughed, "Have you?"

Casey swallowed, "Not really. It doesn't feel so bad this time but I keep having nightmares. I see that man's face all the time. His and the one from Germany."

"I'm sorry you went through so much Casey. And I'm also so glad to see you're clearly not hiding away this time."

"I didn't have a choice, I needed to visit my mom in the hospital every day. You didn't want me to visit."

"I know, and again, I'm sorry. It was nothing personal, I should have explained myself to you."

"So did it help?" Casey asked, "All this alone time? Hiding away like you didn't want me to?"

Emily smiled wryly, "You know, it really did. I've realised something these last few weeks. I didn't want to be a victim, but that's what I was. I definitely didn't want to be a survivor either, fighting to keep my head above water, but that's what I was, and it certainly didn't feel like anything to be proud of, which I've told you before. But it wasn't just the actions taken against me, I think a lot of it was the actions I took myself. Sometimes I thought that taking a life meant that I didn't have a right to enjoy mine. And now I've taken a second one."

"Did it makes things worse? What happened with Phillip?" Casey asked, not meeting Emily's eye.

"If anything, it made it better." Emily said simply. "I was so sure I had killed Stan for me, which I did really. But knowing that Phillip wanted to hurt people I cared about made it really easy for me. I would do it a hundred times over, knowing that it was protecting you or anyone else I cared about from him. I feel no guilt, maybe guilt is the wrong word. I feel at peace with what I did to Phillip, and I think, seeing how sick he was, how crazy his father and uncle had made him, helped me to know for certain that I did the right thing with Stan too. Does that make sense?"

Casey nodded, "It does."

"So I think," Emily said, reaching for Casey's hand, "after all this, I really am ready to start living because I want to."

Casey was silent for a while. "I really hope I get there soon."

"You will. I have no doubt." Emily smiled. "We'll both have days that overwhelm us, and nightmares that threaten to pull us back into the ocean, but I think we just need to keep reminding ourselves that the shore is always within reach, we just need to keep heading in the right direction."

"I'm never going to see you again after he's born am I?" Casey asked sadly.

"That's totally up to you. I'll always be there if you need me. And I'd like to think we've been through enough that we will continue to keep in contact. But only as much as you want."

486

# Four Months Later

Paige smiled at her daughter, "Are you ready for this?"

Casey grinned back, "I can't wait."

"You're going to be amazing." Paige told her. "Where's your father gone?"

"He's there, heading back to us." Casey said, pointing across the small hallway of the airport.

Daniel joined them and handed Casey her boarding pass, "Everything is set, you're bags are checked in, all seven hundred of them."

"Thanks Dad." Casey said with a laugh. She hugged her father tightly, then hugged her mother, holding onto her just a little longer.

"Your cousin will be waiting when you get off the plane. Let us know when you land." Daniel said.

"I will Dad, don't worry." Casey smiled at them both, "I love you guys so much." She looked over their shoulders towards the doors one last time.

"We knew there was a chance she wouldn't make it." Paige said kindly, knowing who her daughter was waiting for.

Casey shrugged, "It's okay, I can always text her later."

Casey gave her parents each a final hug then picked up her carry-on and walked towards the terminal.

"Wait!" A voice yelled from behind Paige.

Casey dropped her carry-on bag and rushed over to Emily to give her a hug.

"Shew, just in the nick of time." Emily said smiling.

"You just had to make an entrance." Casey laughed, hugging Emily again. "Thanks for being here." She whispered in Emily's ear.

"Anytime." Emily whispered back. "Now go be amazing. And text me every day. I want all the news and updates."

"I will." Casey promised.


As Casey walked away, Paige stood beside Emily watching her daughter take the steps to a new life.

"Thanks for coming." Paige said.

"Wouldn't have missed it for the world." Emily replied, smiling at Paige.

"Where's Lucas?" Paige asked as they turned towards the exit where Daniel was waiting.

"Liam took him to the station to say hello to Muriel. I wasn't quite ready to travel too far without him." Emily said sheepishly.

"A mother's prerogative." Paige smiled.

"Cathy and Christian have asked us to come for lunch as well, I think we're going to spend the afternoon making wedding plans."

Christian had seen Cathy leaving Emily's hospital room one afternoon when he was on duty and had asked Emily if Cathy had upset her. Emily had told the surprised doctor that they had made peace before anything had happened with Phillip and Dave and that Cathy had been visiting most days. Cathy for some reason, was one of the few people Emily hadn't minded having in her space.

Within a week, Christian and Cathy had announced their engagement to Emily and Liam and Cathy had been happier than anyone had ever seen her.

"I suppose they have to make plans whenever you guys are in town long enough." Paige said, looping her arm through Emily's companionably.

"Landen isn't exactly far away Paige." Emily pointed out.

Liam had taken a position in a high school as a sports coach in Landon, a larger town less than an hour away. He hadn't wanted a life as a cop anymore, so he, Emily, Sophie and baby Lucas had all happily moved to Landon shortly after Lucas was born. Emily was incredibly grateful that Glynis had followed them there. Glynis had claimed the city life was no life for an older woman and she assured Emily she was following the gorgeous baby and not her grumpy boss.

"Speaking of which, are we still on for Sunday?" Paige asked as they reached the car where Daniel was waiting.

"Of course. The house will probably be a mess because we're going to church first, but we'll see you around midday?"

"Sounds good." Paige hugged Emily tightly. "Are you heading straight to Cathy's now?"

"Not yet. I'm going to drop Liam and Sophie so long, then I need to make a quick stop."

Emily dropped Liam and Sophie in Cathy's driveway, giving them both a kiss and telling them she would be back soon. She made Mutt get out the car with Liam, wanting to do this next step with her son alone. Then she made her way to the other side of town, arriving at the cemetery just as the midday sun was reaching its peak. Emily unstrapped Lucas from his car chair and carried him through the cemetery to her mother's grave.

She stood with her baby boy sleeping peacefully in her arms, listening to the leaves rustle gently in the breeze. She didn't say anything to her mother this time. She didn't need to. She just stood, cradling her child and kissing the silky soft hair on his head.

Driving back through town, Emily passed Amy and Erik as they headed in the opposite direction and waved at her friend who grinned back from the passenger seat. It turned out that one of the women Nick the bartender had been seeing was none other than Lorraine. Erik was so relieved that Lorraine was the one wanting out of the relationship that he had happily moved out of his house and back in with Amy where he belonged. Nick and Lorraine were expecting their first child and Amy was happy with her small-town life for now, especially now that she had Erik back. It hadn't taken either of them long to realise how stupid they had been and how much they belonged together.

Emily's next stop was at the house she hadn't been to since she had left town all those many years ago. Emily knocked on the door and waited.

Mitchel Winter opened the door in surprise. He hadn't seen his daughter since the hospital, he had felt too awkward to visit her again once she started recovering, especially since she hadn't wanted to see anyone.

"Hi Dad." Emily said with a small smile. "I thought maybe you might like to meet your grandson."

Mitchell smiled, tears in his eyes, "I would like that very much."